SILENT JOURNEY

Silent Journey

E. Ayers

Silent Journey
by E. Ayers
© 2018, E. Ayers
All Rights Reserved
ISBN: 978-1-62522-123-0

PUBLISHER INFORMATION
Indie Artist Press
P. O. Box 131
Brackettville, TX 78832

Paperback version
Library of Congress Control Number: 2018951726

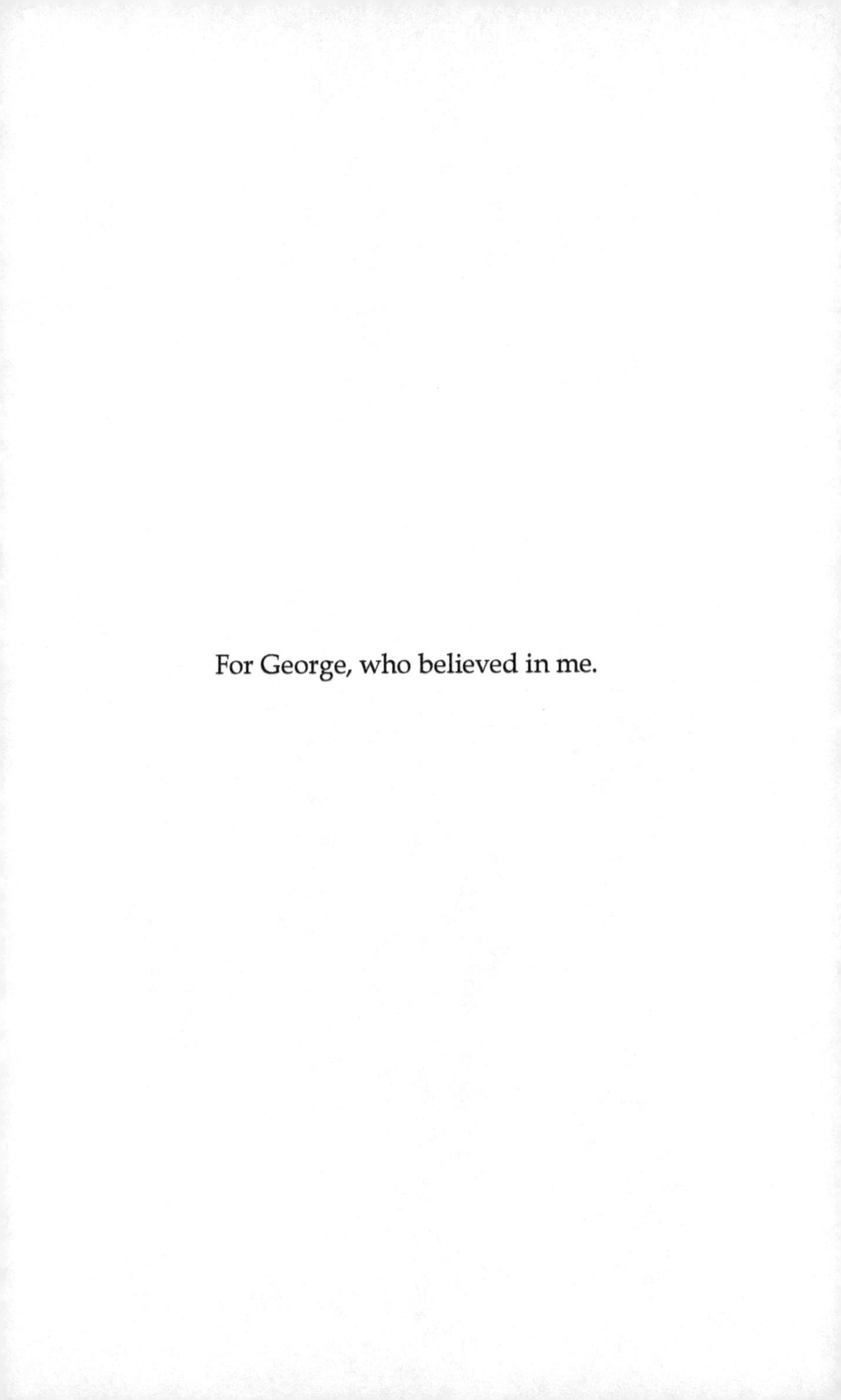

For George, who believed in me.

Savannah's Letter to Readers:

My silent journey started a few years ago. I saw Alex and instantly fell in love. How could I not? He was gorgeous! I was certain he was just another student. Well, he was, except he was a Deaf student.

Fortunately, I'd attended Prof. Stockton's American Sign Language (ASL) classes long enough to at least begin to understand the difference between deaf as in "not hearing" and being Deaf as a culture, sort of like saying someone is Spanish, German, or Japanese. At first, the concept of the cultural aspect of being Deaf was difficult for me to understand. Eventually, I became aware of the long history of the Deaf people and their language. Alex was Deaf with an uppercase D. Born of a Deaf father, he was considered Deaf of Deaf. He has a long lineage of Deaf ancestors. It's a little like having a pedigree.

It took me a while to understand that ASL is speech. The Deaf speak with their hands. When someone who is Deaf speaks, it's handled grammatically the exact same way as our spoken words are handled. What they sign gets quotation marks.

As I was learning ASL and about the Deaf culture, Alex was on his own journey into the hearing world and away from the protective enclave of family, academia, and the Deaf community. It hasn't always been easy for either of us.

The journey isn't over; it's only just begun...

Savannah Chisholm stared at her new adviser as though he'd grown horns. "I don't want to take Spanish. Wasn't it enough that I had it in high school?"

"No, you've declared your major in communications. You'll need it for your degree. Spanish is the most logical, being you've already had three years in high school. If you can pass the test, you will need two semesters." He sat back in his leather chair as he pushed his computer mouse around. "You can take the test online during regular hours. The testing rooms are down that hall." He pointed towards the hallway leading to the bookstore.

Her guts began to tangle like a ball of snakes. *Test?* "Do I have to give you an answer today?"

"Of course not, but if you wait, these required classes fill up very quickly."

She swiped at the screen of her tablet until it showed the languages available. "What's ASL?"

"Sign language, American Sign Language."

"May I take ASL and have that count?"

"Yes, but you will need at least three semesters."

Sign language has got to be easier than Spanish, even if it is an extra semester. "I'll take ASL."

"Monday and Wednesday at 3:10 is still open, as are our evening classes."

"Afternoons will work." The sinking sensation in her abdomen had to be from knowing that she'd committed to one too many classes this semester. Three of her classes were going to require a lot of research and writing. And Visual Production… She'd talked to others who had that class and the majority loved it, but a few said it was one of their most demanding classes in the whole curriculum.

A printer, on the stand behind where her adviser sat, spit out papers. She signed her name on each one and then thanked her advisor. *Okay, sign language. That should be a breeze – a few hand movements. So much for the idea of having a light class load on Monday.*

She stepped out of the office and spotted her friend Ashley. "Guess who has to take a foreign language?"

"Seriously?"

Savannah nodded. "I'm taking sign language. Anything is better than taking more Spanish."

Ashley laughed. "Don't count on it. Since when has any class been easy?"

Savannah squinted her eyes at her friend. "Don't even say that. I'm swamped this semester. I have no clue how I will survive."

"We'll take it together. I know I need elective credits." Ashley pulled out her phone and tapped the screen a few times. "What class?"

"Stockton, on Monday and Wednesday at 3:10."

"Got it! I'm signing up for it now."

Four days later, Savannah and Ashley walked into a packed room of Professor Stockton's ASL class. By Wednesday, attendance had dropped to less than half, and the Monday after that, there were fewer than fifteen students. Savannah knew why. It wasn't easy. She began to wonder if transferring to Spanish was still an option.

She could barely manage the alphabet and, most of the time, she was completely lost. Ashley studied the manual and attempted to coach Savannah whenever they were together. But it didn't take long for Savannah to realize that sign language wasn't child's play. ASL would take concentration, and she didn't have enough time to devote to it. Not with the amount of work that she had to do for other classes. *This is what I get for thinking ASL would be easy.*

Professor Stockton began to write on the board.

**For additional credit: Aldo's, Thursday evening,
Silent Spaghetti Supper.**

Huh? Savannah wondered why. Aldo's was the Italian restaurant next to the campus, but it tended to be a little pricier than Sal's Pizza. Aldo's was more of a date place than a hangout. But for extra credit, Savannah couldn't turn it down, even if it cost her money. She'd have to skimp on something else.

As soon as her last class on Thursday afternoon ended, she rushed back to her dorm, knowing she needed to change for the Silent Spaghetti Supper. Wearing jeans to a place like Aldo's seemed wrong, but jeans were what Savannah owned, except for a pair of beige slacks and a pair of dress pants. She decided to wear her beige slacks with her peachy-pink pullover and figured casual-nice was as good as it was going to get.

"Are you ready?" Ashley called from the threshold of Savannah's dorm room.

"No, come on in. I'm not even certain I'm dressed enough for this."

"You look awesome. You could wear a burlap bag and

look terrific." Ashley flopped into the comfy chair by the bed. "Did you know that they will take our meal cards for these events?"

"What? Really? I wondered how I would pay for this." Savannah walked into her tiny half bathroom and began to apply some makeup.

Ashley continued to talk. "Oh, and I found out why they call it Silent Spaghetti. No one is allowed to talk, including the wait staff."

"What? How are we supposed to order anything?" Savannah held her eyes open extra wide as she applied light brown mascara. She stared at the image in the mirror. *I'm too pale for a lot of color.* With her hair brushed and pulled into a long ponytail that fell below her waist, she secured it with a wrapped elastic band in the same peachy-pink color as her top. She thought about Ashley, who looked wonderful with her bright red lipstick. If Savannah had to describe herself in one word, it would be white, milk white, much too white, whiter than a sheet, whiter than newly fallen snow. *Even my hair is white.* She decided she was lucky she didn't have pink irises because she'd heard albinos had terrible eyesight. "Okay, I'm ready."

Brindlewood dorms were on the far side of the campus from Aldo's. The dorms needed a serious facelift and most students did everything they could to keep from staying there, but Savannah really didn't mind. The place was quiet and cheap. Everyone had their own room and a half bath. Partway down the hall there was a large kitchen that everyone on the floor shared, but hardly anybody used it except to make a cup of coffee or reheat a slice of leftover pizza. Across the hall from kitchen were the showers. They didn't provide much privacy, but they were clean. Compared to the other dorms that looked like luxury apartments, Brindlewood was about as modest as possible.

Living off campus wasn't an option for her or Ashley. The one thing they both had in common was lack of money. Ashley's mom was a single parent and struggling to make ends meet. Savannah's parents weren't in a much better position. Ashley and Savannah, like most of the other young women in Brindlewood, were surviving on scholarship monies.

The evening was clear and the walk pleasant. The daytime heat had faded, and the nighttime temps were only going to be in the sixties. The campus still bustled with students going to evening classes. Taller, more modern buildings surrounded the original portion of the campus. That historic area was nicknamed The Heart. They cut through The Heart and went to Kings Street. Aldo's was situated across the street between an art gallery and an upscale boutique. Taped on the door was a warning.

Silent Spaghetti Supper Tonight, Absolutely no talking allowed! Public welcome.

"Here goes." Ashley opened the door and held it for Savannah. The place was strangely quiet. Not completely devoid of sound, because there was still the sound of movement and dishes. But there wasn't even music playing softly in the background. A hostess held up two fingers and, when Ashley nodded, the woman picked up the menus and led them to a table.

The table contained another warning about no talking, a small pad of paper with Aldo's logo, and a plastic-coated sheet with some suggestions should they need help. The menu was simple: spaghetti: white, rosé, red with meat, or marinara, with a choice of plain, meatballs, shredded chicken, or sausage. Then there were some specialty items such as shrimp, but they couldn't use their meal cards with those. Savannah chose the creamy rosé sauce with chicken.

Then she looked around.

That's when she realized there were sounds, vocal sounds, just not words. They were primitive sounds. The slapping of hands, low dissonance of grunts, and punctuated higher notes that were almost animalistic. It was disconcerting and fascinating at the same time.

Most of those in attendance were using sign language. Now she knew why Professor Stockton gave extra credit for attending. A redheaded waiter came to their table. Savannah instantly recognized him as Andy. He frequented the coffee shop in the technology building where she often stopped between classes. She smiled at him and pointed to the items she wanted, but then couldn't figure out how to tell him she wanted unsweetened iced tea with lemon. Finally she took the pad of paper on the table and wrote it. Andy grinned and signed what she had written. She lifted her eyebrows at him, and he shook his head as though admonishing her.

Next to what she had written, he wrote.

You will learn. Is this your first semester signing?

She nodded.

Ashley did a little better and Andy left them.

All the normal small talk was gone. She wanted to sneak her phone from her purse, but there was a huge warning not to use phones or to allow them to ring. It was a little boring staring at Ashley who seemed to be struggling with the same silence.

Andy brought their drinks and salads to the table. The salad was appealing, not that horrible shredded lettuce that was served in the cafeteria. This was mixed greens with lots of feta crumbles and Kalamata olives. About half way through her salad, Savannah stopped with her loaded fork poised in front of her face.

Across the room, there was a young man sitting with an older couple, a female around his age, and a younger female teen. *Maybe it's his family.* He was a golden blond and the only description Savannah could think of was drop-dead gorgeous. He was signing with one hand as he ate. The younger girl seemed to be playing with him, as though they were teasing. Someone must have chastised the teen by the look on her face and the way she sat back in her seat.

Ashley touched Savannah's arm and made a face as if to ask what was happening.

Savannah lowered her fork and motioned for Ashley to look behind her.

When she turned back to Savannah, Ashley grinned and fanned her face.

Silent Spaghetti Supper is getting interesting. But Savannah decided that catching the eye of such a guy wasn't going to be easy when he was across the room, and not looking in her direction.

She ate her spaghetti and instantly rated it the best she had ever tasted. But she kept watching the table across the room with the hopes that *he* would look at her. The young man left, never once gazing in her direction. As he walked away, it felt as though something had been pulled from within her.

Ashley tapped her foot against Savannah's. In Ashley's hand was the pad of paper.

Stop staring!

Savannah snatched the pad and wrote,

I want a date with that guy.

Ashley stifled a laugh, but a small sound squeaked out, causing several people to look in the direction of the table.

Savannah ran her hand over her forehead hoping to shield herself from the deadly glares. *I didn't do it. But we know who hears us.*

When she was certain she could no longer eat another bite, Andy placed a small plate of grapes, apple slices, and sharp cheese on their table. Between Ashley and Savannah, they ate every speck. *Oh, roll me out of here after this meal.*

That night Savannah tossed and turned in her bed. She attempted to tell herself it had to have been all the food she had consumed, but deep inside she was certain it was that guy. It was like a magnet pulling them together, but he must not have felt it. *It's the food. I'm not used to eating that much.*

No longer did she walk the campus oblivious to the students around her. Now she scanned the landscape for *him*. Nothing. It was as though *he* didn't exist and had merely been a figment of her imagination.

She tried a little harder in sign language. Her motivation was to go back to the restaurant and at least not sit there with a pencil and paper the whole time. But with a test in Early Forms of Communications on Friday, she didn't have time to study all those little hand movements. She was slipping further behind.

When Professor Stockton reminded the students about the next Silent Spaghetti Supper, Savannah pressed her lips into a thin line. She couldn't remember the signed words for the family members or even how to count to twenty. Her only hope of passing was to attend classes and go to Aldo's Silent Spaghetti Suppers. Stockton gave them the equivalent of an A on a quiz. She needed those extra points.

Thursday afternoon it decided to rain. Not a little drizzle, but a full downpour that showed no signs of stopping. Savannah pulled on her beige slacks and paired them with a soft sage-green cable-knit sweater. She studied herself in the mirror. *I don't care if it's raining. I want to look good. Besides,*

I'm not a child who will play in the puddles. I'll wear my boots and my raincoat, and I'll stay dry. This time she tried wearing a little more makeup. That meant she used some eyeliner and a dash of green shadow on her lids. *Please be there and notice me.*

"Ready?" Ashley called.

"Yes, let me grab my slicker." She slipped her feet into her orange rain boots and pulled on her yellow slicker with an orange-billed hood.

"You look like a goofy duck!"

"It keeps me dry."

"Why can't you wear an ordinary poncho?"

"Because I have this. And for your information, it was the rage a few years ago."

"And how old were you?" Ashley groaned. "Two?"

"No! I had one when I was eight. I found this one before I started college and couldn't resist."

"You look so ridiculous."

Savannah grinned at her friend. "Maybe the bright yellow will catch his eye."

"Are you going to Aldo's to practice signing or to wrangle a date?"

Savannah rolled her eyes as she pulled her door closed. "I'm going because I need that extra credit. If I get a date out of it, that's even better."

Ashley opened her umbrella and squealed as she stepped into the pouring rain. "It's raining sideways!"

"Ahh! We'll be soaked."

Both of them took off in a run towards the large, decorative baldachin that protected the entrance of the art building. Then they made another mad dash to another covered area. By the time Savannah reached the restaurant, her wet slacks clung to her legs and the moisture was seeping down to her boot covered feet.

"Ugh!" Savannah pulled open the door to the restaurant, then gasped as her hand flew to her mouth. Wide-eyed, she prayed that they wouldn't be tossed out for making noise. Ashley stifled her laughter.

"You are early," the hostess said. "The silence doesn't start for another few minutes."

Savannah's gaze caught the droplets of water that ran off her billed hood and dripped onto the floor in front of her. *Oh, no. I'm a drooling duck.* She flicked the orange bill so that the hood flopped onto the back of her slicker. "I'm so sorry." Her words were forced as she caught her breath. "We just ran all the way from Brindlewood dorms."

"Oh, you live in those? Didn't anyone tell you that they are the pits?"

"They're cheap!"

Someplace from within, someone started a countdown from ten.

"...three, two, one, silence begins now!" The hostess picked up two menus and showed them to a table on the far side of the almost empty dining room.

Savannah hung her slicker over the back of her chair and looked at the menu that hadn't changed, knowing she'd order the same thing, except she wanted a cup of hot tea. She tried to sign to Ashley but kept messing up. Her frustration level was rising along with the growing chill that covered her legs and feet.

Several people entered the dining room and took seats, but then *he* came in with the same people he dined with the last time. *It's got to be his family.* Savannah couldn't prevent herself from staring. He was tall – not too tall, maybe the height of her dad. She figured that meant he was at least six feet, but probably not much more. The whole family seemed to sign with ease. *I wonder if my parents would learn to sign? Wouldn't that be fun? Dad wouldn't have to hush us when he was watching something on the TV.*

Ashley kicked Savannah under the table and she realized she'd been staring at the family for too long, but she couldn't help the feeling that flowed through her. Never had she been that attracted to anyone in her life. It was as though some inner part of her leapt towards him and refused to return.

She managed to tell the waitress what she wanted to eat by pointing.

Ashley rolled her eyes and signed her menu choices.

Savannah scrunched her nose at her friend and mouthed show-off.

Ashley shrugged and made a face. Using the pad of paper, Savannah wrote the words.

Ashley grinned and stuck her nose in the air.

It was all Savannah could do to keep from laughing at her friend's smug response.

When the waitress brought the hot tea, Savannah picked up the cup and wrapped both hands around the steaming warmth. She wasn't certain if she wanted to drink it or pour it over herself in an attempt to get warm. Drinking it was the proper thing to do in public, so she politely lifted the cup to her lips and sipped.

When their salads came, Savannah ate hers, but constantly slid her gaze to the table where *he* sat. It wasn't until she was halfway finished eating her spaghetti that she caught him staring at her. He quickly looked away, and her heart fell. *Maybe he doesn't like me and that's why he turned away.*

She swirled some pasta on her fork and attempted to keep her attention on her food, but she couldn't help glancing in his direction.

He was looking at her.

She smiled. *Did he? Was that a smile? Was it directed at me or at someone else?* Her heart decided to do little flip-flops. She put her fork down and tried to steady the jitters that had taken hold of her guts but she couldn't resist looking in his direction one more time.

He was signing to someone at the table. But the young teenage female member of that table was now looking at Savannah.

Ashley stuck a note in Savannah's face.

STOP STARING!

Savannah grimaced and reached for the pad of paper, but Ashley was too quick, snatched it back, and wrote,

BEHAVE!

"No!" Savannah mouthed. But deep inside she knew she had probably made a fool of herself. How many times had her mother told her it wasn't polite to stare? That's what she had done almost through the entire meal. She tried to finish her spaghetti, but her appetite was gone. Part of her was elated and the other part was busy berating the euphoric portion. The waitress took their school meal tickets and scanned them. Savannah would forward that emailed receipt to Prof. Stockton for her much-needed credit.

She pulled on her slicker and caught the young man's gaze. There was no question in her mind that he smiled at her. She winked at him as she snapped her slicker closed. A warm pulse shot through her as she turned away and left the restaurant with Ashley.

The restaurant door had barely closed behind them when Ashley let loose. "Have you lost your mind? You were worse than a love-sick preteen with a first crush."

"I was not. And he smiled at me."

The rain had slowed to a drizzle.

"He was probably laughing at you. I can't believe you spent the whole meal with your eyes glued to him." Ashley fumbled with her umbrella.

"I did not."

"Yes, you did!" The umbrella opened as a gust of wind caught it, snapping a little metal piece. "I think my umbrella is hosed."

"My slicker still works."

"How did I manage to gain a best friend who impersonates a duck and acts like a fool in front of a guy? He's probably going to be looking over his shoulder to make certain he doesn't have an oversized yellow duck stalking him."

Wind whipped down Kings Street and brought with it more rain. They both yelped and took off running at full speed towards their dorm.

Ashley swiped her electronic key, allowing them to enter the main lobby of the old building.

"What are you going to do now?" Savannah whispered. Every student in the building had signed a no excessive noise contract before moving in. It was extremely rare to hear more than muffled voices, even in the lobby.

"A hot shower and I've got to study. I've got that test tomorrow in chemistry. What about you?"

"I'll take my shower before I go to bed. I've got a paper to do on propaganda techniques over the years." A little chunk of frustration fell into Savannah's overly filled stomach as she faced the evening's workload.

"How boring." Ashley rolled her eyes.

Savannah nodded and raised her hand in a wave as Ashley opened the door to her room. Savannah stepped into her own room and closed the door. She knew she needed to concentrate on her paper, but that little part of her wiggled and jiggled over his smile. No matter how much Savannah tried to concentrate, the memory of his handsome face seemed to constantly flash in front of her. *I don't even know his name.*

Over the next week, she watched for him on campus, but she didn't see him. It wasn't a huge campus compared to those with enough students to create a small city, but the campus covered a lot of acres. *Maybe he is someone who lives in the community and doesn't attend the university. He does look older.* She tried to conjure up every possible explanation for not running into him. *Maybe I should ask Prof. Stockton. He's probably in an advanced class, perhaps taking it at night.* The best that she could do was content herself with the hope of seeing him at the next Silent Spaghetti Supper. That's not what she wanted. She wanted to spend an afternoon talking over a cup of coffee or maybe laughing about the day's events while eating pizza at Sal's.

I could get lost in that man. Sharing days, plans, and dreams for their future… *Oh, yeah!* There was no question in her mind that she was hopelessly hooked on a total stranger.

All she needed was an actual chance to talk to him. *Conversations that will last all night…oh, and kisses…yes, kisses… lots of those.* Her mind wandered to places where it didn't need to be. *Where are you hiding?* When she wasn't in class, she checked all the normal places where students hung out, but she never saw him. She finally came to the conclusion that he was not on the campus.

She rushed to her textual mediums class and took a seat just in time to hear the professor say to take out a piece of paper and pen. *What? A quiz? Paper? Really, paper? Oh, I hope I have a pen.* She dug through her purse until she found one. A half hour later, she sighed with relief. Now, she was glad she had studied. But she was facing a test in ASL, and she probably had more than two hundred words to memorize. *I can do it. It'll be easy. I just need to concentrate.*

2

Alex lifted his backpack from the dining room chair and tossed it over one shoulder. He smiled to himself. This was his final year and it was going well. Against his parents' wishes, he had moved out of the house two years ago and into an old house off campus. The place was small in terms of square footage yet felt specious after being in cramped dorm rooms. The house had recently been revamped. The wooden floors had been refinished and were as smooth as glass. When he moved in, he did everything he could to prevent marring them with furniture. He loved this little house and appreciated its charms.

After he closed the front window, he walked through the downstairs, checked the coffee machine one last time to be certain it was off, walked out the back door, and got into his used Prius. Although his parents had raised him to accept challenges and face them head-on, they had panicked at his decision to live on his own. That thought made him laugh. *I'm not exactly a party person anyway.*

He drove to Kings Street and parked his car near the campus' newest building. Then he sprinted his way to The Heart. His mom had asked him to stop by her office before he headed to class at nine. He smiled at the secretary as he entered the wing of the building.

"Hi, Alex, go on in. Your mom's expecting you."

He nodded, went to his mom's door, and pushed it open a wee bit before peeking into the room. "Hi. I got your message."

"Oh, I'm glad to see you. I was thinking about planning a party for your father's birthday but wanted your ideas. I'd like to surprise him."

"You brought me here for that? You could have texted."

"I didn't want him to pick up my phone and see the text accidentally."

He shook his head.

"I want to do something special. Any ideas?"

He shrugged. "I'll think about it."

"Try to come up with an exciting idea, maybe a theme."

"I've got to get to class. I'll text you later." He gave his mom a quick hug and kiss. Not wanting to be late for class, he hurried in the proper direction, but spotted the long white-blonde hair of the woman he'd seen at the Silent Spaghetti Supper. There was something about her smile that he liked. One thing he'd learned in the last ten years of life was that pretty women didn't get serious with him. They might flirt for a moment and then they'd walk away. He consoled himself with the thought that they didn't deserve him. He had a lot to offer. It was their problem, not his.

Maybe she's Deaf? No. If she were Deaf, I would have seen her in the community. Most likely she's taking Stockton's class. That's a good indicator that she can speak my language.

He made it to class, took a seat, and watched as the professor walked into the room. The man started explaining the stress and breakage of steel in this particular design when under the strain of an earthquake. Then he turned his back mid-sentence and started writing on the board.

Damn! Alex tapped his hand on the desk. Frustration rose inside of him. This particular professor seemed to constantly forget. *Why can't he remember?*

"Sorry, Alex. I was explaining the..."

Twice more the professor forgot and turned away from the class. Ben Weaver showed the notes he'd taken, and it was enough for Alex to realize what he'd missed. The little speech to text app on his laptop didn't work from this distance, and it never worked if someone mumbled. And this professor often mumbled, making the class twice as difficult to understand.

Alex wasn't one to complain. If he protested, everyone looked at him as though he had some sort of free ride, especially since his mom was a dean at the university. But no one ever gave him a break that he was aware. He was expected to perform like any other student. When class was over, Ben bid him goodbye.

He could see himself partnering with someone like Ben, even though Ben didn't sign. Of course, a college town in the middle of nowhere was not where they would succeed. They'd have to move to a big city someplace, but they both had to do an apprenticeship. Alex had his eye on several architectural firms. He also knew how hard it would be to get into such prestigious firms. And it would be twice as difficult for him because such firms would be hesitant to hire someone Deaf when there were plenty of other applicants who weren't.

After the rain the other night, the temperature had dropped considerably. The leaves were turning color, and a few had already begun falling to the ground. A bright orange maple caught his eye, and then the longhaired blonde in a green sweater. *It's her!*

He took off across the grass and tapped her on the shoulder.

Startled, she turned, and that beautiful smile flooded her face. "Hi!"

He smiled back. "Hi. Want to grab some lunch?"

She studied his hands before she looked into his eyes and laughed. "Don't do that to me. I don't understand any of that mumbo-jumbo."

"What did you call it? Are you serious?"

"Stop it!" She grabbed at his hand. "Stop!" Her smile was so bright, and her eyes reflected her merriment.

He broke free of her grip. "Okay, I will slow down."

She laughed and grasped at his hands again. "I can't do it. This is my first time ever taking sign language. I have no clue what you are signing."

He began to laugh as he , again, broke free of her grip and signed some more. Seeing that smile filled him with joy.

"NO! Stop it." She attempted to stop his hands and push them down. "It's not funny. I've got to know over two hundred words by tomorrow, and I can barely do the alphabet. I should have never taken the class."

Seeing her concern struck him. "But if you don't sign—"

"Stop it!" She captured his wrists with a death-like grip. "I said I can't. Just talk to me."

He formed the letter I.

She repeated each letter. "I A M D E A...K"

He shook his head and mouthed the letters slowly until she caught on.

"I am deaf... Oh n-n-no." The smile drained away from her face and her mouth opened slightly. Her eyes stared into his, but they were filling with tears.

"It's ok." He smiled and then pursed his lips. He motioned for her to smile, but she didn't. Instead, she covered her face, and he was certain she was fighting tears. He didn't understand. If she had turned on her heel and walked away, he would have understood, but her reaction perplexed him. He gently tugged her hands away from her face. "It's ok."

She shook her head.

He reached out, wiped a tear from her cheek, and then slipped his hand in his jacket pocket for a small notepad.

Lunch?

She took the pad from him and started to write.
He took it back.

Just talk. I can read your lips.

She stared, and he could tell by the look on her face that she was confused.
He wrote on the pad.

You are beautiful. I love your smile.
Have lunch with me. I don't have another class until 2.

She shook her head. "You know what I am saying? You can *read* my lips? I though that was a joke, maybe a few words or something."
He nodded.
"I have class in another fifteen minutes. I can't stop for lunch."

Ok, meet me here at 4?

"I can't. I won't be available until five."
He smiled and wrote.

At 5, I will see you here.

She stared at him with the sweetest expression. "At five. Then I have to study, unless you want to coach me on sign language. I've got to pass my test tomorrow."

At 5. I'll make certain you pass it.

"I'm so sorry. I had no idea you were Deaf. You look…"
He reached out and touched her cheek again. She didn't have to finish her sentence. He fingerspelled, "NORMAL."

She shook her head. "Handsome."

This time she turned and walked away. He wanted to reach for the stars, but instead he stood and watched as she headed towards the Lee building.

He bought a salad at the cafeteria and texted his mom while he ate. A big party was something that he knew his mom wanted, but he wasn't so certain his father would. His father wasn't antisocial, but he was uncomfortable in a world where everyone spoke. Within the Deaf community, his father was fine, but his mom lived in both worlds and would probably invite some of her friends who couldn't communicate with his dad. It was awkward for them, but it was twice as difficult for his father.

Alex chewed on the salad and thought about his dad. Growing up in schools that catered to children with special needs had given his father a fine education but had left him out of the hearing world. Alex was glad his mother had resisted and fought for him to enter regular school. She didn't want him to be placed in special classrooms. It wasn't always easy, but he learned to live in the world of the hearing. He learned to cope and pay close attention. But many people still looked at him as though he had three eyes and couldn't tie his shoes without help. For some reason people assumed that being Deaf also meant that person was mentally challenged.

So many times, he wondered what it must be like to hear things. Having never heard a sound, he couldn't grasp what that experience must be like. He'd felt the vibration in music. But actual sound meant nothing to him.

He stared out of the narrow cafeteria windows that failed to provide much light. Then it dawned on him. He didn't get her name or her phone number. Texting on cellular phones had opened up the hearing world to him. It would be the first thing he'd ask when he saw her. *She's so pretty.*

He had a design class to take at two and he'd have to concentrate, but for now, he allowed the images of her smile to flash before him. Her pale blue irises were filled with what appeared to be white lines like lightning streaks. Her skin was clear and milky white. Her very white teeth were perfectly aligned. Her hair, the color of sun-bleached wheat, hung to her waist, and she was slender without being too thin. He liked that.

What was left of his salad became soggy under the avocado lime dressing. He tossed it out, picked up his drink, and headed for his car. *Five o'clock. I have a date with the most beautiful girl on campus.*

After class, he went to his place, showered, and changed his clothes three times. He finally settled on his blue and white checked shirt. The check was so fine that the shirt looked blue unless someone looked carefully at it. Then he matched it with a better pair of jeans. He threaded his belt through the loops and slipped his feet into a pair of casual boots. He brushed his teeth one more time and stared into the big mirror over the bathroom sink. Keeping a close eye on the time, he attempted to make certain his place was spotlessly clean. The thought of changing the sheets went through his mind, but then he decided that's not what he wanted. Something told him she wasn't that kind of girl.

Satisfied, he pulled the door closed behind him, pulled his hood up on his jacket, and faced another deluge of rain. *I'll take you to dinner and teach you to sign. I want to talk to you forever.*

Savannah slipped out of class a few minutes early and discovered it was pouring rain. Not a little, it was what her grandfather called a gully-washer, the kind of rain that prevents someone from seeing more than a few feet.

She looked out from the covered entrance and barely saw anyone across the greens. He had said to meet him about fifty feet from where she stood. She wasn't going out there and get soaked. She only wore her denim jacket and she'd be drenched in seconds.

She waited and watched. She checked the time. She continued to wait and still didn't see him. *Where are you?*

At five thirty, she gave up and went to her dorm. After a hot shower, she pulled on her yoga pants and an old tee shirt before making a cup of Earl Grey tea. *Maybe it's a blessing. Do I want a guy who is Deaf?* She pondered that situation. Her head was telling her to steer clear and her heart was breaking. There was something about him – something that drew her to him. She fixed a bowl of instant oatmeal and began to study the paperback textbook on sign language. Opening her eyes, she realized dawn was breaking and she had fallen asleep. After chiding herself, she fixed a cup of coffee and started studying again. She had to do this. She had to pass the test.

Certain she probably could remember the nouns, she tried to combine them with verbs and couldn't. It was as though her brain turned to mush. So far she had one C, two D's on quizzes, and two A's for going to Aldo's. She figured that was a C, and she had to do much better on this test or chance ruining her grade point average.

She fixed another cup of coffee and continued to study. In the back of her mind was that handsome guy. She wanted to communicate with him. She wanted to know who he was.

"Hey, ready?" Ashley called from the other side of the door.

Savannah jumped up and unlocked her door. "Not exactly."

"You actually were studying for this test?"

"I fell asleep studying. I've been up since a few minutes after four trying to cram this stuff in my brain."

"How'd your date go?"

"What date? I think I got stood up."

"You?" Ashley checked her hair in the mirror that hung over Savannah's desk. "Why do I even try? It's still raining."

Savannah chose a pair of jeans and a clean shirt. "How cold is it?"

"It's forty-five, but headed to a balmy fifty-five around three. They are talking about a heavy frost tonight."

"Ugh!" She stepped into her bathroom, pulled on her clothes, brushed her teeth, and braided her hair into a single long plait. "Okay, I'm ready."

"No makeup?"

"Why bother." She frowned at Ashley.

"Aren't you going to ask me how my night went?" Ashley handed her friend her backpack.

"Fine. Tell me." Savannah pulled her door closed.

"Are you in a foul mood or what?" Ashley flounced down the concrete and steel stairs as though she were six years old and headed to a park to play with friends. "Just because someone stood you up doesn't mean I didn't have a great time."

"Really? What happened?" Savannah wasn't certain she wanted to hear, but Ashley would tell her anyway. There was a theatrical side to Ashley that usually made Savannah laugh.

"Well, while I was at the library working, this guy by the name of Matthew came in and wanted some help locating some old newspaper articles on a murder about twenty years ago." Ashley looked over her shoulder and raised her eyebrows at Savannah.

"Let me guess, he's a law student?"

"Nope!"

"Um, criminal justice, wannabe cop?"

"Nope!" By now Ashley's grin was so large that Savannah was certain it couldn't get any bigger.

"Okay, I give up."

"Journalism major."

"I'm intrigued. Tell me more." She pulled her slicker's hood over her head and made her way to the cafeteria.

"You really want the details?"

"Not about the murder, only about this guy."

"Well, he's tall, dark, and handsome. And he's from Texas, so he has that tw-wang when he talks." She tried to mimic his accent. "I found what he wanted, and he was so happy that he's asked me out to dinner Friday night."

"That's wonderful."

Ashley continued to rave about Matthew. She seemed to be falling madly in love, and that was something Ashley just didn't do easily.

In the cafeteria, Savannah selected the scrambled eggs and bacon, the citrus fruit cup, and a cinnamon apple muffin with a package of cream cheese. It would be some time past two before she'd have a chance to eat again, and after last night's cup of instant oatmeal, she was starved.

In the midst of devouring her breakfast, she stopped mid-bite and held up her hand. She swallowed. "You are not going to believe what I just figured out that I did!"

"W-w-whaat?" Ashley answered with her mouth full.

"I'd run over to the art building yesterday because I needed to ask Ella something and I knew she hung out there."

"Ella?"

"I found a shirt on the laundry room floor and I was positive I'd seen her wearing it. So I washed it with my stuff and took it to my room because it was too late to knock on her door. I didn't want her to think it was lost or that I'd stolen it."

Ashley made a face. "Was it hers?"

Savannah nodded and took a sip of her coffee. "Well, I left the building, ran into that guy, and went to class. That means I went into the Lee building by the back entrance, not the front. But when I came out, I came out the front door.

That's why I didn't see him. I was at the wrong door, facing the wrong direction."

"How did you manage to make such a stupid mistake?"

Savannah's head began to pound. "I have no clue." *I was the one who stood him up. What have I done?*

They cleaned up where they were sitting and headed for their classes. Every chance Savannah had she went through her manual and looked at the pictures. She wasn't certain if she could pass the test with much more than a C, but that would be better than failing it. *I should have taken Spanish.*

"Miss Chisholm," Prof. Stockton said sternly. "Please call the dog and tell him that his dinner is ready."

Savannah stood, started to touch her hip, and then realized that wouldn't work. A dog wouldn't hear her. She clapped her hands, waited a moment before touching her hip and motioning eat.

Prof. Stockton stared at her. "Call the cat for dinner."

Savannah looked at the professor and almost laughed. Her family's cat, Gray Socks, never would come if called. Chances were, he was curled up sleeping in some odd spot. But grab a can of cat food and start to open it… That cat would dash into the kitchen.

"Cat," she signed and shook her head no. "Can opener. Cat run." She couldn't remember the word for kitchen so she spelled it out. "Spoon, dish, eat." She smiled and prayed it was enough, hoping she'd made herself clear.

The professor knitted his brow and asked her several more things before she could return to her seat. Her stomach was knotted. She'd have to wait and check online to find out how she had done.

She watched several other students, and she wasn't certain she was any worse. When Ashley was called, Savannah paid careful attention.

"Those of you who I have tested may leave," Prof. Stockton

announced.

Savannah slung her backpack over her shoulder and started to walk out.

"Miss Chisholm."

She stopped and turned to the professor. With effort, she signed, "Yes, sir."

She watched as he signed back to her. She smiled, but she wasn't positive. *Did he say that I did well?*

Twice after class, she checked for her grade, but it wasn't posted. Ashley came through Savannah's door and made herself at home in the tiny room. "I don't want to eat in the cafeteria. I'm sick of chicken, instant mashed potatoes, green beans, and tasteless chocolate pudding."

"Okay, what do you want?" Savannah put her computer to sleep.

"Something decadent. Something that tastes like home."

"Well, if we want to use the kitchen, I'll cook, if you'll clean it up."

Ashley made a face. "Depends, what are you cooking?"

"I have fourteen dollars to my name."

Ashley left the room and returned about five minutes later. "I've got twenty-one. What can we get on that?"

Savannah swiped the bills from her friend's hand and picked up her coat. "Let's see what the supermarket has on sale."

"Go. I have to study for a test."

"Fine. I'll do it myself. Keep your phone handy in case I need to ask about something."

The walk to the supermarket wasn't bad. The evening was chilly, but the sky wasn't quite dark. The walk back would be pitch black, and she wasn't thrilled. The faster she was, the happier she'd be. She took a cart from the parking lot and made her way inside the store. Bright lights flooded every aisle, and she instantly felt the pangs of hunger. Veggies that she hadn't seen in ages called to her. Fruits begged to be taken from the large display bins. Roasts and steaks… She put her hand to her mouth and prayed she wouldn't salivate. *Why can't they feed us decent stuff in the cafeteria?*

At the end of the meat counter, there was a bin of marked down meats. Towards the back was a lonely, marinated pork loin that had been reduced in price to almost nothing. She put it in her cart. *Now, what to go with it?*

She found a bag of bib lettuce and an avocado. *A few sweet potatoes will taste good with pork and be easy to bake.* Mentally she tallied the cost. She was well under, but cooking time was also a problem. She wanted something delicious for dessert. Backtracking, she found a small shaker of cinnamon and went to the fruits. *Apples…baked…in puff pastry.* She selected a bag of apples, figuring she'd bake enough for tonight, extras for tomorrow's snack, and the rest they could eat raw. Then she went to the frozen food department. She opened the glass door and reached for the puff pastry as someone took the door and held it for her.

She backed away from the cold blast and realized who was holding the door. "Oh!"

He smiled. "Hungry?"

She put her fingers to her lips, signed eat, and nodded. "I'm so sorry. It was pouring rain and I—"

He shook his head at her and motioned smile.

She smiled at him and he smiled back. In her cart was more than enough food for two people so she decided to ask. "Have you had dinner?"

He shook his head and pointed to his cart.

"Want to come with me? I promise I know how to cook."

He looked at his cart and then at her. He signed something, but she had no clue what.

3

He thought his world had crumbled when she hadn't appeared after class. There was something about her – about the way she looked at him that made him think she was different. Dating outside the Deaf community had its drawbacks. He'd make friends, but they often slipped away. They felt awkward.

As a child growing up, he decided he was a freak. He'd spent a summer playing on a little league team. The other boys would get together after games and do things, except he was never invited, not even to the birthday party for the coach's son.

He wasn't supposed to attend a regular school. The reasoning was that the teachers weren't skilled enough to handle his *special* needs. He didn't have special needs other than the need to be accepted.

They were the ones with the problem. He could read and write and do everything they could. Why didn't people understand that? He knew what they were saying, so why couldn't they understand what he was saying?

Something told him she was different. She didn't look at him as though he had a problem. It was as though she realized that she was the one who couldn't hear him. Her inability to sign was a barrier, but she was learning.

Before they left the supermarket, he pulled out his phone, found his contact app, and passed it to her. She took it and typed in her name and phone number. Then she touched the little hand set icon and sent a phone call to her phone. She smiled and touched her phone's screen, then passed him her phone. He typed his name into the box and handed it back to her.

"Alex Van Doorn, pleased to meet you."

He pointed to the parking lot and she seemed to understand.

"I walked here. Brindlewood dorm."

He signed, "Unsafe."

She knitted her brows and shook her head slightly. She clearly didn't understand the sign. Taking her elbow, he led her to his car and opened the door.

"Okay, you are handsome, but I don't know you. It's one thing to ask you to dinner and another to get into the car with you."

Signing would be too much for her. He took out his phone and texted. -I'm not going to molest you. I'm saving you from a long walk on a cold, dark night.

She hesitated for a moment. Then stared intensely at him before she shrugged and got into his car.

A few minutes later, he pulled his car in front of her dorm and parked in one of the guest spots. He carried her grocery bag and followed her up the stairs. She rapped on a door and kept walking down the long hall to a small kitchen. Soon the friend who had accompanied her to the silent suppers appeared.

With effort, Savannah spelled, " A S H L E Y." Then she spelled, "A L E..."

He added the X for her. Then fingerspelled it again, "ALEX"

Ashley nodded at him and rolled her eyes at her friend as she walked to the counter where he had placed the bag of groceries. "What's for—"

He disliked it when people turned away from him, but

most didn't know, and those who did would forget that he couldn't read lips unless he could see them.

He could tell Ashley was talking by the movement of her body and her hands. She turned so her back wasn't to him.

"It'll only take me a few minutes." Savannah slipped an electronic key from her pocket and handed it to her friend. "Would you get my computer for me? I need to study while this is baking." Then she smiled at him. "Do you need to study? We can sit here at the table."

He started to spell computer, but she caught on before he finished.

"In the car?"

He nodded.

She shrugged. "Let me get everything going. Then we'll walk down and get your computer."

He pointed to the counter where she was standing and signed, "Me H E L P"

She shook her head and mimicked the sign for *H*.

"A B C D E F G H"

"Am I ever going to learn?"

He smiled brightly, nodded, and again spelled help. He made a *V* with his fingers and pointed to his eyes.

She nodded.

He made a fist with his left hand and brought his right palm up to it as if trying to lift the fist. Then he fingerspelled, "HELP."

She mimicked the sign and said, "Help."

He gave her a thumbs up.

"No, it's easier for me to make the meal without interference."

Ashley returned with two computers and pods for the coffee machine. She held one out to him. He nodded and smiled. She proceeded to make everyone a cup.

Savannah must have said something because Ashley turned to Savannah and then looked at him. Ashley shrugged and motioned for him to follow. He realized she was walking him downstairs to get his computer. She was like most people who didn't know how to communicate with someone who was Deaf. She clammed up and didn't say a thing.

He retrieved his computer and thanked her as he stepped into the building. She smiled and motioned for him to follow. A few minutes later, they were all sitting with computers at the kitchen table. Savannah reached over and touched his arm. "I'll be right back."

He watched her leave. Her loin roast smelled delicious, and the aroma was making his stomach react by behaving as though it were filled with shifting marbles. She returned with more coffee pods and her ASL textbook. Then she sat at her computer, and he realized she had pulled up a screen with grades. She touched him again and turned her computer for him to fully view. She had an A on a test in sign language. He spotted Stockton's name. He was lenient with beginners.

"Help me?' She made the sign for help and pushed her manual in his direction.

He looked at the pages she had covered and then scanned several more. It was an introductory class. He signed. "Watch."

It took several times, but she began to catch on to the flow of the words. Then she jumped up as if startled and Ashley had done the same. Savannah pulled the roast and sweet potatoes from the oven and set them to one side. Then she set the table. With each item she placed, she attempted to sign its name.

"You need to learn to put them together."

She frowned at him. "I wish I knew what you are saying."

He smiled. *You will learn.*

He decided the meal was delicious, and her baked apples were a tasty treat. Other mothers cooked meals. However, his mother's meals were plain or were bought and brought home. She said she didn't have time to cook. Once he moved away from home, he bought a cookbook that claimed to contain simple recipes. Using that book, he had learned how to cook a few things, not much, just enough to get by on his own.

Ashley cleaned up the dishes as he helped Savannah with signing. When the manual showed a two-handed, palms-down sign for walk, he frowned and showed her the two-fingered sign that he typically used. The problem was that such learning guides showed the correct or formal sign, but very few people were that precise as they signed. In fact, some of his Deaf friends were downright sloppy with their hands because they rarely interacted with people outside of their small circle of family and friends.

An hour later, Savannah put her hands on her head and shook it.

"Too much?"

She shrugged but took the manual from him and placed it on the far side of the table. She signed thank you and pointed to his computer. He pulled up a screen that showed mathematical problems and her eyes grew wide. "What are you studying?"

He touched the notepad on his screen and typed,

Architecture, final year, Master's degree, and then go for licensure.

He pointed to her.

"Junior, communications with a minor in marketing. That's why I had to take more credits in a foreign language."

He grinned and went back to his screen. Having already lost his own study time, he needed to concentrate. But his ability to do that was waning. He kept looking at Savannah. She reminded him of a pure, silver moon on a clear night, all pale shining light. At ten o'clock, his little clock began to flash in the corner of his screen. It was time to go home, but he didn't really want to leave her.

"I have to go," he signed.

She nodded.

He packed up his things, but she motioned for him to leave them. She led him down the hall and opened a door. It was the guest bathroom. After three cups of coffee, he wasn't about to pass up the opportunity, but that wasn't what he'd meant when he signed that he had to go. She'd misunderstood, but it was truly adorable.

When he returned to the kitchen, another young woman was there. She smiled at him. Long legs were topped with a tee shirt that left nothing to the imagination. He didn't need that image stuck in his brain. Nor did he need to see the tattoo of what appeared to be salmon swimming up her bare thigh at such an angle. He didn't need to think about spawning. He smiled politely when she said hello. Then he caught Savannah's gaze.

It was useless to sign what he was thinking, so he reached for his phone. -Worth noticing but not what I want.

She texted back. -What do you want?

He raised his eyebrows and pointed to Savannah.

Her eyes narrowed as though questioning him and she tilted her head slightly.

He went back to his phone. -A lifetime.

He put his coat on and slung his backpack onto his shoulder. -I have my own place off campus. I'd love for you to come with me.

She shook her head no.

He laughed. -*Do I at least get a kiss?*

-Pushy aren't you. Do I get credit for feeding you?

-I can provide the late-night dessert.

She narrowed her eyes as she typed. -You are so bad!

He took her hand and they walked down the stairs to the front door. When he reached the door, he stopped. "Thank you for my dinner."

She smiled, and he knew she understood.

He wanted to tell her more, wanted to tell her how he felt, but he knew it was too soon. "You make me happy."

She stared at him.

He tried again and this time used the word smile.

She smiled back.

He put his backpack on the floor by the door and looked around. There were a half-dozen cameras in that foyer. Two years before, the university had spent a fortune updating all sorts of security systems and installing cameras everywhere. He pointed to one and she shrugged.

He raised his eyebrows and pulled her to him. Her hands slipped around his waist and then up his back to his shoulder blades. He held her tight and stared into blue eyes. She closed them and her mouth opened slightly. It was his invitation.

His mouth covered hers. His body heated. Her gentle curves pressed against him. The desire to hold her so tightly that she would be forever molded to him was intense. Her fingers stroked his back as her tongue skimmed his lips. This was nirvana and he knew it. His mind no longer processed rational thoughts; it only knew sensation.

She pulled her head back, away from their kiss, and exposed her neck to him. His lips slid down her silky skin, and then back up where he toyed with her ear. He nibbled and caressed it with his tongue. Then he worked his way to her other ear and began to stroke and fondle that lobe with his lips.

He felt the tremble in her throat and knew she was lost in his kisses. Her hips were tight to his. He laved her neck and she tensed, gripping his shoulders. There was more than sparks between them. This was hot and filled with passion.

With cameras running, he didn't dare do more, but the

need was there. He wanted to touch bare skin, and to kiss her from head to toe, leaving no part of her untouched. Every fiber of his being seemed to tighten and there was no question in his mind that she felt it, too.

She leaned tight to him and looked at him through half-closed eyes. A slight smile turned her lips upward. He covered those lips and her tongue found his. The involuntary movement from the heat of their kissing sent a pulse of concern through him. She responded by moving her hips ever so slightly like a gentle stroke, letting him know she was aware with the same desire. He had to stop – had to put an end to their antics, but he didn't want to cease.

She pulled away and he drew her back to him.

She raised her eyebrows. "Need a moment to compose yourself?"

He nodded and signed with slow calm movements so that she could understand him. "Come home with me?"

She shook her head.

Kissing her with cameras all around them may have been a mistake, or maybe it was the best deterrent. Otherwise they might have wound up naked on the floor. He leaned down and lightly kissed her lips. They were soft and slightly swollen from their fervor. He had to go home. It's not what he wanted, but it was the right thing to do.

She leaned up and returned the light kiss. "You are—"

He touched his fingers to her lips. Then turned, picked up his backpack, and left. He couldn't handle another moment being that close to her. It was too much, and he needed to analyze the whole thing. He didn't want easy, but he did want her. There was a lot to consider, starting with what he was feeling.

It only took a few minutes to drive to his place. He needed a shower and some sleep, but he fixed a cup of coffee, slipped his phone from his belt, and texted her. -Are you awake?

-Very.

-I need to know what you feel.

Savannah looked at Alex's text and froze. She knew she could ignore it, but she wasn't certain how to respond. Rational thoughts and strong emotions whizzed like lightning through her mind. -IDNK

-That's not a good answer.

She fought with herself for a moment and then replied. -I'm trying to figure out what I feel.

-OK I will give you time.

Her fingers trembled as she touched the letters on her screen. -R u feeling what I'm feeling?

He returned the text almost instantly. -IDNK what u feel.

She smiled at her phone. -I like ur kisses.

-Then I will kiss u often cuz I like kissing u.

-I need 2 take my shower + go 2 sleep. Early class. Nite!

She put her phone down, took her shower basket, and went down the hall. *Why didn't I tell him what I'm feeling?*

With water sluicing her body, she seriously began to think about the whole situation. *I'm a total idiot!* Thoughts of being married to someone who was Deaf played through her mind. How many times had she avoided contact with someone who was handicapped? She remembered the people she'd known growing up, the girl who had Down's syndrome, and the woman with the malformed body who walked with strange crutches. Then she wondered what her parents would think if she told them she'd fallen in love with a guy who was Deaf. *Who will hire him? How will he be able to work?* Deep inside, she knew the whole relationship was crazy. *Does he really think someone will give him a job? The last thing I need in my life is to be involved with someone who is disabled.*

She rinsed the conditioner from her hair and stepped out of the shower. Wearing her pale lemon-yellow terry robe, she wrapped her hair in the towel. Certain nothing had been left behind, she exited the shower room only to run into Ella in the hallway.

"Who's the handsome guy?"

Savannah smirked, knowing what Ella really wanted. "His name is Alex."

"A classmate?"

"He's a grad student."

Ella grinned. "I think he liked my tattoo."

"I'm sure most men would find it intriguing."

"Men like tattoos."

Savannah wrinkled her nose. "I can't stay and chat. I've got an early class."

The last thing she wanted was to be conversing with Ella, and she knew Ella was fishing. There was nothing her dorm mate liked more than to put her hooks into someone's boyfriend. She'd stolen Ashley's boyfriend last year. Savannah had spent at least two months convincing her friend that if a guy could be that easily swayed by Ella, he wasn't worth keeping.

Would Alex be the kind of guy to succumb to Ella's flirtations? Savannah couldn't answer that question, because she practically knew nothing about him. All she knew was that he was cute, a good kisser, and Deaf. She frowned as she climbed into her bed and pulled the covers over her. *I'm insane!*

At a few minutes before seven, her phone pinged a message. She rolled over and focused on the small screen.

-What's ur class schedule? When can I c u?

She texted Alex her schedule and waited.

-C u @ 2 then I have 2 b @ work 3:15.

Work? Where? She tried to imagine him working and wondered what he would be capable of doing. Going back to sleep didn't come easily, and an hour later when her alarm awakened her, it was all she could do to drag herself from her warm bed.

She pulled on her clothes and headed for the cafeteria. It was the best meal of the day, and that wasn't saying much. Paying attention in classes was difficult because she wanted to know more about Alex. With so many questions going through her head, she started to make notes on her phone. She needed answers.

Alex was waiting for Savannah as she walked out of her class. She appeared to be surprised to see him standing there, and her face lit up with her smile. He loved her smile. It was genuine and showed in her eyes.

"Hi, walk with me?"

She nodded.

"You need to sign as you talk to me. It's practice."

She made a face.

"Sign the words you know."

He pulled out his phone. Sign the words you know.

She pressed her lips together before she spoke. "But it is so hard. I don't know enough words."

He watched what she was trying to sign, and she often didn't get the words right. Very slowly he'd re-signed the words so that she could see her mistake. They walked to the coffee shop, and he bought them both a cup of plain brew. They didn't have much time, but he wanted to spend it with her. When she pulled out her phone and began to ask questions, he knew there were plenty more. Then she asked about his working. He could almost guess what was on her mind.

"Yes, I work. I teach."

She shook her head.

"TEACH MATH AT HIGH SCHOOL." He spelled each letter to her.

"How?"

"SKIP STOCKTONS CLASS WATCH ME." He fingerspelled.

She looked at him as if he were lying. He motioned for her to come with him.

"I can't skip ASL class."

He took her hand and just about yanked her off her feet as they made their way to where she took her class. She followed him into Stockton's office and stood there trying to figure out exactly what Alex was saying.

Prof. Stockton made the sign go. "Go ahead and go. Maybe it will help you learn."

"But I don't want to miss class."

Stockton crossed his arms over his chest and stared at her. Alex tried to contain his laughter. He knew the professor wasn't doing more than acting tough. The man was a total pussycat. Alex nudged her with his elbow. "Sign to him."

She scrunched up her nose and tried to say that she didn't want to miss class. She wound up spelling half of it.

Stockton nodded and then handed her a worksheet. "Bring this with you to the next class."

Alex said, "Thanks, I'll take good care of her."

Stockton smiled. "You'd better. I'm going to assume you are coaching her. She's done better lately."

"Yes."

"Good. She needs help. At least she hasn't given up."

Alex looked at Savannah for a moment and then at Prof. Stockton. "If I can help it, she's going to learn."

"Are you two an item?"

Alex grinned. "Working on that."

Stockton laughed.

Alex signed thanks, so Savannah did, too. From the look on her face, she had no idea what they had discussed.

A half hour later, they stepped into Kennedy High School and went to the office. She had to show her driver's license and her university ID. She quickly produced both. Then they walked down several halls and into a classroom. Two boys and a girl sat waiting for him.

Savannah watched as Alex opened a book, looked over the homework assignment, and went to the board. After a few minutes, the girl raised her hand, and Alex pointed to her.

"I don't understand how you…"

The two boys signed, but the girl didn't. When she spoke, Alex was signing.

Savannah sat stumped by what she was seeing. It took her a little while to figure out that Alex was signing to the boys what the girl was saying. *She can hear but doesn't sign. So how is he managing to teach the girl without speaking aloud?*

Watching him explaining geometry was spellbinding. Sometimes he wrote words on the board and other times he pointed to the equation. The three students were glued to him as he taught a particular theorem. She discovered she could follow along even though it had been years since she had taken geometry. The way he taught and the patience he displayed showed his ability to communicate.

He taught for more than an hour, and then the students left the class.

"What do you think?" Alex signed.

"I understand you were teaching Deaf boys, but the girl?"

His hands circled in a flurry of movements, like a ballet set to music that only he could hear. It was lovely, but confusing.

"When you sign, you need to slow down. I can't follow when you go too fast."

He signed it again, but this time he was slower, and she understood. "She hears. She wanted additional help. She'd come in and sit, so I informed the office that she was welcome, too."

"So there are special classes for the boys?"

"They go…" He quit signing and took out his phone. -I went to school here. My mother insisted because I live in a hearing world. There is nothing wrong with me intellectually. So it's a bit experimental. The parents must agree, and the teachers are given some direction rather than being specially trained. The school brings in additional help as needed.

"And you are that help?"

"Yes. My sister also teaches." He wrote his name in the visitor book in the office and pointed for her to do the same.

"Is your sister Deaf?"

"My family is Deaf except for my mother."

"Oh. Then it is hereditary?" They walked out of the school and to his car.

He signed, "Yes. Small."

"That's not the answer I wanted."

He shrugged and fingerspelled percentage. "You want a number?"

She nodded.

"I don't have a number. Because I am deaf, it is possible, but not always. My father's family is mixed."

One more thing to consider. He held his car door for her.

He signed dinner.

"The cafeteria is fine."

He shook his head. "I'll take you to dinner."

He drove to a restaurant, and she realized she was nervous. This wasn't near the campus, and it wasn't Aldo's. Would she be expected to order for him? Could he manage in a regular restaurant?

The hostess led them to a table, and he looked over the menu. He pointed to the rib eye and indicated it was good. The price was more than Savannah could imagine spending. Then he pointed to her and the menu again.

She shook her head. "That's too much money."

She wasn't certain what he signed before he pointed to the menu, but she knew he was adamant. "Ah, medium rare."

When the waitress came, he pointed to the steak and made it clear that he wanted two orders.

Savannah placed her napkin on her lap. "You are spoiling me."

"I will spoil—"

She shook her head.

"I will SPOIL you FOREVER."

She leaned forward and whispered, "I don't know. I have concerns."

He leaned forward and did the equivalent of a Deaf whisper by signing very small, "Tell me."

"I worry because you are Deaf."

He took out his phone.

-I'm living in a hearing world, so are you worrying that I will not succeed or that I will not be accepted?

"Both."

-I am the one making allowances because those of you who hear cannot hear me.

She knew he was right. She sat back in her seat and closed her eyes for a moment. Without opening her eyes, she signed, "My heart wants you."

He reached across the table and took her hand in his.

She opened her eyes. He was smiling at her and his hand in her palm formed the sign for "I love you" that just about anyone could recognize.

He nodded and signed that his heart wanted her, too. Then he texted that he understood they had much to work out, but he did not question what he felt.

"Now what?"

He shrugged.

-We give ourselves time. I graduate this year but I must apprentice. That will pull us apart unless you transfer to a different university. Are you willing to step into the Deaf community? Will your family and friends be able to accept me? And if not, then how will you handle it?

Tears formed in her eyes as the weight of his words came down on her. She batted the moisture away, but it returned. She wiped one tear from her cheek, and then wiped both eyes with her fingertips. "I don't have those answers. I've been trying to figure everything out, and I can't. I don't know. It's all happening so fast."

She didn't want to look at him. He'd stare into her eyes so intently that she was certain he knew what she was thinking. She was glad when the waitress brought them their salads, as it saved her from trying to explain.

She glanced at him several times and returned her focus to her salad. As she forked her last bite, she once again raised her gaze to him and realized his eyes were filled with pain. Unsure as to how much Alex sensed the gravity of the situation, she concentrated on her now empty plate.

The waitress removed her salad plate and replaced it with the beautiful rib eye. Except her appetite was waning. She cut into the steak and it was the perfect color. The baked potato was beautiful, and the grilled vegetables couldn't have looked or tasted any better. But her heart pounded in her chest. It was as though she had been covered in a lead blanket that was threatening to push her deep into the ground with her negative thoughts. She put her fork down and noticed that Alex had barely touched anything other than his potato.

Gathering some courage, she touched his hand. "I want us to be together. But I don't know how we can do it."

He signed, "Eat."

She forced herself to eat as much as she could and asked for a box. She didn't want to waste it, but she had reached the point where she could no longer put another morsel in her stomach.

Alex finished his and paid for their meals.

Thinking they were driving home, she was baffled when he pulled into a residential area not far from the campus. He parked in a driveway, and then escorted her inside.

She stepped into a cozy, yet modern kitchen. Two metal bar stools were tucked under a raised stone counter, and from the looks of it, that's where Alex ate his meals.

He turned and placed a few things in the kitchen sink. He made a pot of coffee and then gave her the grand tour.

In the dining room was a table filled with books and papers. Through an archway, the small living room was sparsely furnished with a plain gray couch and a matching recliner. A few large ottomans, she decided, served as additional seating. On one wall, opposite a stairwell, was a large screen TV.

He motioned for her to go up the stairs. There were two bedrooms, but only one contained a bed. The other had an old side table, a big upholstered chair, and multiple bookcases filled with books. An extremely small room contained a few boxes. And there was a bathroom. She looked at his bedroom and noticed his bed had been made. The room appeared to be neat except for a pair of running shoes that were casually lying near the foot of the bed. *Even the bathroom looks clean and tidy.*

Maybe she had figured all guys lived in pigsties. She mentally kicked herself for being unfair to him. Why had she thought that he couldn't survive? Slowly she descended the stairs to the living room. The whole house was utilitarian, yet it appeared to be comfortable. She stared at the TV. *Does he have those closed caption words that run across the screen when he watches? He must.*

She had questions about the simplest things. How did he know when the dryer beeped or the oven buzzed? Would he ever notice a sink dripping? Everything appeared to be normal. "Alex, how do you…" She realized she had started to call to him and went into the kitchen. When she was sure he was looking at her, she asked, "How do you know when your laundry is done?"

He took her hand and showed her the laundry area. He pointed to the dial where it said *OFF* and grinned.

"So you just check?"

He nodded, but then took her back to the kitchen and showed her a timer. He set the timer for thirty seconds, allowing her to watch the dial countdown to zero and start flashing.

He took her to the front door and showed her how the doorbell flashed a light. Then, in his dining room, he showed her how his phone worked by dialing her number. Suddenly she felt very foolish for even questioning how he could survive. Her heart strummed until she could feel her pulse in her fingertips. She reached out to him and pulled him close. "I'm so sorry for questioning your ability to liv—"

His mouth crashed on hers, and she was lost in the glorious sensations he created in her. Hot and passionate, she knew her heart would never stop him. The loss that overtook her as he broke the kiss made the deep recesses of her body feel as though they were being pulled from her.

He stepped away and then went into the kitchen. She

followed him. His forearm was on an upper cabinet and his head rested against his arm. That kiss was ready to lead to more. She knew it and apparently, he did, too. But she wasn't ready to take that step. Not yet. She went to him, took his free hand and intertwined her fingers with his. He squeezed her hand and she knew they were on the same page.

He stepped back, opened a cabinet, withdrew two mugs, and filled them with steaming coffee. He didn't have creamer, so he offered her milk. She accepted it and added the milk to her cup. A moment later, he vanished out the back door, and when he returned, he had their backpacks.

She smiled as he placed hers on a dining room chair, but the smile he returned was hungry. That little niggling feeling went through her. Would he expect more? She wanted more. She wanted to be lost in him forever, but that was in fairytales, and this was real life.

She sat, searched her bag, and began to pull out materials to work on a paper that was due the following week. A few times, she'd reach across the table and touch his arm. Or he'd do the same. He refilled her coffee. Quietly, they studied for hours. In the total silence of his house, she was able to concentrate and actually finish her paper. She closed her computer and opened her sign language manual.

He closed his computer, slid it to one side, and took her manual from her. Then he led her to the couch. "Talk."

"My heart wants you. My head says everything is wrong."

"Why?"

"Because you do not hear. I know it might not make sense to you, but how will it affect us? How will it affect your… Who will hire you? I mean, not everyone signs. Not everyone wants to sign or even cares about making the extra effort to try to learn."

"The company who hires me will do so because I am good. If they cannot accept the fact that I am Deaf, then I don't want to work for them." He took her hand and brought it to his lips and kissed it. "I can live in a hearing world. I can communicate. We communicate, yet you still can't sign more than a few words."

"But what about friends?"

He raised his eyebrows. "Do you think your friends will turn away from you because of me?"

"Maybe. Or maybe, they'll learn to sign."

He nodded. "There are many who will back away because they don't understand." He narrowed his eyes slightly. "Today those boys have it easier than I did. And why do I have a girl with hearing in there?" He furrowed his brow as if to ask Savannah what she thought, and then smiled. "She needs as much help as they do, but she doesn't need words. She only needs to understand. Numbers are words. She needs to know how to use the numbers. I can give that to her."

"I was watching you teach. You're very good."

"I am a better designer than a teacher. I love what I'm studying. But I could not design if I did not understand math."

She realized she was getting used to his signing. Sometimes he would spell the word out, but often she could tell what he was saying by the other words he signed, as long as he did it slowly. Plus, there was the expression on his face as he talked. It was an indication and almost a part of the signs that he made.

They talked for more than an hour and finally she curled next to him and tucked her head into that soft spot between his chest and his arm. She gently reached for his hands and stilled them. He held her close with his arm tucked around her. Listening to his heart beating, she wondered what it must be like not to hear. He'd never heard the call of a bird or a dog bark. It also meant that he would never hear a child cry or a baby's first word. That stopped her. *How would I cope with a deaf child?*

Savannah closed her computer and called to Ashley, "Come in; it's unlocked."

"Where were you last night?"

"No 'good morning'? Just instant interrogation?"

"Of course. I want all the juicy details." Ashley flopped into the comfy chair.

"It's not what you think. I got permission to skip class because I was going to be with Alex while he tutored high school students in Geometry. Then we went out to eat. Afterwards, we went back to his place and studied. Hardly exciting." She slipped on her heavy sweater.

"Seriously? Is there something wrong with your sex drive?"

"Okay, he kissed me, and we talked."

"That's all you did was kiss?"

"If that kiss was another second longer, we'd have been in deep trouble."

"It's fun. You need to drop those puritanical ideologies from your head and get with the times."

"Oh, Ash, I'm not that bad!" She lifted her heavy coat from the hook in her closet, slipped her computer into her backpack, and went to her door. "Ready? I'm starved."

As they walked across the campus lawn, Ashley asked, "How do you talk to him?"

"As long as he signs slowly, I understand him. Sometimes he texts, and other times, he has to spell the words."

"This is serious between you two, isn't it?"

"Maybe. We're working on that." Savannah pulled open the door to the cafeteria. "He wants us to join his family tonight at Silent Spaghetti."

Ashley looked wide-eyed at Savannah as though something was terribly wrong.

"I know. I'm scared to death. I can barely sign."

Ashley frowned. "Great! Meet the Van Doorns. It's serious if he wants you to meet his family. What is it about his last name? It's so familiar."

Savannah shrugged and took a lunch tray from the stack in the cafeteria.

The rest of her school day sped by, and when she finished her last class of the day, she groaned. She knew she'd be up all night working on her one paper. As soon as she reached her dorm, she took a quick shower and blew her hair dry. She braided a small section of hair and wrapped it around her head like a hair band. Wanting to at least look sophisticated, she wore her black dress pants with a fuzzy, light-blue sweater. Then she checked the weather report. It was beginning to feel as though every time they'd had Silent Spaghetti it rained. Tonight's prediction was seasonably cold. She checked the mirror one last time to be absolutely certain her makeup was perfect.

When Ashley didn't knock on the door, she went to Ashley's room and rapped lightly. Ashley opened the door wearing sweats. "I'm not going. I'm sick. I feel terrible. I can't breathe through my nose and my throat hurts."

"You're doing this to get out of going. Just throw me to the lions!"

"I'm not. I promise I'm not. I was sitting in class and I could feel my throat getting worse by the minute." Ashley sneezed.

"Want me to bring something back for you?"

"Yes, one of those slushy drinks. Any color but red."

Savannah nodded. "Okay, keep your germs. I'll go without you, but I swear you are doing this to get out of going with me."

Ashley sneezed again. "Just make certain I'm not dead when you get back."

Savannah rolled her eyes and left her friend. When she opened the door to step outside, Alex stood there with his bright smile.

"Where is Ashley?" he signed.

"Sick. Seems she's come down with a cold and sore throat today."

"Does she need to go see a doctor?"

Savannah shook her head. "Not at this point. It's probably a simple cold. I'll check on her when we get back. She wants me to bring her one of those frozen drinks from the convenience store."

Alex's expression said volumes about Ashley's poor choice of nutrition.

"I know. But that icy cold feels so good on a sore throat. I'll pick up some of those chewable vitamin C tablets to go with it."

"My car?"

She nodded.

They walked to his car, and he held the door for her. He always made her feel special, and she liked it. She signed, "Thank you."

He shook his head.

"What? Did I do it wrong?"

He closed her door and went to his side of the car. Once seated with his belt on, he looked at her and began to sign. "Talk and sign together."

"But you don't."

She watched him inhale.

He said something, signing too quickly and she frowned. "Huh?"

He pulled out his phone and texted to her what he had said. -I sign. That's what I do. But you are still too new not to talk while signing.

"But--"

He shook his head and texted. -Using your words as you sign is very much a part of your signing.

"I truly do not understand."

-Believe me.

She held her hand up, as if to ask him to wait. "Your parents know I'm coming?"

He nodded.

"Do they know that I'm really lousy at signing?" She could tell he was laughing on the inside. "What's so funny?"

He tucked his phone away and signed, "Do you think they won't be able to talk to you or you to them?"

"I don't know. You talk slowly to me, and you know that I don't know all the signs."

He put the car in reverse and backed out of the parking space.

She knew not to attempt to talk to him while driving because he couldn't read her lips and watch the road. But the uneasiness inside her was building. *What are his parents going to think of me?* Then she remembered what Ashley had said about the relationship being serious if he wanted her to meet his parents.

She shifted in her seat, and then clasped her hands in her lap only to move them to her seat and under the edges of her outer thighs.

Alex reached over and took her left wrist. Bringing her hand to his lips, he kissed her fingertips. If he was trying to reassure her, she wasn't certain it was working even though his kiss sent tingles through her.

He pulled into the parking lot behind the restaurant and then led her through the alleyway between the buildings to the front entrance.

"Wait!" She tugged on him to stop before he could open the restaurant's door. "You just told me to sign with my words, but this is a no talking zone. I'm not allowed to talk!"

He fingerspelled, "PRETEND."

"They are going to hate me. I'm no good at this. Take me back to the dorm or"–he attempted to cut her off, but she ignored him and kept talking–"never mind; I'll walk back." She started to turn away, but he caught her arm. "No!" she continued. "I can't do it. I'll make a fool of myself, and they will think you are crazy for being with me."

He shook his head and gathered her into his arms giving her a light but earnest kiss before releasing her. He signed, "They will like you because you are with me. Meet my family."

She took her gaze from him and realized several people were standing beside her. Magically sinking into the concrete of the sidewalk would have been better, but she tried to smile as she held out her hand to his mother. "I'm Savannah Chisholm. Pleased to meet you."

"It's our pleasure." The woman spoke and took Savannah's hand. Then she began to sign as she spoke. "This is Alex's dad."

Savannah smiled and offered her hand to him. "Pleased to meet you, sir."

"And his sisters, Gwen and Emily."

She offered her hand to each one.

Now she could tell that Gwen was older than her brother and pregnant. Emily looked like a high school student. Alex's parents appeared to have a few years on her own parents, but Savannah wasn't certain how many. The entire family was blond and blue-eyed. Alex resembled his mom with her honey blonde hair, smaller bones, and angular features.

Alex was about the same height as his dad, but his dad had a bigger build and his hair was fading to white. Then she caught Alex signing behind her. She turned and faced him. From the mischievous expression on his face, she surmised he'd been saying something about her. She narrowed her eyes at him and could tell he was now laughing.

Alex's father pulled the door open and they all stepped inside. The father signed seven or at least she thought it was the number seven. She looked at her fingers and attempted to count in ASL. They were given a large table, and a minute or two later, another young man joined them. It didn't take much to figure out that Alex's older sister was married.

Alex nudged her and pointed to the shrimp scampi on the menu. She shook her head and pointed to the box pertaining to her meal ticket. He frowned and indicated for her to choose whatever she wanted.

"Don't you like shrimp?"

"I love it," she mouthed, and then pointed to the meal ticket warning. "I must stay within my meal ticket."

He made it clear that she didn't have to use her ticket, but she shook her head. It was obviously going to be a long night with his family. In a way, she was pleased to see Andy would be their waiter because he knew she was limited with her ability to sign. She pointed to what she wanted, and he smiled as he wrote it. At least now, she knew how to order her tea the way she liked it. Then she watched Alex as he ordered. Alex didn't sign as quickly to Andy as he did to his family. In fact, the entire table signed slowly to Andy.

Savannah realized the family was signing at the speed of light to each other and she had no clue what they were saying. When Alex nudged her, he signed that his parents wanted to know if she liked going to the university.

"It's good," she mouthed the words and signed good.

Alex nudged her again and indicated for her to keep going.

"I'm a junior. One year left."

She looked at Alex and could tell he was laughing as he signed to keep going.

She returned her gaze to his parents and tried to sign as much as possible but had to fingerspell a few things. "I'm taking ASL with Prof. Stockton. It's my first semester. I thought it would be easy, but it's not."

Judging from the look on Mr. Van Doorn's face, she figured he didn't like the idea that she thought sign language would be easy. At least when her salad was served, it gave her something to do other than talk. She felt totally uncomfortable. She was failing the meet-the-parents' test and she didn't like failure.

Alex watched Savannah and his parents throughout the meal. He knew she was nervous, but she was doing well. Several times he touched her leg in an attempt to assure her that she was doing fine. Her focus remained a little too intent on her salad. He wanted her to relax and enjoy the evening with his family. When the main course was served, he pushed a side plate of shrimp scampi at her. He'd ordered two servings because he wanted her to have one. The look on her face alone was worth it.

She protested.

"Eat. It's good." He stabbed a shrimp with a small fork and passed the impaled crustacean to her. He let it be known that he would not accept a refusal. "I got it for you."

She carefully removed the curled delicacy from the end of the seafood fork and ate it. He could tell by her expression that she enjoyed it. When she was involved with him, she relaxed and was herself. But as soon as her attention was drawn back to the family, she seemed to tense.

"Dad, please slow down when you try to talk to her. She's

still learning." He turned to Savannah. "My father wants to know what your parents do?"

"*My* parents?"

He nodded.

She turned to his father and attempted to sign that her father worked in a large factory, and her mother did childcare in their home.

Halfway through her signing, his little sister dissolved into a fit of giggles. The whole table tried to hide their laughter.

Gwen signed, "Tell her."

He took Savannah's hands and showed her the sign for work. Then slightly out of sight of everyone, he showed her what she had signed. "Bad. I'll tell you later."

Savannah swallowed and put her hands to her lap as though afraid to try to sign more.

He knew the dinner was not going well for her and decided it had been a mistake to invite her when she'd be so restricted. It would have been better if she had met them in their home. Talking wasn't allowed and her ability to sign was much too limited. He did manage to get her to eat the scampi, and she insisted on sharing her spaghetti with him. He motioned to the waiter and asked for a box when she indicated that she couldn't eat another bite.

There was a bit of chaos as the check was brought to the table. She passed her meal ticket to his dad and he took it. Andy must have split her meal from the others because Alex watched as she touched the school's logo on her phone and spotted the Aldo's logo. Then she started to leave a tip.

Alex took the cash and handed it back to her. "No. My father has taken care of the tip."

"But it was my meal and I paid for it with my ticket."

He shook his head, and then smiled as he raised his eyebrows and bumped his wrists together under the table.

You have to work? She mouthed.

He winked. "No." He signed, "We."

She looked at him with a perplexed expression as he held her coat for her. His younger sister tugged on his sleeve and he signed, "Just a moment."

She frowned.

Emily was jealous of Savannah. Emily would have preferred to sit by him, garnering his attention the whole evening. Instead, tonight his attention was given to Savannah.

He looked at his little sister. "Hey, squirt, want to play tennis Saturday morning if it doesn't rain?"

"No, it's too cold."

"Pick something else."

"Really, anything?"

He frowned. "Depends. Text me."

She hugged him and he dropped a kiss on her head.

The family walked outside, and he could tell by the way Savannah stuffed her hands in her pockets that she was glad to be out of the restaurant.

His mother turned to Savannah. "I'm so happy you joined us. I know this was difficult for you, but you are doing well for your first semester with ASL. What is your major?"

"Communications. I'd like to be able to work in a corporate environment and develop methods for instant and accurate information exchange. I'm getting a minor in marketing instead of information technology because I felt as though marketing will give me a slight edge. It's not just information, but how it's presented."

"It appears you've given this some thought."

"Yes, ma'am, I have."

"Did my son tell you that Communications is my specialty?"

"No, ma'am, he only told me that you worked for the university."

"Stop by my office tomorrow at ten. I'm in The Heart.

We'll chat some more."

"Thank you, ma'am. Which building?"

"Gales Court, 10-C."

Savannah nodded, and his mom smiled. Alex considered that to be good. A few more pleasantries were exchanged with the family members, and then they all left.

He walked Savannah to his car. "Let's get Ashley's drink."

Savannah nodded but seemed distant.

When they were both in his car, he asked, "What's wrong?"

"Everything."

"Why would you say that?"

"You said that I signed something bad."

He laughed. "This is work. I will show you what you signed when I take you home."

She grimaced. "What else did I do wrong?"

He showed her the difference between left as in left turn and amount of time left. "It's OK, an easy mistake to make. Year is another. You are trying and that's what counts."

"No. I made a fool of myself and of you."

"No one condemned you." He took out his phone. Too much effort to fingerspell. -Communicating with you, at this point, is slow and tedious. But everyone knows you are just starting to learn. I think my mom was impressed that you are doing so well. Your effort is showing.

"I have a good tutor."

He smiled, put the car in gear, and went to the convenience store for Ashley's drink. He remembered the first time he got sick on campus. He also had to endure the embarrassment of his mother getting him from the dorm and taking him to the local hospital's emergency department. That little *I'll-get-over-it* cost him three days in the hospital and another week of lost classes until he was well enough to come back to school.

-I'll bring her a drink tomorrow morning. I'll phone you to

come get it from me. What time? Is 7:45 too early?

"Too late. Make it seven. I've got an eight o'clock class. I need my breakfast, too."

-OK 7:30 and I will bring you something special you can eat on the run.

He wouldn't let Savannah pay for her friend's drinks, and he made her get two. He also picked up a bottle of ginger ale along with several other items he decided Ashley might need, including chewable vitamin C and a bag of cough drops. -You don't have the money and I do. My treat.

She frowned and got back into the car carrying the two big iced drinks while he carried the two bags of other stuff they had bought.

When they reached her dorm, he told her to wait before getting out of the car. "This is…" He bumped his two wrists together. "This."

He leaned over to where she was sitting and put his arms around her, drawing her near. When she was close enough, he inhaled her wonderful scent and placed his lips on the tender skin of her neck. He kissed her. That wonderful sensation sizzled within him, growing in intensity with each tiny kiss. He knew it would plague him for the rest of the night.

avannah ran downstairs and took the package from Alex. Then she delivered the drink to a still groggy Ashley who readily accepted it. But Ashley refused to even consider the protein bars, swearing she couldn't swallow any food with her throat being so raw. There was no question in Savannah's mind that Ashley was dealing with more than a simple cold.

Savannah made her way across the campus, chomping on the cream cheese filled granola muffin before washing it down with the orange-flavored protein drink that Alex had given her. She made it to her class with plenty of time to spare.

She sat through that class, and then headed over to The Heart in plenty of time to meet Alex's mother at ten o'clock. It didn't take much to find Gales Court. Some of the buildings dated back to the 1700's, and Gales Court was one of the oldest ones, according to the little plaque near the door. It was a three-story brick building with two long wings on each side. The interior of the building looked like a posh mansion compared to the rest of the buildings on campus. Just inside the door, a sign pointed the way to the various departments. The Colonial décor was beautiful. Gold cords pulled heavy burgundy and gold drapes to the side of the large, deep windows. The wallpaper looked like silk that had been printed in shades of gold. She wanted to touch the wall covering to be certain of its material. But when she saw an old globe that stood taller than her waist, she strode to it. For thousands of years, people had to walk or travel on horseback to reach the nearest town. News would take weeks or months. She stood staring at the globe as her imagination took her back in time.

"Savannah! I'm so glad you came. Follow me, and we'll go into my office."

The jolt of hearing her name made her almost jump. Then she realized it was Mrs. Van Doorn. Savannah struggled to sign as she spoke. "I apologize. Alex told me how many things I signed wrong last night."

"Savannah, I can hear as well as you can. You don't have to sign around me when it's just us, unless you want to practice."

"Oh." She put her hands in her jeans pockets. "Signing is difficult."

"It is, yet most of the signs make perfect sense when you understand the origin of them. Signing is as old as civilization. Unfortunately, you will only have a minimal amount of Deaf culture history during the first two semesters. But Alex will teach you."

Savannah nodded and followed the older woman into a room.

"Have a seat." Alex's mother pointed to a comfortable-looking chair.

On her desk was a nameplate engraved Marianna Van Doorn with several initials after it, and the second line said Dean of Communications. What was left of the undigested granola muffin rolled up the back of Savannah's throat, forcing her to swallow to keep it contained. "Alex didn't tell me you were a dean, Dr. Van Doorn."

His mom smiled. "Obviously, you weren't paying attention the first day of orientation."

"Probably not. I was so excited to be here, and I had so much to do. Sitting listening to speakers welcome us wasn't exactly…um…"

Mrs. Van Doorn laughed. "You and every other student on this campus. I've been telling them that for years. You've done well; your grades speak volumes."

"Thank you." All those little nervous vipers in Savannah's guts seem to come alive during her moments of panic. At the moment, they were twisting everything together and snapping at her innards. *What else can go wrong?*

"I want you to be totally comfortable coming to me with any questions you might have. I know it's difficult to step into the Deaf community. I grew up with it." Alex's mother smiled. "My father lost his hearing in an industrial accident. I was too little at the time to actually remember it or even remember my father with hearing." She brushed her blonde bangs to one side. "I grew up signing. It was easy for me to fall in love with a man who was Deaf. But I know what it's like from both sides of the playing field. Learning to accept can be the most difficult thing."

The woman continued to talk about deafness and the Deaf community. She explained how the Deaf consider themselves to be part of an elite society with their own culture. But she also spoke about the challenges of being Deaf and the many misconceptions. "You will find yourself straddling the two worlds."

"Thank you, Dr. Van Doorn. I appreciate your openness. And I'm truly sorry that I'm not better at signing. Is there anything else before I leave? I have a class in ten minutes in the Colburn Building."

"No, Savannah. Go to your class. Just remember I am here."

"Thank you." She stood.

"Oh, one more thing," Dr. Van Doorn said. "I'll warn you

my son is a terrible tease. Don't take him too seriously. I'm afraid he's taught his little sister all his tricks."

Savannah grinned. "At least he has a little sister. I wanted one the whole time I was growing up."

"No siblings?"

She signed zero and left. *That wasn't too bad...I guess... maybe. I hope she doesn't think I'm a complete idiot.*

She walked to her next class as fast as she could and got there just before the professor closed the door. Pulling her tablet from her backpack, she was ready to take notes. Part of the way through class, she received a text message.

-Dinner tonight? Let's do something special on Saturday, but first I have that date with my young chick. I'll be available after 1:00 or we can grab a late lunch.

She tried to tell herself that she had jumped into this crazy relationship without really knowing Alex. And if he had another girlfriend, then she didn't need to be wasting her time with him. She swiped the message from her screen and went back to taking notes. She had another problem. His mother was her dean and she had three full semesters to go. *What have I done?*

When class was dismissed, she headed for her dorm. She had leftover spaghetti, her half-eaten steak, and a dozen snacks that Alex had brought this morning from which to choose for lunch. Hunger was the least of her problems. But when she walked up the steps to her room, she discovered Ella in the hallway.

"You do have strange taste in men. He's certainly handsome enough to make anyone want to jump him. I wouldn't mind giving him a few spins around the dance floor, but he just doesn't talk." Ella made a face and began to walk away. "I offered to show him all of my tattoos, but he just stared at me."

"Ella, did anyone ever teach you not to pee in the pond where you swim?"

Ella turned and gave Savannah the most horrified look.

Get over it, Ella, before someone does something really mean to you. Stop trying to steal everyone's boyfriend. Savannah went down the hall to the kitchen. *I'll eat my spaghetti and then check on Ashley.*

There in the kitchen sat Alex. *Oh, that's why the weird comment from Ella.*

He smiled brightly and began signing.

She ignored him and reheated yesterday's spaghetti in the little toaster oven. She didn't want to talk to him. She didn't want to sign. She wanted him to go away.

"What's wrong?" Alex asked, but Savannah had purposely turned her back to him. He clapped his hands to get her attention. Nothing. Frustration filled his chest to the point of feeling as though it would burst any second. It was obvious that she was angry with him over something, but he had no clue what.

He went to where she was standing and physically turned her. She closed her eyes.

He hated trying to speak. Knowing his voice was considered flat, whatever that was, he only knew it apparently lacked something called tonal qualities of the hearing. He had given up trying a long time ago, even though he'd been given voice lessons when he was little. He didn't want to speak. But the need was too great. He had to communicate on her level. Awkwardly he uttered, "Oopen yur eyess. Don't sshut meh hout."

She opened her eyes and glared at him with such a hostile expression that he wondered what was going through her mind.

"You speak?"

"I ham deef, not moot," he verbalized.

"But you speak."

He nodded.

"You can talk."

He partially shuttered his eyes as he looked at her, and he signed, "Don't lock me out. What is wrong?"

She stood looking at Alex trying to figure out what had happened. The frustration from trying so hard to communicate with him and his family, only to discover that he could talk, felt like betrayal. The feeling whipped through her with tornado speed.

He seemed to be searching her eyes for something. Yet somehow as she looked at his face, she also felt that strong attraction that she wished would leave. "I don't want to sign. I'm lousy at it. I've made a fool of myself in front of your family. Furthermore, you never bothered to tell me that your mom is the Dean of Communications. I have three semesters to go! And now I find out that you can talk? I've struggled trying to figure out what you've been saying, and you thought it was funny."

He kept his lips pressed into a thin line, but she could see the movement in his mouth as though chasing a piece of gum.

"I hhate to tahlk."

"But you can. Do you think that is fair to me?"

"My voice…not goud."

She winced as he spoke. *What do I say?* She heaved a few breaths. "Here's the difference; I'm not laughing."

His brow wrinkled, and he said, "You are oopset behcause I lafff?"

She put her hand to his mouth. "This is horrible." She looked around the room. "Let me eat. My classes are over for the next few hours. I can go to your place. This kitchen is not conducive to this conversation."

He raised his eyebrows at her.

"Let's discuss our problems where we can be alone."

He fingerspelled A S H L E Y.

"Mostly sleeping. If she's not better soon, I'll make her go to the clinic on campus."

She offered to share the food that she had prepared, but he turned her down. A half hour later, they left for his place.

Once inside his home, she turned to him and started. "Do you have any idea how frustrating it is to try to converse with you? I've barely had six weeks of ASL and you assume that I can just pick it up as though it is as natural as brushing my teeth. Well, it isn't. I was lousy at Spanish, too! Languages don't come easy to me, even if this is English. I do it this way and it means one thing, if I *goof,* it means something else! How am I supposed to keep it all straight?" She sucked in a few deep breaths. "Now I find out you can talk, too! Why are you doing this to me? I'm supposed to make all the effort while you sit back and laugh." Then another bolt of anger took her. "Then you will see me after your big date with someone else? No. I don't play those games."

He got that same thin-lipped, chasing-the-gum-in-his-mouth look. Then he spoke. "My date iss wiff my lidtil ssisster." He stared at her for a moment and then continued. "My moother wahnted meh to sspeak. Sso I had lessons. How chan I talk when I hannot hear mysself? I know words cohme out, but I do not know if I ssay sem right. There iss no way to tell."

"Okay, you sound horrible. You are too loud and you sound like a sick, squawking seagull." She went to him and touched her fingers to his mouth. "We have problems, don't we?"

He nodded.

She moved her fingers from his mouth to his cheeks, and then ran them through his blond hair. That attraction made her want to kiss him, but she was still too angry and frustrated to let go of her feelings. She turned away and then raised her arms slightly from her sides before turning back to him. "How?" She shook her head. Frustration welled inside of her like a gusher. "You have me meet your parents and I look like a total fool. How do you think that makes me feel?"

He reached in his pocket and withdrew his phone.

"No, don't text me."

He swiped the screen and held it up to her.

It was a text from his father. -She's lovely.

He motioned for her to keep scrolling.

She did and saw where he had asked his dad about her and further up was the text prior to her meeting them for dinner. -She can barely sign, but she's trying so hard.

Frustration turned to foolishness and fell into her stomach like lead weight.

He pushed the screen a little further and she read what was there. -She's incredibly beautiful and I love her. She sees me and not my deafness.

Tears welled in her eyes, and she wiped them away.

"Do oou have da sahme fehlings?"

She touched a finger to his lips and picked up his hands. "Use them or I will never learn." She smiled and could see the relief in his eyes. She never realized how much he spoke with his eyes or how much was written in his expression when he signed. "Your face is such a part of your signing."

"So is yours when you speak, but you forget to look at such things. You rely on your hearing." He pressed his lips into a thin line. "But you haven't answered my question about your feelings towards me."

"The feeling is like a magnet making me want to kiss you forever. You'd better make some coffee, and I do have a class at four."

He made coffee and when he turned to her, she spoke. "I don't know how we can have a serious relationship. I know now that your mom lives in a world that hears, but she also grew up with deafness. How will *we* make it? How will *we* live? I'll never be able to make enough to support a family and live the way I want. I don't want to accept the standard of living that my parents have. I want more. There's this side of me that doesn't want to settle for mediocrity. I want that good job and a nice home. I want children. And what if our children can't hear? Oh, why? What are we going to do? Don't you see that from my perspective everything is so scary?"

Alex poured them each a coffee, took a sip of his and began to sign. "We will succeed. Do you think I'm getting my master's degree for the fun of it? I'm coping with people who forget I'm Deaf, yet I am succeeding, and not because my mom is a dean. I've earned every grade I have. I've always graduated top in my class and I will do it again."

Savannah wrinkled her nose. "You sign too quickly. I only got about five words out of that."

He pulled out his phone and texted what he'd signed.

"You really intend to work? I mean become an architect with an office and clients who speak? How?" Her face was filled with confusion.

-Why not? I will need a partner who speaks, or I sit in a back office and draw whatever someone else tells me. I want my own company. With the right people, I can do anything. I know I can't do it alone in a world where people who hear think that those who don't should be relegated to that back room. I'm going to do it or die trying.

He watched Savannah as she read what he wrote, looking for the clues that told him what she was thinking. When her lips curled slightly upward, he knew she understood.

"But where will you find a partner who signs and speaks?"

He stared at her and signed, "It doesn't have to be another architect."

She scrunched her face and pursed her lips. He could tell she was thinking. If she could see the situation from his angle, then she would understand.

A few minutes later, he took her back to campus for her late Friday class. Watching her as she walked to her class sent his mind and body to places that he tried to reserve for only the very private moments. But she had a way of triggering the flames within him and at the worst of times.

As she approached the door to the building, she turned, smiled, and signed her goodbye.

Oh, I'll wait for you, but it won't be patiently. You have no idea what my feelings are for you. Nor have you realized what we can accomplish together.

Savannah had a love-hate relationship with this marketing class. Three short classes a week filled with proven techniques, but the homework was horrendous. She knew she'd walk out of class with plenty of writing to be done. It wasn't so much the reports that were constantly due, but the research behind each one. When the professor wrote the assignment on the board, Savannah's mind began running with ideas at high speed. The entire class that day had been dedicated to the concept of doing things outside of the box, and how it was a worn-out term when so much of it was simply applying known techniques to new media or audiences. The assignment was to create a marketing plan for a product that existed, such as dish soap, but was being offered by a different company as though it was totally a new thing. The draft would be her midterm grade.

At least this assignment allowed her to create a comprehensive marketing plan. She liked that idea. Plus, she had the ability to choose a product. Certain that there would be plenty of plans generated for various household products, makeup, perfume, jewelry, and even computers or cellular phones, she wanted something different.

Alex was waiting for her as she walked out of the building. She waved and made her way to his car. "Hi, I'm done until Monday morning."

"Good." He pointed to two slushy drinks in the cup holders.

"For Ashley?"

He nodded. "Then I'll take you to dinner."

By the time he drove across campus, she knew she could have walked there faster. She swiped her key and opened the door to Brindlewood dorms, and then headed up the stairs to Ashley's room.

"Hey, Ash, it's me. We've got drinks for you."

Savannah could tell as Ashley greeted them that she'd taken a shower and changed her clothes.

"Feeling any better?"

Ashley shrugged. "Now my ears hurt."

Alex signed for her to go to the hospital. "Ears are important for you."

Ashley looked at Savannah.

"I can't tell you what to do. But you should at least go to the clinic here on campus."

Alex frowned and pointed to his ears.

Savannah signed no. "We'll take her to the clinic."

"I'm starved!" Ashley whined.

Savannah giggled. "Granola bar or protein bar?"

"Soup?"

Savannah nodded. "Give me your meal ticket. The cafeteria will have it."

Ashley handed over her ticket and Savannah and Alex left. The cafeteria was crowded as usual. They chose several things including the soup for Ashley and then took it all back to the dorm. Alex handed over her meal card and Savannah placed all the food on the dorm's kitchen table. Ashley ate both bowls of soup, took a bite of the pizza slice, and then ate the chocolate pudding.

"Let me brush my teeth and change my clothes if you are taking me to the clinic." She pulled at her baggy top. "I don't want to wear this in public."

Alex nodded and signed yes.

Savannah cleaned up the mess they had made. "I'll be right back."

She went to her room, made some changes to her backpack's content. Her tablet sat on her desk. Picking it up, she slipped it in her bag next to her laptop. For some odd reason, she opened a drawer and scooped her flash drives, grabbed her coat, and headed to the dorm's kitchen to wait on Ashley. She stopped short of the kitchen's doorway and listened.

"I've never had a man refuse to talk to me."

Savannah leaned against the wall and crossed her arms over her chest. Ella was up to her tricks and Savannah couldn't wait to see how it played out.

"What's it going to take? You know, dating Savannah is like howling in the wind. It might feel good, but it's not going to get you anything. I've got the goods and I know how to use them."

Ashley started to come out of her room and Savannah held a finger to her lips, signed tiptoe, pointed to her ear, and cupped it.

Ashley stood near Savannah and listened. Her mouth opened and she knitted her brow as she fingerspelled, "HOW DARE SHE?"

"I have toys if you like kinky. Kinky is fun."

Savannah held her hands out as though to claw at the air. Then signed to Ashley, "I'm so angry I can't see straight."

Ashley nodded.

Savannah stepped from where she was and entered the kitchen.

Alex was standing by the window with his back to Ella.

"Gee, Ella, I thought you didn't like the quiet types?"

Ella stuck her chin out. "I can't help it if men like me."

"Did it ever dawn on you that some men might not hear a word that you are saying? Or that they might not care to hear what you say?"

"I don't have to listen to this. You're jealous because I can get any man that I want. I can have your lover boy eating out of my fingers if I wanted him."

"Do you really want him?"

Ella did a one-shoulder shrug. "No. He's rude. He walked away from me."

Savannah walked to where Alex was standing and tapped him on the shoulder, causing him to turn around. She winked at him. Then she turned her attention back to Ella. "He's not rude at all. He merely saved you from a little wrath. Not every man wants you."

"Guess he likes nerds."

Savannah turned and faced Alex. She couldn't hide her smile. "Am I a nerd?"

Alex nodded and grinned.

She moved so that she created a triangle between Alex and Ella but knew Alex could still see to read her lips. "Well, that solves it. Since he likes nerds, you don't qualify. Some of us will make a living in our chosen careers by using our brains, while others will spend their days on their backs. I'd much rather use my brains and save what I have for the top drawer that will never stray because I have what it takes to keep a man."

Ella wrinkled her nose and let out a huffy breath. "Have him, because I certainly don't want a dweeb."

It was Ashley's expression that made Savannah turn her attention to Alex who was glaring at Ella. His hands were fisted at his sides, but it was that thin-lipped mouth movement that he did before he attempted to speak that worried her. She touched his lips.

He moved her fingers and said "No."

Ella seemed to jerk backwards. "Eew! Now I know why he's quiet."

"No, you don't." Ashley said in her cold-laden, nasal voice. "Did it ever dawn on you that he turned his back so that he didn't have to *hear* your nonsense?" She had raised her hands and made quote marks in the air as she said hear.

Ashley had Ella blocked from leaving.

"Let me out of here. You can keep your weirdo."

Savannah raised an index finger and pointed it at Ella. "You wouldn't know what is worth keeping if it fell into your lap. And as for your name-calling, let me teach you one. Slut!"

"How dare you!"

"Knock it off, Ella. You are what you are, and he's deaf. He's graduated as Valedictorian every time, and he will probably do so again this Spring with his Master's degree in Architecture. Furthermore, he's done it while attending regular schools. He's done it in an environment where everyone hears, without anyone to translate or pave his way. He's worked twice as hard to prove himself." She inhaled a few breaths as she watched Ella's eyes. "You don't even have the brains to recognize someone who is deaf."

Savannah took Alex's wrist with one hand and her backpack and coat with the other, and left with Ashley in tow. As soon as they stepped into the cold air, Savannah's ire flew up the back of her throat and she began to rant.

Ashley clasped Savannah by the shoulders. "Calm down. But you were so good! She deserved it."

"What?" Alex signed. "I turned my back to her."

Ashley grimaced. "You don't know what she's done. She had all of that coming."

Savannah's neck still prickled at the thought of Ella. "I'm lousy with confrontations. I should have never lost my temper. But some of the things she was saying—"

"CLINIC," Alex fingerspelled.

The clinic was filled with students and most of them seemed to have the same cold-like symptoms as Ashley. There was nothing to do but wait. Ashley looked bleary-eyed and tired as she watched the TV.

"I can't hear what they're saying. Why don't they turn it up?" Ashley whined.

Alex laughed. "Read their lips."

Ashley sneezed.

Savannah tried to sit still, but the anger she had felt towards Ella lingered. *Maybe if I work on my paper it will take my mind off her.* She pulled out her tablet and began to work on one of her assignments.

Ashley was finally called to the back. Savannah continued to work but realized Alex was watching the TV. She found it annoying that the TV was on with no sound. *Either turn up the sound or turn the TV off.* Then she was irritated with herself because she knew she'd failed to consider Alex who had never had sound on the TV.

When Ashley reappeared, she seemed happier. "I have a double ear infection and a sinus infection. They tested my throat for strep, but it was negative. Did you know when snot is any color other than clear, it's often an indicator of infection?"

Savannah wanted to gag as she packed up her tablet. "Oh, gross!"

Ashley held up the paper with her prescription for an antibiotic. "Will Alex take me to the 24-hour pharmacy on Sebastian Steet? I need to fill this."

Alex nodded. "I told you caraches are not good."

Savannah looked at her phone. *It's after eleven. Three and a half hours here still beats going to the hospital. Strange night.*

It took almost another hour to get Ashley's prescription filled and get back to the dorm. Ashley would have done the same thing for her, but sitting in the university's clinic was not a great way to spend a Friday night.

Alex walked them to Brindlewood's door. Ashley went inside, leaving Savannah alone with Alex.

"I'm so sorry tonight has been horrible. I don't like drama, and there's been too much of it."

Alex took out his phone. -You didn't need to come to my rescue. I ignore people like her.

"Oh, you have no clue. She prides herself on stealing boyfriends." She looked off into the distance and took a few deep breaths. "You know the joke about getting a degree in basket weaving? Well with her, it's not a joke. Her degree will be in something like material arts if she even passes. She'll cheat and steal in a heartbeat."

Alex wrinkled his brow. -Those are serious allegations.

"She's been caught several times, but nothing has come of it."

-Cheating can get a student thrown out.

"I know. That makes the whole thing even stranger. She was caught red-handed during the final exam in History. There's a theory as to why she passed that class and wasn't expelled. And it has to do with the professor."

Alex narrowed his eyes.

"I know. When students know that sort of thing happens, it makes us all wonder why we try so hard."

-Integrity.

She nodded. "I'm so sleepy I can barely stay awake, and after being in that clinic with everyone around me sniffling, I want to get a shower and climb into bed.

-In the morning, I'm taking my little sis to the game store. She wants to buy a new game. Then she wants us to play it.

Savannah leaned against Alex, and he kissed her goodnight. She went inside and started up the stairs. Part way she stopped and texted Alex. He texted back, and it made her smile. She walked the hallway to her room, and as she about to unlock the door, she realized it wasn't latched. She pushed it open with the tip of her electronic key. Then screamed.

Ashley and several others who lived on the floor stuck their heads out of their dorm rooms. Ashley hurried to Savannah's side and stared into the disheveled room. "Omigosh! Do you think *she* did it?"

"Of course *she* did it. I'm not going to pretend that it didn't happen." Savannah punched the number on her phone to call the campus police. As soon as they answered, she told them who she was, where she was, and what happened. Then she texted Alex. She looked at the others who had come to see what had happened. "Esther, will you let Alex in and the campus police when they get here?"

Esther was studying accounting. Her long ash-brown hair hung almost to her knees. Normally she kept it confined in a braid and the braid twirled into a bun, but tonight her hair looked slightly wet and hung free down her back. Esther was one of those quiet people who kept to herself, but she was an excellent student.

During the first two years, Savannah frequently had Esther in classes. If Savannah needed any sort of help in math, Esther was a willing tutor. As a way of saying thank you, Savannah would often invite Esther to pizza at Sal's or would bring back some other treat. Esther's family lived on a small farm. She was as dependent on scholarship money as Savannah.

Standing there looking at her ransacked room sent Savannah's mind to her friends. Ashley was the closest friend, but when Savannah thought about the others, they all had similarities in background, in their dedication to their classes, and their desire to make something of themselves.

Savannah knew she had little to steal. Her laptop and her tablet were in her backpack. She didn't own much, just a few clothes. Most of the things that decorated her room were thrift store finds, a few coins or a couple of dollars here and there. Her parents only sent a few dollars when her dad got paid. But now the little bit she had was ruined.

Alex appeared with Esther. Seeing him gave her a certain amount of comfort. He rubbed her shoulders and she leaned against him. Then she turned to him, wrapped her arms around his waist, and started to cry. He held her tight. All of the anger that had been gripping her the entire evening dissolved into a pit of misery. It was as though the fiber that kept her going and glued together had also melted away.

The police came and eventually Ella stepped from her room in a much too skimpy, see-through nightgown, acting as though everyone had disturbed her sleep. She ran to Savannah and in a syrupy sweet voice said, "Oh, how horrible! Everything you have is ruined. You don't even have a toothbrush. What will you ever do? Who would do such a thing?"

A campus police officer looked at Ella and then came to Savannah and asked her to step into the kitchen.

"Come with me?" She tugged on Alex's hand.

He shook his head and signed, "I'm reading."

She knew exactly what he was doing. Reluctantly, she left him in the hallway and went to the kitchen. The combination of the evening's events draped her in a cloak that sapped every bit of energy from her system. After giving the officer her basic information, she was hit with dozens of questions. He kept asking over and over if she or anyone else had entered the room.

"No, I pushed the door open with the edge of my electronic key." She raised the credit card-like thing on a key chain and dangled it in front of him. "I've not touched a thing and no one has gone in there since I pushed the door open. I called your office and was told not to go in until you guys got here and gave me permission."

"Are you sure?"

"Yes. I'm sure."

"Can you give us the names of everyone in the hall?"

"Yes."

It was after four in the morning when she was allowed to leave. The campus police called the city police department and their crime scene investigations unit. Only once was she allowed to step into her room. Nail polish had been poured on her clothes. Her toothbrush and several other things were in her toilet. If her things didn't have nail polish on them, they had been ruined some other way. She didn't even own nail polish. There were several small things she knew were missing including some money. The dish she kept change in was broken and the coins were gone. Why she had picked up her tablet, she wasn't certain, because she already had her laptop. Now she was glad she had. If it had been left in the room, it would have been ruined.

"I'm taking you home," he signed.

She shook her head.

"You have no choice and no place to go. You can't sleep on the hallway floor. Hot shower and a soft bed. Come."

She followed Alex out of the building and into his car. She was too tired to even care. When they reached his place, she was half asleep. He handed her a pair of his sweats with a drawstring tie and a tee shirt before he sent her to the bathroom to shower. The warm water felt good on her aching body and so did his super soft, big towel. She pulled on his clothes and had a terrible time trying to get the pants tight enough to stay up. But as she stepped out of the bathroom she realized he was gone. Then she saw car lights in the driveway.

When he came inside, he handed her a bag from the 24-hour pharmacy that contained a toothbrush and several other personal care items.

She was almost too tired to thank him. But she took the toothbrush and went back to his bathroom to brush her teeth. He tucked her into bed and vanished. Somehow, in her semi-conscious state, her brain told her she was not alone. She snuggled against his chest. But when she opened her eyes, he was gone. After making her way to the bathroom, she found a note.

I promised Emily we could do that game thing today. I'll be back around 2. I'll take you shopping. Use my clothes washer or whatever you need. Push start on the coffeepot when you are ready for a cup. There's OJ and food in the refrigerator. Pretend it is your house and make yourself at home.

She held the note in her hand and realized how thoughtful he was about everything. After washing and drying the clothes she had been wearing, she got dressed and called Ashley.

"Did you get any sleep?" Ashley asked.

"Yes. Omigosh, Alex was so wonderful. I think I was asleep before he got into bed."

"You slept with him?"

"Um, sleep. Only sleep, well, maybe not. I remember being curled up to him."

"Well, it's about time."

"Ashley, we slept. That's all we did."

"You have this wonderful guy and you slept. What is wrong with you?"

"Oh, I was up at six thirty yesterday morning, met Alex and brought you breakfast at seven thirty and was in class at eight. I ran all day long, and then had an argument with Ella, took you to the clinic and the pharmacy, and came back to the dorm to discover my room had been broken into and trashed. Talked to the police until the wee hours of the morning, came here to Alex's house, took my shower, and tumbled into bed. I think I had been up for twenty-three hours."

"Hey, something is going on in the hallway, hang on." Ashley whispered, "It's city police. I'll call you back."

8

Savannah paced as she drank her coffee. Then her phone pinged an incoming message.

-Who are you and why are you sniffing around Alex? He's mine.

The text had come from Alex's phone. She texted back.
-Who are you?

-I'm his girlfriend.

-Really? For how long?

-We've been together for years.

The exchanges were sporadic and laced with sexual innuendo. Savannah thought there was something not quite right.

-Be home at four, sorry.

Nothing made any sense, but madness had become the norm since Thursday afternoon when she faced Alex's parents.

Twenty minutes after three, Alex stepped through the door. "I'm so tired. Let me catch a nap and then I'll take you shopping and for a meal."

She was too confused to even attempt to ask him about the text messages. She sat at the kitchen's bar seating and studied. Her phone rang, and she picked it up.

"Savannah, you should have been here." Ashley was breathy

as she whispered into the phone. "Ella's been arrested."

"What? I never said a thing about the argument." That little ball of snakes in the pit of her stomach awakened and began their twisting routine.

"Neither did I. But…"

Savannah listened to what had transpired. Her skin prickled at the events that Ashley relayed. A little part of her felt sorry for Ella, yet another part was still angry. "But what makes them think she did it? Is there some sort of evidence?"

"Apparently. Amanda seems to think that Ella said something last night that incriminated her. That was enough to make the police start checking very closely."

"Ah! She said something stupid about not having a toothbrush. How would she know that?"

"Exactly! And earlier Amanda saw Ella in the hallway standing at your door. She told Amanda that she needed your help on something but didn't want to wake anyone up. Amanda went back to her room."

"Ella has never asked for my help on anything."

"They still have your door taped closed. What are you going to do?"

Alex awakened to a dark bedroom. He couldn't remember if it was morning or nighttime. Certain he'd slept straight through the night, he bolted upwards, thinking he'd left Savannah without food. She wasn't in the bed with him. He found her in his kitchen working on her computer.

"Did I oversleep?"

She slightly tilted her head and looked at him. "Slow down."

"Morning or night?"

She shook her head, and then smiled. "It's evening. I was

going to wake you, but I figured you needed the sleep. I ate a snack after you went to bed. May I fix you some dinner?"

"No food in the house."

She shook her head. "You have lots of food. It's only a matter of putting it together." She slid off the stool and went to the cabinet where he kept some canned goods. Then she opened the freezer section of his refrigerator and slipped two frozen hamburgers from the large package. She opened the refrigerator and took out several items. Curiosity had him.

She turned to him. "Relax."

By using his microwave and his stove, she had managed to make a meal for the both of them in a matter of minutes.

"What is it?"

She shrugged. "My mom called meals like this hobo dinner. She usually used leftovers."

After handing him a soupspoon, he eagerly ate every speck in his bowl. Then he gave her the sign for good.

"I can't tell if you are saying good or thank you."

He moved his lips and signed both. Then he tried again. "This is good. Thank you for making dinner."

"Sometimes it's confusing."

"Watch the face."

"You've told me that. It's still difficult."

She took his bowl and cleaned up the counter where they had sat, but he placed the dishes in the dishwasher and washed the two pans she had used.

When he turned back to her, she asked, "Do you have a girlfriend?"

"I'd better. I'm hoping she's more than a girlfriend."

She raised her eyebrows.

He knew something was amiss. "You are my girlfriend. I want you forever."

"No, not me. Someone else. Was there someone before me?"

He shook his head and unclipped his phone from his

belt where it was attached. -I've dated, but nothing serious. I was beginning to think that I would never find a woman that I would ever want.

"Why? You are handsome, and I would think there are plenty of women who would love to go out with you."

He laughed. -I've probably dated every eligible female within the Deaf community. I've dated several women with hearing and most of them knew how to sign. But nothing ever clicked. No strong feelings or attraction. I wanted someone special.

"There's nothing special about me."

He cocked his head. -How can you say that? I knew it when you smiled at me. The chemistry was there like a giant force field. The attraction was so strong.

She nodded. "I feel it whenever you're around me."

He signed, "Good."

She looked intently at him. "So why do I have one of your girlfriends using your phone and texting me to leave you alone?"

"What?" He swiped the screen on his phone. "When?"

"Where?" Her confusion was obvious.

"No." He fingerspelled, "WHEN?"

She shrugged. "I thought you said you were with Emily this morning, but who were you with this afternoon?"

-Emily. I didn't even get to her until 10:30. That's why I was so tired. I barely had four hours of sleep. He looked at his phone and tried to figure out when such a message would have gone out.

"Here." She handed him her phone.

There were seven messages over the course of about two hours all sent from his number, but according to his phone there was nothing sent. *I was with Emily.* He read each message, and he knew it had to have been her. He also knew she had deleted each text. *Why?* -This was from Emily. She's jealous of you. Don't erase it. I want to confront her. Fun is fun, but this isn't cute or funny.

"How did she do it?"

-I'm not certain but I could have sworn I put my phone down on the table when we were playing her new game. When I went to leave, I couldn't find it. She found it in the sofa cushions.

"I was suspicious that it might have been her. It seemed too juvenile to be anyone you would have seriously dated."

You are in so much trouble, Emily. -Let's get you out of here and do some quick shopping. We'll handle Emily tomorrow. Are you spending the night again?

"If you'll have me. I'm still locked out of my room by the police department."

It took a few minutes to get out of the house and drive to the big shopping complex. But once there, he tried to get Savannah to do some serious shopping. She found some jeans that she loved until she saw the price tag. Then she did the same with a pair of slacks.

"I don't care about the money. Do you want to know how much you can spend?

"That might help."

He gave her a figure based on what he had available on a credit card.

She gasped. "Never would I spend that much!"

"Maybe not, but you need more than a change of clothes. Everything in that room is ruined."

He dragged her into the fancy store that sold women's under things and grinned. "Find something pretty. I like pretty."

"They are expensive."

He shrugged. "For you, pretty."

He lifted a skimpy lace thing and handed it to her.

"I want comfortable."

He finally convinced her to buy one very lacy pair of panties with a matching bra. But no matter how hard he tried, he couldn't talk her into the sexy nightgowns. She refused to go into the boutiques, but she willingly went into a discount store that sold brand names. There she settled on three pairs of jeans, four tops, two sweaters, and a pair of slacks. She also found two bras and a package of underwear. He swiped his credit card and was surprised at the total. She really had not spent much, yet she'd found some cute clothes. She still needed more.

But now he had her sizes on everything, except her shoes. They were running out of time. Several stores were already closed.

"Home?"

She nodded.

He drove to the 24-hour drug store and handed her several twenty-dollar bills, and then shooed her inside to get whatever items she wanted.

She spent quite a bit of time, and he figured she was either searching or trying to remember. He didn't want to go in and check on her because she might be embarrassed about buying some things. She smiled as she came out of the store, and then attempted to hand him the leftover money.

"No, keep it. You might need it for something."

The drive home only took a few minutes, but the feeling inside him began to build. They had slept without problems because they were both exhausted, but they weren't that tired tonight. *Give her the bed and take the sofa. No, I want her in my arms.* The mental battle had begun. By the time he unlocked his back door and flipped on the light in the kitchen, he knew he needed to talk to her. *You already know her answer.*

He motioned for her to follow him as he went up the stairs. "You'll be here for a few days." *Maybe forever?* "I'll make room for your things."

His furniture wasn't exactly to his taste. His mom knew someone in their neighborhood who was about to have an estate sale and managed to let him get a few pieces early.

He bought what had been the guest room furniture and his living room set had been in their sitting room. His dining room table was their kitchen set. Several bookcases and a few other things that he knew would be serviceable were purchased at the same time. The best deal was the TV.

He unloaded one side of the chest of drawers, moving a few things to a shelf in the closet. Then he moved his clothes in the closet to one side and retrieved a few hangers for her. The bathroom wasn't too difficult. There were several drawers in the bathroom cabinet and most were unused. He merely moved his stuff to the drawers on the one side.

It took him longer to move his things than it did for her to add hers. She vanished into the bathroom and the scent of her soap filled the air. When she reappeared, she was wearing his things from the previous night. He grinned as he saw her. "I like you in my clothes. You're hot."

She looked at him and frowned.

"What?"

She signed sleep.

"Yes. Sleep." He fanned his face and signed hot.

Sex was an important topic, and they hadn't discussed it. He sighed and went to the bathroom to prepare for bed. The drawers he'd left open were now closed. Curiosity got him. He opened them and was surprised to see how empty they looked. Maybe he hadn't given her enough money to replace what she needed. He took a shower and then figured maybe he should have taken a cold one. *Maybe she'll be asleep.*

Showered and shaved, he walked into his bedroom to find her sitting on the edge of the bed.

He sat beside her. "What?"

She shrugged.

"Tell me."

The look on her face was of sadness. Then she wiped her fingers across her eyes.

He leaned over and kissed her. Still, he wrapped her in his arms. She clung to him as though hanging on for her life. Heat surged through him. They fell onto the bed. His fingers discovered bare skin, and the storm within him swept fury through his entire being. It's not what he had intended, but the intensity was beyond anything he could have ever imagined. Then he realized there was moisture in her eyes.

He backed away from the kiss and stared deep into her pale blue eyes. Uncertain why she was crying, he kissed the moisture away while trying to tether his own desire. He knew they should stop, but he wasn't certain if that's what she wanted. Her fingers still gripped him.

He rolled over, pulling her on top of him. "Talk to me."

She sat up, but kept her hand on his chest, as if to say, don't move. "I'm glad you stopped, because I don't think I had the heart to say no to you." She wiped more tears from her eyes. "I was taught that I should be married first."

"That's a line that I don't want to cross until you're ready." He wasn't certain she understood what he was saying.

"I don't want what is happening between us to go wrong. I want us to be certain."

He smiled, pulled her to him for a light kiss, and when it ended, he signed, "I know what I feel."

She ran her hands up his chest, and then down his arms until she grasped his hands in hers. She pulled him to his feet.

He couldn't talk without using his hands, so he was forced to watch her expression while withholding his thoughts. She leaned into him and kissed him but kept a tight grip on his hands. The heat her kiss generated had to have been obvious, yet she didn't pull away from him. She had the lead and he didn't dare attempt to change that.

She finally broke the kiss, but instead of backing away she pressed her head to his chest. Her breath was heavy and ragged, matching his own. Letting go of his hands, she slid her arms around his waist.

Maybe it was better not to talk.

After a few moments, she looked up at him with sadness in her eyes. "Now what do we do?"

"We sleep?" He made certain she understood it was a question.

She nodded.

It's not what he wanted to do. He wanted to remove her clothes and kiss every square inch of her body. "Do you want me to sleep on the sofa?"

She shook her head, pointed to the bed and made the sign for together.

This wasn't going to be easy, but he knew he had to be patient. She said she wanted to be certain, and he had no clue what he could do to help her make up her mind. He turned down the bedding and watched as Savannah slipped between the covers. Then he turned out the light and climbed in next to her. If he rolled on his side with his back to her, it would seem rude, but if he rolled on his side facing her... *I can't do that without touching.*

She decided for him. She snuggled to his side and put her head on his chest.

It's going to be a very long night.

When Savannah's breathing became rhythmic, he knew she had fallen asleep. He reached for his phone on the nightstand beside his bed and looked at the time. He still was facing the situation with Emily. If he said anything to his father, Emily would probably lose her phone and be put on restriction. His father didn't tolerate certain things, and her texting trash to Savannah would fall in that category. If he said anything to his mom, Emily would be in just as much trouble, maybe more. He didn't want her punished, but he wanted her to understand that what she did was wrong.

Savannah bolted upright and ran to the window. He realized he must have drifted off to sleep at some point, because now he was wide awake again. Flashing lights went past his window, then more. There was a firehouse nearby, but it never bothered him. He was used to the lights and occasionally he could feel the rumble of the heavy trucks as they drove past. She turned back to him and motioned for him to come. He joined her at the window and figured out what she was seeing. The sky was orange in the direction of the campus. Whatever it was - it was big.

Savannah rushed to her phone and then he watched her response, but she had absent mindedly turned away from him. She walked to his phone and handed it to him. It was flashing an incoming text.

He opened the message from his mom, read it, and responded. -Yes, Savannah is here with me. After the incident the other night, they won't let her back into her dorm room.

-I'm going over there now. I've been informed that Brindlewood is on fire.

He sucked in a deep breath before looking at Savannah. From the look on her face, she already knew.

avannah looked at Alex and mouthed Brindlewood.

"There's nothing we can do." He pointed to her. "Ashley?"

She motioned for him to wait. Then she disconnected her phone call with Ashley, after they had promised to stay in touch. "That was Ashley. She's staying with her boyfriend Matthew tonight. They had been out and as he brought her back to the dorm, they spotted the fire. She's either talked or texted with most of our friends. The only one she hasn't been able to reach is Esther Zookerman. Esther doesn't have a cell phone."

"Do you want to go over?"

"As you said, there's nothing we can do. Someone from the fire department is doing a roll call and I'm accounted for."

She came back to the window, leaned her arm against the top of the lower sash, and stared at the yellow glow that ended in brown smoke. *Now what?*

There was a finality to the fire, an irrevocable end of whatever she had owned. No chance to clean it up or use it again. No Ashley two doors from her. Jill, Amanda, Michi, Aisha, Clarissa, Esther, or the other twenty-some women who lived on her floor wouldn't be her dorm mates. There were over a hundred students in that dorm. Computers, flash drives, textbooks, everything, gone…lost in flames. She said a silent prayer that everyone had gotten out safely. Deep in her heart, she knew that things were just replaceable stuff, but lives weren't. Still it hurt to think she'd lost the little bit that she had.

She paced around as Alex climbed back in bed. But she wasn't ready to go back to sleep. The chaos in her life was almost overwhelming, yet strangely she felt as though she were in a protected bubble watching it, much like standing in Alex's bedroom and seeing the distant glow. She looked at Alex who appeared to have fallen asleep. There was no desire to sleep. Tiptoeing from the room, she went downstairs and into the kitchen where she made a pot of coffee. *He needs a single serve pot.*

There was a surreal feeling to all of it. She listened to the coffee dripping into the pot. *It resembles my life, an unstoppable flow.* As the last drops fell from the basket, she fixed a cup of the dark brew. She took a few sips, and then realized that she was trying so hard not to make any noise because she didn't want to awaken Alex. She laughed to herself. *I could turn on the TV, and he wouldn't hear it even if the volume were set on high.*

She was facing midterms this week. Her marketing plan was her midterm as was another paper for a different class. It didn't matter that her life was in tatters. Everyone in Brindlewood would be expected to carry on as though nothing had happened. She finished her cup and poured another. *I'll never sleep.*

Ella. Why must we make allowances for poor behavior? Was I wrong to stand up to her? Yet I am punished. She finished her drink, turned off the coffeepot, placed her cup in the sink, and returned to Alex's bedroom. The orange glow of the fire cast shadows through the front window. The fire looked worse. Visible licks of flame leapt upwards. *Why? How does a fire burn like that when there are sprinklers installed in the ceilings?*

Suddenly, it felt like a huge weight had been dropped on her shoulders. No longer did she want to stand there and watch the flames like a pyromaniac. She wanted to sleep and sleeping next to Alex was delicious. Slipping between the sheets, she snuggled to his back. His hand found hers and their fingers intertwined. *This is what life is about.*

She awakened to the aroma of coffee and realized that Alex was standing next to her. His smile was contagious. She lifted her arms to him. He leaned down and kissed her.

"Get dressed," he signed. "Lots to do today."

She remembered all the new clothes she'd bought, and like a small child, she couldn't wait to wear them. After pulling on a pair of jeans and an icy-blue turtleneck, she put on some mascara and a tiny amount of eye shadow. Then she twirled her hair onto a knot and secured it with long decorative pins. Whoever was looking back at her in the mirror looked good, and that made her smile

She made the bed and cleaned up any mess before going downstairs to Alex. He had made scrambled eggs, sausage patties, and English muffins. She smiled. "My favorite meal of the day."

He opened a cabinet and showed her his cereal collection. "No time for big breakfasts during the week."

"Any word on the fire?"

He nodded as he sat beside her. "Mom said the whole building is gone. She's at the office working to find places for the displaced students."

"I have an idea. If you stop at the supermarket, we can buy groceries, and I'll make dinner for everyone at your house. At this point, your mom's life has been as disrupted as all the Brindlewood students."

"Too late, Gwen is cooking." He frowned. "You need to know that my sister and her husband both have cochlear implants. But they might not be wearing them. I think they only wear them when in public. Gwen says too much noise."

"Slow down."

"Repeat?"

She shook her head. "I'm trying very hard."

He smiled at her. "You are doing well. Ready to face my family again?"

She nodded.

Alex took their plates and loaded the dishwasher. Then he turned around, faced her, and signed, "Bring your computer if you want to study. There will be a football game to watch."

She laughed. "I don't think I've seen a game since I left home. My father is a Vikings fan."

Alex shook his head.

"Can we go to Brindlewood? I want to see."

He nodded.

They made their way to the campus where they were forced to park by the main cafeteria and walk to where the building once stood. There was a foul odor in the air, and the closer they got the stronger the smell became. Someone had installed orange plastic fencing to keep onlookers from getting too close. Several fire trucks remained on scene, and what was left of the building still smoldered. It hit her that this might have made national news, panicking her mother. She rethought that and decided her mother hadn't called, so she probably didn't know. Savannah called home.

As she talked to her mom, she noticed Alex kept placing his hand over his nose. She motioned for them to leave. There really wasn't anything left to see, and there was that strange, acrid odor. Alex seemed pleased to get away from the stench.

But when Alex drove to a high-dollar community and

pulled through the gates, she inhaled. *This is where he grew up?* Beautiful homes, like mini mansions, were perfectly landscaped. There was a golf course and a lake. She'd never seen such a place. No one back home lived like this. Not that the University sat in the big city, but the town was larger than where she'd grown up. He pulled into a driveway. A three-story stone house loomed before her. *Yikes!*

He took her hand and went to the front door. After pressing several buttons, he opened the door. "Home."

She nodded and followed him through the house. Overhead lights were flashing and soon his father appeared. He touched a panel on the wall and the lights quit flashing. She knew it had to be some sort of security system to alert the family that someone had entered. She signed hi and then remembered what Alex had said about speaking while signing. She extended her hand to him, but he took her by surprise when he drew her into a hug. Then he signed something that she didn't know. Her insides were twisting.

Alex and his dad signed too quickly, and she wasn't certain what they were saying other than something to do with sleep. *Does his father know we've been sharing a bed? Oh, please, I don't need to blush.*

Alex took off through the house with her in tow. The sound of video game gunfire came from somewhere within. She fingerspelled video game and covered her ears.

"You hear it?"

She nodded. "Very loud."

Alex took off in the direction of the sound as though he knew where to find the game. She wasn't certain what the décor of the house would be called, but she figured it was traditional. It was plain, somewhat modern, but comfortable and not stuffy like colonial, Victorian, or one of the more formal styles. One room contained a grand piano, and she wondered why, but decided that maybe his mom played.

As they got closer to the video game, she covered her ears. There, in the back of the house, was what appeared to be a den. Alex walked in, picked up a remote, and the TV ceased. He signed at the speed of light and Emily was signing back. Whatever they were saying was making Emily very upset. Savannah stepped between them.

"Emily, I can't sign very well so pay attention. Your brother is very upset with you, and he has every reason to be. What you did was not nice."

Emily looked away and Savannah went to her.

"No. I want to talk to you. Watch me."

When she had the teen's attention, she smiled. "Your brother loves you. He will always love you. Being with me isn't going to change that. One day you will find a guy and fall in love. Do you think that will change the way you feel about your brother?"

"He's mine!" she said aloud.

Hearing Emily speak with such clarity, momentarily shocked Savannah "Yes, he's loved you and played with you. That will never change. He's your brother, and you are lucky to have him. You aren't going to lose a brother because he's spending time with me." She took a breath and smiled at Emily. The teen resembled her dad. She was blonde and blue-eyed like the rest of the family, but Emily was broader boned with stronger features. The combination made her very attractive. "I never had a sibling. I wanted one so much, especially a sister. Having you around isn't quite the same as having a little sister because you are almost an adult. But maybe…maybe I'll gain a good friend instead."

Emily glanced at her brother for a moment.

"I don't know if you thought it was a joke, or if you were trying to create a problem between your brother and me. That doesn't matter. It's important for you to understand that you used his phone without his permission. And what you said was inappropriate."

"Are you telling Mom and Dad?" she signed and spoke.

Savannah turned to Alex and watched him sign. She wasn't certain exactly what he said. They signed so quickly that she couldn't catch all of it. It seemed as though they didn't always complete a sign. But when she turned back to Emily, the displeasure was obvious. Savannah had tried, but the teen was making it clear that she was still unhappy with Savannah's presence.

From the few things Alex had said about his family, Gwen was a busy teen when Emily was born. He was the one who bonded with the newborn. Then as she got older, he was her sitter. She was attached to Alex, and to make the situation worse, she was spoiled. Alex was probably the one who gave her whatever she wanted.

Alex was signing to his sister and whatever was being said, it wasn't happy family time. Feeling as though she could do no more, Savannah walked to the windows that overlooked the backyard, the family pool, and part of the golf course. She couldn't imagine living in such a lovely place, but she was certain, she could get used to it very quickly.

She heard Alex approaching her and his sister stomping off. When Alex put his arms around her, she covered his with her own and leaned back against him. Whatever happened between the siblings wasn't pleasant. But the way he held her, and the rise and fall of his chest, gave clues to the sadness that he was feeling. He might have been angry with his little sister, but he didn't want her hurt.

Savannah turned in his arms and faced him. "She doesn't understand, but she will eventually."

"We tried. You tried. Thank you."

"I don't want to be the cause of problems between you and your sister."

He smiled and shook his head. She didn't know what he signed, but she got the impression he was telling her that it was the two of them together. Then he kissed her. His shirt twisted in her fingers. She prayed that she'd stay upright and not melt onto the floor.

The feel of his arms and the scent of him drove her over the edge, and reality slipped away as he carried her to where dreams were made. She was adrift in his kiss, and his love for her swirled around and through her like a magical spell.

"Oh, cute, the love birds." The female voice was flat, not at all like his mother's.

Savannah broke from Alex's hold and peered over his shoulder at his older sister who smiled at them.

Alex turned around and greeted Gwen.

Savannah felt as though she'd been pinned into place and forced to endure the heat that flowed from her chest to her cheeks. She signed, "Hi."

"Alex texted that you were willing to help with the meal. So if you can pull yourself away from Romeo, I'd love to have help."

Savannah nodded and followed his older sister into the kitchen. Gwen immediately began to unload bags of groceries. There was so much food that Savannah figured maybe a small army was joining them for this meal. Then Gwen sat a large ham on the counter. Savannah immediately checked the weight and calculated the cooking time.

They both washed their hands. Then Gwen started to unwrap the ham and place it in a shallow pan. Savannah tapped Gwen on the shoulder and tried to sign. She gave up and fingerspelled.

"Talk to me. I have implants. I can hear you."

"Implants? I've heard about them, and Alex said you had them, but might not be wearing them."

Gwen pointed to the small unit that she wore. "It allows me to hear. It's wonderful, but the amount of noise... I don't know how people who hear can stand all the sounds."

"Interesting. Maybe we are used to the noise." She reached for the ham. "May I?"

Gwen nodded. "Go right ahead. You don't want Mom's cooking. I'm not exactly a great cook either. I was thinking a simple meal."

"Simple? You have enough food for a week." Savannah began to open cabinets and familiarize herself with the kitchen. She found the spices and placed the ground cinnamon and the ground cloves on the counter. A little more investigation turned up pineapple rings, a can of mandarin oranges, and some maraschino cherries. Then she found the kitchen knives. *I thought Alex said his mom hardly ever cooks. She's got plenty of food in the pantry for someone who doesn't spend time in the kitchen.*

Gwen left the prep area and leaned against the counter at the far end. "So, you really cook?"

"Yes. My mother taught me. We don't have much money, but Mom likes to fix nice meals once in a while. We'll have a big meal, usually on Sundays, and then she'll fix other meals with the leftovers. I've always been in the kitchen. I'm not gourmet or anything, but I do enjoy it."

"Go for it! We could use a wonderful home-cooked meal."

Savannah prepared the ham and placed it in a large Dutch oven that appeared to never have been used. She could barely believe the size of the kitchen and all the lovely things that seemed almost untouched. *When he said his mom didn't cook much, I believed him.* "My mom would kill to have a kitchen like this."

Gwen laughed, except it was an odd sound. Not at all like the laughter Savannah was used to hearing. Alex never uttered a sound when he laughed, only breathy huffs.

"Want to wash the vegetables for me?" Savannah held up the bag that contained a variety of fresh produce. "I'll make a healthy snack plate to go with that football game this afternoon. Do we have sour cream?"

Gwen shook her head. "No. Make a list and I'll go back

to the store."

Savannah did and thought Gwen was leaving, but she returned to the kitchen a minute later. "The game hasn't started. Dustin will go for me." Gwen smiled. "He's so protective of me and the baby."

Savannah smiled. "When is your baby due?"

"Dustin Junior is due to arrive February 2."

Savannah giggled. "Groundhog Day will never be the same in your house." She wanted to ask, wanted to know more, but she figured it might be rude. *Do you know if your baby will be deaf?*

Gwen laughed. "I'm scheduled to take off from work, starting February 1. And I'm staying out for three months."

"What do you do that you can take off for three months?"

"I'm a lawyer. Didn't Alex tell you anything?"

"No. Not really." She began to cut up potatoes for potato salad.

"Alex is terrible about some things. Dustin is an orthodontist. The kids love him. He got his implant as a teen. Both of his parents hear."

"Do you have a big plate for the veggies and some bowls for the dips?"

Gwen went directly to a cabinet and found a football-themed plate with matching bowls. "When it comes to entertaining, Mom has it all. Promise you'll cook Thanksgiving dinner for us?"

"I'd be honored, but I'd need a slight head start. That's one meal you don't whip up in a few hours."

With potatoes boiling, the veggies cut and ready for the dips, and the ham in oven, there was nothing more to do other than wait until Dustin returned from the store.

They sat in the breakfast nook and drank some coffee. Gwen picked up her cup and sipped the hot liquid. "I guess you've figured out that Alex is stubborn. He's too much like Dad. To be honest, my father hated it when I told him I was getting an implant. It stirred up quite a bit of conversation around here. Mom offered Alex an implant. She thinks he might not be a successful architect without it. He refuses the implant and refuses to use an interpreter."

"Is it dangerous surgery?"

Gwen shrugged. "It's surgery and all surgery has risks, but it's not a dangerous surgery. They put a unit right here, under the skin." She pointed to a spot behind her ear. "And there's a wire piece that threads into the inner ear." She lifted a round piece that was partially covered by her hair. "This is magnetic. It transfers sound to the piece under my skin."

"That's it? And you can hear?"

Gwen smiled. "That's the very condensed version of a very complex and complicated device that gives us sound."

"If you don't mind my asking, why would your dad be against you having an implant? I would think that the opportunity to actually hear…I'm sorry. There's a lot that I don't know about deafness. I'm trying to learn."

Gwen laughed. "At least you are trying to learn. That's more than most people. Actually, most people assume if someone is deaf they are… I hate to say this, but they think we're stupid." Gwen shook her head. "There are some genes that can cause deafness, and also things such as high fevers can damage the inner ears. So it's luck of the draw. Dustin was not deaf at birth." Gwen's face took on a serious expression. "You have blue eyes. You had to inherit the blue-eyed gene from both your parents. When a child is born deaf, they had to inherit a deaf gene. But a child might be a carrier of the gene without being deaf. If one parent had brown eyes and the other had blue eyes, a child could have brown eyes, but can carry the blue gene."

Savannah nodded. "I remember learning that in high school biology."

"Anyway, deafness is not an indicator of intelligence any more than saying someone who has blue eyes is stupid.

Over ninety percent of the children who are born deaf have parents who hear, and two to three children out of every thousand have some form of hearing loss."

"That many?"

"Yes. And being deaf is not something that has to be fixed any more than having blue eyes has to be fixed. It's not pathological. Being deaf is not a horrible thing. We are what we are. Deaf people have existed forever. It's quite normal to be deaf. The hearing world needs to accept it."

"But you hear with implants, so it's fixable."

"I hear to make the hearing world happy when I must interact with them. Your world is much too noisy. I can't imagine living with your sounds all day and night. It must be awful to live that way. I have one implant, so I only hear out of one ear, not both."

Dustin came into the kitchen with the additional groceries. "Game starts in three minutes." He kissed his wife as he withdrew two big packages of chips from one of bags. "Got to have chips!"

Gwen took the chips from him and emptied them into two big bowls. "If you want dip, you'll have to wait a few minutes."

Savannah wished the conversation had not ended. She wanted to know more about implants - wanted to know the odds of having a deaf child.

A lex sat at his parents' dining room table, figuring he was in heaven. Then he kicked himself for eating potato chips, but the dips were just too good to resist. Just when he thought he'd made up his mind as to which dip he liked, he tried the vegetable slices in the dips. Even Emily, who normally refused to eat her vegetables, downed quite a few. Now the table contained a beautiful ham with raisin gravy, potato salad that was better than anything that was bought in a container, asparagus that wasn't pale green and soggy looking, and corn that appeared to have been roasted. Everything was delicious.

The family conversed while they drank their coffee, and Gwen took on the role of interpreter for Savannah. They found out a little about the fire. It was believed to have started in the laundry area on the first floor. Then there were a series of things that probably happened. The building was old and not up to today's codes. It didn't take much for the fire to spread. Everyone got out and was accounted for except for Esther Zookerman.

"Several students said she'd left for the weekend. They said that it wasn't unusual for her to do that, but they didn't know where she went. Her parents don't have a phone, only an emergency contact number that the university called," Alex's mom explained. "There's no cell phone number on file for her. And no one seems to know if she owns one."

Savannah raised her hand to stop his mom from speaking. "It's quite normal for her to leave for the weekend, but no one seems to know where she goes. She never says much."

"She's listed as unaccounted for, but that makes me feel a little more positive. Still we must wait until she's found." His mom smiled. "We have all the students placed elsewhere. Most went to other dorms. One of the hotels has willingly taken in thirty-one students with only a minimal charge to the University. Several students are staying with friends off campus." Alex's mom said, as she looked directly at Savannah. "Are you going to be staying off campus?"

Alex signed yes. "There's plenty of room at my place. And if she makes meals like this for me, I won't let her leave."

"And where did you get such a chauvinistic attitude? I raised you better than that!"

Alex laughed. "Mom, when have you had a meal this good?"

Savannah giggled. "I really don't mind cooking, as long as I don't have schoolwork. But if Alex doesn't get me back to his place, I'm not going to be ready for midterms."

"All the professors with students from Brindlewood have made allowances. Most everyone lost their computers and textbooks."

Savannah nodded. "I have my computer and my tablet, but several textbooks are lost. I should be okay for the midterms, but I'm going to have to replace them. Please excuse me while I clean up."

Gwen frowned. "I'll take care of the clean up. You fixed it."

"Really, I don't mind." Savannah collected several empty plates.

"No, go with my brother and study. Your grades are important."

"I don't want to leave you with a mess. In my house, whoever made the mess was the one to clean it up."

Alex went to her and put his arm around her shoulder. "Don't worry about it, my sister will handle the dishes."

Gwen quickly signed, "Want some leftovers before you go?"

Alex nodded, and with Savannah still tucked to him, they followed his sister from the informal dining room into the kitchen. He took some of everything unless Savannah said no.

"Why? I liked that."

"It's easily made fresh."

"Are you sure?" Gwen asked. "I don't mind sharing. There's plenty here."

Savannah nodded.

It was another half hour before they actually left his parents' home. Then he had the drive to his place. When they entered his house, Savannah immediately pulled out her computer and started working.

She printed out her schedule for the week and he mated his to hers. "I swear I'll fine going to the coffee shop or hanging out at the library."

He opened his wallet and handed her some money for coffee. "Take it. You might be glad to have it."

"I can't keep taking money from you. I owe you a fortune as it is."

He frowned and shook his head. "No, you don't. You don't owe me a penny."

"Okay, I owe your parents."

"No, I have an income. Remember, I tutor?"

She narrowed her eyes at him. "I've spent more money than what you've probably made this year."

"No. I have money. I can tell you about it later, and you don't owe anyone anything."

She left him at the table and went upstairs. He still had

work to do. When he finished, he climbed the stairs to his bedroom. Half way up the stairs it dawned on him that he might be making too much noise. He tried to quietly step, but he had no idea if he'd managed to succeed until he got to their room. She was already in bed asleep. The scent of her shower filled the hallway and room. He wasn't certain if it was her soap or shampoo, but it smelled like a bouquet of flowers with a hint of citrus. That wonderful female scent filled his lungs and fueled his desire for her.

The clock said it was well after one in the morning. He took a quick shower and readied for bed. There was no time tonight to dwell on the physical aspect of their relationship. He needed his sleep and so did she. He slipped into bed beside her. *I need my sleep. I need my sleep. I need my sleep.*

Then he felt her hand on his back. A moment later, she snuggled to him and her legs intertwined with his. *How can she sleep?*

It was the movement of the bed that awakened him. He opened his eyes long enough to see her heading for the bathroom. He must have closed his eyes again because the aroma of coffee filled the air and forced him from the warm comfort. Dressed in a navy long-sleeved Henley and a pair of heavy denim jeans, he made his way to the kitchen.

"Good morning, I heard you, and knew you were awake."

"I smelled the coffee." He stared at her plate. "What did you make?"

"No eggs. Peanut butter and jelly on toast."

He started to go for a box of cereal, but she stopped him.

"You need protein. Eat what I'm eating." She dropped two slices of bread in the toaster.

He shrugged and fixed a bowl of cereal anyway. When he saw the look on her face, he nudged her. "I'll eat both."

He pointed to the exam schedule as he spooned some cereal into his mouth. She obviously didn't understand his one-handed signing. He put his spoon down and tried again. This time she followed what he was saying.

They finished their meal, collected their things, and went to the campus. He dropped her off and then parked. Confident about his exam, he entered the building and went to class. He was a little early and spent the time looking over his notes, as other students slowly filed into the room. This was an advanced class and everyone in it was quite serious. He spotted his classmate, Ben Weaver, and gave him a thumbs-up.

Ben was methodical, but not always the most creative when it came to design. But he knew his materials and the codes. Alex wanted to talk to Ben about his plans after graduating. Alex knew he wanted Ben for a partner. He took out a piece of paper, wrote on it, and then handed it to Ben. Out of the corner of his eye, Alex saw the professor watching.

Ben opened the paper, nodded at Alex, and put the paper in his shirt pocket.

The professor handed out the tests. He stared at Alex and then at Ben, as he handed them each the test. When the professor told them to start, Alex flipped over the paper and began. It was a tough test, but he understood the materials and the formulas. He did each problem, and then checked each one. Satisfied, he turned his paper over and waited for the professor to pick it up. The hardest thing for him to do was nothing. But he tried to occupy his mind with something other than the completed paper in front of him. He looked around the room. Another student was debating the strength of the concrete, based on the words he was mouthing. Alex had considered that the easiest question on the test. Ben turned his paper over and grimaced. The slump of his shoulders told Alex that Ben had also struggled. *Why? It was easy.* The professor began collecting the tests and allowing the other students to leave. *Why hasn't the professor picked up our tests?*

He sat and waited.

One by one, the students finished and walked out of the room. When it was just Ben and he, the professor came to them and asked for the paper that Alex had given Ben.

He thinks we've cheated!

Ben reached into his pocket and handed it over. There was nothing on it other than Alex asking Ben if he would consider going into business with him and a request to meet with him on Friday to discuss it. The professor looked at the paper and tossed it back to Ben.

The man's eyes narrowed, and his nose flared slightly as he crossed his arms over his chest and stared at Alex. "You really can't hear a thing, yet you think you are going to be an architect with your own business?"

Alex nodded.

"How are you going to talk to clients? And who would trust you to design anything for them?"

Alex used the small pad that he always kept handy. -I will have my own company. I'll use an interpreter if and when I need one. As for my clients, they will want me because I'm good!

Alex wrote the note so that Ben could see what was being written.

Ben waited for a moment and then said, "Sir, I've worked on two major projects with Alex in other classes. I don't know sign language, and we've managed without any problem. I have a lot of respect for him. I've watched him taking notes. He is good, and I don't know how he does it."

Alex rolled his hand over and gave the thumbs up sign.

The professor dismissed them. They took their belongings and left the classroom.

In the hallway Alex mouthed thank you.

"Do you have an exam now?" Ben asked.

Alex shook his head and motioned coffee.

"You want coffee at the coffee shop?"

Alex nodded. *I need Savannah to interpret. Oh, how I wish her signing was better.*

They strode across campus and Savannah was waiting for them. Her smile was bright. She must have done well on her exam. He ordered a coffee and sat at the table with Savannah. "I need your help. I need you to talk for me. You need to tell Ben what I'm saying."

"Me?"

Alex nodded and gave her what he hoped was his best smile. *Please do this for me.*

Ben joined them at the small table.

"Hi, I'm Savannah. Apparently, Alex wants me to talk for him."

Alex nodded. He signed and fingerspelled. It was enough for Savannah to understand and tell Ben.

Ben knitted his brows. "So if we work together… How am I going to know what you are saying?"

Savannah started to laugh. She looked at Alex and winked. "This is from me. If you are around him enough, you will learn to sign. He knows exactly what you are saying, and he'll either write or sign his response. I watched him around his family, and he signs so quickly I can barely catch what he's saying. But he signs slowly to me."

A few times Alex used his pad to write his response.

"I don't know. I figured I'd work my way up with a large firm someplace. I've already started to send out letters."

Alex shook his head. -You will wind up drawing electrical lines on a design by someone else. We're a good team.

Ben nodded. "I'm not sure I can learn to sign."

Again, Savannah laughed. "If I can learn, anyone can learn. Most of it makes sense, so it's easier to understand sometimes than it is to remember the signs."

Ben shrugged, but Alex could tell that Ben was giving the offer some serious thought.

Someone had left the paper wrapper from a straw on the table. Alex picked it up and began to play with it. He wrapped it around Savannah's index finger.

She frowned, removed it, and rolled it into a tiny ball. Then she looked at her phone. "I'm out of here. I have another midterm."

Alex stood, drew her to him, and kissed her.

She pulled away and grinned. "Don't do that to me." She waved her hand in front of her face as though to fan it. "I have to take an exam. Kissing you keeps my mind off my schoolwork and makes me too hot."

Now it was his turn to laugh as she stepped away. "I like hot. See you after your exam."

She pointed downward.

He shook his head and signed the word for here. "Yes. Here."

She shrugged and turned away from him.

He used his phone and texted her. -I'll be waiting for you here at the coffee shop.

He turned his attention to Ben. With pen and paper, they'd communicate. He was certain that Ben would learn if he tried. Savannah was catching on quickly, but she still got so much wrong that he worried about her upcoming midterm. Her class was easy, and Stockton knew most of the students were only trying to fulfill a requirement for a language. As long as they attended class, and at least tried, he passed them. But Alex wasn't certain what it would take to do well in the man's class. Savannah was studying from the book, but Alex was certain that she didn't know more than a few dozen signs. He still had to fingerspell too many things to her. He glanced in the direction of the door as if to will her a good grade.

He smiled at Ben and wrote.

We can do it. We'll be an awesome team.

"I'm going to have some heavy student loans to start paying, and if I'm not making enough money…"

Are you willing to make a few sacrifices to build your future?

Savannah took her exam and then went to find Alex. This exam had been tough, but she felt confident taking it. She entered the coffee shop but didn't see Alex anywhere. She texted him. -Where are you?

When he didn't instantly respond, she figured she'd order a cup of coffee and study for her next midterm. She stood in line and chose a toffee hazelnut cappuccino. *A special treat for doing well.*

Time kept ticking, and she wondered what had happened to him. The coffee shop was in the technology building. Against one wall, there were plenty of unoccupied small tables. The long tables with bar seating, tabletop outlets, and diffused lighting tended to be the most popular. There were also soundproof booths. A favorite hangout of hers, she used it as a place to study, but buying a fancy coffee drink was a treat that she only allowed herself on rare occasions. The plain brewed coffee was cheap, but the other stuff wasn't.

She took her drink to a small table and waited. It was almost a half hour later when he texted back. -Sorry. Be there soon. I had to do something.

Alex hoped he had calculated correctly. He'd tossed the balled straw wrapper into the trash and retrieved a fresh straw from the fixings bar on his way out the door. He had about an hour to run the errand. He laughed to himself as he drove across town. *Errands are necessities. This is special.*

He entered the store and began to look around. *I don't want to spend a fortune. I'm going to need money for my office.*

When a shadow fell across the glass case, Alex looked up and saw a woman probably in her forties. Her dark hair was pulled into a tight bun and she was wearing plenty of expertly applied and probably expensive makeup.

"May I help you?"

He shrugged and pointed to his ring finger.

"These rings are for women. Would you like to look at something more masculine?"

He shook his head. Then pointed to a particular ring. Several small diamonds would be much cheaper than one big one, and he liked the way it swirled. She lifted it from the display case and handed it to him. He checked the price tag and thought maybe he'd misread it. It had one too many digits in the price. Handing it back, he shook his head. He tried to sign the amount he wanted to spend, but the woman looked at him as though he'd lost his mind. Then she turned, walked to the back of the store, and vanished behind a door. Sometimes he hated dealing with the general public.

There was a male salesperson who had been waiting on another customer. When the man was finished, Alex approached him. Using his little pad and pen, he asked to see a ring that wasn't going to cost a fortune. The man walked away, but only to another showcase. He pointed at the rings. These appeared to be for children.

No, not a child's ring, a ring for a very special woman. Alex wrote on his pad and showed it to the man.

The man gave Alex a smile that looked more like a smirk.

I'm not stupid, and I've made myself clear. Why can't you get it right? Alex looked at the rings in another showcase and knew they were all wrong. He didn't want fake diamonds. *I'm not here to buy costume jewelry.* He gave up and left the store. Looking at his watch, he still had some time left, but not much. He strode to his parked car and sat behind the wheel for a moment trying to tamp down the burn of his anger. *Why? Why do people treat us this way? Is it that difficult to understand that we know what you are saying when you talk?*

He put the car into gear and drove to an area on Kings Street that was well known for its specialty shops and boutiques. There was a small jeweler there. Probably most of their business was doing repairs or replacing watch and cell phone batteries and cracked screens. He walked through the door, and there was a young female at the counter. She smiled politely.

He signed hello and then took out his pad of paper. I want a ring for a special woman, but I don't want to spend a fortune.

She took the pad from him and wrote. Do you know what size and how much were you looking to spend?

He bit the insides of his cheeks. *At least, she's trying.* -I don't know the exact size, but you can measure something, correct? Just talk to me. I can read your lips.

"What would you like me to measure?"

He took out the straw paper and showed the woman.

From under the counter, she produced a conical tool. "Your paper isn't going to give us a proper size. A ring that fat would be a larger size than a typical ring."

He held out his hand and she handed him the device. He slipped the paper around it and knew she was right.

She produced two sets of plastic rings attached to an elastic band. One set was wider. He took the narrow set from her and began to look at the inner hole of the paper loop and the plastic rings. He calculated the difference between her ring finger and her index finger. He chose one and smiled as he handed it to the young woman. On his pad, he wrote, I don't want to spend the equivalent of a down payment on a house.

ou and everyone else. Give me a second to retrieve some rings that you might like." The saleswoman walked to the back.

Most of the cases were filled with what Alex considered baubles. It was a cut above the cheap jewelry, but still not the high-end designer stuff. When he turned around, the young gal was standing there holding a velvet box.

He went to her, and she had quite a large selection. The box was marked with the size he'd chosen. He picked up one, looked at the price tag, and shook his head. She showed him another ring. It was in his range, but he didn't like it. He kept thinking about the one ring he'd seen at the other store and the way it flowed. Something simple. Plain. But with a wave to it, so that it is different. *Something that flows like my beautiful Savannah River.* He took the ring she was holding and placed it on the paper. This price range.

She vanished with that box and brought out another velvet box. One ring had pale blue sapphires and light green emeralds with tiny diamonds that curved partially around a center stone, but the large center stone was missing, and the four prongs stood upright.

He pointed to the empty prongs and drew a big question

mark on his little pad.

"We can set whatever you want in there. It's the cost of the ring with the cost of the added stone. Would you like to see some diamonds that would fit?"

He nodded.

She turned away from him, and from the way her body moved, she must have called to someone. An older man joined them with several loose stones in another velvet tray.

Alex looked at his phone to check the time. He would be late, but he wanted to finish this transaction.

A half hour later, he was walking to the coffee shop when he spotted Savannah's friend from the dorm who had been missing during the fire. She was talking into a phone. *I thought she didn't have a phone.* As he watched the woman, he realized what she was saying. His mother would have his hide for lip reading a private conversation. Suddenly everything made sense to him. *She probably hasn't told anyone.*

He watched the woman as long as he dared before taking those final steps into the coffee shop. Savannah was deeply engrossed in writing something on her computer. Her half drank coffee was probably stone cold. He reached for her cup and she still didn't see him. He stood for a moment and waited for her to sense his presence. When she did, she jumped.

"More?" he signed.

She shook her head. "No, thanks. I had a fancy cup earlier and was washing it all down with plain coffee. If you want me to cook dinner, we probably need to stop for groceries."

"Not during exams." He sat across from her. "I saw your friend, Esther."

"Is she okay?"

Not wanting to betray what he considered a private conversation, he simply said that she appeared to be fine.

"Oh, thank goodness. I was so worried about her. Rumor had it that she was missing because she was with her boyfriend who apparently lived a few hours away and was going to a different school."

Understatement.

"How did your exam go?"

No point in telling anyone. But I still don't like my professor's attitude. If I wanted to cheat, I could. Then he thought about the student that was mouthing the wrong numbers for the formula. "No problem. Easy. How were yours?"

"The first one was good. The second wasn't as easy. But I'm sure I did well."

"Let's get some food. Then we can study in peace."

She looked at him and laughed. "You mean someplace quiet with no noise to disturb you?"

He grinned.

"Mind if I borrow your ears?"

Savannah was thrilled to be at a nice restaurant. They ordered their meal and waited. She watched Alex as he signed, while she was barely able to follow along and only catching enough words to partially understand. His facial expressions said so much of it. His hands were lovely for a man, totally unlike her dad's calloused ones. Alex had long fingers and immaculately trimmed nails. He had a golden tint to his skin that matched his golden blond hair. His blue eyes seemed to sparkle as he signed to her. She fought the urge to reach out and caress his hands and arms.

The waitress brought them their iced tea and salads.

She forked a mouthful of salad, wondering why he elicited certain feelings in her. From the moment she'd first seen him, there was something about him that attracted her to him. The allure was in his smile, but also in the way he carried himself. That self-assured confidence of a man who knew what he wanted and wasn't afraid to get it. But the way he treated her and his family spoke volumes about the type of man he was. There was no question in her mind that he wanted her. It was in the way he looked at her. He didn't have to do anything more than smile.

He smiled as he stared at her. "You are far away and not paying attention."

She grinned. "Thinking about you. You distract me."

He furrowed his brow. "How?"

She could feel the warm flush rising to her cheeks. She fanned her face.

He laughed. "I'm glad I have that effect on you. Because it's mutual." He looked around. "Never sign anything in public that you don't want the world to know. You have no idea who knows what we are saying."

"I never thought of that."

"It's true. And since I read lips, I often know what someone else is saying across the room."

"I wondered about that, too."

He nodded.

They finished their salads and the waitress brought them their meals. Grilled salmon with a soy topping sat on a bed of brown and wild rice. A medley of colorful grilled vegetables sat next to it.

"Do you think Ben is going to take your offer?"

He shrugged and signed one-handed. "He's...because I'm Deaf. Ben is quiet. He's...man. But...good."

"I'm not sure I understand."

"What I'm saying or my signing?"

"Both. When you only use one hand I get very confused."

He grinned, put his fork down, and used both hands. "I know. No talking when my mouth is full."

She shook her head at his joke. "You are so bad!"

"I'm very good!" He winked. "I don't just want an

interpreter. I want a partner. I need someone who can smile and talk to people. Someone who can assure them that I know what I'm doing, and that I'll do the best possible job for them."

"Isn't there someone else from your classes who would go in with you?"

"I don't need an architect. I need a people person who can also understand sign language."

She swallowed her food. "Then you need an interpreter."

He shook his head. "No. I need you, Savannah. You have the skills. Work with me."

"You mean quit school?" She tensed at the thought.

He shook his head. "We'll work around…important to you. Besides it…before I…my own company. It will take… I…architect."

She sat back in her seat and stared at him. "I don't know. I really don't know what to say. How am I supposed to talk to clients when I know nothing about architecture?"

He shook his head. "You'll be my voice. That's all. I know what they are saying, I can…with them, but they…want a person who can…talk…them. You'll be… They will be…to you."

"Slow down! I can't follow you. You sign too quickly."

"Sorry." He pulled out his phone. -Furthermore you will be able to use all your communications knowledge and marketing skills to help the business grow and gain clients. Didn't you tell me once that you wanted to work inside a company?

She nodded.

-Here's your chance. Except it will be your company, too. Partnership all the way.

She hated how her stomach tangled into knots. She had an almost full plate of food in front of her, and now she wasn't certain it would go down. "I don't know what to say. I need to think."

Alex and Savannah ate the rest of their meal with hardly any conversation. Maybe he'd been overthinking too many things. But time was ticking by and he needed to be ready to set up his office. He had his initial certificate to pass, and that was no easy feat. Getting that board-certified license and then joining the American Institute of Architects would give him the credentials he needed. *Maybe for my personal satisfaction?*

If he opened his own office, he'd be limited, but there was no reason why he couldn't build his business. Networking and gaining clients was the name of the game.

After they had finished their meal, he drove to the campus and parked. The afternoon was waning.

Savannah looked at him with complete perplexity on her face. "Why are we here?"

He grinned. "You'll see. Come."

He walked her to the spot where he had first attempted to talk to her. She was so funny as she grabbed at his hands. He knew then she loved him. It was written in her eyes.

"I brought you here because this is where we first met."

"I'm so sorry. I didn't know then that you were Deaf."

He stood in front of her and this time he took her hands. They matched her. Soft, feminine, and unadorned, her hands still couldn't communicate very well, but she'd come a long way since that first day. He let go of her hands so that he could sign. "I know. You didn't know it at the restaurant. You still didn't realize it as we stood here."

She shook her head. "I wasn't expecting it." She reached up and touched his face. "You are so handsome."

"I don't run around with a sign on me that says I'm Deaf."

"It's as though you aren't, but you are. It's all so confusing.

And I still haven't learned enough."

"I love you, Savannah. I knew it that very first moment I laid eyes on you. Your eyes told me what I wanted to know. Your laughter and your tears told me everything else. I want to spend the rest of my life—"

Abruptly, Savannah turned away from him.

He looked in the same direction and saw Esther rushing towards them.

"What happened? Where is everyone staying?"

Savannah looked at him and then at Esther. "I know they put several students into a hotel someplace, most of the first-year students went to another dorm, and the rest of us are staying with friends."

He texted his mom.

She replied quickly and he showed the message to the women.

He offered, "Stay with us tonight?"

Savannah nodded. "Will you sleep on the sofa?"

"Yes, anyplace. I'll sleep on the floor. I don't mind. It's better than sleeping outside on a bench."

"What did you do last night?" Savannah asked.

"I didn't come back until this morning. I figured I'd drop my suitcase off and head to my first exam. I had no idea."

Alex smiled at Esther, but inside he wasn't thrilled with the intrusion. He had something burning in his pocket, and he didn't like waiting.

When they discovered that Esther had eaten an early dinner after her last exam, they all headed back to his place. They needed to study. He couldn't understand why Esther waited until the last minute to try to figure out where she would sleep. But she had waited, and now he was taking her to his place.

A half hour later, they had settled in and began studying, but his disappointment got the better of him. Several times, he reached into his pocket. He looked over at Savannah who was furiously typing. Whatever she was doing, she was working hard on it. She would stop long enough to fix a cup of coffee and then she was on it again.

Esther was in the kitchen on a stool, studying. Every time he saw her, she had her nose in a book or was making some sort of note. From what Savannah had told him, Esther was a good student and studied every night. But to him, it appeared that both the women were cramming for these exams as though they never studied.

The light flashed on his phone and it began to vibrate. It was a message from his mom. After a few text messages, he decided that Esther could stay at his place. Another text alerted him that his father was on the way over with Emily. They were bringing Emily's old twin bed. He saved what he was doing on the computer and ran upstairs. He didn't want to give up his library room. That left the small room he used as storage. He took the boxes and the three large plastic bins and placed them in his library. He was probably almost out of time, but he took the vacuum cleaner upstairs and gave the room a quick once over.

The hallway light began to flash, and he knew his father had arrived. By the time he came downstairs, Savannah had opened the door. Emily wasn't acting happy about any of it. He helped his father to unload the bed from the SUV and carry it upstairs. As they passed by his bedroom, his father raised his eyebrows and smiled.

It wasn't until they had the bed assembled that Alex even dared to say anything. "I'm not sleeping on the sofa."

"Didn't think you were. She's a pretty thing."

He withdrew the ring from his pocket and showed it off.

His father knitted his face.

"What's wrong?"

"It's too small and it looks like a dinner ring."

"A what?"

"A dinner ring. Women wear them to dinner and parties. Women want a big diamond."

Alex shook his head. "I could afford this."

"What did you do with all the life insurance money?"

"I'm going to need it to open my own business."

"She's not going to like it. Women want to be pampered."

Alex put the ring back in his pocket and made the bed. When he turned around, his father was gone. Emily was standing in the tiny room. Her disapproval was obvious.

"What?" he asked, and then smoothed the blanket.

"I want to see the ring."

He took it out of his pocket with the hopes that Emily might think it was pretty. He didn't get that lucky.

Emily rolled her eyes, told him it was a stupid ring, called him a vulgar name, and walked away.

He should have known she would do that. Her attitude towards him since Savannah had come into his life was terrible. Emily would get over her jealousy eventually. But the little ring wasn't cheap. It just wasn't so darn expensive that it would ruin his plans. Still, disappointment lingered, and that didn't sit well. He picked up the spare set of sheets and the extra blanket that his mom had sent with the bed and placed them in the tiny closet. With barely two feet of hanging space and a tall column of shelves, the closet was probably better suited for a small child than an adult, but it was a closet. Esther had almost nothing.

He took out his pad and wrote on it. Then he walked down the stairs, into the kitchen, and handed it to Esther.

"For me?"

He nodded and motioned for her to follow him.

Her jaw dropped as she entered the little room. "I've never had anyone do such a nice thing for me. This is wonderful!"

She looked as though she might cry.

He walked away. He wasn't good with crying females.

Savannah cries. Crying was something he never quite understood, especially when women cried because they were happy.

Downstairs, Savannah was still writing, and he didn't know if or when she'd take a break. He picked up his keys and left the house. Women liked ice cream. For them, it was comfort food, and maybe they could all use a little comforting.

His excitement over the ring had waned and what was left of his enthusiasm fell into his stomach to be destroyed by an abundance of hydrochloric acid that boiled up the back of his throat. *What have I done? Maybe the whole thing is a mistake. Maybe I shouldn't even try to start my own company. Maybe I should have bought that expensive ring.*

Savannah gathered everyone's ice cream bowls, rinsed them, put them in the dishwasher, and started the unit. After turning in her one paper, she had another paper for her marketing class, and her sign language exam. It seemed that the signs that she was learning never matched what was in the book. *When will I even need to worry about buying train tickets or having to order a continental breakfast in a hotel?*

She sat, opened her book, and looked at the signs. She had all the basics and she understood quite a few signs, but couldn't always remember them enough to sign them when she needed them. Alex often laughed at her and several times said that when he quit having to fingerspell all the time, then she'd know that she was proficient. Until then, she had to study.

Alex took her book from her and scanned the various pages. Then he signed them and she had to tell him what they were. After that, he gave her a list of words and she had to remember the signs. She messed up glass and cup. To her, they were the same. When she failed to remember clothes dryer, her frustration level peaked, and she knew she had to go to bed.

After packing up her things so that she would be ready for morning, Alex kissed her, and she walked up stairs. Her shower felt good, but as she stood there under the running water, it dawned on her that her marketing outline that was to be her midterm exam could be so much better. She had been looking at products as physical things. *Service is also a product and a custom home plan… Yeah, I'm going to do it. Oh, my brain cells are dead tonight.*

She finished her evening rituals and sank into the bed, never hearing another thing until morning.

First thing the next morning, she made oatmeal for everyone.

Esther showed up dressed and ready. "Do you need a lift to campus?"

"Today I have to turn in a paper electronically. I don't need to step foot on campus, but Alex has an exam." She looked at the time on the kitchen clock. "And if he doesn't get down here, he's going to be late. I'd better call him." She started for the stairwell as she called, "Alex—", but stopped before she ever left the kitchen, groaned, smacked her forehead, and turned to Esther. "I forget that he can't hear."

"That's an easy mistake. I know he's deaf, but I don't think of him as deaf."

Savannah took off, and as she rounded the corner upstairs, she spotted Alex going through his jeans pockets and transferring his wallet to the pants he was wearing. She obviously had surprised him from the look on his face. Relief flooded her to see that he was awake and almost ready to leave.

"You don't want to go on campus?"

"No, I'll be fine. I sent that paper electronically last night and got my confirmation back almost immediately. Want some oatmeal?"

"No, I'll grab a granola bar and a protein shake. No time for you to make breakfast."

"It's made."

He placed the jeans next to the laundry basket and followed her downstairs to the kitchen.

"Here, it's ready." She scooped a generous portion into a bowl.

He smiled and held out his hand.

She handed over a bowl and he stood at the counter eating it, never bothering to sit. She smiled at him. He had such an easy way about him – never flustered, never upset, always smiling. It was one of the qualities she liked most about him.

He thanked her and took a protein drink with him as he went out the back door.

A few minutes later, Esther left in her old blue Matrix. Now, Savannah was completely alone in Alex's house. Cleaning the place would be a nice surprise for him, and it was so mundane that it would give her a chance to think about the marketing plan. She started with the bathroom, being extra careful not to bleach her new clothes with the cleaning products. Then she vacuumed the upstairs, gathered all of Alex's laundry, and dusted before heading back downstairs.

She dumped the armful of dirty clothes on the dining room table and began to sort them. Jeans, underwear, a few knit shirts, two dress shirts, and three pairs of slacks, she mixed her things with his to create full loads of like items. She'd seen him check his pockets before tossing his things in a laundry basket. Her dad never checked his. At an early age, she was taught to always check the pockets. *I'm glad I don't have to check Alex's.*

Alex stopped by the vending machine, and as he reached

into his pocket it dawned on him that the ring he'd bought for Savannah wasn't there. It was in the jeans he'd tossed next to the laundry basket. She'd interrupted him as he was filling his pockets and he didn't want to chance exposing the ring while she was standing there. He'd retrieve the ring when he returned to the house. For now, he had to face what was probably his hardest exam, Advanced Geotechnical Design and Thermal Principles. It was an area of special interest to him, but he knew it would be a difficult exam.

He walked into the computer-filled room and spotted a seat near Ben. Ben held out his fist and Alex bumped it with his.

"Good luck," Ben said.

"You, too."

Ben's smile told Alex that Ben understood.

Alex looked around the room. Tametha Tull sat in a seat looking white as a ghost and as if she hadn't slept. She had come to class still wearing her pajamas. *They look like pajamas.* He didn't understand why other students had to wait until the last minute to study something. He also never comprehended coming to class as though they were too lazy to properly dress. He considered his jeans and casual tees to be reasonable, but he usually wore nice shirts with his jeans, or slacks with dress shirts.

The professor called the class to order.

A few seconds later, everyone was glued to their computer for the test. Alex took a deep breath and began. Periodically, he checked the bottom of the screen that showed the time. Next to it was a stopwatch counting the minutes. Each problem took serious thought and careful math. The professor walked around the room. Alex found the man's movement to be distracting. He was used to watching professors to see if they said anything. This particular professor was very good at making certain Alex knew what was being said, but Alex couldn't help but glance at the man occasionally.

Tension built in Alex's muscles. He put his hands at his sides and shook them. He rolled his shoulders, and then went back to what he was doing. *One more problem.* Three people got up and left the room. He read the last question carefully, and then read it again. It didn't make sense. He scrolled down and looked over the design. After rereading the question one more time, he began.

He answered the question and had ten minutes left. Most of the class had finished and vacated the room. Ben was struggling. Alex spent the time going over his answers. He was satisfied with each one, except for the last one. But no matter how he looked at it, he was certain he was right. The little timer at the bottom of the page began to flash. The test ended and the computer screen went black.

Alex took out his phone, pulled up a notepad, and wrote.

It was a design flaw, right?

He stood and stretched. Then he took his phone to the professor and handed it to him.

The professor went to a computer and sat there for a few moments.

Every fiber in Alex seemed to draw tighter by the second. All he could do was wait.

The man smiled at Alex. "You did well. I'll post the grades this evening."

Alex mouthed thank you.

Ben was waiting outside the door. "How did you do?"

Alex shrugged, but gave his friend the thumbs up sign. "You?"

"That last question was a killer."

Alex nodded and showed him the note he'd written to the professor.

"Oh, I hope you are right because that's what I was thinking."

"Don't know. Coffee?"

A few minutes later, they sat in the coffee shop. Alex looked at his friend and wrote on paper.

Since we have to do a few years with a firm, it would be nice if we could both get hired together.

"What are the odds of that?"

Lousy. But we can at least try to stay in the same city. I want you as a partner. We're a good team.

Alex finished his coffee and left for his place. He had a ring to retrieve.

Savannah finished cleaning the house and sat on a kitchen stool to study for her sign language exam. *Any. Every. I'll never keep these straight! Why won't they stick in my head?* She wasn't certain how many signs they had actually been taught, or how many she knew, but being with Alex had definitely helped.

She moved a load of laundry to the dryer and folded what had been in the dryer. Slowly the pile of dirty clothes turned into a several neat piles of clean, folded clothes. As she had worked her way through the clothes, she tried to sign each item, including the color. She went through all the signs for the family members and then started on foods. That made her think about fixing dinner.

Uncertain if Esther would be there for dinner, she went ahead and planned on it being the three of them. She didn't have a lot to work with and she didn't want to do another hobo dinner, but she found enough to cobble together what she hoped would be a good meal. *I need to do some serious grocery shopping.*

Surprised to see Alex walk through the back door, she smiled and waited for him to notice the sparkling clean kitchen. Instead, he ran up the stairs. He returned a few seconds later and stared at the pile of folded clothing.

"Did you…when you…find anything?"

"Huh?"

He fingerspelled, "FIND."

"No. Did you lose something?"

There was an odd look on his face as he walked to the tiny alcove that housed the washer and dryer. Both were still. He lifted the flashlight that hung from a hook on the wall near the back door and went to the washer.

She watched him for a moment and went back to peeling potatoes. When he came out of the little alcove, he walked up to her and smiled.

"Did you find what you were looking for?"

"I found you. You are everything to me." He kissed her cheek. "You cleaned the kitchen." He pointed to the stove and brushed the palm of his right hand across his left palm.

"Yes, I cleaned this, too." She showed him how she lifted the top piece of the stove.

"I didn't know that would open."

"Now you do. The rest of the house was easy. You're very clean and neat."

"I like things that way." He slipped his hands around her waist and pulled her to him.

She loved being in his arms, loved the feel of his body pressed to her, but it was his kisses that carried her away, and he was kissing her. Her body tingled as his lips found her ear and then slowly his lips made their way lower. Each little nibble sent another shot of heat through her until it reached the pit of her abdomen and did delicious things to her. She moaned as Alex held her tight to him. There was no question about him feeling that same heat.

Alex was determined that nothing was going to stop him this time. Their midterms were over, but Savannah was still waiting for her marketing and ASL grades to be posted. Together they had a Saturday night party planned, nothing too exciting, just hamburgers on the grill with friends. He invited his childhood friend Chris Rutledge and his wife Cami who were both Deaf, Ben Weaver and his fiancée Kate, Ashley and Matthew, and the invitation was extended to Esther and her boyfriend. Definitely not a wild group, but Alex figured there were enough people to call it a party.

It was after dinner on Friday night when Savannah checked her grades. Alex didn't need to hear her squeal. He could tell from her expression that she had aced something. He looked over her shoulder at the computer and saw her A in ASL. Near the bottom of the screen was her marketing grade. She had pulled all A's in every subject.

"A good reason to celebrate." He slipped his arms around her. She melted into him.

"Come with me." He took her hand and led her to their bedroom. "I was going to do this Monday evening, but we were interrupted." He fumbled in a drawer until he found the ring he had pulled from the washer. The diamond setting lodged the ring in a small drain hole of the washer's inner tub.

All thoughts of romance had left him as he dropped the ring into his pocket. No longer did he want to do this while bestowing her with flowers or even a fancy dinner. He wanted to give it to her and see it on her finger. To him, it was more than a ring. It was physical proof that they belonged together and that he would always love her. He turned around and motioned for her to sit on the bed.

She followed his instruction with a puzzled look.

He sat across from her and crisscrossed his legs. He knew he had to sign slowly so that she understood. "I love you."

She made a heart shape with her fingers and pressed it to her chest.

"I want you forever. We belong together."

She smiled and nodded.

He inhaled and slowly let it out. "I am not wealthy, nor am I poor. It will be several years before I dare do anything outrageous with money."

She watched him carefully. "I know you want your own business."

"Yes. I must be careful with the money I have until I am making enough as an architect."

"Yes, I understand."

"I want you to marry me."

She clasped her hands together in the sign for marriage and separated the pinkie, index, and thumb from the clasp to form the I-love-you sign. She nodded and smiled.

He reached into his pocket, pulled the ring out, and slipped it on her finger.

Tears began to flow down her cheeks.

No, don't cry. No. Not now.

She practically leapt from where she was sitting, threw her arms around his shoulders, and kissed him.

Savannah thought the party went well. She proudly showed off her ring and her friends thought it was beautiful. Ben did not understand sign language nor did his fiancée or any of Savannah's friends at the party other than Ashley. But even with the communication barricade, Alex managed to have a great party and everyone seemed to enjoy it. Chris and Cami brought plenty of beer and wine, but no one drank very much.

Esther showed up with a guy named Demitri. Dark and handsome, he wasn't exactly the kind of guy Savannah expected Esther to date. A crucifix hung from a heavy gold chain that circled the man's neck. But he was friendly, outgoing, and treated Esther like a fragile bird. There was no question about Esther's love for him. And when the party came to an end, Esther helped clean up before vanishing to her room with Demitri.

The next few weeks fell into a pattern that was comfortable. Sundays were usually spent with Alex's parents, and often the whole family went out to eat at a nice restaurant. As Thanksgiving neared, Savannah was asked if she'd do the honors of fixing the meal. She made pies in Alex's kitchen and several other dishes such as cranberry relish. On Thanksgiving, Alex played eighteen holes with his dad, while Savannah roasted the turkey and prepared the rest of the meal.

Alex's mom set the table with beautiful Waterford crystal, fine sterling, and autumn plates from the Presidential Collection of Lenox china. There was a beautiful matching centerpiece of fall flowers that picked up the colors in the china. Savannah was awestruck at such beauty and excited to be part of it. Spending time with Alex's mom was enjoyable. No longer did she fear that her relationship with Alex would somehow complicate her college experience.

Savannah was certain that her presence made Emily uncomfortable. *I can't fix her problem.*

When the Thanksgiving meal was ready, the family came to the dining table, and everyone, except for Emily, was complimentary of the meal. Savannah beamed with pride, but she also felt guilty for not being home with her parents, even though Alex was taking her to her family the following morning. Having never missed spending Thanksgiving with her parents, the awkwardness of that situation didn't compare to the enjoyment of being in the company of Alex's family and seeing the meal she prepared being served on such a beautiful table.

The family, as usual, signed with such speed that Savannah couldn't keep up. She was lucky if she even understood a few signs. But every time her gaze slid towards Emily, Emily stared daggers at Savannah. Several times, Savannah was certain that Emily was signing something when no one was looking. And when Savannah caught one sign in particular, she nudged Alex, and looked at Alex's dad. "Excuse us, please."

Alex followed her into the hallway and out of range from prying eyes or ears. Certain they were at a safe distance, she looked at Alex, duplicated what she'd seen, and asked, "What does this mean?"

Alex looked at Savannah. "Where did you learn that?"

When Savannah didn't immediately answer, he knew where she had learned such a sign. He shook his head, fingerspelled its meaning, and signed, "Don't use it."

"I can't be certain, but I think that is what is being flashed at me."

"If Mom or Dad catch her, she's in so much trouble. It's useless to talk to her."

"I don't want trouble in the family because of me. I don't want the drama. I've had enough of that in my life lately."

"You are not responsible for anything that has happened."

"I realize I'm not responsible for the fire, but the whole situation with Ella, well, maybe it would not have happened if I'd kept my temper under control."

"What Ella did was wrong."

She shrugged. "But I'm the one who told her off."

He put his arm around her shoulder and gave her a quick kiss. Then he smiled and signed eat. After leading her back to the table, they resumed their meal. He was certain that his parents knew something was amiss.

Emily kicked him under the table, making him look at her.

"What?"

"I want to go to the movies tomorrow."

Alex raised his eyebrows at her. "You already know I'm going with Savannah to meet her parents. You'll have to find someone else to go with you."

"You are doing it on purpose just to be mean to me. We always go to the movies together after Thanksgiving."

"Knock it off, Emily. I'm not doing anything to be mean to you." A moment later, he caught what she had signed to Savannah. "I guess you don't want to go with me ever again."

"What is going on between the two of you?" his mother asked.

He looked at Emily and then at his mom. "Don't worry about it. It's handled."

He finished his pie and asked if he and Savannah could be excused. "I think under the circumstances, someone else can clean up. Savannah made this delicious meal."

Gwen immediately signed that she didn't mind kitchen duty.

Alex took Savannah's hand and they left the table. "I'm sorry my sister is being so obnoxious."

"By not doing things with her, you are making her worse. She wants your attention. If she doesn't get time with you, she blames me."

"I can't give into her jealousy. I'm not going to reward her for bad behavior."

Savannah's gaze drifted from him to someplace behind them. A split second later, he felt the tap on his shoulder. His father motioned for the two of them to follow him.

Once seated in his father's home office, his father wanted to know what had been transpiring between him and Emily.

"She's jealous of my being with Savannah. We've tried talking to her. We even took her with us to the homecoming game and she was…" He didn't want to tell his father what Emily had done or how bad it was getting.

"Why haven't you said anything?"

Alex gave a partial shrug. "We're not children." He looked away and then signed, "I don't want her punished over something emotional that she'll outgrow." He reached over and took Savannah's hand, giving it a quick squeeze. "I'm not going to let her come between us. She has to see that."

"I'm not going to allow her to be disrespectful, and that was what she was doing. I saw what she was signing."

"Dad, it's Thanksgiving. Talk to her tomorrow. Don't do it today."

His father looked at Savannah and slowly signed, "The dinner was excellent, and my son is a very lucky young man. This family is honored to have you."

Savannah blushed and signed thank you.

An hour later, Alex and Savannah left for the comfort of his place. The situation with Emily wasn't going to be easily resolved no matter how much they punished her. He was as responsible for Emily's behavior as they were. Emily was spoiled. The ride back to his place was void of conversation. He couldn't drive and read Savannah's lips, and she didn't understand his one-handed signing. *Maybe it's just as well. Maybe we both need time to let it go.*

Esther had left after classes on Wednesday and everyone assumed she was going home to her parents. But he figured that home was with Demitri. Alex wondered how they had met and how two very opposite people had found love.

The following morning Alex took the suitcases from the bedroom that he shared with Savannah and loaded them into his car. He'd never once asked about sleeping arrangements at her parents' home, but he assumed they would be separated. His parents knew, but he doubted Savannah had said much to hers. She hardly ever talked about her family or growing up. He was walking into the unknown.

The trip to her parents took several hours and they stopped once for a snack and some coffee. According to the

GPS, they were getting close. He hated to admit it, but this was very similar to going for a job interview, except this job was for a lifetime.

Savannah pointed to the next exit. The town was small, barely a blip on the map, but it had a major grocery chain store, a big name shopping mart, and handful of gas stations, a pizzeria, and two fast food restaurants. They made a turn into an older neighborhood. The houses were tiny, but most were well tended. This was a blue-collar neighborhood. She pointed to a house with beige siding and faded brown shutters. It looked like every other house on the street.

She turned to him and smiled. "We are here."

As he got out of the car, she bounded up the narrow walk to the door and opened it. A rather large dog immediately danced around her and then came to him with teeth showing between curled lips.

Savannah caught the multi-colored, mixed-breed dog by the collar and introduced her to Alex as Lady Floppy-Ears Chisholm. "Affectionately called Lady."

He held his hand to the dog that sniffed it warily. *The feeling is mutual.* Having never owned a dog or any pet, he wasn't certain what he should do. But he watched Savannah who beamed with love for the large animal, and the dog seemed to return it.

Meet the parents. Something inside of him crumbled. He stepped across the threshold into a tiny living room and closed the door behind him. Blinking a few times, his eyes adjusted to the interior. A large screen TV glowed with a sports channel, showing a panel of commentators talking about several teams and the players.

Savannah turned to him, pointed down the hall, and signed bathroom. He nodded his response.

By the time he washed his hands, whatever had been crumbling inside him, he decided there was nothing left but the weight that now lay deep in his gut. It was a modest bathroom designed with pale blue tile and white porcelain that looked as though it hadn't had a shiny finish in years. There was a hot-water faucet and a cold-water faucet. The chrome on both was blistered and missing in places. The house appeared to be a WWII residence and he was expecting to see a *Rosie the Riveter, We Can Do it!* poster someplace. The bathroom had been decorated in seashells and mermaids and smelled faintly of bleach. He dried his hands on a little baby-blue guest towel that hung from a ring on the wall. At least Savannah was waiting for him as he opened the door.

"Come meet my parents."

He smiled back at her and followed her down the hall through a dining room and into a kitchen. Any preconceived notions he might have had about her family vanished instantly. Her dad greeted him with an outstretched hand. They were probably close in height. Savannah was a clone of her mother, except her mom's hair was shoulder length and she had bangs.

"Would you like a cup of coffee or a..." Mr. Chisholm opened the refrigerator.

"I have..." Her mother turned to the counter.

Savannah fingerspelled beer, signed coffee, and then pointed to the little kitchen table.

He signed coffee as he slid across the bench of the table's booth seating, even though a beer would have probably helped him to relax.

Savannah's mom put a loaf of white bread on the table and plastic zip bags containing several types of lunchmeat, another group with cheeses, and then added a jar of mayonnaise, along with several other condiments and pickles.

Savannah's father sat at the table with a bottle of beer. "So what are you going to school for?"

Here goes. He signed architecture.

The man looked slightly puzzled and then turned his gaze to his daughter before returning it to Alex. "Is this some sort of joke?"

Alex shook his head, spotted Savannah's giggle, and signed, "I read lips."

"No, Daddy. He's deaf. I told Mom and told her to tell you. As long as you look at him when you speak, he can read your lips."

"Can you hear me?"

Alex shook his head.

Mr. Chisholm appeared to be confused. He looked at his daughter and then at Alex before beginning to prepare his sandwich.

Savannah handed Alex a mug filled with coffee. "Make a sandwich."

Her father passed the loaf of bread to Alex.

He accepted the bread and withdrew two slices from the plastic sleeve.

She passed him the meats and then the cheeses.

Savannah's mom sat across from Alex. "So how do you manage to go to college?"

Alex pulled the notepad from his shirt pocket.

The same way as everyone else.

She took a sip of her coffee. "I thought people like you went to special schools."

People like me? What's that supposed to mean? Stay calm. She doesn't understand.

No. I went to the local public school. No special classes.
But many Deaf will attend dedicated schools.

"And you've always been deaf?"

He nodded.

"So how do you talk?"

Before he could write an answer, Savannah said, "Mom, he uses his hands. It's sign language, and it's a real language. I'm taking it instead of Spanish. I told you that's how we met, the Silent Spaghetti Supper."

"Like Helen Keller used?"

He shook his head and Savannah watched him.

"Not exactly." Savannah interpreted. "It's changed over the years, and she couldn't see. She fingerspelled. We've come a long way since those days. Fortunately, I can see. I am merely Deaf."

"But you're dumb, too."

"Mom, he's mute by choice, not stupid."

"What? What is mute by choice supposed to mean?"

Alex pressed his lips together and then forced himself to answer the question verbally, "I cannot hear therefore my voice is not good."

The look on Savannah's mom's face told him she understood.

Savannah put her hand on his arm. "It's easier for him to use his hands."

The family barely said a word. It was Savannah who did most of the talking.

Obviously, her parents were concerned about his relationship with their daughter. Yet he would make more money and be better able to provide for their daughter than her father had provided for his family.

Mr. Chisholm glanced up at Alex and then turned his attention to his daughter. "I thought maybe he'd like to hang out with me and look at the car I'm restoring. But I guess that won't work."

A little time with Savannah's father might be good. He nudged Savannah. "What kind of car?"

Savannah turned to her father. "He wants to know what kind of car."

"A 1950 Town and Country Newport with only 23,000 miles on it. It was in my grandfather's barn. I inherited it."

Alex grinned and gave the thumbs-up sign. *In the barn? A family owned antique car? Super low mileage? Oh yeah!*

A few minutes later, he followed Mr. Chisholm out the back door and into a detached garage. He was on his own with a man who did not sign. Alex had to win the man's trust.

As soon as the men left, Savannah's mom turned her attention to her daughter. "Well, he's cute as a button. But how is he going to make a living? Or do you intend to support him?"

Savannah shook her head and began to clear the table. "He'll get a job as an architect. I'll never make the money that he will."

"You mean someone will hire him?"

"Yes." She had to tamp down her frustration with her mom, but she also understood for she had asked herself those same questions.

"Is that your engagement ring? It doesn't look like an engagement ring."

"Yes, Mom. Isn't it beautiful?"

"What happened to a simple diamond? Are you certain those stones are real?" There was the sound of disgust in her mom's voice.

"Mom, he bought it from a local jeweler. I think it's beautiful. It's different."

"If you wind up marrying him, what will you do, adopt?"

"You mean because he's Deaf?"

Her mom nodded.

"We haven't talked too much about children. The odds of us having a deaf child are minimal. And Alex doesn't understand why there would be any concern about having a deaf child." She remembered a conversation Alex and she had and began to giggle. "Mom, do you miss your third arm and hand?"

"What?"

"It's simple. Do you miss your third hand?"

"Don't be ridiculous."

"I'm not. A third hand might be super wonderful, but how would we ever know because we've done quite well with two. Hearing is the same for him. He's never had it, so he really can't imagine it – he's never heard any sound in his life. As a result, he can better comprehend having a third hand, because he has two hands, than he can comprehend sound. He can't miss something he never had."

"Oh, Savannah, I worry about you in this relationship."

"Don't, Mom. In three months, I've learned quite a bit of sign language, and his mom says it will take me two years of being with Alex to really learn it."

"I guess you want us to learn it, too."

"It would help." She took the sponge and wiped the table of every crumb.

"Being it's such a pretty day, and we weren't certain when you'd arrive, we thought we'd do hamburgers on the grill tonight, and tomorrow I'll fix a big turkey dinner."

"Sounds perfect."

"I fixed up the guest room for him. You might want to check it. I don't know if he needs anything special."

"No, Mom, he doesn't *need* anything."

They settled into the living room to talk, and Gray Socks appeared from nowhere, curled into Savannah's lap, and began to purr. "Did you miss me, old boy?"

Savannah spent most of the afternoon talking with her mom about everything, including the dorm's fire.

"So what did you do?" her mom asked.

"I stayed with Alex." Her attempt to stop petting the old cat was met with a head butt to her hand.

"He's renting an apartment with extra bedrooms?"

"It's a two-story house, I guess you would call the one room a bedroom. It's very tiny, smaller than my room, and then there's his bedroom. He also has a third bedroom upstairs that he calls the library, which is filled with bookcases. Plus there's a bathroom up there, it's actually the only bathroom. It's been modernized and so has the kitchen. His place is not real big, but it's not small. He's letting a friend of mine from the dorm stay in that tiny room."

"So where are you sleeping?"

She could feel the heat rushing to her face. "With him."

Her mother lifted her eyebrows. "Are you pregnant? Is that why he put that ring on your finger?"

"No, Mom. I fell in love with him the minute I saw him. I thought he was just another student, doing what I was doing, earning extra credit."

Her mother rolled her eyes.

Apparently it was going to be difficult for her parents to accept Alex. Worry over that situation slithered through her, leaving an unwelcome apprehension. She didn't want to be forced to choose between Alex and her parents. She loved them all.

Alex came through the door with Savannah's dad. They washed their hands and Mr. Chisholm, again, offered Alex a beer.

Alex put both hands up and mouthed no thank you.

"Want to help me with the grill? I think we should start now or it'll be pitch dark when we're done."

Alex nodded and held out his hand for Savannah's father to pass him the hamburgers.

Savannah came into the kitchen with a coating of gray animal hair on her.

Alex pointed to her and signed cat with one hand.

She nodded. "Gray Socks." She looked at the front of her. "I think I should change my clothes."

Alex smiled as he went out the back door. Savannah's dad was catching on to the limited communication and doing well. Alex paid close attention as he'd explained what he'd done to the car. The man understood metal and mechanics. He was also a good carpenter and had built the garage without help. Each stud was even and square.

Savannah's dad didn't need any help tossing a few hamburgers on the grill but standing alone on a cold autumn day was no fun. He talked almost constantly as if he needed to fill in the silence. A few times, he asked Alex how to say something in sign language, and Alex showed him.

A tentative bond formed between them. But being forced to spend time alone, without anyone to help communicate, reinforced the need to speak. He knew how to make the sounds, but his speech was terrible. The thought of undergoing speech lessons brought back all those negative childhood feelings. *I don't know how to fix my voice.*

It didn't take much time to cook the meal. The propane grill with its built-in thermostat kept the temperature even, making the job easier. Savannah took away the container that had held the raw hamburger and handed them a fresh plate along with a package of hamburger rolls to toast on the grill.

The aroma of the grilling vegetables and the hamburgers was making Alex very hungry. But he also knew from what Savannah said that her family lived on a tight budget. He doubted their meals were this good every time. The family was putting forward their best to impress him.

When they brought the food inside, the kitchen table was

set. There were crisp lettuce leaves and slices of tomatoes arranged on a plate waiting to be placed on the hamburgers. Ketchup, mustard, and mayonnaise stood like sentries next to the salt and pepper. It wasn't exactly picture perfect. But the food looked inviting to him.

Savannah had poured coffee for him, and she had what appeared to be iced tea. He figured it was probably sweet tea, and she knew he didn't like it. The coffee was fine.

He assumed Savannah's father asked about wanting a beer when the man extended a bottle in Alex's direction. Alex smiled and held up his coffee mug when the man turned around.

The food was delicious, and the grilled vegetables had been seasoned prior to cooking. Savannah's mom knew how to prepare food. It was no surprise that Savannah had learned from her mother.

So far everything was going well. Mr. Chisholm bragged about how he was learning sign language and showed off the words that Alex had taught him. Savannah smiled at her dad.

The evening went well, and when the college football game on TV ended, it was time for bed. He wasn't certain, and he didn't want to ask, if Savannah was joining him.

Savannah laughed when she tiptoed to Alex's room. He wasn't sleeping alone. Lady had climbed on the bed next to him and was now sprawled out and hogging one side. Quietly, she tried to get Lady to leave, but the dog wasn't about to get off the bed.

Savannah signed, "Come to my room."

Alex nodded, but when he attempted to get up, the dog showed her teeth and growled.

"That's what you get for making friends with her and sneaking her treats during meals." Savannah tried to give Alex her sternest look, but it was all she could do to keep from laughing.

Alex feigned his innocence.

"I caught you sneaking bits of hamburger to her. And I'm certain you got into the doggie treat jar that Dad keeps in the garage and fed her those, too."

"Your dad gave me a handful for her."

Savannah crossed her arms over her chest for a moment and then leaned down to kiss Alex.

Lady growled.

Savannah shook her head. "A jealous female at your

parents' home and one at mine. How did I get so lucky?"

She returned to her own room and could barely contain her laughter over the dog's behavior, but she hated sleeping alone. The sheets were cold, and the warm comfort of Alex's arms was missing.

Saturday, they had a turkey dinner with all the fixings. Sunday, before they left, they once again had lunchmeat sandwiches. Her mom insisted that they take some turkey leftovers home with them.

Savannah tried to say goodbye to her parents and to Lady without filling with tears. But she couldn't help the feelings that washed over her. Maybe the worst of it was her mom's disapproval of Alex. The dire warnings that Savannah would wind up supporting a disabled man and how tragic it would be to have handicapped children. Lady demanded her attention until Savannah kneeled in the floor and wrapped her arms around the dog that now towered above her. After a full face washing by the dog's tongue, Lady turned her attention to Alex, who obviously didn't want the same treatment. "Lady, shake hands."

The dog sat and lifted her paw.

Savannah motioned to Alex to shake the dog's paw.

Alex broke into a big grin and promptly took the dog's hand, while Lady swept the floor with her tail. With his other hand, he reached into his pocket and withdrew a small treat.

She watched what he said to the dog and the dog reacted as though she understood every word. But her real surprise came from her dad who walked over to Alex and gave him a big hug.

Then her dad got a stern look on his face and told Alex, "You take real good care of my little girl. And I hope you'll bring her back to us at Christmas. We liked having you."

Maybe you did, Dad, but not Mom.

The drive back to the university was uneventful, but Savannah had plenty to do when they arrived at Alex's home. Neither one of them had even touched their computers over the long weekend. But spending time with her parents was a treat, and not having to take a bus to get there was even better.

Savannah was slightly surprised as Alex pulled into a supermarket before returning to the house. When his basket was filled, he paid for everything and drove home.

Alex sat at his computer and concentrated on his project. He barely had two weeks left of the semester and she knew he had plenty to do, too. Had he been home alone, he would have devoted most of the long weekend to his project. The overhead light flashed, indicating someone had passed through an entrance door.

Esther waved hello as she passed by the dining room table where Savannah and Alex sat. He hardly knew she was in the house with them. Most of the time when she was there, she was in her tiny room or sitting on a stool in his kitchen doing schoolwork. The rest of the time she was gone. She ate her meals on campus.

The university was paying him to allow her and Savannah to stay. Certainly not what they had been charging the students, but from what Savannah had told him, the students were getting some money back. The added income was nice. If he could have found renters like Esther, he would have rented out those extra rooms long ago. But Esther was one-of-a-kind. He didn't ask and she didn't volunteer, but he wondered if she went home to her parents or home to Demitri.

He stared at nothing while his mind wandered into the future. *Savannah has one more year and I have to find a job. We will be separated. That's not what I want. I want my Savannah next to me.*

Classes resumed on Monday, and the cold air whipped the last of the brown leaves across the campus. Already there were signs of Christmas on the various university buildings and in the town. Della Robbia-style evergreen wreaths decorated all the doors in The Heart, with sprays at the windows festooned with red apples, pinecones, pieces of dried straw, and deep red velvet bows. The simple additions transformed the place from old and plain into something welcoming and beautiful.

It was time for another silent dinner at Aldo's. He went to his mom's office where he informed her that he wasn't going to sit at the table with the family. He intended to sit with Savannah and Ashley.

"I don't want a problem between you and your sister." His mother wore her unhappy mother face.

That's not going to work on me anymore. I'm not a child. "It's her problem, not mine. I've tried to spend time with her, but she's not satisfied with that. She's determined to break Savannah and me apart. That's not going to happen."

"She's just a child."

"No, Mom, she's almost an adult. What she texted Savannah from my phone…" He raised his eyebrows. "She's not a child."

"What did she text?"

"Let's leave it with extremely inappropriate for anyone."

"I'm sorry. I will talk to her."

"We already did. Maybe you should talk to her about relationships." He frowned. "I've got to get to class."

"How are you doing?"

He smiled at his mom, came around her desk, and gave her a quick hug and kiss. As he walked out of her door, he gave her the thumbs up sign. He stopped in his tracks and turned. "Don't punish her; talk to her."

He went to his class. This one was by far the hardest class

because the professor tended to talk to everyone individually. Alex was forced to write, but the professor understood and was patient. He'd often scrutinize Alex's design and make comments and suggestions. But today he just looked at what Alex had done and smiled. He told Alex to start on his renderings.

It was a professional building on a small lot. It was something that Alex had noticed many times while driving and seeing commercial lots for sale. The lots were small and often expensive. Maximizing building space, creating sufficient parking, and maintaining some green area could be very difficult. Alex had created a three-story building with good parking and traffic flow, as well as plenty of office space. He liked his modern design that would blend into almost any area. Plus, with his knowledge of passive energy, he was able to increase the efficiency of the building. From the look on the professor's face, Alex was certain that the man liked what he'd done.

Thursday afternoon, Ashley and Matthew appeared on Alex's doorstep. Ashley smiled brightly and, in ASL, attempted to say, "We're ready."

Alex showed her the proper sign and thought she groaned by her facial expression. "You will learn, keep trying."

"Trying to remember everything is difficult."

Alex shook his head and grinned. "Savannah is upstairs."

Ashley grimaced. "You said, 'River up up.'"

Alex blew out a breath. He fingerspelled Savannah and then showed the sign for river, the sign name he'd given Savannah because her fluid beauty reminded him of the Savannah River, and then drew a set of stairs in the air and pointed up twice. "The DOUBLE sign for up will give you UPSTAIRS."

Ashley looked at him with that blank stare. He used his pen and wrote what he was saying.

Matthew duplicated the sign for river and upstairs.

If he used his voice, they would understand. But the thought of taking those lessons… He knew he had to face his fear. He hadn't backed down from anything, ever… *Well, going to school for the first time.*

The memory of being in second grade flashed before him. In a split second everything came back, including the feelings from long ago. He was the smallest boy in his class, and compared to the other boys, he was scrawny. Tommy stood a foot taller and was probably thirty pounds heavier, and the boy insisted on calling Alex names. Tommy would often shove Alex while singing a little ditty about Alex being deaf. One day, Alex had had enough. He balled his fist and nailed Tommy on the nose. He followed that one with a punch to the boy's abdomen. Alex was in so much trouble that he almost wasn't allowed to attend that school. They tried to tell his mom he had behavior problems. Eventually he was told that he should tell someone when he was being bullied. He didn't understand that either because then he would be a tattletale. He preferred using his fists.

Apparently, it worked because Tommy never bothered him again. But the situation came up again as a young teen. He tried to walk away, but it didn't work. He knew not to fight on school grounds, but when the other teen physically pushed him, Alex let loose on the schoolmate. That time Alex had witnesses who stood up for him.

He'd faced a lot of things in his life without fear. But for some reason the thought of speaking, not being able to tell what sound he was uttering, bothered him. Savannah joined him, and her smile always lifted his spirits. He studied her. She'd be honest with him. She'd help him. *Will you teach me to speak, Savannah?*

Savannah waved to Ben and his fiancée Kate as they approached Aldo's. "I'm so glad you came."

Kate answered first. "We figured we'd try it. The food is delicious here, but we have no clue how we're going to manage a whole meal without being able to talk."

Ashley laughed. "There's always pen and paper."

Alex looked at Ben. "Did you get your approval?"

Ben winced and looked at Savannah.

She repeated what Alex had signed.

Ben nodded.

This was going to be an interesting meal. The party they'd had went well, but everyone could talk. And as awkward as it was for them to attend a silent meal, it would be ten times harder on Alex.

She remembered Alex talking about his father not speaking, and how it crimped his mother's parties and created a rift among their friends. His father was uncomfortable with those who didn't sign, and they weren't comfortable with him. *At least Alex is trying to be friendly with hearing friends.*

The meal was fun. They passed around paper. She was certain that Kate and Ben saw a different side of Alex. He was always a serious student, but Silent Spaghetti showed Alex's fun side. Several times Savannah thought she'd die trying to hold in her laughter. But once it ended, and they all walked outside, the laughter broke loose.

Ben looked at Alex. "You are terrible!"

Alex laughed and signed, "I'm very good."

"Didn't you just thank me?"

Alex laughed and waved as if erasing what had been said. Then he gave the thumbs up sign and pointed to himself.

By the time they made it home, Savannah knew they had little time left for studying. But as she worked on her paper, she realized that Alex wasn't studying, he was looking at architectural firms and making notes.

"Four years?"

Alex nodded. "About that. I should have my AIA when I open my own business."

"What's AIA?"

"American Institute of Architects. It's a professional organization. They set the standards and do so much for the field of architecture. It is their exams that I must pass."

She nodded. "Would you do better partnering with an established company?"

"It depends on the company." He looked at her and pushed his lips together. "You can stay here in the house, but you'll need transportation. I must find a car for you."

"Dad can help me with that, I'm certain."

"Can you handle my being gone?"

She saved what she was working on and shut down her computer. "Yes. But I'm not going to be thrilled about being apart."

"I don't want you finding someone else while I'm gone."

"Not a chance. I can't imagine ever wanting anyone but you." She reached out and touched his cheek. "It was love at first sight."

"But a man with hearing, who could give you sound…"

She shook her head. "I don't want anyone but you." She took his hand and gave it a quick squeeze. Not wanting to silence him, she only sought to remind him of that unspoken bond between them. "The man I love put this beautiful ring on my finger. How could I ever want anyone else?"

They sat in silence, allowing their love to pass between them. Eventually she rebooted her computer and he went back to work. When his fingertips touched her arm, she looked up and smiled.

"I need help, Savannah. I need to learn to talk so that I don't squeak. Will you teach me?"

She realized her mouth fell open and she forced herself to close it. But the pain in his eyes was obvious. "I don't know how to help you. Aren't there people trained to do that?"

"It's expensive and the woman who tried to teach me..."

"I know." She ran her fingers over his lips. The feelings welling inside of her were mixed. She had no clue how to teach him to talk, but she understood his desire. *How is inflection taught? How do I...? He sounds awful. How do I get rid of that? I have no idea.* "How do I teach you?"

He shrugged. "I know the sounds. I need to feel your voice."

"How do you do that?"

He put his hand on her face so that it touched her throat, the side of her nose, and her lips. He said aloud, "Say word and I say word. Say your name."

She said her name and then he tried.

"Lower your voice."

He whispered her name.

She shook her head. "No lower your voice into your chest. Oh, how do I explain this? It needs to be deeper. Men have deeper voices. You're not a little boy."

She tried again in a deep voice to say her name and he repeated it. This time it came out as a deep bass. That sounded just as strange and too forced. It took almost two hours until she had him saying things in a range that seemed somewhat normal.

It was still flat and without inflection. He was either too loud or too soft. It would take time and practice for the subtle nuances that those with hearing used automatically.

But it was when they climbed into bed that he turned to her and said, "Iah loveh vu."

Her eyes instantly filled with tears as she kissed him. It was the first time he'd ever spoken those three little words, and she was unprepared for the feeling it created in her. She wasn't even certain why. She just knew that her spirit leapt at the sound of his words. His arms encircled her, and she was lost in the glorious sensation of him.

The following day she went to the library. She couldn't

help Alex, not enough. If he was determined to speak, then she had to find him professional help. She looked over the list of speech therapists in the area and surmised whomever Alex needed would be a specialist. She'd hit a brick wall. She didn't have time to go to The Heart, not when she had another class in less than twenty minutes. Making a quick decision, she looked up Dean Van Doorn's email. It was listed. She wrote a short note and included her phone number.

Almost instantly Alex's mom replied by text message.

Savannah decided her spirit couldn't climb any higher. She barely could concentrate in class. As soon as her marketing class ended, she walked outside to a remote spot and made the phone call.

"Hello, I'd like to speak with Lila McCord, please."

"Speaking."

"I was given your name. I'm calling for a friend who is Deaf. He had some speech lessons about twenty years ago, and hated it, but he would like to try again."

"This is an adult?"

"Yes."

"This might be too quick for him, but I had a cancellation a few minutes ago. Is there any chance you could come in the next half hour?"

Savannah spotted Alex's car pulling into the parking area. "Maybe. We're on campus at the moment. How far away are you?"

The woman gave Savannah the directions.

"If you will give me about five minutes, I'll text you to confirm that we'll be there." She mentally crossed her fingers as she said goodbye to the women and greeted Alex. "I have a surprise for you."

"What?" He kissed her.

"Speech lessons. There is a speech therapist who wants to meet you." She held her breath and waited for his response.

"You teach."

She shook her head. "Give this person a chance and I will help you."

He pushed his lips together.

"It's the same as me taking ASL as a class, and you working with me. You are helping me, and now I can help you."

"Dohn't leave mee."

"You mean stay with you during the lessons?"

He nodded.

She gave him the thumbs up. But then she reached for him and drew him close to her. Immediately he embraced her and kissed her again.

"I love your kisses. But I want an honest answer. Are you trying to talk for me or for you?"

"I do talk."

"Yes. But I mean this verbal thing. What has changed your mind about speaking aloud?"

"Being with your parents showed me a need that I'd never seen before, especially when I was with your dad in the garage. Then I was thinking about the job. Job interviews. Employers who don't comprehend and..." He seemed to look towards the sky as though searching for words. "I'm not mute. Why should I limit myself? I've worked hard to prove I'm intelligent. Being deaf doesn't stop me from learning." Moisture appeared in his eyes.

"No. You can do anything you want to do. You've proven that your entire life."

"I need to learn to communicate using my voice. But please don't ask me to have an implant. I don't want it."

"Alex, I'm not asking you to do anything. I love you as you are."

He shook his head. "Talk to my sister. She says the world is too noisy for her. Not hearing is better."

"I want you to do this because you want to do it. And if that is what you want, then I will help you."

He kissed her again and grinned. He moved his mouth and then spoke. "I don't…" He dropped the timber of his voice. "I don't want to sound like a seagull."

She couldn't prevent the giggle that came from within her. "You are my seagull."

He signed, "Seagulls love the river."

"And I love you." She picked up his hand and signed marriage using her hand with his.

He nodded. "Where are we going?"

She gave him the directions and texted the woman that they were on their way. "It's a consult…"

Alex drove, but the entire time her stomach twisted into knots; those vipers were alive and well. She worried that he was doing this for the wrong reasons. His father had managed to get through life without speaking. Had Alex merely copied his father? Had Alex refused to speak to gain his father's approval?

Her mind shifted to her parents. She had been certain her mom would accept Alex's deafness, and her father would have been the one to disapprove of the relationship. But it was her mom who seemed to be worried, and her father was proudly showing off the few signs that he had learned. Her mom made no attempt or even acted as though she might consider learning.

Now Alex had suddenly decided he wanted to talk. Part of her was excited because she felt as though he had restricted himself in a world that hears, but another part of her was concerned about why he'd changed his mind. An additional thought went through her head. She liked the quiet. Silence didn't intrude. The memory of telling him that he sounded like a sick seagull flashed through her mind. Uncertain whether he was doing this for her, she could feel the guilt worming its way inside her.

Alex drove to the building on the corner of Maple Terrace and Grove Street. It wasn't very far from the campus or his house. It was once a bustling little office complex. Now, it was comprised of cheap office rentals. Four trucks were parked in the corner of the lot with Dylan's Electrical written on them. He remembered when the building was beige brick, but someone had since decided to paint the entire building white and then trimmed it in swimming pool blue.

He opened the door and shook his head. The waiting room was painted in bright primary colors and filled with toys and children's magazines. *I doubt she's going to be able to help me.*

A thirty-something woman greeted them and signed, "Hello, I am Lila McCord."

Alex clasped Savannah's hand and brought her with him as they stepped from the waiting room into the woman's office.

His childhood memories gripped his lungs and his hands.

"I understand you want to learn to talk, and that you've had lessons at some point in your life."

He gave Savannah's hand a quick squeeze. "I sound like a"—he looked at Savannah and smiled—"a sick seagull."

Lila shook her head and signed.

Every time he spoke, he had to let go of Savannah's hand so that he could use his. "If you only sign, she won't understand. She's still learning."

"No problem." She used her voice and signed, "For now, will you use your voice? It will give me a better idea of what help you will need."

The next forty minutes were difficult. But in the end it was decided that he did know his sounds, although he was rusty with many. But Savannah had been right about the fact that Alex needed to deepen his voice.

"This isn't much different from someone who sings but wants to sing opera. They need to train their voice. You know your sounds. You only need to be trained."

Savannah touched his arm. "Will his voice always sound flat – without inflection or intonation? I've noticed that with the deaf."

"That's not easy to answer. Those who once heard have an easier time of controlling their voices, because they have memory of sounds. Alex has never heard any sound. The odds are he will never speak the way we do, but he will be able to control his voice and make himself clear to those with hearing."

"Yes, clear," Alex said aloud with his high-pitched voice.

Lila smiled. "We'll work on your *c-l* sound. I've made notes on several sounds that we will tackle first. Let's start with two times a week."

He nodded and pulled out his phone, which contained his schedule. Once they had agreed on the times, he asked, "How do you know sign language and how to teach vocalization?"

"I trained as a speech therapist, but when my second child was born deaf, I knew I had to learn everything I could to teach him."

"No one else in your family is deaf?" Savannah asked.

Lila shook her head. "Not in my family or my husband's, nor did I have problems during my pregnancy. I had twins two years later, and their hearing is perfect. Deafness can be very random."

"So I've heard." A look of resignation crossed Savannah's face.

Alex could tell that Savannah was still concerned about any children they might have. They had plenty of time to decide on creating a family. He knew what he wanted, but he also knew he wanted his income to be stable before they took on the role of parents.

He and Savannah said goodbye and left for home. Maybe this time, he would learn to speak.

As they headed in the direction of his house, he made the decision to stop for dinner. He wanted real food, not something quick, and he didn't want to burden Savannah with fixing a meal. He stopped at a local restaurant, and since it was Friday evening, the restaurant was busy. They stood next to a large fish tank while they waited. He'd always enjoyed watching the colorful saltwater fish. Touching his finger to the glass, he could feel the vibration. He wondered if the fish could feel it, too. Did the filtration system make noise, did bubbles make noise, or was it only a vibration? He knew he was missing certain things, but he couldn't imagine what it was to hear. Having played with tuning forks, he knew the physical process, but couldn't grasp sound.

When their table was ready, they sat, and he smiled at Savannah. *You are naturally beautiful.* She was also very feminine in her mannerisms, but she had an athleticism that probably would make her a tough opponent in any sport. Her sparkling blue eyes stared at him.

He reached over, took her left hand in his, and touched her ring.

She grinned. "Pretty."

"Pick a day."

She shrugged. "The date doesn't matter."

He looked at her askance. "I thought all women wanted a big wedding with friends and family, flowers, and champagne."

She shook her head. "My parents can't afford a big wedding. I know my parents don't want me to run off and marry unannounced. I think my mom would like me to have the white dress. But I can promise you my wedding won't be like the ones in those wedding magazines."

"Church?"

"That doesn't matter. I think I would prefer to marry in a church but it doen't have to be in my family's church."

"So a little wedding." He grinned. "I have an idea. Have your parents ever had a real vacation?"

"They drove to Illinois once when Dad had to go there for his job."

"That's not a vacation."

She wrinkled her nose her face. "What are you planning?"

"I'm not planning anything until you are ready to plan it with me."

Savannah was staring at finals and spent her evenings studying or working on papers. But she noticed that Alex seemed to constantly be interrupted with text messages. And from the look on his face, he wasn't thrilled with whatever was happening.

She had two written tests, three papers, and her ASL test. It seemed as though Prof. Stockton was being harder on her. She admitted that she often understood what Alex was saying without actually knowing the individual signs. For a test, she had to know the signs.

Usually every night, Alex would stop, and together they

worked on her signing and his talking. He would say the word aloud, and she would have to sign it. If she made a mistake, he would narrow his eyes at her, making her laugh. Often she'd say the word for him and try to show him where he goofed. His voice was still flat, but he had more inflection than he'd had prior to starting lessons, and the clarity of his speech was improving.

When they had finished her words and signs, he would concentrate on the vocabulary of an architect. A few times, she had to look up a term so that she knew how to articulate it. She knew the words when she read them, but she wasn't as confident with their pronunciation.

Often his mouth seemed to move the proper way, but the sound that came out wasn't. She was very aware of the patience he had shown her, and she returned it when working with him. Most of the time, he followed her instruction and watched her face. Occasionally he'd place his hand on her face. But the look in his eyes said everything she wanted to know. They spoke for him and his love for her showed.

He was always checking to be certain she had money for anything that she might need. They would stop by the grocery store twice a week and he often offered to take her to any store. He constantly tried to spoil her. The only thing she could do for him was cook his meals. Then he'd fuss at her if she cleaned without him.

Time sped by. She packed up her things and went upstairs, leaving him at the dining room table to continue to work. He was doing a drawing of a building. She turned on the shower in preparation for her nightly ritual. The warm blanket of his love continued to wrap her.

Every time she thought about a wedding, she'd pushed it to one side. Her parents and his parents, she didn't want to ruin the tender sensation that had filled her. But the thoughts of mixing the families, and the reflection on the various personalities kept intruding. *Maybe we should just quietly get married and then tell everyone. I don't need a fancy white dress. Mom will shoot me if we elope.*

Never had Alex worried about exams, but he discovered he had some concerns this semester. His time was no longer his own. He helped Savannah and worked on his voice. The theft of his study time had been his own doing, but somehow he couldn't imagine life being any other way.

He saved his work and then went to the Internet to find the perfect family vacation and wedding destination. Little cove towns on the east and west coasts begged to be selected. The Big Apple, Charleston, the Florida Keys, and a dozen other locations, including Las Vegas, each had a special charm or excitement, but that was not what he wanted. *Why can't I find something peaceful? Where we can be alone?*

He tried several search possibilities and suddenly he landed where he wanted. *Yes!* Satisfied, he turned off the computer and went to the bedroom. Esther was still in the kitchen cramming for her exams.

Savannah was sound asleep. He took a shower and the scent of her lingered in the air. Never had he dreamed he'd find someone like Savannah. He had watched other friends become involved with someone and their grades slipped along with everything else. He had made some changes, but nothing that would severely impact his grades. But he needed to do some extra studying for one class. *Of course, taking vocalizing lessons is another time buster. Is Savannah the reason why I've changed my mind about verbalizing? Or has she shown me the need?*

Snapshots of Savannah's parents went through his head. The time spent in the garage with her dad. The man did most of the talking often when busy showing something under the hood. Alex couldn't always see his lips, but still managed to piece together the conversation. But his ability to talk to Savannah's father was limited. He didn't want to write every question he had. There were many things he wanted to ask, and they didn't all have to do with an old car.

Then his professor's comments about not succeeding as an architect, because Alex was without hearing, had managed to wiggle its way into his fiber. Sometimes it was the negative comments that made him more determined. But tonight those thoughts swirled through him, sucking his confidence away, making him feel like that little kid who wasn't invited to the birthday party because he was different.

He stumbled into bed and Savannah instantly snuggled to him. He tucked his arm around her, knowing he probably didn't deserve her. She was normal and he was considered handicapped. *I hate that word. Nor am I disabled.*

People wondered why he didn't have one of those tags for his car. They figured he'd get hit crossing a parking lot because he couldn't hear a car coming. *Do people really rely on their hearing for such things? Can't they see the speeding car?*

Now he had Savannah and another set of pessimistic thoughts flowed through him. They probably would be separated for a year until she finished school. Would she wait for him? Would she find another man who would give her things that he couldn't?

He spotted the light in the hallway and knew that was Esther going to bed. He looked at the clock and noted the time. He had an exam and needed his sleep, but sleep wasn't imminent.

His mind wandered back in time to his childhood friend, Ted Carlton. When Ted drove his car off the road at high speed, everyone figured he was just another teen going too fast. But Alex never believed that for two seconds. It was a suicide. Ted felt ostracized, because he was Deaf. He lost his job as a busboy. The new evening manager didn't understand that he couldn't tell Ted something unless Ted was looking at him. That set off a chain of events, and Ted couldn't handle them.

There in the darkness, with Savannah beside him, Alex knew he had to be the best. He had to prove that he could do anything and do it better than anyone else. It drove him and pushed him to his limits. He also learned not to take too much too seriously. Early in his life, he figured out the difference between criticism and intended destruction. Too many people believed that he wasn't worthy of breathing the same air as they did because he was Deaf. And they didn't like it when he did well. *How could I get straight A's when I was Deaf? Because while you were playing video games and watching TV, I was studying.*

His parents expected him to do well – taught him the importance of doing well. He played games and watched movies like anyone else, except it wasn't the focus of his time after school. And when he needed to escape the daily grind, he climbed into a book and allowed himself to be whisked away on an adventure. When he was little, he wanted books with pictures, but then his imagination began to create better pictures.

The clock beside him began to glow. He must have fallen asleep. It was time to get up. He hated to leave the warmth of the bed and untangle himself from Savannah's soft body, but he needed to get ready for class.

He sat on the edge of the bed and stretched his arms over his head. Knowing that when he finished with today's exam, he'd never have to cope with that professor again. *Yeah, I breathe the same air as you, and you don't like it. You don't understand how I can get the grades that I do. I don't think you want me to succeed or get through this exam.*

Savannah took her exam in one class and turned in her paper for the other. Now she had to wait. The test was harder than she thought it would be. Alex acted as if anything short of perfection was failure. She was happy with a B and thrilled with an A. When Alex caught up to her at lunch, she was glad to see him.

"Did you get an A?" He asked her from the other side of the room.

She shrugged. "It wasn't easy. That's not a good sign."

"But you've been studying for it. Think positive."

"I'm not like you."

He grinned at her as he raised his eyebrows. "I like you the way you are. If you were like me, I wouldn't have put that ring on your finger."

She pouted for a moment. "I just want to be certain I maintain my scholarship eligibility."

"It's a matter of paying attention and studying. Remember, I only catch part of some classes depending on the instructor. I have to make up the difference by studying on my own."

"I don't know how you survive. I've noticed that in my classes many professors don't always stand still and teach."

"Every class I take, the person teaching it gets a memo on meeting my need to see them talk."

"And what happens if they don't?"

"It puts the burden on me to complain. I can request an interpreter."

"Have you ever done that?"

"Usually a friendly reminder is all that is needed. I have one professor who always forgets. But if I tap the desk, he realizes what he's done. I also have Ben in that class. He'll show me his notes. But I've had that professor for multiple classes over the years. He's a good man. He just forgets."

"Do you have other problems on campus?"

He shrugged. "Occasionally, like when the prettiest gal on campus laughed and wanted to stop me from signing."

"I'm so sorry." She could feel the blush rushing to her cheeks. "And just how many pretty girls want you to stop signing?"

"Only…" His gaze lifted from her to someplace behind her.

She turned and saw Ella. It was the second time she had seen her since that horrible night. She turned back to Alex. "It's okay. I'm over it. It was a stupid childish thing that she did. There's no way to prove that she did it, but there's no question in my mind." She pressed her lips together and took a few breaths. "She must have been terribly jealous of me, and I have no idea why. I didn't own anything of any value."

He reached across the coffee shop's table, took her hand, and kissed it. "But you are precious to me."

She moved her fingers so they spelled the combined sign for I love you. "If it hadn't been for her, I wouldn't be living with you. Maybe I should thank her."

He laughed. "I wouldn't go that far. But I'm glad I took you home with me. And I'm really glad I didn't spend that night on the sofa."

She gave him her evil-eye look, and then laughed.

A few hours later, after she had fixed a simple dinner and cleaned up, she sat once more at her computer and reread her paper. Certain she had covered all the material and properly used every comma, she asked Alex if he'd like to read it.

He wrinkled his nose.

She had interrupted whatever he had been doing.

He took her computer and turned it towards him.

She watched the smile slowly spread across his face.

"This is for your marketing class?"

She nodded.

He read it and then scrolled to the top to read it again. He made some sort of change and she wanted to know what he'd done.

"You misused an industry term. I corrected it. You did this for me?"

"Well, I could use any product. You'll be providing a product. It fit the parameters because it is not a new product, but a new company providing a known product in a competitive market. Why not put the work I'm required to do into something useful?"

"This is great, but where would I get that much money?"

"The bank, in the form of a loan. You must not have read the footnotes."

He scrolled down.

His face did not reveal his thoughts. Normally he was extremely expressive, but for now, he only occasionally blinked as he looked at the screen.

She watched as he must have reread the paper, scrolling to the end and then back to the beginning again. When he finally looked up at her, the smile on his face created an instant sense of relief. She knew he approved, and that meant more to her than any grade she might receive.

Then his smile turned serious. "It looks good on paper, but do you really think we could do it? It's a lot of money. Would you be willing to go that far into debt?"

lex walked Savannah to ASL class, gave her a quick kiss, and wished her luck. She was nervous. He didn't understand her apprehension. She had gone from knowing nothing in August to comprehending so much now. She knew the signs in the book and quite a bit more from being with him.

Prof. Stockton was an old family friend, except Alex had never told that to Savannah. The man's wife was Deaf. They had met while they were attending college. Stockton had been an English Lit major. But long after he had obtained his doctorate, he realized the need to teach sign language. He went back to school and picked up the required courses that would allow him to teach ASL on the college level. If Savannah thought he was being harder on her, he probably was. *He's tread the same path, Savannah. He knows what you are going through and just how much you will need to know if you marry me.*

That thought struck him hard. He didn't want to lose Savannah. But she had never once mentioned a wedding or even talked about setting a date. Did she not want to marry? He knew some women didn't want to marry or have children. He also knew she had reservations about having his children because of the possibility of their children growing up Deaf.

He hated going to a doctor's office because no one understood him. And this was one time he didn't want to bring his mom to act as an interpreter. *But if I went to a specialist… Someone who could do a DNA test and give us some idea as to the likelihood of having a deaf child…* He still wasn't certain that Savannah would be satisfied. He pushed the thoughts to one side and went to the library.

The need to start sending query letters to architectural firms meant he needed to explore which companies he wanted. Everyone sought the major corporations where they would get the experience of working on big projects. Having his name attached to something that was eighty stories high or higher carried prestige, but that's not what he wanted to do. Those were the kinds of projects that made a company millions and often gained them other projects of similar designs. Nor did he want to build hospitals with their nightmarish wiring, plumbing, and gas configurations. He wanted to build houses and small commercial buildings. He wanted the opportunity to utilize his knowledge of passive energy and apply as much as possible to what he designed. *Solar in every house.* What he really wanted was that one-on-one with the person who would live or work in the building. *Not some massive tower to be filled with apartments or offices that would be occupied by people I will never know. And they won't know my name.*

He got caught up in what he was doing and when he noticed the time, he realized he was late to meet Savannah. He found her in the coffee shop curled in a chair with her tablet's screen dark in her lap. Uncertain if she'd fallen asleep or if she was lost in thought, he approached her and waited for her to realize he was there.

Her eyes fluttered open, but there was no smile. She looked worn out.

"How did it go?"

She shook her head. "Terrible. He handed everyone the test paper except for me. He gave me a different one."

"What?"

She nodded. "I caught a glimpse of Ashley's paper. Totally different."

"That's not right." He held out his hand and she took it. He pulled her to her feet. Using only one hand, he signed, "Let's go."

It only took a few minutes to reach Prof. Stockton's office. Alex ignored the secretary and marched to the man's office. "Why did she get a different test? That's not fair."

"She didn't need to take that test. I gave her this one because she was ready for it." He handed Alex the test along with a red pen. "Want to grade it and save me some time?"

Alex looked at Savannah, wondering if she comprehended anything the professor had signed. Not knowing, he took the red pen and the test, as he seated himself in the chair closest to the man's desk. He looked at the first page and marked one wrong. Each page had at least one mistake. They were words that weren't used very often in normal conversation, yet she managed to get many of them correct. The last page contained ten animals and she had to match the word to the sign, and she had managed to do it. All ten were correct. There were two hundred and ten questions. He looked at Stockton.

The professor smiled. "She gets an extra two points for each animal she has correctly answered. Have you taken her to the zoo?"

Alex shook his head and began to count up the score. He wrote 176+20=196 on the top of the front page and handed it back to Stockton.

Stockton smiled. "How did you manage to get the animals?"

She lifted her shoulders. "Well, some of them made sense, such as the elephant. And I've seen Katy Perry's song *Roar* done in ASL so I knew tiger. And I had to guess—"

"Sign when you talk to me." Prof Stockton narrowed his eyes.

Savannah signed her response, but she was quaking the entire time.

The professor looked over the paper. "You did well." He turned to Alex. "Make sure she knows her higher numbers. She needs help with some syntax, and she's weak on emotions, cities, and places. But I'd say she passed next semester's class, and with flying colors, too. She would have breezed through the exam for the class she just had." He turned his attention to Savannah. "Do you understand what I just signed?"

She nodded but Alex knew she probably only caught half of what the man had said.

Professor Stockton took a handful of papers from a file in a drawer. "Pick one."

She gingerly chose the tip of one as though the stack were tarot cards and her future depended on it.

"I'll save you from doing the booth. Sign what is on that page." Professor Stockton sat back in his seat and crossed his arms over his chest.

The blood drained from her face as she looked at the sheet.

Alex smiled. "Look at me and do it."

Savannah began to sign. "The weather is calling for more rain and the river has reached its…" She fingerspelled capacity.

Alex was surprised that she knew the word for overflow.

Then she signed the rest. "The little children all wore navy pants and yellow shirts as they tiptoed through the art museum."

All he could do was watch her sign because he couldn't see what she was being asked to sign. But when she fingerspelled chemistry, he sucked in a breath and waited for the rest of the sentence. What she signed made sense, but she fingerspelled too much of it.

She took a few deep breaths and stared at him. He wanted to somehow mentally pass her the words that she needed. She started to fill with tears.

"I can't do it. I don't know this."

"Try. Fingerspell what you must. You can do it." Alex smiled, hoping to encourage her.

She looked at Stockton, and he told her to keep going. She closed her eyes, as though she needed a moment to compose herself. Alex could read her like a book, but he couldn't tell her what to sign. *You have to do this. I can't help you.*

Most of the next sentence she fingerspelled. But she did each letter quickly and clearly. He watched her as pride built within him. She'd come a very long way in only a few months and she was trying so hard.

Her hand shook as she gave Stockton the paper.

Stockton smiled broadly at her as he passed the paper to Alex. "What do you think her little performance was worth?"

Alex looked over the paper. She had used the wrong sign for youngest and had substituted smallest. The test wasn't easy for someone like Savannah. Maybe in another four months, but she had tried hard and had made herself clear as she signed. "I think she did well considering she's never taken that class. There were a few errors, but it was easy to understand what she was saying."

"That's not giving me a grade for this."

Alex grinned. "She did make several mistakes, but she tried very hard and did it with clarity. Her fingerspelling was quick and flowed. She was stone faced, because she was scared. I'd give her an A. I'm also prejudiced."

"You're honest." He turned his attention to Savannah. "You did well. Sign up for the class, but you don't need to attend. You've already passed it."

She nodded again and signed thank you.

Alex knew she didn't understand, but Stockton lessened the burden on her. Alex thanked the man but, as he stood to leave, Stockton's hard stare at Savannah meant he had more to say.

"I'm going to recommend that she take ASLIII this coming semester. It's only offered in the evening. I'll put in her file for her to take both. She'll only need to attend the ASLIII."

Alex thanked the professor so Savannah did, too. Alex wanted to laugh at her, but he knew now was not the time. She probably only had picked up part of the conversation. From the look on her face and the tiny quake to her hands, he knew she was still upset.

It wasn't until they were headed to his car that he reiterated what Prof. Stockton had said.

"I'm going to do what?"

This time he laughed as he opened her car door. "He's giving you permission to take both classes but you only have to take ASLIII. You've already passed ASLII with flying colors. Do it, Savannah, you need the vocabulary."

She got into his Prius and snapped her seatbelt. "I guessed at half those answers."

He closed her passenger door, and then went to his side of the car. From behind the wheel, he looked at her. "You've come a long way since we first met. I don't have to fingerspell every other word."

She shook her head. "You said when you could quit fingerspelling that I would be proficient. I'm afraid I'll never be that fluent, nor will I be capable of keeping up with the normal speed you use when signing to your family."

"Yes, you will. Look at how well you do. It takes time. You aren't going to learn it all in a few months." He put the car in reverse, backed out of his parking spot, and headed home.

They sat at the table and worked on their computers.

Movement in the kitchen caught his attention and he realized Esther was on her phone with Demitri. He didn't always see what she was saying, but the look on her face said plenty. His heart went out to Esther. Demitri was a nice guy. Neither family would approve of their relationship, but they were determined to forge a life together, no matter what.

He went back to his computer and the renderings that he was doing. He wasn't doing anything more than playing in colors and landscape elements. He wanted perfection.

After switching between stone and mulch, he chose stone and then traded out the white birch for something darker in color. He almost went with a maple but chose a flowering tree that would add bright color in the spring and then settle into a solid green during the summer. He added a few low-growing junipers. He got up from where he was sitting and looked at his drawing from a distance. This was better.

He watched Savannah pick up her phone and answer a call. She turned her back to him, so he couldn't read her lips. He figured it was intentional, especially when her shoulders slumped, and she raised her hand to her face. She only acted this way when she was on the phone with her mom.

Savannah listened to her mom, and finally responded. "Mom, you aren't going to make me change my mind. I love him."

"But, my darling, you'll have your college education. You can get a great job someplace and find a really wonderful guy."

"Mom, I love Alex. I'm going to marry him."

"Darling, he's handsome. I can understand you've fallen for his looks, but lust is not love. You don't want to saddle yourself with a man who is disabled."

"NO! That's not fair." She stood up and went to the living

room sofa where she was certain that Alex wouldn't see her talking. "He's not disabled. He's just Deaf. You of all people… I can't believe I'm having this conversation."

"I want you to listen to reason. You'll wind up working yourself to death to support him. You've already said his sisters are deaf. Do you want deaf children?"

"I can't have this conversation, I'm in the middle of exams, and Christmas is less than three weeks away." *Why Mom? Why are you doing this to us?* She wiped away the tears that were forming in her eyes.

"I'm trying to protect you from making a horrible mistake that you will regret."

The conversation continued until Savannah knew she couldn't keep going.

Alex's hand touched her shoulder, and then he kissed the top of her head. The tears streamed down her face, as her insides twisted into a hard knot. "Mom, I'll call you later. I can't talk at the moment."

She disconnected the call and let the tears flow unchecked.

Alex kneeled in front of the sofa where she sat and looked at her with such compassion. He didn't ask. He waited for her.

She snuffled, and he brought her a box of tissues. After taking a few to wipe her tears away, she blew her nose. *How do I tell you? I can't.* She reached out to him.

He enveloped her in his arms, holding her tight and rocking her. The pain of her mother's words ripped through her, stirring doubts that she thought she'd conquered.

When she ran out of tears, she gasped several large breaths as she tried to steady her emotions. She had soaked the shoulder of his shirt, and he didn't seem to care. That was her Alex, her steady rock. The man who never got flustered. She looked into his sapphire blue eyes and only saw his love for her. Making the sign for I love you, she placed it on his chest.

He kissed her.

Reality vanished as she allowed herself to dissolve in his embrace.

He picked her up and carried her upstairs. There in the privacy of their room, he kissed her until her insecurity was gone. A few more deep breaths and she began to tell him some of what her mother had said.

He shook his head. "Don't let her fears influence you."

"But her fears have been my fears."

"Why?"

"Maybe I've progressed beyond them."

He shook his head and frowned. "No, you still carry doubts. If you didn't, she wouldn't be able to upset you."

"I worry about deaf children. I worry about you getting a job. Who will hire you?"

"Anyone who wants a good architect." He shrugged. "Yes, I have an additional burden because I need to be able to talk to workers on job sites. That has played on my mind and is part of the reason why I'm taking speech lessons."

She put her hand to her forehead. "Good. I was afraid you were doing it to somehow please me. I wanted to know that you were doing it for you."

He raised his eyebrows for a moment and then went back to a serious facial expression. "I am doing it for you, because I love you. I want to be able to succeed. I want our children to be free to bring friends to the house and for you to have friends who don't sign." He soothingly cupped her face in his hands. "I refused to talk because I knew my voice was not good. And…" He pressed his lips together. "And I was angry that I could learn to read lips, but the rest of the world has never learned to sign. Call it pride or maybe stubbornness. My father gets away without talking, because my mom grew up signing, and his job allows him to sit at home on his computer. He's not hindered by an office environment where he'd have to speak."

"Your father works?"

"Yes. And he makes a lot more than my mom."

"Oh."

"His birthday party is next weekend. Mom's been planning it for months. It's the big six-zero. You will see how difficult it is and uncomfortable he will be with Mom's friends who don't sign." He frowned and then continued. "Parents sometimes teach us more than they think. Sometimes they aren't always right. Life keeps changing."

"Do you intend to get an implant?"

He shook his head. "I have no desire for noise. My sister and Dustin have jobs that would severely limit them if they did not have implants. Society thinks we should have them. But most people I know who have been deaf all their life, when they get them, they hate them. They say the noise is too much and they can't wait to remove the processor and go back to silence. We do quite well without them." He shrugged and winked. "You can keep your sound."

"Don't you want to hear me?"

"Hear you what? I *hear* you with your hands, your body movements, and your expressions. Do I really need more?"

She looked at him and shrugged.

"I didn't need to hear you downstairs. I knew you were upset, but not why."

"I do worry about any children we might have. I've thought about adoption, but I want your seed to grow inside of me."

"We have plenty of time to decide. There are doctors who specialize in DNA testing. Let's figure out our odds before we make those decisions."

"Designer babies?"

He shook his head and placed his hand on her lower abdomen. "We'll find out the odds. Being Deaf is not a problem, it's normal." He smiled brightly at her. "Am I not perfect?"

"You are vain."

He laughed and kissed her again. "Don't worry about your parents. The best way to convince them that I am the most wonderful husband is for me to succeed and to make certain you never doubt my love." He kissed her again. "How much do you still need to do tonight?"

"Not much."

"Let's make some popcorn."

They both ate popcorn while they sat in front of their computers. She looked at his computer and frowned at him.

"What?"

She pointed to the screen and the flowering tree. "It's blooming too late. That blooms just as most of the trees start budding, not after they have their leaves."

He furrowed his brow. "How do you know that?"

"There's one in my parents' backyard."

He popped up another screen that contained a database of plants and smacked his forehead. Then he leaned over and kissed her.

In just a few seconds, all the trees had vanished from the drawing and Alex was redrawing them. "I knew there was something wrong, but I couldn't put my finger on it. I'm so glad you spotted that."

She smiled at him. "Glad to help."

She watched him draw and then pointed. "If I owned that building I'd put two large urns by the front doors and fill them with annuals and some pretty hanging pearls."

He fingerspelled, "PEARLS."

Using her phone, she searched for an example, and then showed him the succulent vine with tiny bead-like leaves. Exhaustion hit her with such force that she packed up her things and left to take her shower. But no matter how hard she tried, she couldn't get her mother's words to go away. To some extent, her mother was right.

Who will hire you? Is it wrong for me to help you search for things? It's not like you can't do it alone. Oh why am I letting my mother's words get to me?

Alex redrew the trees and looked at his drawing. *Much better.* The lacy, leafless trees with their hint of color added a nice, soft touch to the stone building.

Esther left the kitchen for her room and he knew that she, too, was coping with personal problems. She and Demitri didn't share the same religion. They had nothing in common. *When her family discovers what she and Demitri have done, they won't be happy. The odds are she'll be disowned.*

Alex couldn't imagine ever being that upset with his children. He wasn't even that upset with Emily over her teenage nonsense. Twice he had asked her to do things and each time she refused. Maybe that's a good thing. *I don't want to burden Savannah and make her think that she's the problem. That's not fair to her.*

Having swapped the trees in his renderings, he liked his finished project. In the morning, he would print the pages on the school's large printers. He copied everything back to his flash drive and sent it to the school's cloud for safekeeping.

When morning came with the realization that he had to print his renderings, he bounced out of bed with excitement. *One semester left and it's over.*

He hadn't much sleep, and it didn't matter to him. His enthusiasm had already overridden any lack of sleep. He had breakfast waiting for Savannah when she came downstairs. He'd drop her off and then print his drawings. They'd meet for lunch and he intended to take her out to celebrate.

"You're chipper."

He laughed. "It's almost over. Doesn't that feel wonderful?"

She rocked her hand. "I have this test."

"You'll do fine. You've studied, and you know the material, right?"

She shook her head as if doubting her ability to write her name on a paper.

He didn't understand her lack of confidence. She'd studied; therefore, she shouldn't have a problem. "I'll see you a few minutes after noon. I have to turn in my renderings."

"Don't you email them?"

"Not this time. I should have done them yesterday, but I wasn't satisfied."

He took her to class and then went to print his project.

17

He entered the computer lab and discovered the printers he needed had signs on them. They were out of order. He inhaled a deep breath and took off for the engineering building. There was a waiting list a mile long and it was estimated that he wouldn't get his printed until after three that afternoon. He didn't bother to put his name on the list. He went to the art department. It took him an extra minute to get across his desire to use their printer. He breathed a sigh of relief as the first page began to print. A yellow light began to flash on the printer. He looked at the printer and realized the ink had run out. He found the person in charge and signed ink.

Finally, the woman got up from her seat behind a desk and went to the printer. She turned to Alex. "It's out of ink."

"Replace the ink."

She looked at him with a blank expression and went back to her seat.

He tried again.

She rolled her eyes and wrote on a piece of paper.

The printer is out of ink.

He frowned and wrote back to her.

Replace the ink.

She shook her head.

There's no ink. There's no budget for it.

He heaved a few breaths. There were no other large printers on the campus. He took off for his car.

He drove to the nearest copier store, but they said they couldn't do it. They didn't have any printer on the premises large enough, but if he wanted to leave it…

Using his phone, he searched for architects in the area. He found one and went to that office. Using the small pad that he kept in his pocket, he asked if he could use their printer.

The secretary left the room, came back, and shook her head. "We don't allow that because we don't want to chance a virus."

He understood their fear, but that wasn't helping him. He nodded, signed thank you, and left.

He checked the phone again. The next place was a fair distance from him. He had no choice. Getting the pages printed was the only thing that mattered to him. It took forty minutes to drive to another small town. The architectural firm sat in an old 1920s building in the downtown. He parked his car and dropped the three quarters he'd found in his pocket into the coin slot of the old parking meter. Taking a deep breath, he attempted to calm his frazzled nerves. *I only need to get these pages printed.*

He slowed his pace and straightened his shoulders. Opening the door, he discovered he was walking into what appeared to be a maze of old rooms with marble floors. Ornate crown mouldings bordered the ceiling. Heavy mouldings framed the doors. He stood transfixed at what was once considered grand, appreciating the details and craftsmanship.

"May I help you?"

A fifty something women had approached him. He pointed to the details and smiled. Taking his pad, he wrote,

Beautiful. Please, I need help. I am an architecture student and our printers on campus are out of ink. I must get these renderings printed today for my exam.

"Just a moment." She vanished down a hallway.

A middle-aged man entered the room. "Good morning. I'm Ian Kilpatrick. I understand you need some help."

Alex smiled, signed that he was deaf, and then showed the note he'd written to the woman.

The man started to take the little notebook from him. Alex withdrew it. Very slowly he signed. "I can see your lips. Talk."

The man scrunched his face. "You can tell what I'm saying?"

Alex nodded. He handed over his flash drive and wrote what he needed.

I'm willing to pay for your paper and ink. There's only one printer still working. The wait time is too long. These renderings must be turned in this afternoon.

"Your final?"

Alex nodded. He mouthed as he signed, "Please."

The man smiled back and motioned for Alex to follow him. There in a back room sat several large printers and an old plotter. The man also had an ancient machine for making blueprints.

Alex stood patiently as Mr. Kilpatrick opened the file that contained the drawings. He said something, but Alex didn't catch it.

I have to see your lips to know what you are saying.

The man brought the pages up on his computer. "What year student are you?"

Alex knew he needed to talk. He concentrated on making his words come from his chest. "This is my next to last semester. I will have my master's in May."

The man looked over each sheet. "Did you design this for someone?"

"No. We were given…" He pointed to the screen and a file listed at the bottom of the screen.

The man clicked on it. It was the list of what they could and could not do. "And this is what you chose."

Alex nodded.

"This is incredible. Total passive never seems to work with commercial buildings."

Alex pointed to the screen and showed the additional system for cooling and heating.

"I'm impressed."

Alex smiled.

Mr. Kilpatrick pulled up all the renderings and told a printer to start printing. He commented on several things as he lifted each sheet from the printer.

Alex swelled with pride. It was one thing for a professor to tell him he'd done well, but this was a total stranger, an AIA architect with his own company.

"And you graduate this spring?"

Alex nodded.

"What do you want to design when you graduate?"

Houses and small commercial buildings.

Mr. Kilpatrick gazed at Alex with such intensity that Alex knew the man had something important on his mind.

"Have you thought about how you will communicate

with clients and those working the job sites?"

Alex smiled. He signed, "I can do it." Then he mustered up the courage to talk again. "I am taking speetth lessthons." He used his note pad.

Mostly I write. I have no problem understanding what you are saying. I know my ability to talk with my mouth is limited.

"Are you planning to open your own company?"

I've thought about it. It depends on what options I have.

The man motioned for Alex to follow him into another room.

"I have the work and I could use a talented architect." He showed him several active projects.

Alex smiled.

If that's an offer, I'm very willing to consider it.

"Come back and see me after the holidays. Let's see how things work out. If you are capable of communicating with clients and handling job sites, I could use a good man."

Alex stuck out his hand and uttered, "Tank you, ssirh."

They went back to the room with the printers and collected all the papers.

Alex retrieved his flash drive. He asked how much and pulled his wallet from his pocket.

"Nothing. Be here after the holidays. Let me see what you can do out of the classroom. I'll pay you for your work."

Alex nodded and gave the man the thumbs up. Then he mouthed, "Thank you," before signing, "I will be here."

Ian Kilpatrick handed Alex a large tube after drawing some lines through the company's logo. "Got a label? Put your name on it. Show your professor that you can be professional."

Alex inhaled, rolled his drawings, and placed them in the tube.

No label.

The man took Alex to his secretary. "Make a label for him."

Alex wrote his name and course number on his notepad and showed it to the woman.

In less than a minute, he had a label to place over the Kilpatrick AIA logo. He put the tube on a big table. Carefully, he peeled the label and stuck it to the tube. He had a large plastic sleeve carrier with a handle that he'd used several times, but this was perfect.

Thank you, Mr. Kilpatrick.

"Call me Ian. I'll see you after the holidays and good luck. You've done an excellent job from what I've seen."

Alex left smiling. If there hadn't been a problem with the printers, he would have never had a shot at this job. The meter was about to expire, which meant he was late for Savannah. He texted her. -Ran into a snag. I'm off campus. Will be there in about an hour or so. I've got good news but must first drop my renderings in the professor's office.

Savannah checked her phone when it pinged and read Alex's message. She and Ashley were celebrating their end of exams with cappuccino coffees that Savannah had bought with the money that Alex seemed to constantly hand her. Savannah didn't mean to groan. "He's off campus and won't be back for a while."

"How's it going with the two of you?" Ashley asked between sips of her coffee.

She shrugged. "It's good. But I have a big problem with my mom."

"Your mom? Why?"

"She doesn't quite understand. She thinks I'm throwing away my life being involved with Alex, and she's dead set against my marrying him."

"What? That's insane. Alex is a super guy."

"I know, but she worries that he won't be able to support me, and I'll be saddled with a guy who is disabled and a total leech."

"She doesn't know the Alex we know."

"I've tried to explain to her that he will have a job, and he will do well. But then she started on the fact that if we have children, they will be deaf."

"Are you sure they will be deaf? Can't they figure that stuff out now?"

Savannah took a sip of her fancy coffee-based drink. "Maybe. Alex said we should talk to a doctor who specializes in DNA."

Ashley made a face. "Is there such a thing?"

"I don't know. I guess all doctors have to learn that kind of thing now. It's not like it was when we were babies."

Ashley finished what was in her cup. "Are you worried about a deaf child? I mean it obviously doesn't bother you that Alex is Deaf."

"I've asked myself that question from the day I figured out that I loved him. Is it fair to bring a deaf child into the world?"

Ashley propped her elbow on the table and rested her chin in the palm of that hand. "Well, it's not like the child will be a burden, and they are making all these strides to give Deaf people hearing."

"Alex won't get an implant. His sister has one. Apparently she takes it off when she's not working, but she wears it when I'm around."

"That I don't understand. Why would someone not want to hear?"

Savannah shrugged. "There seems to be two different

camps when it comes to implants. Those who have always been Deaf don't seem to care about hearing. But I was reading something the other day about a woman who has always been Deaf, her parents were Deaf, and she thinks being able to hear is the most wonderful thing."

"Hmm."

Savannah looked at her friend. "Does it make any sense if I say I want Alex's child, I just don't want a deaf child?"

"No." Ashley raised her eyebrows and sat up. "What if there was some magical potion you could take to prevent the child from being deaf. And you took it. Then after the child was born, you discovered that baby was deaf anyway. Would you love that child any less?"

"Of course not."

"So what are you worried about?"

"Having a deaf child."

Ashley shook her head. "Do you love Alex any less because he's Deaf?"

"No."

"So he's had problems with the general public not comprehending that he's smart and capable of doing almost anything. Isn't that minor in the grand scheme of things? What if you had a normal child, except that child winds up with some horrible disease? Are you going to blame yourself for passing on the wrong DNA to that child?"

"Eww! That's a terrible thought."

"No, it's not. The truth is simple. If Matthew and I get married and we have a child, what are the odds of that child being perfect and growing up perfect with no problems whatsoever, not even needing a pair of glasses?"

"I don't know. Slim, I guess."

"Right. So what if Alex's parents never had him because there was a chance of passing on some deaf gene."

"Okay, I get what you're saying. His sister was trying

to explain to me that it's like blue eyes. It's just something that makes them what they are, and there's nothing wrong with that."

"Exactly. No one is perfect. There are a lot of really awful things that can go wrong and that never stops us from having children."

"Let's get more coffee."

"Yeah, I want a regular cup of coffee this time. This is yummy, but how many calories are in it?" Ashley groaned.

Savannah nodded. "Probably too many."

They went to the counter and ordered plain coffees. Once they had them, they returned to the small table where they were sitting. Savannah looked around and then checked the time.

"Want to grab some lunch when we're done? I'm hungry."

Ashley stared at her coffee. "I think that Freshmen Fifteen was more like twenty-five and I'm still gaining. How will I survive another year?"

Savannah laughed. "You're not fat."

"Not yet. But at the rate I'm going, I will be."

Savannah's phone pinged again, and she checked the message.

-Be there in just a few must drop off my presentation.

She smiled and then pulled her tablet out of her backpack. "I want to see if anyone has posted my grades. The wait is killing me." She ran her finger across the screen. "ASL class is up."

Ashley checked her grade. "I got an A. How did you do?"

"An A, but I already knew that grade."

"How?"

She didn't want to tell her friend what the professor had done. "I saw my test. Alex took me to Prof. Stockton's office about something and my test was there."

She swiped her screen a few more times and still no other grades appeared. She was certain she'd done reasonably well in all her classes, but curiosity was getting the best of her. She checked her marketing class one more time. Nothing.

Ashley squealed, "I got another A. I was scared to death about that grade."

"Do you realize that in ten years we are not going to remember what grades we got or in what classes?"

"Yeah. I know, but for now those grades are everything if we want to stay in school. Just promise that you'll always be my best female friend."

Savannah laughed. "There's nothing that will undo our friendship, even if one of us moved to the other side of the world."

"I think you're right." Ashley leaned in and whispered, "How's Esther doing?"

Savannah shrugged. "I get so caught up in my own studying, I never pay much attention. She sits in the kitchen and studies, while Alex and I spend most of the time at the table in his dining room."

"Maybe she shouldn't spend so much time in the kitchen." Ashley looked around. "She looks like she's really packed some weight on."

"I noticed that, too. We've told her she can use the kitchen, but she eats every meal in the cafeteria."

"Is she still going with Demitri?"

Savannah nodded. "I like him. He treats her like a princess. And to see them together… It's so obvious they are in love."

Ashley's face lit up. "Look who has finally decided to join us."

18

Savannah turned and realized Alex stood behind her. "What's kept you away?"

He started to explain. She watched him sign but Ashley intently stared at him with a slightly confused face. Savannah knew then that her best friend who had once coached her couldn't keep up even though Alex was signing at half the speed of what he considered normal.

He explained what happen and his complete panic over the printers not working.

She was bad about worrying over grades and such, but Alex was completely obsessive.

Yet his grin grew wider as he picked up speed.

Savannah was totally unsure of what he had signed. *"What?* You've got to slow down! Did you just say that you got a job?"

He grinned and nodded. "I start in January. I'm certain I won't be doing anything other than drafting, but it's a start." He pulled a chair from another table and joined them. "I'll have a forty-minute commute. That means I can stay in the house."

"And he plans to keep you on after you graduate?" Savannah asked.

"This is a trial. I think he wants to know that I can do the work, but that I can also communicate." He stared at Ashley. "What do you have this afternoon?"

Both women shook their head and signed, "Zero."

"Did the two of you eat lunch?" Alex asked.

Savannah and Ashley both signed, "No."

"Let's go celebrate. I'm buying." He pursed his lips and stared at Ashley. "As long as I don't make Matthew jealous."

Ashley glanced at her phone. "If we wait ten more minutes, he can join us."

They waited almost fifteen minutes and when Matthew joined them, his face was pale, and his hands shook. "Worst. Exam. Ever."

"Want to go to lunch?" Ashley asked.

"Sure. Why not?" He turned to Alex. "Sorry. I forget."

Alex smiled. He didn't seem to mind too much when people forgot occasionally. It meant that they accepted him and didn't think about the fact that he was Deaf. But when it was important, he often got frustrated.

Without trying to be conspicuous, Savannah pulled her tablet out of her backpack and checked her grades again. Her one exam had been posted and she had an A-. *That's better than a B.* But she wasn't positive it was enough to give her an A for the class.

She checked another screen and still nothing. She didn't really expect to see her marketing grade until much later. *No surprises. I don't want anything unexpected. Oh, please like the marketing plan I did for Alex.*

Ashley talked to Matthew. Savannah's thoughts turned to Alex, and how she would handle the holidays. There had been some talk about having Christmas Eve dinner with his parents, and then driving to her family so that she might be there for the morning. She didn't want to be driving late at night. She would rather get up early and go. They needed to talk.

A few minutes later, they all went out to eat. The Hawaiian chicken salad was delicious. Everyone laughed and had a good time. Ashley tried to sign the entire time that she talked, and a few times, Savannah and Ashley signed to each other.

Savannah remembered what Alex had said about signing and others knowing what they were saying. *If anyone wants to hone in on our conversation, they are going to be very disappointed.*

She looked at Alex who was writing something to Matthew. With her friends, he didn't have a problem communicating. They all made the necessary allowances, and they genuinely enjoyed Alex's company. It was his quick smile and easy-going personality that made him so likeable. Plus, for a man who never seemed to watch much TV, he managed to stay up on sports and could add to almost any conversation.

She was proud to call him hers. The feelings inside of her swelled, she loved him, and her mother's protests hurt. Not wanting to be put in a position of choosing between her mother and her future husband, she was smack in the middle. She was going to have to face her mom at Christmas, and she wanted Alex with her. *Why does life have to be so complicated?*

With classes finished for the semester, Alex could have kicked back and relaxed. Instead he used the time to get a jumpstart on his final semester. The entire semester would be design-oriented, and the professors already had issued the projects. He handed Savannah the keys to his car and asked her to do some grocery shopping.

He started to worry when she didn't return from the store in a timely manner, but then, she really hadn't had much freedom. If he were really worried, he knew he could text her, but he didn't want her to get the impression that he didn't trust her. He convinced himself she probably had met up with a friend. Ashley had left campus for her parents' house, and Esther had left, leaving a thank-you note that said she would return before school started again. The house was empty, a rare occurrence since Brindlewood had burned.

Savannah and he had cleaned the entire house in a few hours and had even washed several windows. They talked about a Christmas tree, but decided for the two of them when they wouldn't even be there for Christmas, it probably wasn't worth the effort. But he wasn't about to turn down her offer to bake Christmas cookies.

He sat at his computer and began to think about some new designs for the coming semester. All of his formal classes were completed. He'd taken that geotechnical class, because he wanted that knowledge, and he was glad he had. Profs. Zinnski and Han encouraged him to pursue every interest.

It was late in the afternoon when Savannah returned, and she had all sorts of packages, plus groceries to last them until the holidays. She put her groceries away and then began to show him what she had bought. She'd obviously been to the thrift store.

"I need to steal some greenery from your yard."

"What?"

"For the wreath. Why do you think I bought these?" She held up a pair of strange looking scissors.

He pointed to the door, totally unsure what she was about to do.

A half hour later, she returned with her arms laden with snippets from the bushes and the ivy that threatened to overtake the entire yard. He sniffed the air and the fresh green scent of the outdoors added a refreshing aroma to the room. Then he watched her as she put it all to one side and began to fix a meal for them.

It was after they had eaten that she began to rework the pitiful used wreath she had bought. But when she was finished enhancing the wreath with her cut greenery and adding a fluffy red bow, it looked full, rich, and beautiful. Then she took a green pottery bowl and began to add snippets of greenery to that. She had made a holiday arrangement.

"Where did you learn to do that?"

She smiled. "When I was sixteen, I got a job at a florist after school. I swept floors and did a few odd jobs. But I watched what the woman did who owned the place. I learned."

"I like."

"The bowl was only a few pennies and I figured green was very versatile and will work with any season." She held up a box of candles. "They were cheap." And then placed them in some glass candlesticks. "Since they are glass, I can use them for any season. Call it shabby-chic."

"Did you have enough money for everything?"

She nodded and kept going.

By the way she arranged the candles on the table, she probably had intended a candlelight dinner.

"What's in the other bags?"

She had thoughtfully chosen a variety of used woodworking tools, including an electric router for her father. There were several little things for her mom, but she also bought things for his family, including a fancy assortment of nail polishes in a kit for Emily.

"Will you go shopping with me? I need to buy some things for my family," he asked.

"Of course. I love to shop. What female doesn't?"

"I cheat." He pulled his computer closer and began to look a few things up on the web.

"What are you going to get for Emily?"

He shrugged. "I wish I knew. By now, she's normally given me a list a mile long of what she wants."

"Have you asked her for her wish list?"

He shook his head. "After her behavior at Thanksgiving, I don't want to give her anything."

"That would be wrong. You can't ignore her."

"Jewelry?" He rolled his palm up as if to question his suggestion.

"I don't know. Okay, I'll think about it. Surely there is something that she would like."

"Good luck." He looked up dishes and then spotted a set of china that he thought her mom might like. It wasn't expensive, but it was pretty. "Here, for your mom?"

"She'd be afraid to use it." She scanned the online store until she found another set.

The price was about the same, but this looked less formal. "Red? You want red for her?"

"She'll love it, and it comes with serving pieces. But it's a lot of money. Are you sure you want to spend that much?"

He nodded. "Your mother lacks dishes."

Savannah laughed. "She doesn't *lack* dishes. She lacks matching dishes."

"How many place settings, eight?"

"I think that would be good. Can you buy extra serving pieces?"

"I think so." He checked the fine print and added the dishes to the cart. "Done."

He did another search in the store. "Here."

"My mom will think she's died and gone to heaven if you buy her that too."

"It's on sale."

Slowly they made their way through the family members until they reached Emily. He turned to Savannah. "I think you already bought her the perfect gift."

"It's not enough."

"It's not. She expects more."

Savannah touched his arm. "We'll figure it out."

If she thought having a few weeks off would be a time for resting, she discovered she was wrong. It seemed there was plenty to do and tons of events to attend, starting with Alex's father's birthday party.

Alex took her to buy an evening dress for the occasion. After spending hours looking for something suitable, he texted his mom. Almost immediately she called Savannah.

"I'll pick you up tomorrow at noon. We'll do lunch and then shop. I need a new dress, too."

Savannah's frustration melted away only to be replaced by astonishment at his mother's offer. "Thank you, ma'am. I'll be ready." She glared at Alex. "She wants to take me to lunch and shopping!"

He laughed.

"You always think it's funny when things don't go well."

"You get upset over the silliest things. You need a nice dress. Let Mom help."

"I have tried on a dozen nice dresses and you don't like them."

He shrugged. "Mom will find you something to wear."

When morning came, it was cold and miserable. Twice Savannah changed what she was wearing. She tried not to overthink the situation. His mom had always been nice to her.

As soon as his mom pulled into the driveway, Alex kissed Savannah and wished her luck. "It's girls' day out."

Savannah frowned. "What do you know about that?"

"Go have fun and buy a pretty dress."

She pulled on her coat and scarf and ran out to the car.

His mom drove to a restaurant on the far side of town. "I made reservations for 12:30. We're a few minutes early. With luck, we won't have to wait."

But wait they did. When they finally were seated, Savannah looked at the menu and swallowed. Growing up, her family rarely ate dinner out. Alex thought nothing of it, and apparently his mom thought nothing of spending big money on lunch.

"Have you decided what you'd like, Savannah?"

"No. I was thinking about a soup and salad, or one of the sandwiches."

"The peanut soup, if you've never had it, is delicious, and their salads are wonderful. But if you want a sandwich and like ham, the Smoky Tavern is wonderful."

"I've never had peanut soup, and I can't imagine the taste."

"Order it. You'll love it. It's a favorite of my son's."

She knew she had to order it. Since it was Alex's favorite, she'd learn to make it for him. "Okay, I'll have the peanut soup, and I was thinking about the avocado salad."

They ordered their meal.

Alex's mom smiled as she asked, "How are things progressing between you and my son? Have you set a wedding date?"

She shook her head. "I don't want to lose my scholarship money. If I marry, I think I'll foul that up because it's based on my family's income."

"You're on a Meredith scholarship?"

Savannah nodded.

"Don't worry about it. I'll help you fill out the papers. There's plenty of money for fourth year students, especially ones with your grade point average. Besides, being married to my son will give you a huge discount."

"Huh?" She didn't mean to say that aloud.

"The family of faculty gets a huge discount."

"Oh."

Their food was served. The peanut soup was delicious. But no matter how hard she tried to decipher the ingredients, she couldn't.

"I must learn to make this for him. It is scrumptious."

"He also loves French onion soup."

"You'll have to tell me all of his favorites."

Alex's mom took a fork to her salad. "There's not much he doesn't like. He doesn't mind food that's a little spicy, but he doesn't like it super hot." She took a bite of her salad. "Nor does he like fish with bones in it. If he sees a bone – that's it for him. Don't even try to get him to eat shad."

Savannah had never eaten shad so she had no clue, but the idea of eating fish bones... She shuddered, and then gave it a little more thought. "No anchovies or sardines?"

"No. It's about the only thing he won't eat."

Savannah nodded and ate her meal savoring every bite. But in the back of her mind were the questions that always seemed to haunt her. She gathered her courage and asked, "Were you worried about having deaf children?"

"Not in the least. Being Deaf is not a problem."

"How can you say that when you've had to fight for your son to attend a regular school?"

Mrs. Van Doorn swallowed before she answered. "There's actually pride within the Deaf community. They consider themselves to be special. You've probably heard Deaf of Deaf."

"I think from Gwen. It means they are Deaf from Deaf parents."

"People lose their hearing for all sorts of reasons but being born deaf of Deaf parents immediately creates a bond within the Deaf community. You'll discover they are tight-knit. And survival for many depends on the community." She took another bite of her salad, ate it, and then continued. "The Deaf community provides tremendous support, not just emotional but in a variety of ways, including information exchange. If you need a plumber or an electrician, you'll call someone in the Deaf community."

"So you don't call four different companies to find the best price?"

"Remember most of these people hardly use the phone.

They'd rather deal with one of their own, besides if you were Deaf and had a question or needed something explained, wouldn't you rather deal with someone who signs?"

Savannah nodded. "And I guess that a Deaf electrician probably needs to work to keep his family fed."

Mrs. Van Doorn nodded. "Exactly. Furthermore, being an advocate means making certain everyone in the Deaf community succeeds. The problem comes from the hearing population not understanding. Surely Prof. Stockton has given you the general history of sign language. You'll get more detailed history during your third semester of ASL, but sign language has always existed. Remember English is the newcomer."

"We learned that."

"There are those who think that the people with hearing who can't sign have the problem, and my son is one of them. Quite honestly, he's correct."

"Not even a twinge of concern about deafness being hereditary?"

She shook her head. "We've come further in the last thirty years, but there's no reason to fear having a deaf child. There's DNA testing that will give you an idea what your odds are of having a deaf child, but it's nothing more than a gamble. Will the X override the Y? In theory, my children had a very small chance of being deaf. It's a complicated formula with DNA. My girls could have been perfectly normal but carriers of one of several deaf genes." She ate the last bite of her salad. "I never had my DNA tested. It's possible that I'm the one responsible for my children's deafness."

"So you didn't worry about it?"

"No. I loved my husband, and knew that no matter what, I'd love my children. And if they were deaf, I would be certain they received the education and the opportunities that they deserved. They *are* Deaf and so far everyone is doing well."

"Emily?"

"We let her get away with too much for too long. If she doesn't straighten up in school, she's not going to have the grades for college. I know you think you are responsible for the rift between Alex and her, but I don't believe that for one second. Her grades took a nosedive long before you came onto the scene."

"She's very jealous of me. I'm certain."

Alex's mom began signing as she spoke. "No. Don't feel that way. She might be jealous, but she's going through a rough patch." Her brow furrowed. "We're putting her in a special school after the holidays. She doesn't know it yet. We've had it with her choice of friends and some of the things she's been doing."

"A Deaf school?"

Mrs. Van Doorn nodded. "It was a difficult decision. It's still a public school. They handle all sorts of children with additional needs, not just Deaf children. Emily will be placed in the Deaf program."

"I hope she's not going into a worse situation."

"My husband and I have been there. We've talked to the teachers and we know many of the students." Alex's mom shook her head. "We've taken Emily's phone from her, which is quite crippling when you don't hear."

"Alex and I text often."

"Emily speaks quite well. She's intelligent, but she's going through a phase of thinking she can do whatever she wants and get away with it. Unfortunately, she manages to get away with way too much."

"Is she driving?"

"No! She's not old enough. And at the rate she's going, we aren't going to allow her to have a license. Gwen and Alex had their licenses and a car when they turned sixteen, but they were by far more responsible. At this point, we can't imagine giving her permission to drive. She's hard enough to control. Can you imagine if she had a car?"

"I had my license at sixteen but not a car. I've never had a car. There's only my dad's pickup truck, and my dad takes it to work. If my mom needs to go someplace, she takes my dad to work."

"That must be tough on your mom."

Mrs. Van Doorn paid the check, and they left for their afternoon of shopping. They stopped at a boutique in an upscale shopping area. Savannah recognized the names of several of the stores, but not the one where she'd been taken.

"Now, see if you can find something suitable."

Savannah inhaled a few deep breaths. Never had she been to such a place, but Alex's mom was insisting that she would pay to have Savannah look properly attired. *If this is what it was like to have money, I might as well enjoy it. Nothing seems very real.*

19

$\mathcal{S}$avannah decided not to even look at the price tags. She tried on three things, and none of them seemed to be good enough to suit Alex's mom.

"Try this. I think it's perfect for the holidays and you have the figure for it." The saleswoman brought a dress into the dressing room.

Savannah took the dress and looked at it, certain she would hate it. The thing hung like an old rag on the hanger. But upon close examination, it was an icy gray snowflake lace over an under-dress and it had been trimmed in tiny rhinestones and bits of silver thread. She put it on but couldn't zip it. The under-dress was low cut and the lace covered her skin, but the back was so low that she knew she couldn't wear a bra with it. But the way it draped... *It looks terrific!* She stood admiring herself in the mirror.

"Do you need help with that zipper?" the saleswoman asked.

"Yes."

The woman entered the dressing room and zipped her. "Oh this is lovely on you. I knew it would be. You need some jewelry to match it."

Savannah stepped out of the dressing room with a smile on her face and showed Alex's mom. "What do you think?"

"Perfect. I think you like it, too, from your expression."

"I do."

"I love the way the skirt flares from your hips. It shows off your figure."

The saleswoman chimed in. "She needs some jewelry for it."

The woman went to a glass case and removed some snowflake jewelry, and immediately Savannah shook her head. "Maybe something a little less bold?"

The woman frowned and retrieved a long string of rhinestone earrings.

Savannah looked at Alex's mom and shook her head. "Maybe something small."

Not liking anything, Savannah retreated to the dressing room to remove the dress. She looked at the price tag and inhaled, as a fog seemed to surround her. The world threatened to vanish into that gray mist. Taking a few more deep breaths, she carefully hung the dress and tried not to think about it. How would she ever manage to wear such an expensive thing? *Get a grip. This is Alex's life and I'm stepping into it. And my mom's afraid he won't be able to support me? My mom doesn't spend this much on groceries in six months.*

She put on her clothes and left the dressing room. His mom swiped a credit card while the saleswoman put the dress on a special hanger covered with a cloth bag that displayed the store's name. Once the dress was tucked in the car, they went to another store, this time for his mom. The sales woman there knew Mrs. Van Doorn and immediately brought out a dress.

"I held this just for you. I knew as soon as I saw it that you would love it."

Alex's mom took the hanger with the dress and vanished. She returned a moment later wearing the peacock blue dress that seemed to shimmer with a purple hue.

Savannah stammered, "It's beautiful."

Alex's mom transformed from mother and conservative educator to an alluring middle-aged woman.

Alex's mom told the saleswoman, "You're right. I love it."

Then they went shoe shopping. Savannah suggested a discount store that sold brand names at a fraction of the original cost. There, Savannah found a pair of strappy, high heels in silver and a pair of warm boots that she really needed. Alex's mom found several pairs of shoes that she loved and a leather handbag. As his mom went to pay for everything, Savannah spotted the perfect earrings for her dress. They were cubic zirconium set in silver.

"I can't believe we got all this for less than what a pair of shoes normally cost. I'm going to have to check out this place more often."

"Nice things that are cheap are important to me."

"Alex said that you were frugal."

Savannah shrugged. "My parents live on a tight budget."

"I'm afraid my son will be on a tight budget until he gets established. The starting salary for an architect isn't very good. He'll be lucky if he makes a median income. Unfortunately, he'll wind up accepting slightly less than the average graduate because he is Deaf."

"That would be discrimination."

The woman nodded. "It is, but he's going to have to prove that he can do as well as anyone else."

Alex knew his mom would find Savannah something wonderful to wear. When she appeared in the pale gray lace dress, it was all he could do to contain his feelings for her. She was ravishing.

"Ready?" he asked.

She shook her head no. "My zipper please?"

He circled behind her. She was holding her dress together with one hand. A tiny zipper, the same color as the fabric, started way below her waist. He held the bottom of the zipper with one hand as he slowly moved the slider upwards, covering her bare back with lace. When he reached the top of the teeth, there was a tiny hook and eye that had to be fastened. With the job completed, he dropped a kiss on her lace-covered back, and inhaled her sweet scent. His hands cupped her waist as he planted more kisses on her back and neck.

She turned and faced him. "Do you know what you do to me when you do that?"

He nodded and smiled. "You do it to me all the time."

"I've not done anything other than ask for help with my zipper."

"The zipper was low. Your skin is soft and," he fingerspelled, "ENTICING."

He knew she was nervous. She always managed to hide her feelings except for one. She'd blush over the slightest sexual innuendo, and the color would run to her cheeks. At the moment, pink was flooding her cheeks.

He stared deep into her eyes. Her hunger showed in the ragged way she breathed. *Why wait? What difference does it make? You will be my wife one day.* He touched her cheek with his index finger, and then dropped a light kiss on her lips.

"I'm worried about meeting everyone. You've already said most do not hear."

He nodded. "It will take everyone all of three seconds to realize you are of the hearing, and they will forgive you. Remember we're used to dealing with the hearing population, and they usually fail to realize that we're Deaf. Everyone will love you."

She shook her head. "They will think you are wrong for falling for me."

"No, they won't. They will think I'm lucky to have such a

beautiful woman who is willing to learn my language." He dropped another kiss on her lips. "You'll find yourself being a liaison between whomever is working at the party and the guests. If you don't understand a guest, just ask them to slow down and fingerspell. They know you are putting forth the effort."

He left a small light on in the living room and another in the kitchen. "We forgot something."

"What?"

"A dress coat for you. I'll pull into their garage, so you can leave your coat in the car."

She shrugged as if it didn't matter to her.

His own coat was already tossed across the back seat of the car but wearing his navy pinstripe wool suit was more than enough for him. He escorted Savannah out to his car and held the door for her. She was exquisitely dressed. But her real beauty came from deep inside her and showed in her smile.

The trip to his parents didn't take long. He hit the remote for the garage door, and it opened. Gwen had arrived and pulled into what he considered his parking space. He parked his car by the garage wall knowing that barely gave Savannah enough room to open her door.

He got out and held the door for her. She squeezed out and smiled, as he apologized.

"I'm not the one who is pregnant."

He helped her remove her coat and tossed it over his in the backseat. Then he snatched the box of monogrammed golf balls wrapped in birthday paper and tied with a large bow that also was on the backseat.

"Do I look okay? Is everything still in place?" She smoothed out the skirt of her gown.

He laughed. "Looking at you makes it very difficult for me to keep what I have in place."

She gave him her evil glare, and he laughed some more. "Ready for a Deaf night like you've never experienced?"

Savannah walked into the house where Alex's mom was giving last minute instructions to several people in black and white uniforms with embroidered interlocking letters that formed the caterer's logo. The amount of food in the kitchen was unreal and more was in the ovens and on the stovetop. If the white aprons were any indication, there had to be three people cooking and at least five people listening to Alex's mom. In the other room, there were even more uniformed people. *So this is how the rich throw parties.*

Arrangements of white lilies accented with tidbits of midnight blue and silver decorated tables and the place seemed to glow with a party atmosphere. Alex took her hand as they walked to his father's office. There they left the box on his dad's desk, along with the card they had signed. Then they went upstairs to what was once his childhood bedroom.

He closed and locked the door behind him. "I can't handle looking and not touching you. You are incredibly beautiful. And that is doing things to me."

His lips devoured hers. She was lost in his kiss and the sensations he produced in her. And when his kiss ended, he stood staring into her eyes with such intensity that she couldn't catch her breath. She touched his cheek and gasped for air, without letting go of his gaze. There was no question in her mind that their feelings matched.

He went to his bathroom and she waited for him to return. After checking the decorative mirror on his bedroom wall, she slipped her lipstick from her small silver purse. She inhaled a few times before redoing the pink gloss on her lips. Even though it was a special occasion, she still didn't like wearing much makeup. The colors she wore with her gray dress were as pale as always, light brown mascara with just a touch of pale blue shadow that shimmered on her lids. As she stared into the mirror, she thought of Ashley with her dark hair and eyes that allowed her to wear bold colors. Savannah envied her friend.

Alex reappeared and smiled, but his smile was a little sheepish.

She went to him and wrapped her arms around his waist. "I love you. You look so handsome in your suit. How did I find you?" She stared into his eyes. With heels, she was almost equal to him in height. "Maybe I should thank Prof. Stockton."

He grinned. "You can do that tonight. Because I can't imagine him not coming."

"What?"

"Old friends of the family. Remember I said his wife is Deaf."

"Oh, I guess with your mom being a dean she has lots of friends within the faculty."

He nodded. "Don't concern yourself. This will mostly be Deaf friends. My father is not comfortable around the hearing, and it's his party."

"Your father seems to like me."

"He thinks you are adorable. But don't forget my mom hears, and he fell in love with her."

"I never asked. How did they meet?"

He shrugged. "On campus, except someone set them up. Someone knew that she knew sign language. And if we don't go downstairs soon and join the party that's about to start, we'll be in trouble."

She captured his hands and held them. The look in his eyes said everything she wanted to hear. Bringing his fingers to her lips, she kissed them. "Yes, we need to join the party before I totally chicken out."

His mouth moved before the sound came out. "You'll be fine."

She kissed his fingers one more time.

Downstairs, guests had begun to arrive. It seemed as though everyone signed, yet a few voices rose above the sounds of those in attendance.

Savannah spotted Gwen who called to her, "Come meet my in-laws."

Slowly Alex and Savannah made their way through a group of people who were excited to see Alex and wanting to know who she was. Alex introduced her to so many people that she knew she'd never remember all the names. But when they reached Gwen, she was standing with two people who could hear. Dustin's parents were probably feeling as out of place as she was. She also realized that their ability to sign was rather limited. Knowing Dustin had spent his life deaf, she found it odd that his parents struggled to sign. *Didn't they learn to communicate with their own son?*

Another couple came to Alex and hugged him. As though being pulled by a tide, Alex continuously introduced her as he chatted with so many people. And when they landed by Prof Stockton and his wife, they both embraced Alex.

"Welcome to the Deaf community," Prof. Stockton signed and gave Savannah a hug. "You have a lot to learn, but you also have a good teacher. This is my wife, Kathy."

Savannah signed that she was pleased to meet her professor's wife and then quickly signed, "Slow down," as the woman signed at the speed of light. She hardly caught anything the woman had said. Apparently Alex knew that, because he laughed silently. She turned to Alex. "What is so funny?"

Alex kissed her and she could feel the blush rushing to her cheeks. His sign of affection was a bit much in front of her professor. Then Alex slowly signed that Stockton and his wife were his godparents. He took her hand and showed off her ring.

Savannah caught the word pretty from the professor's wife, but by the look on the woman's face there was no question that she loved Savannah's ring.

"Savannah, you'll need to work extra hard. There's a lot you still don't know." Prof. Stockton warned. "Not only do you have vocabulary to learn, but you will need to pick up some speed. You have to learn to automatically sign and not think about each word."

She nodded her response.

As the night went on, she discovered that this crowd seemed more tactile and openly affectionate. Even the men hugged one another. But when a pretty blonde came up to Alex and hugged him, Savannah could feel that green jealousy running through her veins, especially when Alex returned her hug.

"Meet Elise." Alex practically pushed Savannah to the woman. Then he held out Savannah's hand and showed off her ring.

The young woman instantly hugged Savannah. "Make him happy. He's impossible."

"I am not!"

"Yes, you are. I want to know what she did to grab your heart." Elise laughed as she signed.

"Chemistry," Alex answered. "She's got it."

The woman looked around and then signed, "She can also hear."

Alex nodded. "She's learning to sign, but…" he looked at Savannah, "Who needs to talk when you are in love? I can think of better things to do with my hands."

Savannah had been following along, piecing the conversation together because Alex was signing slow enough for her to understand, but with that last comment she thought she'd hit him. Elise did it first, except hers was playful.

"You are so bad!" She turned her attention to Savannah.

"Savannah, make him behave." Elise signed extra slow. "He's terrible. I've known him all my life. You've captured the top dog, and every eligible female in this room wishes that ring was on her finger instead of yours."

Savannah smiled and signed, "You?"

"Of course. Together since we were old enough to see a movie."

Savannah smiled at the young woman, but deep inside she wasn't happy. Whoever this gal was Savannah figured she would be waiting in the wings to snatch Alex back, except he seemed to take it all very lightly.

The evening progressed much the same. Delicious finger foods, and a variety of miniature desserts graced doily-covered silver platters, fine china, and crystal plates. Candies sat in little dishes in every room. Drinks of every sort were available, and Dustin or Gwen manned the bar, acting as interpreters to the hearing-only bartenders. But the punch and fruit juices seemed to be most popular.

Alex tried to explain but gave up and texted that the valet parking meant people turned over keys and couldn't get them back unless they could pass the breathalyzer test.

"Do they know that?"

Alex nodded. "But this isn't a wild crowd. Can't say there aren't a few heavy drinkers. But everyone knows who they are, and they probably came with a designated driver."

About eight o'clock, word seemed to circulate for everyone to gather in the dining area. An elegant tiered cake was brought out and candles that seemed to cover each tier, as though they were part of the design, were lit. Instead of the normal song Savannah had heard all of her life, the guests began to sign something with happy, wishes, and many more. To Savannah, it seemed too strange. Before he blew out the candles, she went to her future father-in-law and touched his arm. She began to sing the traditional happy birthday song. Several people in the group, including Alex's mom, chimed in, and sang it with her.

Alex's father blew his candles out, and then hugged her. Alex's family was becoming her surrogate family. But there was one member missing from the party, Emily. Knowing this was one group who would read her lips no matter what she said, she pulled out her phone and texted Alex. -Have you seen Emily at all tonight?

-Ask Mom.

Savannah went to Alex's mom and covered her mouth as she whispered, "Emily is missing. We haven't seen her all night."

Alex's mom eyes scanned the room, and then she took off. Alex's phone must have vibrated because Savannah's rang. Gwen looked up and so did Dustin. Everyone took off for different parts of the house. The party continued, but no matter where the family looked, Emily was still missing.

Gwen texted and said Emily's jacket and good coat were still hanging in the front closet.

Savannah and Alex checked all the bedrooms, closets and every possible hiding spot. Then Savannah had an idea. She texted Alex's mom and got a quick response. Emily was supposed to be wearing a blue dress piped in black and a pair of black heels with straps that went over her ankles. Savannah ran back to Emily's room and Alex followed. The shoes were stuffed in a bag in the closet, but the dress was missing.

Savannah looked in every drawer and possible normal place Emily could have hidden her dress. She even looked under the bed before reaching between the mattress and foundation of the bed. Nothing.

They began to search every bedroom and every possible nook and cranny. Savannah went back to Emily's bedroom. "Where did you hide it?"

Knowing that children had places where they hid things,

she tried to remember the places that she used over the years. Then she remembered her favorite spot. She had hid love letters that she had written in the foundation of her bed. She immediately began to remove the covers from Emily's bed. She pulled the queen-sized mattress off and then managed to grab the foundation. Alex helped her. Once the foundation was off, it was obvious that it was intact. Savannah took off for Alex's room and did the same thing to his bed. A spun fabric cloth covered the bottom of the foundation except the cloth had been cut along the one edge. The dress had been stuffed inside.

She looked at Alex and said, "I'll make bets she's not in the house."

Alex shrugged. "It's too cold to go without her coat. She's got to be here."

Savannah shook her head. "The way she keeps her room, I can't imagine her hanging her coat in the front closet."

"No. She usually comes home through the garage and into the mud room." Alex ran down the stairs to the closet by the back door where the family kept their everyday coats. Emily's old corduroy jacket was gone.

Alex tapped Savannah's arm. "She's run away."

Savannah looked at Alex. His words were more of a question then a statement. She nodded.

Alex pulled his phone from the clip on his belt.

"Don't bother trying to reach her. Your Mom took her phone away the other day."

It was late when Alex brought Savannah back to their place. The fun of a large party evaporated and concern for Emily vacillated between fear for her welfare and anger over her childish prank. Everyone was taking the situation very seriously, but Savannah clung to the idea that maybe Emily had run off to spend the night with a friend. Alex didn't believe that. This was a thought-out plan to escape. The only thing in the family's favor was the fact that Emily was Deaf, but even that might not be picked up by an untrained ear. Emily's ability to speak was excellent.

The police questioned the family about the amount of cash Emily might have. No one knew. But Alex indicated it might be a substantial amount. The family had money – plenty of it, and his parents were always generous with their children. Depending on how long Emily had been planning to run away, she might've had a hefty amount.

Nothing was found that looked as though Emily was involved with drugs. But the police said that any paraphernalia she might've had probably went with her. He knew his mom's heart had dropped into her stomach. Being on a campus meant his mom had seen plenty in her day and was not unaware of the drug situation or the signs. As much time as he had spent with his little sis, never was there any indication that she was involved with drugs. But that wasn't bringing her back home.

In a way, he hated being trapped at his parents' home talking to the police. He would have been happier out looking for Emily. He knew some of her haunts, but also knew that most of them were closed. Had she run away as a way of punishing her family and rebelling against the change in schools? He was certain Emily knew she was being moved away from her friends. It wouldn't take much for her to figure out what her mom was planning.

When he was able to return to his home, he unlocked the back door. Part of him expected to see Emily with her smiling face beaming at him, but he knew that wasn't going to happen. He was as torn up over it as his parents, maybe more. Emily and he had been tight once upon a time, but that had been gone for a while. Looking back on it, he could see that Emily no longer wanted to just be his buddy. She was on a gimme kick. What could he give her? But once Savannah entered the picture, everything changed. There was no question in his mind that Emily was jealous.

Upstairs, he took his suit jacket off, undid his tie, and turned to Savannah. "I'm sure you'll need help with that zipper."

"If it wasn't almost impossible for me, I would think your offer was an excuse to touch."

He grinned. "I love touching bare skin. I wish you'd allow me to touch more."

"Do you need to sleep on the sofa?"

"Any other night, I would say I needed a cold shower, but tonight…" He shook his head.

She turned and put her back to him.

He unzipped her and offered for her to use the bathroom first. Her silence told him more than anything she could have said. She felt as though she was responsible for Emily's bad behavior by intruding on the family's dynamics. Convincing her otherwise was fruitless. If it weren't for Savannah, it would have been something or someone else.

He thought about the ski trip several of the young adults from the community took to the Rockies last year. Emily was livid that she couldn't go with him. The trip wasn't meant for teens, only the adults. But that didn't stop her poor behavior. *Maybe that was the start of it? Then I failed to realize it.*

When Savannah finished in the bathroom, he took his shower, hoping that the water would wash away the night's problems. But it didn't. He climbed into bed and took Savannah's hand. She squeezed it. Their wordless communication was sufficient for him. She was his other half – the woman he'd always wanted. And in the bleak night, she understood.

Where are you Emily? Don't you know how much we love you?

As Savannah made the morning coffee, she wondered if they'd hear something about Emily. It was pushing sixty hours since her disappearance and still no word on her since a female matching Emily's description was seen at a local convenience store entering someone's car. The police had checked the bus station, and the police issued an alert that covered several counties. It was as though she had vanished into thin air. It made Savannah wonder if the teen was holed up at a friend's home even though the police were checking all of her known friends.

Alex joined Savannah in the kitchen and poured a cup of coffee. Between sips he signed, "I think we need a change of pace. Staying here isn't doing anything but dragging us downward. We can't spend hour after hour worrying about Emily. She's done this to herself."

"I agree. Your mom will continue to call or text a dozen times every day wanting to know if we've heard from Emily. Do you want to go to my parents' early?"

He shrugged. "We weren't supposed to go until the evening of the twenty-fourth."

"I'll call them." She picked up the phone and wondered if they were only walking into another problem. "Hi, Mom."

"Have you had any word on his little sister?"

"Nothing. I think she's hiding someplace."

"It's Christmastime. What child wants to miss out on all the presents?"

She turned her back to Alex. "What do you buy the teen who has everything? In a way, it's sad."

"Yes, but children love presents."

"Mom, she's got a larger TV in her bedroom than what you own, and every game for it. She's got more clothes than you can imagine, and she cuts them up to look in style."

"What?"

"Yes. Expensive designer jeans and she slices them. Her mom buys her pretty knit tops and she takes the scissors to them. There's enough makeup in her bathroom, with big name brands, to open her own store. She's been totally spoiled. She's never had to wait on anything. She says she wants it, and she gets it."

"That's ridiculous."

"I agree. But Alex and his older sister don't act spoiled even though I know they are." She cracked a few eggs into a bowl as she listened to her mom.

Savannah put the pan on the stove and added a pat of butter. "Would you like company? Staying here is getting to both of us. Alex wants to get away and I'd really like to come home. We can always come back if there's any change."

"I would love to have you. I've missed not having you. You've always spent your break here." She sounded happy.

"Have your grades been posted?"

"Yes, A's in everything except Visual Production. I got a B+ in that. It was a hard class, but a good learning experience. Alex has all A's." She dropped the bread in the toaster and added shredded cheese to the eggs.

As soon as the eggs were done, she got off the phone and fixed their plates. "Mom will be thrilled to have us. But are you certain you won't go stir crazy during the extra days?"

Alex smiled at her. "I don't think so, better there than here. I can't seem to concentrate enough to even conceive of building designs. I probably should text home and let them know that we've gone to your parents."

She nodded and watched him text. Instantly he had a reply and he showed it to her. His father was in favor of him getting away and promised that they would let him know if Emily was found.

They cleaned up after breakfast and left for her parents' house.

"Tell your mom I'll take everyone out to eat when we get there," Alex signed while stopped at a rest station.

She called her mom, but her mother had already started dinner. Besides her father had to work, which meant he'd come home grubby and would be expected to clean up to go out to dinner. That was not his idea of fun.

"You've already said they don't have a lot of extra money. We'll go for groceries tomorrow, or I can give you money, and you can take your mom."

His one-handed signing while driving was difficult to understand, and since he couldn't read her lips and drive, she had to sign a response. She merely gave him the thumbs up sign.

Alex knew the way to the house, but when traffic slowed to a stop on the interstate, they lost quite a bit of travel time. There was nothing they could do but sit in the traffic jam and wait for the problem to clear. Even though darkness was beginning to descend as they pulled into the driveway, the house was already lit with Christmas decorations. This year there were new lights across the front. She assumed they were supposed to look like icicles. From someplace in the yard, there was a light shining on the house that made it look as though it had a bad case of measles.

She expected Alex to say something, but he didn't. This was home. It's where she'd grown up. Her family was here.

Lady barreled around the corner of the house. When she saw who came, she wagged her tail so hard that her body seemed to wag with it.

Savannah jumped out of the car and greeted the large dog. Alex carried their suitcases, and together they made their way to the front door. She just hoped her mom would be more accepting of Alex this time.

As soon as they stowed their suitcases in their rooms, Alex went back to the car and brought in the Christmas gifts to her parents and placed them under the tree.

Alex stood by the tree and pointed to several ornaments. They were the little things that had been added over the years. He found her fourth grade picture that had been framed with painted Popsicle sticks.

She groaned and Alex smiled.

"A tree of memories?" Alex signed.

She nodded.

He found baby's first Christmas and a dozen more from her childhood. He leaned in and inhaled. "Fresh pine. I love the scent."

She nodded and signed, "Me, too."

Her mom had grown up in the country and that meant going into the woods for the perfect tree. But Savannah knew her parents had bought the tree from the local stand in front of the grocery store, just as they had done for as long as she could remember. It was a cut pine, and it did smell delicious.

Alex had told her that his parents didn't put the tree up until after his father's birthday, and what they had came out of a box. She wondered if anyone there would even bother to place a wreath on the door. The family was worried about Emily and not in the mood to celebrate the holidays. Alex was right, getting away was a good thing.

"Look who's here!" Her father greeted them.

"I'm so glad to be home, Daddy."

Her father gave her a big bear hug and then hugged Alex. Shortly after that, they sat down to their meal.

Her father did most of the talking and seemed to aim it at Alex.

Alex looked at her and fingerspelled a few things for her to say to her dad. But her mom was strangely quiet. Savannah knew her mom still had not accepted Alex. *Time, it will take time.*

Alex's mom would text one of them almost every two hours. It would say the same thing. No word yet.

On Wednesday night Savannah, her mom, and Alex went to the small church her parents attended. It was their Christmas chorale production and Savannah's mom wanted to go, but she couldn't figure out why Alex was going to go with them.

"I thought you said he can't hear."

Savannah shook her head. "No, Mom. He's used to living in a hearing world. He can handle sitting through this. He wants to be with me."

"I don't understand."

"We'll sit in the very front by the speakers so that Alex can feel the music." Savannah led them into the sanctuary.

"What? If he can't hear it, how can he feel it?"

"He can feel the vibration." Savannah took them to what she considered the best spot in the church. Alex could reach in front of him and touch the speaker stand. She moved it closer to the pew and then took the seat between Alex and her mom, leaving Alex on the very end of the pew.

Mrs. Updyke came and wanted them to scoot over, Savannah shook her head. "I'm sorry, ma'am, but please sit beside my mom. Alex needs to sit there."

She realized that the older members occupied most of the church's front rows and she was certain they were there so that they could hear. Several people greeted her, happy to see her home for the holidays, and introduced themselves to Alex. She found it awkward, but Alex just smiled and signed back to them.

When everyone bowed their heads, he didn't. He watched what was being said. And when the music started, he touched the speaker stand. She attempted to sign what she could, but too many words she didn't know. Alex smiled and patted her leg. Then she noticed Mrs. Swenson was signing. She nudged Alex and motioned for him to watch Mrs. Swenson.

Mrs. Swenson had been her second grade teacher. Her hair had been pure white even back then. Long since retired, the woman sang in the church's choir and stayed busy in her garden.

A big smile crossed Alex's face as he watched the woman sing and sign. Relief coated Savannah as she had been liberated from a tough job. Otherwise, Alex would have had an extremely boring night. But it made her wonder how Mrs. Swenson knew how to sign.

The whole thing lasted for over an hour, and when it ended, Mrs. Swenson made her way to Alex and Savannah.

"Darling Savannah, you are home from college. I'm so glad to see you."

"Yes, and thank you for what you did. This is my fiancé, Alex."

Alex began to sign in earnest, and Mrs. Swenson smiled broadly as she kept up with him.

Savannah looked at her mom who seemed totally shocked.

Mrs. Swenson turned back to Savannah. "Where did you find this handsome man?"

"On campus. I took ASL to fulfill a language requirement. It's a rather convoluted story, but I can thank a wonderful professor." Savannah smiled at her old teacher. "But how did you learn to sign?"

She laughed. "When I was little, a friend and I thought it would be fun to learn, like a secret code. It wasn't a recognized language back then. So for us, it was a game. Then about twenty years ago, my friend's granddaughter was born deaf. We dusted off our old skills and began to sign to her. Had to teach her parents. Since then, I've taught quite a few classes in ASL and I'm certified to interpret. I often go to organizations to speak or I get asked to interpret." She turned to Savannah's mom. "Jennifer, come over and see me. I'll give you lessons. Certainly, you'll want to learn."

Savannah's mom smiled weakly. "With only one car..."

"Pick a day, and I'll come to you. I promise it's fun."

Savannah signed, "No, it's not. It's hard work!"

Alex laughed. "She's learning and very quickly."

"I do hope you enjoyed our music."

Alex smiled and nodded.

A young girl came to him and fingerspelled, "HI."

He grinned at her as he signed, "Hello."

Then slowly he fingerspelled asking if she was learning sign language.

She looked around and spelled, "YES."

"THAT IS WONDERFUL." He dropped to one knee so that he was on the same level as the child. "WE USE BIGGER SIGNS FOR MOST WORDS. IT IS FASTER THAN SPELLING."

Savannah could now appreciate the patience he had shown her in the beginning. She had come a long way in one semester. Yet he had been forced to spell so much of their original conversations. Now it was rare that he had to spell to her. She often had to spell to him because she didn't know enough signs, and she hardly ever finished a word because Alex caught what she was saying.

Alex smiled at the child, gave her the thumbs up, and then returned to Savannah's side. There was a small crowd that had gathered around Savannah. Most were pleased to see her home for the holidays, but a few seemed to be interested in Alex. She introduced him to everyone. The reaction of the various members of the church took her by surprise. A few smiles turned to frowns. One woman made a derogatory comment in a low breath.

Savannah wrapped her arm around Alex's waist and leaned against his chest. Such comments had to hurt him, but he always acted as though it was the other person's problem. She looked up at him and smiled. If there were a way to place him in a protective bubble, she would have done it. She loved him too much to see him hurt by ignorance. But her biggest problem was her mom. Getting her to see Alex as a wonderful guy who was very capable of supporting a wife and family would take time.

Pastor Smith came to them. "So happy to see you, Savannah. And I'm glad you've brought a guest." He turned to Alex. "We have such a wonderful choir. Maybe you'll join us. We could use a few more male voices."

Alex started to sign, but Savannah said it first, "He's Deaf."

"Deaf? You brought someone who is deaf? I'm sorry that he can't enjoy our choir."

"He can feel the vibration, and Mrs. Swenson signed as she sang."

"Oh, I wondered why she was doing that. She knows that sign language stuff."

"Pastor Smith, this is Alex Van Doorn, my fiancé."

The man did a double take, and then smiled as though it was an afterthought, but he was at least trying.

He raised his voice a little louder. "Welcome to our church."

"Pastor, he's deaf. He reads your lips. He doesn't hear you, no matter how loud you speak."

The man frowned and then smiled at Alex. "We welcome everyone here."

They didn't get out of church until late. But most of the time they stood there, the one little girl stayed at Alex's side. Her father finally claimed her. She proudly announced that she had been signing to the man. Her father apologized. Alex smiled at the father and then turned to the little girl.

"This is the word for signing." He rotated his hands in front of him.

Savannah interpreted.

"This means I'm learning." He showed her those signs. Then he grinned. "This is friend."

Savannah recognized the former star football player of her high school but didn't realize he had a little daughter. "Bill, this is Alex, my fiancé."

Her old classmate hesitated and then held out his hand to Alex. "Sorry my daughter bothered you. She got hooked on sign language about a year ago." He looked at Mrs. Swenson. "When you came to Amanda's preschool and showed the kids a few things."

"I'm glad she remembers so much." Mrs. Swenson said.

"It was that little handout you gave them. She acts as though it's pure gold."

Alex laughed. "It's golden to me. She's adorable. Encourage her. Growing up bilingual is good."

Savannah laughed as she interpreted. She put her hand on Alex's arm. "He's considered bilingual, because he knows ASL and English, but he also knows Spanish."

Bill looked at her as though she'd lost her mind. She merely nodded, led Alex down an aisle, and out of the sanctuary. The cold air hit them as they stepped outside.

Her mom asked, "How can he know Spanish?"

"The same way he knows English."

"We had to take a foreign language in school." Savannah repeated what he signed.

"That makes no sense."

"Mom, he went to a regular public school. He took all the classes that everyone takes. The requirements are the same."

Her mom shook her head and got into Alex's car.

Savannah signed, "I don't understand my mom's attitude."

"Don't worry about it. She'll learn. She worries. You are her little girl."

Savannah rolled her eyes at him, and he laughed.

"You need to stop worrying. I can handle the hearing world. They are the ones with the problem, not me."

"Except it's my mom with the problem."

21

Daily, they found things to do in Savannah's little town. Several times, they merely walked through her neighborhood or went to the park in the center of town.

But as Christmas drew near, he wondered about his sister. Mostly he wondered about her safety. He also worried about his mom spending the day alone. This would be the first Christmas without someone in the house. His sister would go over for the day – in an attempt to provide moral support to his mom who was taking Emily's disappearance very hard.

He and Savannah had talked about it several times, and he thought Savannah was right. *She's hiding at someone's house. When she runs out of money, she'll come home.* But he still thought it was strange that she had not shown up. *Certainly, she wants her Christmas gifts.*

He found it odd that Savannah's dad had to work on Christmas Eve day. When he returned home, he took a shower and they all went to church. That put Alex back in the company of some of the same people from the other night. He was glad he'd decided to bring his sport coat and a tie with him. He had no idea that he'd have to dress up for anything with her family.

Christmas morning was bright and clear, but the wind blew hard. They all gathered in the kitchen. Her mom fixed breakfast and when everything was cleaned up, they went into the living room to open the gifts. Savannah gave him a nice deep royal blue sweater that would complement his blue eyes.

Her mom had given Savannah several pieces of clothing, and Savannah's dad received socks and a pair of heavy canvas work gloves. Alex motioned to Savannah to hand out their gifts. Savannah gave her mom the big boxes and when her mom opened them, she was obviously floored and excited in spite of her protests about the expense. There were also all the little things that Savannah had picked out for her mom. Her dad was thrilled with his gifts, especially the Vikings signage and sweatshirt.

The two women disappeared into the kitchen, and Alex wound up with her dad in the garage.

"How's school going?"

He gave the man a thumbs up.

"Savannah's mom said you think you're going to get a real job."

"Yes." Alex chuckled as he took his pad out of his pocket and wrote that he was tutoring math two days a week at the local high school and had been offered a job with an architect a few miles away.

"Someone is going to hire you? Do they know you don't hear?"

Alex nodded. "I've talked to him."

"He knows how to do that signing stuff?"

Alex shook his head.

After being out in the garage with her dad, they went back inside to catch a football game.

Her father turned to him. "You getting disability?"

Alex shook his head and signed, "I'm not broken."

Mr. Chisholm looked at Alex, so he wrote his response.

The man furrowed his brow. "Being deaf isn't considered a disability?"

Alex rocked his hand, and then wrote that most Deaf do not consider themselves disabled. They merely speak another language.

The game started. Alex reached over and snatched the remote. A few clicks and he had turned on the closed captioning. He smiled at Savannah's father. When the game was over, Savannah's mother called them to the kitchen table.

The table had been set with the new dishes. The ham was sitting on the platter and the vegetables were in the matching bowls. The meal looked scrumptious.

Her mom was thrilled. It was in her smile and the way everything was neatly arranged. The same pride his mom took in setting the dining table for formal meals showed in the less formal Chisholm kitchen table. "Your table is beautiful, and the food looks even better."

Savannah interpreted for him.

Her mom smiled. "Thank you."

Winning her over would be difficult, but he thought by now she would have warmed up to him. Instead, she kept him at arm's length. She was wary of him and acted as though he would never be good enough for their daughter. There was nothing he could do beyond what he had done.

Three days later, they were on their way back to his place when his phone vibrated. He pulled it from its clip and handed it to Savannah, but she was answering her phone.

She took his phone and looked at it. "Same message." She attempted to sign because he was driving. "Emily is home."

Relief washed through him. Taking a few deep breaths, he pulled to the side of the road. "What else?"

"She's home and okay. Apparently dirty and miserable.

She went upstairs to take a shower. Your mom called the police and texted us at the same time."

"Thank goodness."

Both phones alerted Savannah at the same time. She glanced at both screens. "She's putting out combined text messages. Gwen is on the way to your mom's."

Alex texted his mom. -We're on our way back. It'll be another hour before we are there. We'll come straight to your house.

Savannah said, "I'm glad she's home, but I still think it's a childish prank."

He took another deep breath and resumed driving. His mom would never punish Emily for what she had done, she would only be grateful to have her youngest home. But the closer he got to his parents' house, the more he wanted to give Emily a piece of his mind.

Savannah knew Alex was livid with his little sister. She called his mom. "Can you talk?"

"Yes. She's still upstairs."

"Do you know anything?"

"Nothing. She only said it was horrible, and she couldn't take being away any longer. I need to get off here. I'll let you know when I know more."

She signed to Alex. "Your mom knows nothing."

Savannah watched him inhale.

When they pulled into his parents' driveway, Alex rested his head on the steering wheel for a moment. She reached over and put her hand on his leg. There was nothing she could do for him or for Emily. At least the teen was home.

Savannah thought back to when she was that age. Her little job at the florist was only a few hours a week and barely paid for anything. But she learned to balance schoolwork with a job, be prompt, and take orders from her boss. Emily had never experienced any of that. She'd been too coddled and protected.

When Alex got out of the car, Savannah did as well. She had a feeling things were going to explode with Alex. They found the family in the den.

Emily had hacked off her hair and shaved one side of her head. It was obvious she had been crying. When she spotted Alex, she ran to him and tossed her arms around him. He pushed her off and began to sign at the speed of light.

Savannah couldn't keep up. She was only catching a few words here and there. This was a family matter and she felt out of place as though she wasn't supposed to be privy to the private matters of this family. In her house, when the family gathered over something important, her mother fed them. Retreating to the kitchen made sense.

Savannah found several sweet potatoes and she continued to poke around until she found a mandoline to slice them. With wafer thin slices, she made homemade chips using the microwave. The refrigerator produced enough ingredients for her to make a dip. She took the chips and dip to the den.

She went back to the pantry and found several cans of chickpeas. She made Parmesan roasted peas and put them in a bowl. The chips were devoured by the time she brought out the chickpeas. *For a woman who doesn't cook, she seems to have plenty of food in the pantry and an odd variety. And she's got more gadgets than anyone I know. I wonder if she knows how to use them? Maybe she watched some cooking show and figured she couldn't follow the recipe without the gizmo.*

Emily was still in tears and Alex sat across from her. His jaw was jutted and locked.

She just hoped Emily had learned a good lesson from what had happened.

Gwen didn't seem very happy with her brother, so

whatever transpired while Savannah was in the kitchen was not pleasant.

Alex's father wasn't saying anything, but his mom was saying something about school, and Emily was nodding. Savannah didn't know if she should return to the kitchen or stay with the family. The general impression she was getting was that Alex's parents were being lenient, and Alex was fuming with rage. Alex got up and as he went past her, he took her wrist and pulled her into the kitchen with him. He started signing furiously. His anger showed in his movements. Telling him to slow down would be futile. Leaning against the counter, she allowed him to rant. In all likelihood, she'd probably find out everything later.

She understood his parents were thrilled to have their daughter home. But she also understood Alex's position that it was wrong to run away. There were more pieces to the puzzle. Where did Emily stay, and what happened to her while she was gone? Not that knowing could undo anything, because whatever happened had happened. The unforeseen consequences of Emily's escapade were cause for more concern, but only time would provide the answers.

A little while later, Alex and Savannah walked out of the house to the car. She wasn't certain Alex should be driving, considering his mood, but he drove to his house without a problem. When they got in the house, she avoided asking anything that might trigger another burst of anger from him.

She unloaded the suitcases and sorted clothes for washing. Alex paced. His anger still smoldered. As soon as she finished the laundry, she went upstairs. Alex didn't follow. It was as though his anger radiated towards anyone within twelve feet of him.

Alex never seemed to let anything get to him. This was a side she'd never seen, but she understood why he was angry. Alex had a very protective streak in him, and this time he couldn't protect Emily from herself.

It was the afternoon of New Year's Eve before she discovered what Emily had done. Running off to stay with a hearing friend who lived with less restrictions seemed like a wonderful thing. But once Emily got into that household, she discovered that life wasn't exactly as perfect as she thought it would be. Her friend's mom entertained a variety of company or was never home. Emily's friend had her boyfriend over who spent the night in the room with them. That didn't set well with Emily, nor did the drugs he brought with him, or his obvious overtures directed at Emily. Meals were non-existent. People came and went. When the friend's mother slept, they were expected to remain deadly quiet. The whole thing had been a fiasco.

It hadn't taken her long to realize that she missed the security of a family who loved her and protected her. Life with her friend was not what Emily wanted, but she was afraid to come home, afraid of the punishment she might be facing. But the stakes had risen on her to the point that she had to return home.

Savannah listened to the whole tale from Gwen, who had taken her little sister to a hairdresser. The mess that Emily created by trying to cut her own hair, Gwen paid to have re-cut and styled. Of course, there was no growing back what had been shaved, but at least now it looked cute and trendy.

"She's not allowed out of the house for the next two months without one of us being with her, except for school. She'll be going to the area's magnet school for children with special needs."

Savannah shook her head. "I knew that's what your mom was planning for Emily because her grades were slipping. I've heard such places are terrible. They're dumping grounds for all sorts of problems."

"You've heard wrong. Not every school is as good as it

should be, but in this county, they are. They are under all sorts of state and federal pressure to maintain standards and provide a proper education to children who have needs beyond the regular school's ability to provide. Besides, I know several people who teach there. Emily *will* get a good education. Furthermore, there are schools across the country dedicated to the Deaf that are absolutely phenomenal."

Savannah scrunched her nose. "I don't understand. If she was managing at Kennedy High, then why move her?"

"Emily wasn't. She was falling behind. At McKinley, they will catch her up in subjects where she's lacking. She'll get more individualized attention, and she's going to discover that she knows quite a few teens from the Deaf community who go there. It wasn't a matter of taking her video games away. Studying something that she doesn't understand isn't going to help her."

Savannah knew it wasn't her place to question where Alex's little sister went to school. But deep inside, she cared about Emily because she was Alex's sister. And Savannah knew how much he loved his little sis.

There was a big party planned for New Years' Eve and Savannah had wondered what would have happened if Emily hadn't returned home. From what Gwen said, the party would have happened anyway. It had become a family tradition.

The caterers came and the house slowly filled with family. Alex's dad arrived and brought his parents from the airport. Alex introduced Savannah to his paternal grandparents who were both Deaf. Then Alex's mom's parents arrived but vanished without introductions. After meeting several aunts, uncles, and lots of cousins, Savannah no longer had any idea who anyone was. Both sides of the family signed and appeared to get along.

Hors d'oeuvres were placed on crystal plates and set out

in various spots, but the hot ones were to be offered by a wait staff that carried them on silver trays. Dinner would not be served until eight o'clock, and she wondered how anyone would have room for a meal if they sampled all the finger foods.

But the family greeted each other, chatted, and laughed as any family would. And a little before six, everyone began to vanish. Alex dragged Savannah to his room, where they changed into party clothing. As Savannah put on the dress that she had worn to his father's birthday party, her mind drifted to Emily running away. In a way, it seemed like yesterday, and yet it felt as though it had been long time ago. She reminded herself that it had barely been two weeks since that horrible event. A knock on Alex's door interrupted her thoughts.

Alex's mom walked into the room with a dress bag. "For you, Savannah. I knew your size, so I took the liberty of doing this."

Black was not her best color, but the bodice of the long-sleeved, black velvet dress was edged in pale blue rhinestones and several more created drifts down the skirt. In the bottom of the bag was a box that contained a necklace and earrings that matched the dress perfectly.

"It's beautiful. I'm beyond…oh, it's… Thank you."

Alex grinned.

"Well, you must wear black tonight. I insist upon it. It's New Years, the end of the old and the birth of the new year. A rebirth of sorts, meaning we must bury the past." Alex's mom smiled as she hung the empty bag in Alex's closet. "I know it will be perfect on you." Then she vanished out the door with a swish of her long, black silk dress.

Savannah vanished into the bathroom long enough to take off the gray dress she was wearing and put on the black one. She wasn't certain, but she thought the new dress had what was called a sweetheart neckline with its heart-shaped bodice. Except there was nothing *sweet* about this one, and the jewelry emphasized her décolletage. She stood in front of the big full-length mirror in Alex's bedroom and stared. It looked like something from the 1940's. This family was conservative, so she wondered if Alex's mom knew her selection would look this sexy.

Alex dropped some soft kisses on her neck and stared at her in the mirror. His grin told her how much he liked what she was wearing.

She attempted to lift the dress' bodice slightly, but it didn't work.

Alex laughed at her. "If you've got it, flaunt it."

"Huh?"

He traced the graceful curves of the dress' neckline. Then he fingerspelled, "FLAUNT."

"Oh, this looks way too much like I'm displaying goods for sale."

Alex shook his head, but he had fallen into a round of hysterics. "This is my family. They know you belong to me and only me. You look lovely. A little cleavage is perfect. It's not too much."

Savannah inhaled. This was not the way her family gathered, but then her parents weren't known for parties, especially lavish parties where everyone dressed in formal clothing. Occasionally they might have a barbeque during the summer or maybe friends over for a Super Bowl party, but never anything like Alex's parents.

When she and Alex arrived downstairs, Alex took her to visit with his paternal grandparents. His grandmother was a pretty blue-eyed blonde, and very petite. The grandfather appeared to stand an inch taller than Alex, and the two men had similar builds. Long since retired, he had worked as a surveyor. Now he worked as an advocate and a mentor within the Deaf community. Alex's grandmother had stayed at home with her children. They were both welcoming to Savannah, and she felt relieved.

It was Alex's maternal grandparents that were more like her parents. That grandmother had red hair, streaked with white. She had her hearing but was completely at home with deafness. She warmly received Savannah with a hug.

"Welcome to the family. I already know my daughter is thrilled to have you and my grandson loves you so much."

Prof. Stockton arrived with his wife. The house was filled with family and very close friends, all dressed for the formal evening. Piano music floated through the air and Savannah followed the sound. Alex's mom played, but soon was joined by her mother. They played a series of duets together. Several people touched the piano.

Alex nudged Savannah's arm. "My maternal grandmother was a concert pianist. That's how she and my grandfather met. On weekends, my grandfather used to handle the lighting at the local theater. But after they married, she played in the church and gave lessons. My grandfather will tell you that his only regret is not being able to hear her play. He loved classical music."

"That must have been difficult for them. How did he lose his hearing?"

"He was working. There was an explosion and he was blown off his feet. He woke up days later in a hospital with no hearing." Alex scowled. "My mother was a little girl. They all learned to sign. Then they moved. It was the Deaf community that had rallied around them. They helped my grandfather get a job, and they taught sign language to everyone. Technology knocked my grandfather out of that job, but by then he learned computers. Now he's retired, and he occasionally does cartography jobs for a gaming company. He enjoys drawing, has quite a reputation as an artist."

"Smart family."

Alex nodded, and his grin widened. "Good genes."

Savannah leaned up and kissed Alex's cheek as he stroked the nape of her neck.

"My Aunt Caroline married a deaf man who was also Deaf of Deaf and they have three children with hearing. Their oldest isn't here. He joined the Navy and is stationed in California. His wife has hearing, and their child is deaf."

Savannah raised her eyebrows. *Good genes? Seems more like roulette.*

Alex watched Savannah. She was trying so hard to sign and fit into the family. It wasn't necessary for her to strive as much as she did, because the family had already accepted her. Except for Emily who was obviously absent.

He went to her bedroom and pressed her doorbell, triggering the light on the other side of the door to flash. A moment later she appeared.

"What?" She was still dressed in jeans.

"It doesn't matter what you think of me or Savannah. Get dressed and go downstairs where you belong. Stop acting like a child." He turned and walked away from her.

He returned to the party and found Savannah talking to his paternal grandmother. He could tell by the look on his grandmother's face that Savannah had charmed the older woman. There were no problems with his family accepting a hearing person. It was not unusual for the hearing to be sprinkled amongst the cousins.

Unlike other Deaf family members, he and his sister Gwen had not attended a school or a college for the Deaf. They survived attending schools without interpreters and straddled both worlds.

"Have you started applying for jobs?" Alex's grandfather asked.

"Yes." He smiled brightly. "I've also received an offer from someone local who wants to take a chance on me. He wants me to come to his office this week."

"Are you going to get an implant or only work for the Deaf community."

Alex scrunched his nose and shook his head. "No cochlear. People will want me because I'm good. They won't care about my deafness. They will only want me to design a beautiful house or office building."

His grandfather raised his eyebrows. "The community will come to you, but I hope you are not being naïve or miscalculating of the hearing world. They are afraid of us." He laughed. "They should be. When it comes to jobs, most of us can eat them for breakfast."

Alex laughed at his grandfather's analogy. He understood what his grandfather meant, but he didn't always agree with it. The Deaf were no different from the rest of the world, other than they had pride in their deafness. Their Deaf lineage set them apart.

The night progressed without any problems and Savannah was a total success the entire time, poised and confident. He knew she was anything but self-assured in the Deaf community. She hid her uncertainties. Knowing she'd tell him later of all her misgivings, he'd assure her that she was perfect and tell her how proud he was of her. Then she'd settle down and snuggle next to him. A smile crossed his face as warmth pooled within him. *She's perfect for me.*

An uncle clamped him in an embrace. "How is my nephew?"

He smiled warmly at his uncle. "Fine. But I am hungry."

Lights flashed, and Alex's father appeared and signed for everyone to come eat. They weren't eating in the small dining room that was used for intimate dinners. They were eating in a large room that his parents used strictly for special gatherings. Tonight it was filled with a long table. Both his grandfathers would sit at the ends and then everyone took their places. He knew the family would be back for his graduation, but tonight was the end of the old year and a chance to put everything behind them.

He found Savannah and took her to the table. Aunt Sally and Uncle Harold were to sit between another aunt and uncle and a cousin and his wife. Aunt Sally was having a fit. After the year that she rearranged all the nametags on the table, Alex's mom decided it was best to lock Aunt Sally out of the room so that she couldn't make any changes to the seating arrangements. That also meant the staff was locked out until the very last moment. Gwen offered to trade places with the aging aunt.

"I am not sitting beside anyone who has a cochlear. They think they are too good."

"Really, Aunt Sally, there's no reason to say that. Just because you don't want one doesn't mean someone else doesn't." Gwen tried to cajole the older woman.

"At least you don't have one."

Alex hid his laughter. Gwen had styled her hair to cover hers, but hers was in place, probably for Savannah's benefit.

Gwen ignored the comment. "Sit here, and Dustin and I will sit over there."

Aunt Sally stared at Savannah, then blew air between pursed lips. "That puts me across from her." Aunt Sally pointed to Savannah. "She can't even sign."

"She's learning," Gwen replied.

Another family member said, "She can barely spell her name. I have no idea how Alex fell for her, but he loves her."

Professor Stockton made a face. "Are you implying I haven't taught her enough? I'm teaching her and Alex is too."

Savannah attempted to sign that she would not interfere with the family. She left the room.

Alex went after her as she dissolved into tears.

"I've tried so hard, and your family hates me."

I totally understand. You mother doesn't make it easy for me. "We all know how hard you've tried. My family understands. They don't hate you; they love you, and they love you even more because you are trying. Don't pay any attention to Aunt Sally. She's old and set in her ways. She's my father's aunt. I swear she's the Devil in human form, but my father swears the Devil doesn't want her. She's too mean."

Savannah shook her head. "Someone said I couldn't spell my name."

My cousin meant no harm by that. She thinks it's amazing that we're together."

"No-o-o…"

Uncertain if she was failing to understand what he had said or if she was heartbroken after trying so hard, he enclosed Savannah in his arms as he took her to his room.

The elder Mrs. Van Doorn appeared at his open bedroom door, and he signed for her to enter.

"Savannah, don't let her comments get to you. Sally's a somewhat-senile little witch who is getting worse with each passing year. She's also a mean gossip, except she never gets out of the house anymore. Harold won't let her go anywhere. Now you come back downstairs and sit with us. Everyone else thinks you are lovely. We all know you are trying hard to sign." She patted Alex on the shoulder. "We love him, and anyone he loves has to be special."

Alex handed Savannah a box of tissues and watched as she tried to compose herself. But his grandmother went to Savannah and gave her a big hug. He knew Savannah was in good hands. His grandmother signed extra slow when she was with Savannah. He left the two women, figuring his grandmother would restore Savannah's confidence.

Aunt Sally had traded with another couple, but she was

sitting with her arms crossed over her chest. His mom had worked hard on the seating arrangement to keep the younger members together and the older members with their families. Aunt Sally had sat next to Alex's cousin the last time she visited, but this time she decided she didn't like the cochlear. It was in his left ear and she was sitting to the right of him. She wouldn't even see it. His cousin's decision to get an implant was about the same as Gwen's and Dustin's. Their career choices meant they had to get the cochlear or be relegated to only serving the Deaf community. With an implant, they could serve the hearing as well as the Deaf and make much more money.

Alex understood their choices, but he didn't want an implant. He'd gotten this far without one. His mom had even tried to come up with some numbers for him, specifically the number of Deaf architects. Of course, the numbers were small compared to architects with hearing. World Deaf Architecture showed how small the numbers were, but they were also a strong worldwide group that contained some extremely successful men and women. He wasn't venturing into some uncharted territory. Others before him paved his way. But nothing said he had to have an implant to succeed. It might help, but he was used to dealing without one. He didn't need to hear his clients. He could read their lips and communicate with them. And he was certain that the Deaf community would rally behind him. He'd get work, and he'd get more work. It was the same theme that played in his head over and over, reassuring him that he would prosper.

Everyone waited for his grandmother and Savannah to return. They didn't have to wait long. Whatever transpired between them must have been good. Savannah smiled and took her place next to him. He wanted to ask, but Aunt Sally was busy complaining, and not one person paid her any mind.

Finally, Emily appeared for the meal. All the women rallied around her and complimented her new stylish haircut. Alex thought she wore too much makeup.

The first course, an appetizer of fish topped with a crab mixture, was served. Then a colorful mixed greens salad with noodles and quinoa came next. Each item was supposed to represent prosperity in the New Year. His mom was like that, always looking for just the right combinations for the perfect meal. Then she'd give the caterer her requests.

The pork roast was delicious and so were the lentils, but Alex was filling up and he knew there was more to eat. When they finally got down to the beautiful ring cake, he thought maybe he would explode. A platter was placed on the table with eight little wrapped gifts. Eight small charms were baked into the cake. Each trinket allowed the owner to pick a gift to go with it. *Savannah, do you need me to explain the game?* He glanced at her for a moment. *No, you'll figure it out.*

Whoever discovered a charm could choose a gift to open, or they could offer the little package to another member of the family…for a price. They played this game every year, and every year was more entertaining than the last.

A cousin found the first one and everyone smiled when he reached for a gift. He held it up and asked who would give him fifty dollars for it. Aunt Sheila offered him twenty-five. He shook his head, and when he had no more takers, he opened the package. Several tens were coiled into a rose.

Morgan, a distant cousin, found one and reached for a package. She tried to get someone to buy it from her. Aunt Sheila offered another twenty-five and Morgan took it. The package Aunt Sheila opened contained a winged Origami bird made out of two one-dollar bills.

Prof. Stockton's wife found charm and the bidding for the package became serious.

Alex nudged Savannah. It was obvious that she had

caught on to the game and began to fork her piece of cake until it was a crumbled mess. Everyone knew the smallest prize had been taken, and the remaining ones were large.

Another cousin garnered the very top prize. When they were down to two prizes, the bidding got crazy. One cousin offered a fair chunk of money and the package was traded. Far from being worth what was paid for it, the package contained an interesting bracelet made with coins. The male cousin passed it to his teenaged sister. The final prize was opened to reveal a wad of twenty-dollar bills.

With everyone in a good mood, the party continued until midnight. They raised their hands above their heads and counted to zero. Then everyone smiled and congratulated each other with wishes for the New Year.

Alex realized this was going to be a very important year for him. With his education behind him and his career ahead of him, facing all of it with Savannah by his side was what he truly wanted. Several bottles of champagne were opened and toasts were offered. Quite a few people raised their glass to his future and to a female cousin who was to graduate from high school. After everyone completed the traditional kissing and bestowing special wishes, Alex took Savannah and slipped out a back door to an enclosed patio.

"Pick a date, Savannah. We need to plan a wedding."

Classes would start again in another week and Savannah had plenty to do. But when Alex announced he was going to visit the architect, she inhaled a breath. He had talked about different architecture firms. There was one in particular that stood out, but he said he didn't want to design schools. That wasn't his dream.

Ian Kilpatrick had a small firm and that seemed to

appeal to Alex. He'd already said he didn't want to design skyscrapers or hospitals. He wanted to design homes. Homes worth having. Comfortable homes. To him, it wasn't just a house. It was life.

After being around his family and so many members of the Deaf community, she began to understand the importance of home and family. She loved her family, but the bonds of family in the Deaf community were different. They were tighter. Her parents expected her to fly the coop, and begin life on her own, but Deaf families didn't. Homes were frequently multigenerational.

Several times Alex had taken her to tour old houses nearby. He even took her to The Heart and told her about the buildings there. The old craftsmanship was something he appreciated, but his real love was the new modern buildings. He wanted glass and openness to go along with private space.

She smiled. "What do I say? Break a leg? Maybe it should break a window?"

His silent laugh came though. "Just cross your fingers for me. This will be either the best thing or the worst thing that can happen. But at least I will be close to you, and we won't be separated."

She held up crossed fingers and he put his arms around her. She looked into his blue eyes as his mouth captured hers. Every time he kissed her like that, she lost all sense of reality. She was part of him.

When his kiss broke, it took her a second to regain her balance. "Do you know what you do to me?"

"I love doing it to you." He smiled. "Do I look like a professional architect?"

She nodded. "Very handsome."

His eyes showed his excitement as he signed. She captured his hands and kissed them. She figured she was more nervous for him than he was.

Alex arrived a few minutes before nine. Taking a deep breath, he got out of the car and headed for the building. Considering he had parked in a municipal parking lot two blocks away on such a bitter cold morning, he zipped his heavy jacket as a blast of cold air struck him. Quickly he strode to Ian Kilpatrick's building.

His mom had given him a light board as a Christmas gift. It was a child's toy, but sturdy. Before leaving the house, he slipped it onto the case with his computer. Having no idea what he might need or would be expected of him, he stuffed his case with all sorts of things that he thought might be useful.

Ian Kilpatrick was unlocking the door as Alex approached. The man smiled broadly. "You're early. Come on in. The first thing I do is grab a cup of coffee while I check the day's schedule."

Once inside, Alex showed Ian the light board.

"That's a child's drawing toy."

Alex wrote on the board. It's perfect for communicating. I touch it here and the screen clears instantly.

"Well, you'll have the chance to try it. I have new clients coming later this morning."

At ten o'clock, Alex and Ian met with the couple that wanted to build their dream house. They brought their plat and a dozen photos they had taken of the property along with several photos of houses and rooms they cut from magazines.

Alex's job was to sit and listen, but when the couple contradicted themselves while trying to explain what they wanted, Alex began to write on his light board. He showed the board to them and they looked at each other. Ian agreed with what Alex had written.

Alex cleared the board and began to just do a rough sketch. The couple watched him, and Alex realized that Ian was talking. He looked up in time to catch what was being said.

"…how he does it. He can't hear, but he sees what we are saying."

Alex smiled and showed off the sketch. Ian began to sketch on his pad.

Alex cleared the screen and did a fast floor plan. You have pre-teens. They need room, privacy, and a place to be by themselves and away from you. But the family center is here where it belongs – a place to come together and interact.

The wife looked at her husband.

Alex pointed to one space.

For them. Computer space or TV. Friends. A place away from you.

Ian nodded. "Think of it as a teen den or a more grown up play area."

The father wrinkled his brow as if concerned. "I was thinking about a man cave over the garage."

"No problem, it really won't add to the footprint. And we can keep the bedroom strictly as a sleeping area. What Alex showed you makes the den a more family-oriented space. We can balance that space by giving you an office area."

"I'd love a library. It seems I collect books," the wife said, and her husband shot her a look that showed his disapproval of her hoarding.

Alex didn't want to step on the architect's toes by thrusting his ideas into whatever Ian had in mind, so Alex sat back and watched the banter. He needed to curb his enthusiasm. But when the couple turned to him and asked what he thought, he jumped back in and wrote on his board.

Adding sunlight is important. We're happier with

natural lighting. But there's one more thing you've not mentioned — how old are your parents? What are the odds that you will need to move one in with you someday?

"My parents are in good health. My father retired last year. I guess it's always a possibility." The man looked at his wife.

She nodded. "I never thought about that."

Anything can happen to anyone any time, but by adding the space now or at least designing for a possible addition is a good idea. Remember there is a flow to a house.

Ian looked at him. "Alex is right. You don't have to add it on now, but if you did, it could be re-purposed as a guest area." Alex sketched the exterior.

A wing could be added here, giving the house a more traditional look. If we stepped this back, then the additional space will look like it belongs.

It was lunchtime when the couple left. Ian asked Alex to join him at the small sandwich café down the street where they both had a Rueben. Alex waited for Ian to say something about the client meeting. He had failed to just sit back and observe. It wasn't his place to talk.

I'm sorry, sir. I should have stayed quiet.

"Don't ever feel that way around me. I want your ideas. In fact, I was surprised at how well the Addisons interacted with you. You handled yourself very well."

"Thank you."

When they returned to the office, Alex found himself

doing grunt work. He expected as much and really didn't mind. It was all part of paying dues that had to be paid in sweat. No matter where he went, he'd be dealing with ductwork, waterlines, and wiring.

At four thirty, Alex looked up and realized Ian had been standing in the room. Alex grinned.

I didn't hear you come in.

The man laughed. "Guess not. How far have you gotten?" Alex pointed to the computer screen.

I don't like the angle of this duct.

"What would you do with it?"

By the time Alex walked to his car, he decided his day had gone well. Not perfect, but overall, he felt confident. Ian said he'd work around Alex's schedule, hoping that Alex would work three days a week. The pay was minimal, but this was nothing more than a paid apprenticeship. He had a lot to prove before he'd receive a raise. There was no question in his mind that he'd never be paid what his peers would because he was Deaf. *It's not fair. I'm every bit as good, if not better.*

His mom always said deafness is not an excuse. If something is wrong, then change it. He would do everything he could to change it. *Is it possible to change someone's perception of the Deaf?*

Savannah was waiting for him when he walked through the door. Her bright smile added to his already terrific day. She had made lasagna, and it was great. But after dinner, she dragged him into the living room. Sitting on the sofa, she began to talk. "Spring break. Let's go home to my parents and get married."

He shook his head. "I have a better idea." He retrieved his laptop. "Your family and my family, Ashley and Matthew. We'll keep it simple."

"I like simple. But I still want a real wedding."

"You mean the dress, etc."

"Long and beautiful, with flowers. But my parents can't afford much."

He found his computer's bookmark and went to the site. "Here, everyone goes on a wonderful vacation."

"That's much too expensive for my parents."

"No. I pay."

"No, not there. But I like the idea. They call them destination weddings."

He grinned as he went to another bookmarked site. "Then this place. It's not as glamorous, but it looks nice."

It was nothing more than a small island resort, and it was within driving distance. He pointed to several things and then watched her face. She was thinking, and he knew she was interested. He pointed to the ferry that would take them there.

"It's still expensive."

"I'm paying. A few days for everyone to get to know each other and then home." He went to the next page. "Beach or garden wedding."

"Oh, that garden is beautiful."

He flipped to another destination. "Or this."

Little cabins surrounded a lake. It was closer to camping in his opinion, but it still looked like fun. There were plenty of activities on the lake and a little town nearby with restaurants.

She shook her head.

"Then this one."

"That's got to be expensive, but I love it! A Caribbean vacation without the cruise."

He shrugged. "You said your family has never had a real vacation. Let's give it to them. They will see that I can take good care of you."

"So, we fly there? My parents can't afford that."

"Don't worry about it. I'll buy the tickets."

"You would do that for my family"

He nodded. "It looks more like a corporate destination than a wedding getaway. But it will still work."

"That pool looks fantastic."

"All weather."

"I think the last time I owned a bathing suit I was twelve."

"Do you swim?"

She nodded, and he could see the excitement in her eyes.

"Then let's see if it's available." He pushed a few keys and filled in the dates. The full week wasn't available, but Saturday through Thursday was. "Enough days?"

She nodded.

"Okay, honeymoon and wedding all in one. We'll get married on…" He pointed to her.

"Wednesday. That will give everyone a chance to have fun first."

"Can your father get off work?"

She crossed her fingers and found her phone. "We hope."

He watched her as she made the call, reading her lips the entire time. He wished he could have known what her mom was saying to her. All he could do was watch as she talked. She ended the call and smiled at him.

"Dad will have to request the time off, but he has vacation time coming to him and she doesn't think it will be a problem."

"We can invite more people if you wish. There are plenty of rooms."

"You mean like grandparents? My grandparents would love to come."

He nodded. "I will pay the airfare for your grandparents. We'll get a head count, and I'll make the airline reservations."

He pulled her to him and kissed her.

When he told his parents what they intended to do, his father insisted that he would pay the airfares for whomever was going. Inwardly, Alex could feel the relief from the financial burden.

Tuesday, he met with his professors. He had to tell them what he wanted to do and what he wanted to accomplish. It was easier to listen to them than it was for him to communicate with them. He asked Prof. Stockton to interpret. It was rare that he ever asked for help, but this meeting was important.

For almost two hours, they grilled him on his goals and what he wanted to achieve. But when the one professor mentioned that he'd have a more difficult time as an architect because he was Deaf, Alex's insides instantly reacted.

"I will succeed. I'm good and people will want me because I am good. I will have my AIA, and I will join the World Deaf Architecture. Some of the top architects in the world are Deaf. Being Deaf will never stop me. Never!"

"To be honest, I didn't know how we were going to conduct this interview." Another professor said. "I wasn't expecting you to bring Prof. Stockton with you."

Alex raised his eyebrows. "If I feel as though I need an interpreter, I will use one. It's not my fault that you do not speak the same language as I do. If I spoke German, would you understand me?"

The other professor smiled at him. "Alex, I speak French. It was what was spoken in my home. I learned Spanish in school, but I was never given the opportunity to take ASL. It wasn't considered a language back then." She smiled. "I've admired your guts, and I know you will face and have faced many of the same problems I did because I was the only female in my class to graduate with my degree in architecture. I worked for several years. Then I stayed home and raised my family. I went back to work. After careful consideration, I decided to return to school for my doctorate and began to apply for a teaching position. I continued to work as an architect. It took another three years before I was hired to teach. This is still a male-dominated field. You have that edge in your favor but being Deaf will make it more difficult for you. Have you started to apply for a job? Do you expect to work for a WDA firm?"

"I've already found a job working for an architect. He's not a member of the World Deaf Architecture. He hears. He's giving me the opportunity to prove I can handle myself in a hearing environment."

The one professor looked slightly shocked and asked, "Who?"

"Ian Kilpatrick. I'm grateful he's giving me a chance. So far, so good."

"You won't be able to talk to clients."

Alex shrugged and smiled. "I managed to do that the other day with a new client. They didn't seem to mind my deafness. It was a lively discussion about a house they want to build."

When Alex walked out of the conference room, he was exhausted. The tension of the meeting still held a tight grip on him. He thanked Prof. Stockton.

Stockton signed, "Jane Hilcomb is right; you will face all sorts of problems because you are Deaf. But I know you too well. Anyone else would have crumbled in there. No one said that you couldn't do it, only that you were going to have a harder time doing it." He smiled. "You are strong with a huge support system behind you. You will do well."

"Thank you."

"I hope you don't plan on living with Savannah forever."

"Meaning?"

"Marry her. She loves you."

"Want to go to Texas during spring break?"

"What on earth for?"

Alex grinned. "A wedding."

Stockton laughed. "Spring break?"

Savannah found that getting credit for a class that she didn't have to attend failed to lighten her load. She still had to take the evening ASL class. And the way her schedule fell with Alex's, she'd be in class the nights he came home from his apprenticeship.

Alex went to school two mornings a week and tutored during the afternoons. Then Monday, Wednesday, and Friday, he worked for Ian Kilpatrick. Tuesday and Wednesday evenings, he'd go to Lila McCord's for speech therapy. But his nights were spent drawing at the computer. Some days, Savannah barely saw him except for dinner, even though they were in the same house.

Online, she looked for the perfect dress. She wanted formal – a chance to be the fairytale princess marrying her Prince Charming. But she didn't want to spend a fortune. Ashley gave her the name of a shop that several people had used and loved. She ordered the fitting kit and sent an email explaining what she wanted. The following day, she had a friendly email with several suggestions. Each dress was made individually for a perfect fit, and she had all sorts of options with each dress.

She pored over the catalog and then she saw it. It was the perfect princess dress. She looked at the materials and the various trims until she found the ideal ones to match a seaside wedding. A little dash of sparkle and some pale blue… It was exactly what she wanted.

Ashley helped her with measurements. And then she did the same for Ashley. Ashley was shorter and curvier. Her dress was simpler but also had that same seaside vibe. And with Ashley's darker coloring, she would look great in blue-green. Satisfied, they ordered their dresses. It was more than either one of them could afford, but they did it anyway.

When Alex came home, she told him what she had done.

"Don't tell my mother what you paid, or she'll think you bought junk. I'm certain she spent more than that on your New Year's dress."

"She thinks nothing of spending an outrageous amount."

"That's Mom." He reached for his phone and checked his bank account. "I'll give you the money and help Ashley. What do you want me to wear?"

She rolled her palms up. "What does Prince Charming wear? A short jacket with epaulets."

"No. I'm not wearing gold braid and epaulets."

"How about this. The only gold is on the buttons." She showed him a picture of a suit that had a short jacket. "And the epaulets will color match the trim on my dress."

He rolled his eyes at her and she laughed.

"I'll settle for the short-fitted jacket without epaulets. It'll look super on you."

He frowned. "Are you serious?"

"Yes. Every little girl wants to marry Prince Charming. Except I'm about to marry him for real."

"Don't do that to me. I'm just a man."

She smiled. "You're *my* man."

He raised his eyebrows and then grinned. "For you, I would wear anything."

She laughed. "Let me measure you."

Afterwards, Alex went to his computer to draw while she called Ashley. Sitting in the living room made it easier to chat because Esther was at Alex's house. She seemed to always occupy the kitchen even though she'd been offered the room upstairs. Esther swore she liked sitting in the kitchen. But being in the living room seemed polite to Savannah, who realized how much she'd come to appreciate the total quiet in Alex's house.

When Savannah returned to the dining room table, Alex looked up and smiled, then resumed what he was doing. Her mind was swirling with wedding plans and her ability to concentrate on her studies was gone. She packed up her computer and went upstairs. She heard Esther retire but still no Alex. She awakened and realized Alex had not come to bed. She got up and found him at his computer, totally lost in what he was doing.

"It's late. Are you coming to bed?"

He nodded and turned off his computer.

"What were you doing?"

He shrugged. "It's for a client. Ian had a design idea and intends to propose it the end of this week. But I'm seeing something different. I like my idea better."

"Is there something wrong with Ian's?"

"No. But this couple wants something… I can't explain it. It's a feeling that I have. They constantly contradict what they are saying. Ian put a lot of work into a design for them last week and they rejected it. I think they will reject his next one, too."

"That doesn't sound good."

"Ian says clients want houses, but frequently change their minds about things. Nothing goes as planned."

Savannah shrugged and followed Alex upstairs. In the bedroom, he continued to talk. Finally, she asked him, "Was your parents' home custom built?"

He nodded.

"Are they happy with all of it?"

"Not exactly… most of it, but not everything. If they ever sell it, that kitchen is in the wrong place."

She looked at Alex as though he'd lost his mind. It was the most beautiful kitchen she'd ever seen. He continued to ramble, and she pointed to the clock. He nodded and continued to sign.

He's not sleeping because mentally he's busy building houses. So why am I awake? Are our lives going in different directions? Maybe the wedding is a big mistake. Maybe it's premature. Maybe we should wait? What if he hates me in two years? Are our hopes and dreams too far apart? Why must everything be so difficult? Why am I still struggling with ASL. I'll never learn. That's not fair to Alex.

When Alex attempted, to kiss her goodnight she told him no.

"What? Is something wrong?"

"I want to sleep."

He leaned over her and stared into her eyes.

She closed them and turned her back to him. Guilt ran through her. She wasn't angry with him. It wasn't him. She was sorting out feelings that she couldn't explain even to herself. The constant strain to communicate, some tough classes, even her contact with her best friend was limited because they were no longer staying in the dorm. Now she was on the verge of a fairytale wedding, and she felt as though she wasn't going to be able to enjoy it. *Everything is wrong and now I've hurt Alex.*

She stared into the dark space that filled the room. His hand rested on her shoulder. Normally a welcomed touch, but tonight it was the catalyst for guilt that circulated through her system in a slow crawl to her heart where it stabbed her like the thorns on a rose. She rolled over and found him staring at her. She tenderly touched his cheek, planted a tiny kiss on his lips, and whispered, "I love you."

She awakened to the beeping alarm of her cell phone. Lack of sleep made it twice as difficult to climb from the warm cocoon of the bed. After pulling on her jeans and the striped sweater that her mom had given her for Christmas, she braided her hair and slipped her feet into her boots. The only thing she wanted to do was climb back into bed, but she had a class.

Alex looked about as bad as she felt. The lack of sleep showed in the dark circles under his expressionless eyes.

"I'm sorry. I should have never shut you out. I only wanted to sleep last night, and it wasn't happening. I had too many things on my mind. Now, I don't want to go to school – I want to sleep."

"We both have to go. I have to meet with Prof. Hilcomb. She's one of my instructors this semester."

"And then you teach at Kennedy High this afternoon?"

He nodded.

"I should be done class by eleven."

At eleven o'clock, Savannah spotted his car in the parking lot. Flurries speckled the air and the only thing she wanted to do was take a nap.

"Car's warm." Alex held the door for her.

"I'm so glad you are here. I don't think I have enough energy to even walk across campus."

"Are you getting sick?"

She shook her head. "I just need my sleep."

"What was wrong last night? You're never like that."

"Everything on my mind from this semester's course load to worrying about the wedding."

"Are you changing your mind about being married?"

Savannah shook her head, forgetting that Alex was driving, and his eyes were not on her. She signed no as he pulled to a stop sign. As soon as they reached the house, she scrambled inside, dropped her things in the dining room, and headed upstairs for the comfort of the bed. Alex did the same thing. She snuggled against him and fell asleep. Later, his movements awakened her. Her little catnap had lasted almost three hours.

She sat up and watched him get ready to teach. He wore jeans with a camel colored Henley, and then put on his boots. He smiled at her and she smiled back. *Totally delicious.*

There were only flurries swirling through the air when he left for Kennedy High School. Two hours later, the flurries that had dotted the air had turned into a real snowfall. They started to cover everything. It wasn't much, but she worried about him driving through it. And when he walked into the kitchen, she breathed a sigh of relief. "Thank goodness, you're home."

He raised his eyebrows. "The only thing predicted was flurries. That's more than flurries."

"Hungry?"

"Starved. I think we skipped lunch."

"I've made up for it. I have chicken smothered in a sausage-mushroom gravy, salad, corn pudding, and something yummy for dessert."

He grinned and scooped her into his arms as he gave her a big kiss. When he released her, he asked, "How did I get so lucky? But what's for dessert so I can be certain to save enough room for it?"

"Lemon lime bars."

"Trying to make me fat?"

She laughed. "It's better than the stuff they feed us on campus. Breaded mystery meat, instant mashed potatoes, canned green beans, and chocolate-flavored pudding."

He laughed. "No thanks. I know that food. I ate it."

She finished fixing the meal and served it. As soon as they had eaten and cleaned up, she dragged him into the living room. Sitting on opposite ends of the sofa so they faced each other, she began to sign as she spoke, "I've been thinking."

He grinned.

"No, it's not funny. I'm being serious."

He wiped the smirk from his face and stared at her. "Something has had you worried."

"Okay. I love you, but can we package that up and put it to one side for a little while?"

He knitted his brow and spoke as he signed. "Yes."

"I've been reading up on all the gene stuff until my head is swimming. I'm not a science major. But also, your sister said something to me, something that made me stop and think hard. Well, actually it wasn't the only time I've heard it. So follow my train of thought, okay?"

He nodded.

"What if your mom never had you because she was concerned about having a deaf child?"

"My mom?"

"No, I mean, what if? If she hadn't, I wouldn't have you."

"True."

"Okay, I fell in love with you even though you are Deaf."

He narrowed his eyes. "Why should that matter?"

"I don't know. I've been asking myself that question. If I could answer it, we wouldn't be sitting here while I try to understand something that makes no sense."

"Keep going."

"Well, little girls don't dream of growing up and marrying Prince Charming who happens to be Deaf."

"I'm not Prince Charming."

She couldn't help but smile at the face he made when he said it. "No. You are not Prince Charming, fairytale hero, but you are the guy that I drooled over long before I actually met you."

"And you were shocked when you discovered I was Deaf."

She nodded. "My whole image of you shattered in a single instant." She held her hand up because she was certain he was about to say something. "But as soon as it shattered, it was replaced. I had this super good-looking guy smiling at me. That's who I fell in love with – not the Deaf guy. I didn't stop and say to myself. 'Oh he's Deaf and I need to find someone else.' But I did wonder why I didn't walk away."

Alex ran his fingers through his hair, moving a stray lock from his forehead. "I'm surprised that you didn't. Anyone else in your shoes would have."

"No. There was something about you. I feel it when we're together."

"I feel it, too"

"Well, no one is perfect. And loving you is… Because you don't hear, I have to learn to understand you. I have to learn to sign."

"You've worked hard."

"Thank you." She put her hand up again. "I love you. I love the wonderful guy that you are. I love the man who is more than the pretty face. I could make a list of wonderful attributes that would fill a book." She grinned at him. "But I have questions about being married to someone who is Deaf, and how your deafness will affect us. Being in love with you means I have to sign, I'm willing to do that."

"What's the problem?"

"Children."

"Why? Do you fear they will not hear?"

"Yes." Her stomach knotted, and those little biting snakes began to chew at her innards.

He stared at her. "Explain hearing to me, because I have no clue what it is."

She shook her head. "I can't. It's just something that is."

"Do you think I care that I can't hear?"

"Okay, maybe you don't care about the sounds, but you said you felt isolated growing up. You knew you were different."

"I am Deaf. And yes, I must live in a world filled with people who communicate with their mouths. People forget to look at me when they talk. They watch me when I sign as though I were an animal in the zoo. Or they look at me as though I will eat them. They think I am stupid because I do not hear them."

"And you want to bring a child into this world to face what you have?"

He narrowed his eyes and made a contorted face. "You like someone calling you a dumb blonde because everyone knows blonde women are stupid?"

She rolled her eyes at him. "If someone wants to think I'm stupid because I'm blonde, that's their problem not mine."

"Well, I don't want a dumb blonde child." He crossed his arms over his chest.

She smiled. "Okay, I get it."

"Are you certain?"

She nodded. He held his arms out to her and she climbed

into his embrace. "I want to hear your heartbeat."

"I want to feel yours."

She snuggled to him. The peaceful aura of his love bathed her. Savannah's phone alerted her of an incoming text message. But she didn't want to move – didn't want to leave the warm comfort of Alex's embrace.

He reached for his phone and unclipped it from his belt. Then he turned the screen so she could see it. School was cancelled.

"It snowed that much?" She jumped off the couch and ran to the window.

Everything was blanketed in white and more was falling. Then the electricity went out.

In the dark house, Alex made his way to the kitchen, took two flashlights from a drawer, and handed one to Esther. From a cabinet, he withdrew two battery-operated lanterns, and found his box of votive-style emergency candles, passing them to Esther along with a lighter made especially for candles.

She nodded as though she understood.

Then he lifted jackets for Savannah and himself off the coat hooks.

"What? I need my boots." Savannah ran upstairs with the flashlight to put on her boots. Alex took the flashlight by the back door, followed Savannah, and did the same thing.

He signed, and she shook her head.

He fingerspelled snowman.

"But the electric is out."

"Nothing we can do about that. The power company will fix it. Let's have fun."

She grinned and vanished down the stairs. He found her rummaging in the recycle bin with the flashlight tucked under her arm. He watched and wondered what she was doing. She kept stuffing her coat pockets, but he couldn't see what she was putting in them. When she turned around, she held two blue bottle caps to her eyes, and then showed him the brown ones that had been removed from some juice bottles.

He smiled and gave her the thumbs up. "Bring extra, in case we need them."

An hour and a half later, they returned to the house frozen to the core. They took off their wet things and hung them from the kitchen bar stools to dry. Savannah ran upstairs first, took a hot shower, and pulled on heavy pajamas. He followed her but knocked on Esther's bedroom door. He showed her where he had stored more blankets and invited her downstairs. From the look of confusion on her face, she obviously had a hard time following what he was trying to say, but she smiled as if trying to be polite. He was certain she didn't understand anything he'd signed. He verbally spoke to her.

She stepped back slightly. "I didn't know you could speak."

He nodded. "Come downstairs. I made the kitchen warm with oven. It is gas. Leave your door open. Warm air rises."

The bathroom was steamy but not comfortably warm. He hopped in the shower and enjoyed the gas-heated water until it warmed him to his bones but stepping out took his breath away. He pulled on heavy sweats and his robe over that. When his mom gave him several robes for Christmas, he had laughed. She said he needed them with Esther in the house. *It's not like I walk around in my underwear. I'm always covered.*

Savannah was telling Esther they had rolled two large snowmen and placed them together in a neighbor's yard, knowing the neighbor had two small children. With bottle cap faces on the snow couple, they were adorable. "Alex managed to take a few selfies of us and the snow couple."

Savannah asked for his phone and checked the photos they had taken, showing them to Esther.

Esther took off for her room and returned with an old pink scarf that had a hole in it. Using a pair of kitchen shears, she cut two strips from an aluminum soda can using the kitchen shears and fringed the strips. She asked to borrow Alex's boots and his phone. Then she went out the back door. Returning few minutes later, without the scarf, she handed Alex his phone. Their snowwoman now had a pink scarf and eyelashes. "That was adorable! Facing them to the house so the children will see them in the morning was so sweet of you. Do you think anyone saw you making them?"

Alex laughed and signed, "I didn't hear anyone."

Savannah was giggling but managed to interpret. Esther started laughing.

Savannah began looking in the cabinets and handed him two large pans. "Fill these with snow. It'll help keep everything in the refrigerator cold."

He raised his eyebrows and Esther took the pans from him. Savannah opened the refrigerator and withdrew the milk. When Esther returned, Savannah put a pan of snow in the almost empty freezer and another in the refrigerator section. Then she made hot chocolate for everyone.

Savannah and Esther both jumped and ran to the front of the house. Something was amiss. He followed to see what had alerted them. Savannah pulled her phone from her pocket and made a phone call. He watched what she was saying and realized she was saying something about a transformer. From where he was standing, he just wasn't certain whom she had called. Looking out the window, there were still a few sparks falling.

Then both the girls jumped as another transformer a little ways down the street did the same thing. This time he could see it from a side window. It created quite a little light show. Explaining to them what was happening wasn't worth it. Instead, he told them it was a type of surge protector.

It was hour later when he spotted the yellow flashing

lights coming from the electrical company's truck. They had big spotlights and were checking the power lines. The wet snow had made wonderful snowmen, but the snow had clung to the power lines and damaged them.

Savannah made more hot chocolate. With Savannah's back to him, he motioned to Esther by holding his fingers somewhat meshed together in front of his tummy and pointed to her. Then he signed baby. Esther nodded. He pointed to Savannah and motioned to tell her.

Esther looked at him as if confused.

He then pointed to Esther's ring finger before pointing to Savannah. He found a piece of paper and a pen.

Tell her. I know. I've known for a long time – since the fire.

From the exaggerated way she mouthed, he was certain she asked, "How?"

I saw you talking on the phone. I've seen you with Demitri. You love him.

She nodded.

When Savannah served the hot chocolate, Esther told the story of how she and Demitri met and fell in love.

"We were married last July, but we've not said a word to our parents. It was a civil wedding, and his parents will never accept that. My getting pregnant was our big mistake. It's too soon. He's got another year to go and so do I. When he's finished his classes, he still has a residency time to fulfill. I already know I can stay on campus and put the baby in daycare there, except it will increase my expenses. I don't know how I'll make it."

Alex waved his hands and then signed, "No, stay here. I will fix the library room for you and the baby can have the little room."

Savannah interpreted for him.

Esther started to cry. "You would do that for me?"

He hated when women dissolved into the tears. His insides turned to mush, and confusion muddled his mind. He could understand grieving, but not how women could turn on the waterworks over the most ridiculous things. He signed no crying, but it was useless, because Savannah had joined Esther's watershed. Unable to sit there and watch, he left the two women. His little house was darn cold.

He returned to the kitchen and turned off the oven. "The crews are working on the power lines. It's late and we need to go to sleep. Pile on the extra blankets."

Picking up a battery-operated lantern, he took it upstairs and placed it in the bathroom. Savannah climbed into bed and snuggled extra tight to him. He held her close, wishing he could do more, but he didn't want to break the thin veil of trust. *I want you Savannah. Damn, it's cold!*

The power flickered and then went off again. He lay there and watched the darkness. Uncertain how many lights had been left on, he waited. It was too cold to even bother to turn over and check the time.

Savannah awakened to sunlight in the room and the feeling of being too warm. She couldn't remember sleeping so late in ages, but then she wasn't one to stay awake almost the whole night. And going to bed at three in the morning was late for her. She quietly slid open a drawer and then reminded herself that Alex wouldn't hear her. She wondered what it was like to never hear sounds. *How many times have I asked myself that question?* She dressed for the day, brushed her hair, and went downstairs. With the power restored, she discovered several lights had been left on and flipped them off as she went into the kitchen to make a pot of coffee.

As the coffee brewed, she looked out the window and could no longer see their footprints in the snow. A pristine white blanket covered the backyard.

From the living room windows, she could see more of the neighborhood. Because of the angle, she could just barely see the snowmen they had made. They'd had so much fun making them, playing in the snow as though they were still children.

Alex wasn't the type of person to get upset over little things. His constant lightheartedness was contagious, but he also could be serious about his grades and studying. He was trying hard to speak clearly and worked on his vocal skills every day.

When he walked away from his computer screen, it showed his bank account. She couldn't stop herself from peeking. Catching her, he grinned and turned the screen so that she could see it better. *Maybe this is why he can be so carefree about some things. But what drives him to be the best?*

She didn't know how much her parents had in bank, but she didn't think it was that much. Now she understood why he was so generous when he took her to buy clothes or would hand her some cash. That's when he told her there was more money.

"I had just gone to college when my high school math teacher, Tom Wilson, discovered he had cancer. I always knew he liked me. He couldn't understand sign language, but he knew I could understand him. He must have gotten my phone number from my mom, because one day he texted me and wanted to me come to his house. Slightly confused, I went. He was preparing for his final days. He'd never married, but his sister had a child. Apparently that boy got involved with drugs and overdosed. Tom Wilson left his house and belongings to his sister, but since his nephew was dead, he made me the beneficiary of his life insurance policy. He said I'd need it to start my own company. That money is held in trust until I turn twenty-five. I can get it sooner, but I don't need it. I only get the interest right now, and I save most of that."

It was a tidy nest egg for someone starting out. It surprised her, and yet it didn't. Now she understood why he could do the things that he did, but he was also careful with what he had. He could have had a really nice car or any number of things. Instead he was content with what he did have. She liked that about him.

She heard footsteps on the stairs and looked in that direction.

"I could smell the coffee," Esther said.

"I'll make a pot of decaf for you. I almost bought Alex one of those single serving coffeepots at Christmas, but brewed coffee tastes so much better to me." Savannah pushed her chair away from the dining room table, stood, and went into the kitchen. "I always wondered why you'd make decaf."

Soon Alex joined them. "Anyone need to go out or should I skip shoveling?"

Savannah rolled her eyes at him. "Why bother? I love the look of the pure white blanket."

"We have enough groceries?" Alex asked.

Savannah nodded. "We used a lot of milk last night, but there's still plenty."

Esther looked at Alex. "If you don't shovel, I can't get to campus for my meals."

"Eat with us. I'm certain the only cafeteria open will be the main one. They really can't close it because too many students need to eat. But the food is limited to things that don't require refrigeration or cooking." Savannah interpreted what he was saying. "According to electric company's map, the power is out on most of campus.

"I promise, there's plenty of food in this house." Savannah smiled at Esther. "In fact, I was thinking about making something fun and more time-consuming since we have the day off. Want to help?"

Savannah watched Esther put together a batter for cupcakes made with raisins. She didn't have a recipe. "I've been making these since I was old enough to pull a chair to the counter and help my mom."

"I can do a few things, but I've got to have a recipe."

Esther rolled her eyes. "My mom has a recipe book, but she hardly uses it."

"My mom has quite a few books, and now with the Internet, I'm collecting recipes one at a time. Because when I find something I really like, I print it out and save it to the cloud. Those printed recipes, I send them home to Mom so she'll have them. Except I've hardly cooked since I've been in school."

"You were lucky you didn't lose everything in the fire."

"Did you lose much?"

Esther nodded. "I lost my laptop and everything that I owned, including a quilt from my great grandmother."

"But your—"

"Demitri bought a new laptop for me. And most everything was in the school's cloud. I only had to sync. He also gave me some money for clothes."

"Alex took me shopping."

Esther put the pan in the oven to bake. "Demitri's dad owns a restaurant. He wants Demitri to marry a nice Greek girl. That's why he won't tell his father we're married."

"And you haven't told your parents?"

Esther shook her head. "Demitri is too worldly for my family."

"So, it's going to be a surprise. Are you going to go home and say, 'I'm married and I have a baby'?"

Esther nodded. "My father will never accept my marriage

to Demitri. My family has a friend outside of the community. I will go there and have her get my mom and bring her to me. I know she will want to see the baby, but after that I will no longer be welcomed. And I doubt anyone else from my family will be allowed to go to college."

"My mom seems to think my marrying Alex is a big mistake, but at least they aren't turning me away."

"I've watched you talking with Alex. You're getting very good with sign language."

Savannah grinned at her friend. "You've picked up some of it."

"Maybe in context. Alex often asks me if I want something, but I really don't know much." Ester knitted her forehead. "I really like Alex. If it weren't for him, I have no idea where I'd be living. I also understand your mom's concern. He's going to have a tough life in a hearing world."

"He knows that. He says we all have tough lives; his is no different."

"But I think Alex is going to make it. He's not going to let anything stop him." Esther smiled broadly. "Are you ready for your wedding?"

Savannah nodded. "I'm very ready to be married, but there are all the little things concerning the actual wedding that must be handled. I'm hoping we can finalize our plans this weekend."

"Demitri and I are planning to be there. We'll fly down ahead of you. He has a friend in Austin, and we're spending a few days with him before leaving for the coast."

"I'm glad you're coming."

Esther smiled. "So am I. I have a gut feeling that Alex Van Doorn will be an extremely important name. He has all the qualities that make someone famous."

"Are you being serious?"

25

Alex worked on his idea for the Addisons. He'd drawn a simple floor plan but then added renderings to it. He added what commonly is called a mother-in-law suite and showed the floor plan with and without it. The Addisons said they wanted a large house but complained about having to clean what seemed like wasted space. He knew that feeling. In a way, he was grateful that his kitchen wasn't exposed to the entire house, yet sometimes the living room seemed like wasted space because he hardly ever used it. *Well, until Savannah came into my life. She likes to talk to me while sitting on the sofa.*

He thought about where on the lot the Addisons wanted to build and changed it from being on top of the hill to having the hill be the view. He angled the house to catch more light and curved the driveway. It was all laid out on paper.

Monday morning, he showed Ian what he'd drawn. Breakfast churned in his stomach as he watched his boss's face for clues to his thoughts. A few times the man frowned, and Alex tightened his abdominal muscles. He pushed that one lock of hair off his forehead and mentally crossed his fingers that Ian would approve.

Several times, Ian looked at the pages of notes that Alex had written to correspond with various things on the drawing. It was Alex's way of explaining what he'd done. He'd written it for the client but knew Ian would carefully read it.

The number of times his mom had told him not to fidget was innumerable. Now he knew why. Standing perfectly still, he waited for Ian to say something. He knew the drawing was good, knew it encompassed what the Addisons wanted.

Ian looked up and without much expression said, "Print it and show them."

Alex signed thank you and said it as he did. It wasn't exactly what he hoped for, but at least he'd be allowed to show it to the Addisons.

He didn't have long to wait. It was Ian's secretary who alerted Alex of their arrival. He joined Ian and the Addisons at the big conference table, smiled, and wrote on his light board. I didn't hear you arrive.

The Addisons laughed.

Ian presented his modified plan and both of the Addisons seemed to agree that they liked the new design.

Ian looked at Alex for a moment. "Alex has come up with a completely different design and would like to present it to you. I'm sure you will find it very different, but earthy and comfortable."

Alex handed them each a copy of the notes he made, and then showed them the placement of the house on the lot. The exterior renderings were followed by the interior ones and, lastly, he handed them the floor plan.

Latoya Addison looked surprised and excited as she studied the floor plan. And Bill Addison kept looking at where on the lot the house was going to be placed and referenced Alex's notes.

"This is going to block the cold weather?"

Alex reached for his light board. He showed the sun's movement and showed from which direction most of the winds and weather came.

"May we have some time alone?" Bill Addison asked.

"Certainly." Ian motioned for Alex to follow him.

They walked to the room that Alex used for his office. It was the same room that contained the coffee pot, a sink, and a few cabinets. But it also contained a big Formica table probably left over from the 1960's judging by the color and design. The table gave Alex plenty of room to work, and that's all that mattered to him.

Ian fixed a cup of coffee and then faced Alex. "I think they liked your design."

Alex nodded and spoke. "But you don't. May I ask why?"

"It's too modern. People think they want modern, but really they don't. They are more comfortable in a traditional layout. You've also added some high dollar items that will up the cost of the house." He raised his eyebrows. "A few thousand usually never stops someone. And your idea will save them in the long run because it will be more energy efficient." He shook his head. "Those big windows... That adds up fast."

"But it has the look and feel of a classic home with added light."

"I do like that center room with its wonderful view. It's a buffer between both living spaces and gives the feeling of a living room without invading private space."

Alex nodded. The differences between them were stylistic and Alex respected those differences. He wrote on his board.

I know I can draw. You have the experience that I can't get in a classroom.

Ian grinned. "If they take your design, you will have a crash course in coping with clients. You'll get some experience."

Alex followed Ian out of the room and back to the conference room. Ian had a beautiful old building but wasn't taking advantage of it. There were at least two full-sized rooms, but they were filled with boxes. He wished he knew reasons for not utilizing those spaces. Maybe it had started when everything connected to the computers had to be hard-wired, but those days were long gone.

The Addisons smiled as Ian and Alex entered.

"Have you made any decisions, or can we answer any questions that you might have?" Ian returned to his seat.

Alex sat and watched the couple. They turned down his design, but then asked for a few of his elements to be added to Ian's design, such as the big bank of windows in the den. Disappointment crept through Alex, chilling him like an unexpected cold evening. But he paid careful attention to what elements they did like and their reasons for choosing the one plan over the other.

It was after the Addisons left that Ian began to talk in length about the design that Alex had done. Ian agreed that it fit the couple and what they said they wanted. Moving the house down the hill preserved the view and all the other things that Alex had intentionally incorporated. Ian actually praised the design.

"Do you know why they chose my design and not yours?

Alex wrote on his light board.

I moved the house down the hill. In a few months, they will lose that wooded view as other people buy the land around them, but they don't understand that. Also, my design was probably too modern for them, considering they preferred the design of a square house with lots of steps. They will wind up ditching the house in a few years to care for aging parents or because they will find those stairs to be too much.

Ian nodded. "Exactly. Very few people will want something truly different. It's a shame because your design was excellent."

"Thank you," Alex said it aloud and signed it.

Alex went back to the design he was working on for Ian. He told himself there was no cause to act like a spoiled child who didn't get his way. There would be plenty more designs that clients would turn down. It was a learning experience. At least Ian wasn't critical, nor did he reprimand him for taking the initiative to design something without being asked. Ian had been complimentary of the design.

A little after two o'clock, Ian came into Alex's room. "Don't toss unused designs. You never know when you might use them again or elements from them."

Alex grinned.

My professor, Jane Hilcomb, has already told us never to toss designs even those we do for class. I've already collected quite a few.

"I wondered how you would communicate. Guess I should have known you would manage. But it's rare you say anything. Why don't you talk more?"

He moved his mouth until he was certain where to start forming the words. "I am taking speech lessons. I need to learn to use my voice and not squawk like a seagull. Leaving academia and venturing into the hearing world is forcing me to communicate using every possible means."

Ian looked at him. "How do you know what a seagull sounds like? Did you lose your hearing?"

Alex smiled, and signed, as he spoke, "No. I was born deaf. I've been told I sound like a seagull. All I know is that they have wet mouths when they nip your fingers while taking a French fry." He grinned and raised his eyebrows. "They say some birds are beautiful when they sing. Apparently a seagull is not."

Ian laughed. "No, they aren't. And you don't sound like a seagull. Keep trying to talk. I'm sure it's like anything else, practice makes perfect."

Alex nodded.

"That little electronic toy you carry works very well."

Alex wrote.

Thanks. It's handy, but it's too big for everyday use. Alex pulled the tiny notepad from his pocket. For some things this works better.

Working for Ian Kilpatrick was going to be Alex's most difficult "class" this semester, but it would also be his most important one. By comparison, his professors were easy. *It's giving me experience and exposure. I can do this.*

One day a week, Savannah sat with Alex during his speech lessons with Lila McCord. By watching what she did to help Alex, Savannah learned things about speaking that she had never considered. Often she found herself doing what Lila was making Alex do. Feeling the sounds as they were made and the amount of breath that was forced out to make certain sounds was something that Savannah had taken for granted. She just spoke. She wondered what it was like to talk without hearing.

Lila turned to Savannah and signed as she spoke. "Keep working with him. He's doing great. He's much more consistent, but he's still monotone and a little sloppy with his sounds."

"Will he ever lose that flatness?"

Lila looked at Alex and then returned her gaze to Savannah. "Without any hearing or help from implants, it is very difficult to overcome." She looked back at Alex. "Time and practice. It is up to you to decide how much you want the inflection. You have improved so much in a very few weeks."

Alex smiled at Savannah. "We work together. I teach her to sign and she helps me with my voice."

Savannah took Alex's hand and gave it a little squeeze as they left the office. He leaned over and kissed her cheek before opening her car door. There was something special about having Alex hold the door. It was so thoughtful of him. He was always doing little things for her and making her feel important. When he sat behind the wheel, she signed that he was doing much better.

"I am trying," he said aloud.

As soon as they returned to Alex's house, Savannah immediately began to study. Her class schedule didn't give her many lengthy breaks during the day, and with ASLIII three evenings a week, her study time was limited. Going with Alex to Silent Spaghetti on Thursday evenings, and then one night a week to Lila McCord's office filled her evenings. Her ASLIII was on one of his speech therapy nights. He would tell her what he did on those nights. The only good thing about her new schedule was having Friday free of classes except for ASL in the evening. She used Friday to do most of her writing assignments.

But the upcoming wedding loomed over her. When Alex's mom texted asking for Savannah to come to the office, Savannah gulped. She made the appointment between two classes. It didn't sound like a friendly mother-of-the-groom meeting.

Savannah watched the little digital clock in the corner of her tablet, ticking away the minutes, hoping the professor would let them out early. When he did, Savannah went out the door, wishing she had wings on her feet like the Roman god Mercury. She bought a bottle of coconut water from the cafeteria's vending machine, unscrewed the top on the drink, took a big swig, recapped it, and cut across campus to The Heart.

"I'm here to see Dr. Van Doorn."

"You must be Savannah." A middle-age woman behind the reception desk smiled brightly.

"Yes."

"Go on in. She's expecting you."

Savannah tapped lightly on the dean's door before opening it. "Hi. You wanted to see me?"

"Yes, darling, come in and have a seat. I was looking at your transcripts. Do you realize that you almost have enough credits for a double major?"

Savannah raised her eyebrows. "Huh?"

"Savannah, you only need a few more credits and you will have your marketing fulfilled. I was looking at the upcoming schedule, and you can pick up two of those classes over the summer and another class for your communications degree. You'll have a double degree. If I were in your shoes, I'd stick around and grab my master's." She did something on her computer and a printer spit out a sheet of paper. "Here, you'll need these classes."

"At the moment, Ma'am, I don't think I can even consider a master's degree. Trying to get my bachelor's is tough enough. And the notion of a double major..." Savannah grimaced at the thought. "I'll think about it, but... I'm dealing with too much to give such an idea the serious consideration it deserves."

"Oh, please, don't call me ma'am. I'm hoping you'll feel comfortable enough to call me Mom."

Savannah smiled. "I would love to call you Mom. You treat me like a daughter and I haven't even married your son yet."

"Just a formality. Which brings up another thing. Those little invitations that you sent to the family were adorable.

Did you make them or someone else?"

"My friend, Ashley, helped me.

"I loved the whole seaside theme. But you do need to have formal announcements made. After all, you are not sneaking off. Would you like my help?"

Think! "That might be a good idea. I'm certain we can do this on the Web and probably save some money."

Dr. Van Doorn shook her head. "No. The Rogers own a small printing business. We'll have them print the announcements. Remember the Deaf community sticks together."

"How do they stay in business with the competition on the Web?"

"From people like us, and a few jobs that they bid."

"Do they have a Web presence?"

Alex's mom shrugged. "No clue. I'm sure they probably have a page someplace." Then she smiled. "I can tell you are thinking, and I'm certain I know what you are mulling. Do what you can for them, but don't charge them."

"I've got to run, or I'll be late for my next class. Can we visit the Rogers on Saturday?"

"I'll set it up. Let's do it in the morning and then we'll have lunch."

Alex checked with Savannah, and as soon as she knew for certain that her dad would get off for the week, Alex purchased the airline tickets for everyone. Alex appreciated his father's promise to reimburse cost of the airfare – the little wedding was growing. He had taken a list of close friends, Savannah's family, and went to his mom for her to add the family from his side. In a way, he was glad that the resort limited the number of guests. They had twenty-two people coming for almost a week at the beach.

It cost him extra, but the resort was going to provide the wedding cake. They offered to bring in a band or a DJ, but Alex politely turned that down. But he did appreciate the offer to have a local minister perform the wedding ceremony. Savannah asked about flowers and he contacted the resort. Savannah had suggested roses but the gal at the resort recommended they use some of the tropical flowers that were available. A few more emails and some photos… Savannah was happy. As far as he was concerned, the wedding was handled. But he knew Savannah still fretted about everything, especially mixing her family with his family.

The biggest hurdle they had was midterms. Except his weren't exactly midterms, they were just projects due. He was beginning to think that working for Ian Kilpatrick was a mistake. Just about every waking hour, he was drawing for his classes.

Sometimes he'd give himself a break from drawing and do housework. Savannah usually handled the meals and the dishes. He'd clean the bathroom, but with three of them using it, he realized that someone was keeping the sink and mirror spotless. He'd clean the shower and check to see if the floor needed mopping. *Someone is keeping this clean.*

The little vacuum cleaner traveled up and down the stairs so many times that he gave up and bought a second one online. He picked out the little robot vacuum and bought it, figuring that saved a little time. With everyone living in the house, it stayed amazingly clean and neat.

He clapped his hands and Savannah came rushing down the stairs. She grabbed her coat and her backpack. Then she smiled and signed, "Ready."

"I hate making you spend so much time on campus."

She answered him verbally. "I don't mind. I spend my time doing my assignments."

"You need a car."

"I need a," she fingerspelled, "CLONE"

"I don't think I need two women in my bed." Alex laughed. "Maybe once to see what it's like."

Savannah playfully smacked at his arm and gave him a mean look. "Okay, I need a sexless clone who can do some of my schoolwork. And your mom wants me to pull off a double major."

"Do it. You will never regret your education."

"Just drive. And don't try to talk while you are driving, I can barely understand your one-handed signing."

He smiled, but inside he felt as though a part of him was crumbling. Their time together was so limited. She'd help him with his voice, but he could tell that it was an interruption in her study time.

It was their lack of time together that was making life difficult. He needed to buy her a car. *That would help.* But he hated to take that much money from his savings. That was part of the reason why they had chosen plain gold bands for the wedding. *Am I forcing her into this marriage because of my own sexual desires? I should have bought her a decent used car, instead of paying for a wedding.*

The first day of February blew cold air under gray-clouded skies. Two days a week, Savannah was stuck on campus until Alex retrieved her. She'd go to the coffee shop where she worked on whatever projects she had or rewrote her notes from classes. This was one of those days.

With less than an hour to go before Alex came to pick her up, she looked out the windows. Savannah wanted some sun. Her notes were carefully typed into her tablet, and the current topic she studied bored her to distraction. A lazy haze threatened to overtake her and send her into a catnap. She stood and stretched. *Oh, a nap would feel wonderful.*

Her phone pinged an incoming message. It was Alex's mom. *What now?*

She tapped the screen and the message appeared. -Gwen is in labor. I'm going to the hospital. Want to come?

She looked at the screen and tried to think how to politely decline. Somehow, she couldn't imagine herself wanting everyone there for the birth of a baby. She considered that to be a private thing between a husband and wife. Then it dawned on her. *If Gwen has her mom, she might be better able to communicate.* Savannah gave the situation a little more thought. Gwen spoke well and had the cochlear. She was quite capable of hearing. *Maybe she just wants her mom.* Savannah texted Alex's mom. -No. You go. This will be your first grandchild. I'll wait for the good news. If Gwen wants, we can come later.

She wasn't sleepy anymore. That wonderful motherhood euphoria flowed through her. *I want a family – a baby of my own.*

Now she paced. No longer did she want to study or take a nap, she wanted to know how Gwen was doing, how the baby was doing. Alex pulled in front of the building and she packed up her things and vacated the little table.

As they ate dinner that evening, she could tell he was as excited about this baby as she was. When her phone rang, she answered it.

"Come visit. It's going to be a little while, and Gwen is bored," Alex's mom said.

Savannah smiled. "Are you certain? We really don't want to intrude."

"Not at all. She hates using my phone, but I promise she's right here telling me to make certain that the two of you come."

Savannah looked at Alex and said, "Your sister is bored and wants company."

Alex grinned, pointed to their food, and one-handedly signed, "We go. Eat first."

"Let us finish our dinner, and Alex wants to be there."

A little while later, they walked into the hospital and went to the Birth Center. Having never been in one, Savannah was surprised. It didn't look much like a hospital, instead it looked like a fancy hotel.

Gwen was thrilled to see them. Emily was there and so was their dad. But he took Emily home around eight o'clock, and Savannah and Alex left a little while later. Alex had to work, and Savannah had an early class the following morning. But that didn't stop Alex from beaming a big smile the entire time he visited with his sister. He was excited about the birth of this child.

Savannah's phone rang a little after three a.m. Dustin Junior had made his way into the world. Mom and baby were fine. Dustin was there with Gwen, and he had no intention of leaving her side or the baby's.

"Oh, that's wonderful news. I'll tell Alex."

"I'll go to the hospital in the morning. I left shortly after you did." By the tone of her voice, Alex's mother was thrilled.

"Congratulations, Grandmom." Savannah giggled. "I'm going to say goodnight, and I'll tell Alex before I go back to sleep. We've got to get up early."

Savannah nudged Alex and told him he was an uncle.

She pulled the covers up to her chin and then couldn't sleep. She got up and phoned Alex's mom. "Can Dustin Junior hear?"

"Apparently not. They tested him as they took his length, weight, and all those little things that they do to newborns. There's another doctor coming in the morning to verify that."

"Thanks for telling me."

"Savannah, don't let deafness scare you. Alex will support you and we will support you with whatever decision you make. Deafness doesn't define a person. It is part of who they are. That doesn't make them less perfect."

Alex took Savannah to Gwen's house. Dustin was there waiting on Gwen as though she were an invalid, and she was making it known that she could stand and walk around without any help.

Alex laughed at them, but he couldn't wait for the baby to wake up so that he could hold the tiny bundle. And when the baby began to stir, he looked at his sister, who nodded. Scooping the newborn into one arm, he gently caressed the baby with a delicate touch. *Beautiful little boy.* He signed to the newborn, "Wake up, sleepyhead."

Gwen came to Alex and peered at her son. Then she began to sign to the newborn. "Meet your Uncle Alex."

"I think he's still too sleepy to pay attention." Alex watched the baby put his little fists to his mouth. Alex held the baby's fist and put it to the tiny lips. *Like this.*

The baby squinted his eyes and opened his mouth.

Gwen removed the baby from her brother's arm. She sat in a large overly stuffed chair and pulled the blanket over her shoulder.

Alex turned to Savannah. "Sorry, I was going to give him to you, but I think he was protesting."

Savannah grinned and signed, "We say he has good lungs. That was one loud protest." Her smile dissolved into a perplexed look. "But why are you signing to the baby? The baby certainly can't understand sign language."

Alex shook his head. "Think about that. If this baby had hearing, would you use your words?"

"Of course."

"Do you think newborns understand those words or do they learn them?"

Savannah wrinkled her brow. "I guess they learn them. The words in the beginning are nothing more than comforting sounds."

"And deaf babies will find comfort in our words."

Savannah nodded. "And if Little Dustin had hearing, you would still sign to him."

Alex nodded. "He would need to learn both languages. But little Dustin needs to learn both anyway. He will learn to read your lips."

Alex went to where Savannah was and sat beside her. "He is Deaf. He will grow up bilingual. Do hearing children grow up bilingual?"

Savannah wrinkled her brow. "Some do. When the parents speak more than one language. Or they grow up with whatever language their parents use in the home, and they learn English once they are old enough to play with other children."

"Our children are the same. They learn our touch and our words. They see our expression."

"I'm sorry. I wasn't thinking along those lines."

"He will complain, smile, and do everything a hearing child does except hear. He doesn't need to hear. He only needs to be loved."

Gwen brought the baby to Savannah and she willingly took him. Watching Savannah with the newborn told of her love for children. Total serenity crossed her face. She rocked the baby in her arms as she caressed him with her fingers.

Alex wasn't certain what Savannah was saying to the baby, but she snuggled the newborn and spoke as if the baby could hear. *Teach him, Savannah, as my mother taught me to read lips.* Alex's heart swelled with joy. *One day you will hold our baby in your arms. Until then, we get to play with and spoil this one.*

With a strong cup of good coffee, Savannah climbed into her study mode, almost oblivious to everything around her in the coffee shop. Lost in her studies, she never noticed another thing around her until a hand waved in front of her. She looked up and saw Alex's face. His presence emanated such joy that it was as though bright sunshine poured into her. She smiled back.

"I love your smile," Alex signed.

"Yours is better."

"It's Silent Spaghetti Supper tonight."

"I know."

They stopped by the house long enough for Savannah to change her clothes, and then they went to Aldo's. Alex's parents were already there, and Ashley and Matthew were seated with them. Gwen and Dustin were staying home with the baby.

Savannah took the seat that Alex held for her and realized she was sitting directly across from Emily. The teen wore heavy makeup, but Savannah wasn't going to say a thing. If Emily wanted to express herself by wearing lots of makeup, it wasn't a permanent thing. It was probably a phase.

While signing with Ashley, Savannah realized that Alex was signing to Emily.

"I love McKinley. I'm not isolated. I have friends and I can talk to them."

Alex raised his eyebrows. "How are your grades?"

She smiled as she signed, "Better. Mom is going to give me back my phone."

"What about your old friends?"

She shrugged. "These are better friends. They can actually converse with me."

"I'm glad you are happy."

Savannah smiled at Emily. "I'm glad you have some good friends now. Everyone needs friends."

"I didn't have too many friends. No one wanted to be with me. All I ever had was Alex and you took him away."

Alex signed, "You didn't lose me, Emily. You gained Savannah."

Emily shrugged. "It's better for me at McKinley."

Alex nodded. "I'm glad I was at Kennedy. It was difficult, but I learned about living in a hearing world." He smiled. "We are lucky that Mom supports us. She's given us choices."

"They were talking about doing an Individualized Education Program for me. I know what that would do. I am not..." Emily's eyes began to fill with tears. "There's nothing wrong with me. I am Deaf!"

"Yes, you are Deaf." Alex nodded. "Your personality is different from mine and from Gwen's. What is important is that you get your education. How you get that is up to you. If you are happier at McKinley where you have Deaf friends and teachers who sign, then that is why such schools exist."

"I couldn't do what you did."

"It's okay. There are universities with Deaf programs."

"But Mom is here."

"And she will stand behind your decision to go to whatever school you choose. Get your education, Emily. Too many doors close because we are Deaf. Education is the key to our success."

Emily nodded.

The waitress took their orders. Savannah kept her hands in her lap until it was her turn to order. Her mind wandered back to those first few times and her inability to sign. Now she watched Matthew struggling because he knew nothing more than a few words. Her heart went out to him.

"Are you ready for the wedding?" Alex's mom signed.

Savannah nodded and signed, "I think I am. I even bought a bathing suit."

"I still can't believe you ordered your dress online."

"It's exactly what I wanted."

Savannah no longer felt like an outsider who didn't belong with this family. She couldn't always keep up with what they were saying, but often she caught part of what they said. She still didn't know all the words.

Alex's dad asked about Alex's job.

"I am learning. He likes me."

"Will you stay after you graduate?"

Savannah watched Alex's response very carefully.

"If he'll have me. Savannah has one more year. I don't want to be far away. Ian does the type of work that I want to do. He's going to show me how he bids the commercial jobs."

Savannah couldn't hold back her smile. It was obvious that Alex was feeling better about working for Ian. Although, the man still had not offered Alex employment after graduation.

The meals arrived, and everyone concentrated on eating with less talking. When they were finished, they left. It was bitter cold, so no one stood talking for more than a minute before going separate ways.

Emily hugged her brother and then came to Savannah. Savannah hugged the girl who would soon be her little sister, too. "I'm glad you like your new school. I really am happy for you."

"Thanks." Emily smiled and went off with her parents.

Savannah turned to Alex. "Wouldn't it have been easier on you to go to McKinley rather than Kennedy?"

Alex shrugged. "Mom always gave us choices, but we also knew we'd have to survive in a hearing world. School is a training ground." He motioned for Savannah to walk towards the car. "If I hadn't learned to survive at Kennedy, I wouldn't have been able to endure the collegiate environment without interpreters. It isn't easy."

"But if you needed them, you could have had them."

He opened the car door for her, then went around to his side and got behind the wheel.

Savannah turned the heat to high and tried not to shiver.

Alex sat in the parked car talking to her. She paid careful attention to him.

"If Emily is happier there, she needs to be there. Sometimes I hated Kennedy. I hated that I was Deaf and that my peers didn't understand my words."

"I didn't understand you when I met you."

"No, you didn't. You still don't." He smiled brightly. "I've never questioned your feelings towards me. You've never indicated that you considered me to be less of a man because I am Deaf."

"I've worried about how you will make it as an architect. How you will be with clients, and how well will they accept you. I've questioned a lot of things." She pushed the heater's fan on full force and held her hands to the louvered vents on the dash for a moment. "I've questioned myself and looked for the answers to those questions. Why did I fall in love with a Deaf man? Why did I fall in love with you before I even got to know you?"

"Why did you?"

"I don't know. Maybe we are meant to be together. I was attracted to you. And even when I discovered you were Deaf, I still felt that attraction. I was so afraid that you would turn away from me because I couldn't sign."

"And I thought the same. Attractive women might flirt, but when they discover I am Deaf, you would think I had some contagious disease. They can't get away fast enough."

"I'm glad they ran away, because I got you."

"It's not fair the way the Deaf are often treated."

"I had to learn for myself that being Deaf is merely different." The car was still cold and the heater still wasn't putting out enough heat.

He grinned and put the car in Drive but kept his foot on the brake. "People need to learn our language."

"It helps when the Deaf speak." She watched Alex frown. "My mom said that Dad found a book on sign language and is trying to learn."

"I'll have to teach him the name of all the tools."

Savannah giggled. "What do you call a SCREWDRIVER? A pointed turning thing?"

"You got it." He held his one finger up and twisted it in the air. "Turn twice."

"Very funny."

"That is the sign, I'm not joking. May I drive now?"

E. AYERS

Alex sat at his computer and worked on his project for class. It wasn't what he wanted to design, but his professor wanted him to do it for the experience. Savannah sat across from him, working at her laptop. The feelings inside of him were intense. Holding Little Dustin had stirred his desire for marriage and for children.

His sister had waited several years, and then discovered she was having problems getting pregnant. She only needed a little help, not major intervention to produce a child, but that inability played on his mind. *Will I have problems, or will Savannah?*

He watched Savannah studying. She was so involved with what she was doing that she didn't look at him. *Don't be afraid to have my children. There is nothing wrong with being Deaf.*

Savannah glanced up for a split second, smiled at him, and returned to whatever she was doing.

Her beauty had captured him. It was natural, and she didn't seem to even realize how pretty she was. *You think you're too pale. You will never be too pale for me. I love you the way you are.*

Savannah glanced up again. "What?"

"Nothing. Looking at you."

She furrowed her brow. "Why?"

"How did I get so lucky to have a woman who is everything I could ever want?"

She rolled her eyes at him. "I am the lucky one. I got you."

"How do you feel about the Deaf community now that you've been involved with it?"

She scrunched her nose and shrugged. Then she smiled. "They are people. Some are nicer than others. Some have wonderful jobs and others have lousy jobs. But what I've really noticed is that no one considers themselves disabled in any way."

"Do you think of us as disabled?"

She shook her head. "When you say disabled, it conjures up an image of someone who can't do something or do it well. The Deaf don't hear. They don't hear my words. They… you miss so many things because you can't hear them. But that doesn't stop you from living."

She sat back in her chair. "When I saw you and Gwen with the baby, I think something inside of me…something clicked…changed…I realized that ASL is a true language. Little Dustin will learn that language. He will learn to say Mommy and Daddy just as any other child. But he will say those words with his hands and not his mouth."

"Don't be surprised if Gwen has him speaking with his mouth as well as his hands."

"I've noticed that your Dad does not verbalize. Ever! You have emulated your father." She raised her eyebrows. "Did you refuse to use your voice because it would please him?"

"Not exactly. My mother taught us not to make sounds as we sign because our sounds are not the sounds of the hearing world. Those with hearing do not understand and often look at us… It's part of the prejudice against us. People pre-judge without getting to know us."

"What would have happened if Little Dustin had hearing?"

"Nothing. He would be raised the same way. He would be taught to sign. Gwen would expose him to the vocal world so that he would learn to speak, just as my mother exposed me. At two, I was in a pre-school program. It was to help me to learn to sign, speak, read lips, get along with other children, and prepare me for school."

Savannah crossed her arms over her chest and looked at him as though he'd grown an extra head. "You went to school to learn to sign, but you expect a baby to learn?"

"And I learned to write my name and everything that every other small child does. The only difference was we had to learn vocal English and learn to read."

"Okay, I get that, but what about signing?"

He shook his head. "Remember you've discovered that the book shows a sign one way and you have learned another way to say the same thing from me."

"Yes."

"That is because there are proper signs and the slang that is used in the home. It's not that what we use is wrong, but it's not as…formal."

"Great! Are you telling me I'm learning sloppy ASL?"

Alex grinned. "Do you always use proper English?"

27

Savannah waited inside the airport's atrium. She paced and fretted. *Where are they?*

Alex came to her and tried to get her to calm down.

"I will feel better when they get here."

He shook his head. "Stop worrying."

"I can't. What if something has gone wrong?"

"Nothing is wrong. We got here early."

"Is that their car? Where's Ashley?"

Alex said something, but she didn't catch his words, only his exasperated expression.

She turned her back to him. He took her arm and stood in front of her. "What is wr—"

She closed her eyes. When she opened them, she knew she had angered him. She went to him. "I'm sorry. I shouldn't have shut you out."

He glared at her. "Don't do that to me. When you get upset, I worry about you. I love your smile. I want you to always smile."

She tossed her arms around him and he held her in a warm embrace. He dropped a kiss on her head.

"Stop worrying. I think I see them," he vocalized.

She turned and spotted her mom, dad, and her grandparents, walking towards the building. She ran for the entrance doors. "I've been so worried about you. I was afraid you wouldn't make it in time."

"I was lost in the maze of parking areas. I had to find the long-term parking." Her dad hugged her.

One by one her family greeted her with hugs and kisses. "Grandmom, Granddad, this is Alex."

Alex extended his hand to Savannah's family. Her grandfather frowned slightly as he took Alex's hand. "How are you going to manage being married when you can't talk?"

Alex grinned. "I do talk. It is a different language." Savannah interpreted. Then he moved his mouth and she waited for his vocal words. "I have learned your words, but I cannot hear them. I read your lips."

Her grandfather seemed skeptical from the way he stared at Alex as though Alex was some unwanted creature.

"Well, I think he's just as cute as can be," Grandmom said. "He looks like he's a real gentleman, not one of those thugs with all the tattoos and piercings."

"Grandmom, that doesn't make someone a thug. It's actually quite normal today for men to decorate their bodies."

Her grandmother rolled her eyes. "Well, he looks real nice."

Alex signed, "Thank you."

A few minutes later, Ashley and Matthew, Esther, Ben and Kate, Chris and Cami joined them. At the last minute, Demitri couldn't take off from the hospital, and Esther almost didn't want to come, but Ashley and Savannah talked her into it.

"Where are your parents?" Savannah's father asked.

"They will join us tomorrow. Dad had an important meeting for work today."

Everyone made their way through security and to the concourse to catch the flight. There by the boarding area, they had to sit and wait.

"I hate this," Alex signed.

Savannah signed back, "Flying or waiting?"

"Time waiting."

"What are you two saying?" her father asked.

"We were talking about the wait time."

"This is time?" Her father pointed to his watch.

"Yes. You've been studying."

He nodded. "I brought the book with me. Just in case Alex says something that I don't understand."

"Dad, if you don't understand him. Tell him."

"I can do the alphabet now." He showed off his new skill.

Alex gave her father a thumbs-up and her father smiled.

But the way her grandfather and mother were sitting together, and their expressions, gave Savannah the feeling that it wasn't exactly a positive conversation.

She heard her grandfather say hocus-pocus and she caught Alex's expression.

"I'm sorry. He doesn't know you and doesn't understand."

"His attitude matches quite a few people. You will run into that all the time with me."

When the light flashed for boarding, Alex produced the passes for everyone. They were flying first class.

Savannah sucked in a deep breath. *Here we go. My very first flight. Lots of people do this.*

Once inside the jet and seated, Alex squeezed her hand. She formed the sign for I love you and signed marriage using his right hand with hers. Peering out the window, she watched what was going on below on the tarmac, and then watched a plane land and taxi out of sight.

"You ok?" Alex signed. "It's easy."

She nodded. "Excited and nervous."

"Never thought I'd see the day when I would fly first class. You must have been saving up for this for a long time."

Her maternal granddad was talking to her dad.

She waited to hear what her dad would say.

"Not me, this is too rich for my blood. Savannah said Alex is paying for everyone. He wanted Savannah to have a memorable wedding."

"A deaf guy has money for something like this? He must get plenty of disability money."

"Granddad, Alex works and he's getting his Master's degree in Architecture. His father is Deaf, has his PhD, and he makes very good money."

"Never heard of such a thing."

"It's okay, Granddad. Give Alex a chance. Get to know him."

A steward came in, asked everyone to buckle their seat belts, and then began to go over the emergency procedures. Alex looked at Savannah and she signed, "Sorry. When we tumble from the sky, you won't have to worry what to do."

He winked.

The steward finished and brought Alex a plastic-coated emergency procedures sheet. Alex looked at it what it was and handed it back. "I fly often."

Savannah interpreted.

The man nodded and pointed to his mouth. "Can you read my lips?"

Alex nodded.

"Then you shouldn't have any problems."

Alex had arranged for the resort's limousine to pick them up at the airport. Given their number and luggage, it had been a wonderful idea. And when they arrived at the resort's lodge, Alex let the weight of not knowing much about the resort slide from his back. He was glad they decided on this particular place. The rooms, decorated with an artful Spanish-Caribbean flair, were beautiful with every possible amenity.

As soon as everyone had signed in, they were sent to the dining room for lunch. Alex knew his parents wouldn't have blinked an eye over the meal, but Savannah's family was impressed.

Most of the meal was taken up with conversation about how to spend what was left of the afternoon, and it was decided that they wanted to relax at the pool.

Gwen, Dustin, and the baby came later in the afternoon, and that sparked another round of introductions.

"Oh, your baby is beautiful. May I hold him?" Savannah's mom asked.

"Certainly," she signed, and Alex assumed she was verbalizing. "His name is Dustin, but we are calling him Dusty. We didn't want him to grow up being called Little Dustin."

Alex watched as Savannah's mom took his nephew. The baby had grown so much in barely more than a month. He was certain the woman was cooing over Dusty because the infant was smiling.

Dustin was his usual, gregarious self, and Alex watched as he talked with Savannah's family.

"Do you sign so that Alex knows what you are saying?" Savannah's grandmother asked Gwen.

Gwen smiled as she nodded. "I sign as I speak because it is natural for me to sign. It doesn't remove anyone from the conversation."

Savannah's father nodded but stared hard at Dustin. "That's a strange looking hearing aid you are wearing. I thought everyone was deaf in Alex's family. He didn't tell us that you were only hard of hearing."

"I'm not hard of hearing. I am Deaf. This is a cochlear implant that allows me to hear when I am wearing it. Gwen has one, too." He pointed to the small oval device that sat behind his ear. "Without it, there is total silence. Your world is very noisy. But as an orthodontist with a large practice, it was important for me to communicate with my patients who have hearing."

Dustin went on to explain how the implanted device worked and how the piece on the outside transmitted sound. "But I read lips just as Gwen and the rest of the family do."

Savannah's father turned to Alex. "You gonna get one of those?"

Alex shook his head.

"Why not?"

He didn't feel like trying to explain that he was Deaf, and he had no need for the noise. He verbally answered, "Don't need one."

The following few days were well packed with activities, but almost everyone seemed to enjoy being in the pool and looking at the Gulf more than they did being in the Gulf water. Savannah's mom was certain sharks were going to eat them. And all the older folks, especially the grandparents, seemed more comfortable in the pool. But the younger generation had fun in the waves.

Tuesday night, Alex took Savannah's hand. They walked to the beach and sat on the sand. He could feel the tightness in the pit of his abdomen, while every negative thought that spun through his head seemed to tighten his gut even more. "This is your last chance to cancel the wedding."

She smiled as she leaned back and rested on her elbows. "I know, but I don't want to cancel it. I fell in love with the most wonderful guy. Why would I not want to marry him?"

"Babies?"

"I still have school. You have to work for your AIA. We have time." She leaned to him and covered his mouth with hers. Then she pulled away. "When we are ready, I want to carry your baby." She sat up and ran her fingers through the sand for a moment. "I think being around Dusty has taught me not to fear deafness for our child. It's a genetic pool game and the eight ball holds the deaf gene."

"The odds of sinking that ball are probably greater than our having a deaf child."

She nodded. "Your being Deaf has made me rethink so many things."

"What?"

"What makes a perfect child?" She shrugged. "Blue eyes and blond hair, or dark hair and dark brown eyes? Either way that would be denouncing many of our friends. No one is perfect. We all have flaws."

"I thought you said I was perfect."

She grinned. "You are perfect for me."

He ran his finger down her cheek and stared into her eyes. "You are beautiful." Reality forced him to be as honest as possible. "I'm Deaf. I'm Deaf of Deaf. You will discover that being married to me will have its problems."

"What do you mean?"

"People look at you differently. You will hear their snide comments. They will even think less of you because you have married me."

She shrugged. "I don't care about them."

"But you care about your family."

"I want them to see you the way I do."

"They will probably never change their minds about me, even if I became the most famous architect to ever live. They will stand there in the shadow, expecting me to fail and wind up living in a box under a bridge."

She shook her head. "My family will learn. My mom still doesn't understand how you have money to do this or that your family has money. They think your mother is supporting everyone."

"Mom makes less at the university than she would

elsewhere, but the savings on our education compensates for it. But what she makes is hers to spend as she pleases. My father pays the bills."

She smiled at him. "What about tomorrow? Will someone interpret for you?"

"To ask me if I will take your hand in sickness and in health until death do us part? I don't need anyone for that. All I need to say with my mouth is I do." He looked at her in the darkness of the late evening and wondered what force of nature put the two of them together. "How did I find you?"

She grinned. "You didn't. I found you. You were too handsome to ignore."

"I think we ask ourselves that all the time."

"I think you're right. I am amazed that I have found a man who is intelligent, handsome, respectful, who treats me like a princess, yet allows me the freedom to be myself. He's loving, and he has a good career in front of him."

He shook his head. "You forgot something. I am Deaf."

"That doesn't matter anymore." She looked up at him and slowly closed her eyes as her mouth opened slightly.

It was an invitation to kiss her. He pressed her to the sand and wrapped her in his embrace. Her hands slid up his back. He could feel her undulation beneath him. Her gentle curves pressed him. She exposed her neck to him and he nibbled at it, feeling the vibration in her throat. The need to take her was strong, but he only had to wait until tomorrow. He'd made it this far, certainly he'd make it through one more night. He broke the kiss and leaned up. Inhaling a few deep breaths, he tried to compose himself.

In the partial moonlight, her lips looked swollen and her chest heaved with each breath. He ran his finger over her lips and the tip of her tongue caressed his finger. Tilting his head, he looked at her.

She captured his finger and sucked on the tip.

His fortitude was slipping. "Maybe we should go back. Our families and friends are waiting for us."

He stood and then helped Savannah to her feet, but he couldn't resist a quick kiss. They walked up the wooden path that protected the dunes and the natural grasses. In the distance, the lights from the resort twinkled.

"I'm sorry that my mom is still trying to figure out how you will manage to work because you are Deaf."

"There's a few of my family members who are wondering why I'm not marrying a woman who is Deaf."

"And Professor Stockton is always fussing at me. He constantly tells me that I need to be better at signing. He says I don't study hard enough."

"He is saying that to make you study harder and learn more. He knows you study. He wants you totally proficient in ASL."

As they approached the private resort, Alex could see the various family members and friends playing corn hole. He inhaled and then said verbally, "We have some serious players. Are you ready for a not-so-friendly game?"

Savannah stretched and stared out the big windows at the sun rising. *This is it. This is my day.*

The knock on the door was from Ashley. "Are you up? You have a breakfast to attend!"

Savannah opened the door to her friend.

Ashley immediately strode to Savannah's closet and selected her dress. "You know you should have bought a white dress for this morning."

"This wedding has cost Alex a fortune."

Ashley rolled her eyes. "What's another dress? Compared

to all of this, a dress is a minor expense."

"There's nothing wrong with this sundress for the breakfast. The white dress comes later."

"Uhh!" Ashley held her hands, palms up in a frustrated protest. "Have you even had your shower?"

"I took one last night and I washed my hair to get all the pool chemicals out."

"The only thing in that pool is salt."

"Okay, I washed my hair to get the salt out. Is that better?"

Ashley folded her arms over her chest. "Get a very fast shower and get dressed. We're running out of time."

A short time later and not properly attired according to Ashley, Savannah, wearing her pink floral sundress, followed her friend to a patio. The tables were covered in tablecloths and decorated with beautiful flowers. All the women had gathered for this ladies-only event. Savannah had bought little gifts for her mom, Alex's mom, and her friends. As soon as they had finished eating the scrumptious breakfast, Savannah gave out her little wedding mementoes. Alex's mom insisted that she buy something nice with meaning. She wound up at the jewelry store next to the campus and chose gold bangle bracelets that were encrusted with tiny diamonds. She decided that the bracelets represented wedding bands. But once at their destination, she found something else to go with the bangles. She couldn't resist buying seashell earrings with matching necklaces from a vender with a small cart of trinkets parked by the sand. To her, those little seashells represented the beautiful Gulf coast destination.

It was an odd mix of females at the breakfast and those with hearing outnumbered those without. Alex's mom interpreted for everyone. But Savannah's real surprise during this vacation was that both mothers seemed to have forged a bond.

Alex wanted her to have a wedding to remember. Putting

both families together had been a good idea. Her family had never had such a vacation. Every morning, there had been some sort of activity such as a boat tour to see the lighthouses. And one afternoon the guys chartered a fishing boat. Her dad trying to sign was almost hilarious, but she realized she was just as bad in the beginning. Seeing her parents have fun was worth every penny spent, but watching her family get along with his family was priceless.

Her wedding morning was filled with stories and warnings about Alex and every lousy habit of hers when she was little. There were word games and all sorts of silly things that obviously Alex's mom had planned. And at noon, they were brought cheeses, crackers, fruit, and chocolates. Savannah was certain she'd never fit into her wedding dress after eating so much.

"Ready?" Ashley asked as she tugged on Savannah. "It's my job to be certain you look perfect. And you will look perfect."

Once Savannah was in her room, a woman came to do Savannah's and Ashley's nails. *This has got to be my future mother-in-law's doing.* As soon as that woman left, two other women came to give them a facial and then a massage. Some sort of misting device was sending out gentle puffs of a light fruity fragrance into the air while ambient nature sounds played softly in the background. Savannah was certain she'd fallen asleep under the soothing touch.

When those women left, another showed up to do their hair.

Savannah laughed when she discovered that Ashley was also to be pampered by this hair stylist. Ashley's idea of an up-do was a messy bun on the top of her head.

"I was going to put it into a bun. O-o-oh, this should be fun. We're going to be glamorous."

"I will make it beautiful. I'll create a braided bun, an elegant up-do," the woman said.

There was another knock on the door. "How are you both doing?"

Savannah smiled at Alex's mom. "I believe you are probably the one behind all this."

"Of course. It's your wedding day. You want to be at your very best. There's another woman coming to do your makeup." She looked around the room. "Where are you hiding your wedding dress?"

"In the closet, and I'm not hiding it."

Alex's mom opened the closet door and withdrew the dress. "Oh, it's lovely. It's so casual."

"Um, this is a beach wedding." Savannah flinched as the hair stylist poked another hairpin into Savannah's bun. Too many times it felt as though the woman was trying to push those hairpins into her scalp.

Another knock on the door came with the voice of Savannah's mom. "Darling, I came to check on you and see if you needed any help."

Alex's mom opened the door. "Jennifer, I love your dress."

"Savannah picked it out for me. I feel like royalty in it."

"Well, you should. It's beautiful on you," Alex's mom replied.

"Oh, that's your dress! It's gorgeous, Savannah!" Savannah's mom stepped to the wedding dress for a closer view.

Then the woman came to do Savannah's and Ashley's makeup. Savannah begged, "Oh, please, I don't like a lot of makeup and no bright colors."

With nothing to do but sit in a robe while being tortured with makeup brushes that tickled, Savannah began to worry. "Is anyone helping Alex? Or is he totally on his own?"

Savannah's mom waved her hand through the air. "Help him? The last that I knew my father, and Alex's grandfather, with some help from Chris and Matthew are trying their hardest to get Alex drunk."

Alex's mom got a wide-eyed, horrified look on her face. "I'm going to kill my father! How dare he get Alex drunk! Where are they?"

Savannah's mom pointed to the floor. "Downstairs in the bar."

"So help them if they've gotten my son soused on his wedding day." Alex's mom rushed out the door.

Alex had reached his limit three shots ago, and his stomach had begun to churn. But when his grandfather proposed another toast, Alex knew he couldn't handle even the tiniest sip. He clinked his glass with his grandfather's and then fled to the nearest bathroom.

With the contents of his stomach gone, Alex knew he had to sober up. He dropped into the nearest chair and hoped the room would stop spinning. He needed a bottle of water and then some coffee. *Oh why?*

He saw feet and looked up. There stood his mom. He held his hand up to her to indicate for her to stop. Then he signed water bottle.

She vanished, but he knew she would return. He leaned his head back and closed his eyes. When he felt something cold on his hand, he opened his eyes to find his mom handing him a chilled bottle of water. After unscrewing the cap, he downed the entire bottle of water in a few swigs. He made a fist with his right hand and tapped his left elbow. Then he signed coffee.

She motioned for him to follow and took him to her room where she used the house phone. He wanted to sleep, and his parents' bed was calling to him. He stretched out on his stomach and closed his eyes. He no longer cared about being married.

Savannah vacillated between wanting to sit and wanting to pace in the little room where she waited, while everyone took seats for the wedding. She paced because she didn't want to wrinkle her dress.

"Oh, please stop, you're making me nervous watching you." Ashley scrunched her nose.

"Is everyone here? Are we ready to start?"

"We have at least another five minutes." Ashley peered out the door. "From the looks of it, Alex's grandparents haven't shown up. His mother is missing. Your mom is turned in her seat as if watching for someone, and I don't see Matthew."

Ashley returned her gaze to Savannah and asked, "Has your mom gotten over her panic that Alex isn't good enough for you?"

"I truly hope so. At least she's warmed up to him and made friends with Alex's mom. Of course, Alex's mom keeps assuring my mom that Alex is a fine man with a bright future." She pushed at a flower petal in her bouquet that sat in a holder on the table next to her.

"Leave your flowers alone. Do you want it to come apart?"

"I wasn't doing anything to it."

Ashley rolled her eyes, took the bouquet and the stand, and placed them on another table out of Savannah's reach.

Savannah flexed her fingers. "I want a drink. I'm thirsty."

"You are not going to drink anything while in that dress until you've walked down the aisle."

"If I don't get a drink, my tongue will have glued itself to the roof of my mouth, and I won't be able to say I do."

"And who is being the drama queen? Isn't that what you accuse me of being?"

"I want a drink!"

"Okay, I'll get you a drink. But don't you dare leave this room!" Ashley shook her finger in front of Savannah.

The moment Ashley stepped out, Savannah cracked the door just enough to see what was going on. Alex was still missing and so were his mom and dad. The large patio was surrounded in torches that were lit and the sky began to take on shades of purple and pink with the setting sun. She quickly closed the door when she heard footsteps approaching.

Ashley handed Savannah a small bottle of water. "Only take a sip!"

There was a slight tap on the door and it opened a crack. Alex's mom whispered, "We've got everyone, including Alex."

"How bad is he?"

Alex's mom glared at Savannah. "Let's just leave it with he's alive and so are those responsible."

Savannah rolled her eyes.

It took another minute and piano music began to play. She was certain it was Alex's maternal grandmother playing. Savannah overheard a bit of conversation and playing the piano was something that the grandmother very much wanted to do for her grandson's wedding.

Ashley checked Savannah one more time and then handed her the bouquet. "Ready? Listen for your music."

"I know."

Ashley pulled the veil over Savannah's face. "You are a beautiful bride."

"Thanks."

Ashley stepped out of the room, leaving the door ajar, and took Chris Rutledge's arm as they walked down the white carpet, edged in real flowers, to the front of the patio and faced the Gulf of Mexico. Savannah could see her father waiting for her. Suddenly she could feel her eyes filling with moisture. She pushed away the tear that slid down her cheek. *Buck up.*

She smiled at her dad, and when the music changed, she stepped from the little room and took his arm. At the far end of the patio, Alex stood waiting for her. He was a little pale, but he stood so erect with a smile that melted her heart. Her father led her down the aisle until they stopped a few feet from Alex. The minister asked who gives this bride. She watched her dad respond, and felt the tears welling in her eyes again.

Her father lifted her veil enough to place a kiss on her cheek. "I love you, baby girl."

"I love you, too, Daddy."

Her father brushed his calloused thumbs over her wet cheeks. "No more tears," he whispered. "Go to Alex."

She took two steps, clasped Alex's arm, and beamed him a slightly teary-eyed smile. Ashley took the bouquet and placed it on the tiny table in front of her.

Savannah signed so that no one other than Alex would see her, "Are you okay?"

"No."

"We are gathered here today…"

She attempted to sign enough that Alex knew what was being said as he watched her and not the silver-haired minister who appeared to have some strong Mexican blood in him.

Alex signed very small as though a whisper for someone Deaf. "You don't need to do that. I don't care what he says, only that we are married."

The minister wanted to drape their hands in a cloth and they both pulled away. Instead, he held it slightly above their moving hands.

Savannah listened to the minister and generalized what was being said. A few times Alex glanced in the man's direction, but his gaze always returned to her. Chris nudged him and handed over the wedding bands.

"Alexander Henry Van Doorn, do you take Savannah Leigh Chisholm…"

Alex must have memorized the wedding vows because he signed them slightly ahead of the minister.

When Alex was finished, she looked at the minister and mouthed, "I do."

To Alex, she signed, "Now."

Alex signed, and he clearly said, "I do."

Then it was Savannah's turn. She repeated the vows and signed them. Simultaneously with her hands and her voice, she said, "I do."

They placed the rings on each other's fingers, tiny gold bands with their initials and the wedding's date engraved on the inside. Then it was time for Savannah to speak her personal vows. She simultaneously signed and spoke.

"I fell in love before I knew you. My heart knew what my head did not. I was not prepared to work so hard to love a man, to learn his language, and to understand him. Your love has made it possible for me to step into your world. It has been the most wonderful silent journey. May it never end. This is my vow to you, my expression of love. I will always be there for you. I will walk beside you as your partner in life, because my love for you, Alex, is infinite. Like the rings on our fingers, there is no beginning and there is no end to my love."

Alex looked at her and his smile faltered slightly as his eyes grew wet. He blinked a few times, and moved his mouth as though he might verbalize, but he began to sign, "Your eyes and your smile showed me your love. You've asked why, and I could ask the same. There are no answers to those questions." He took her hands in his for a moment. "You've stood beside me, accepted, and embraced Deafness. Your hands say so much, but they say more with their touch. Like the never-ending flow of a river, I shall always and forever love my Savannah."

Alex reached over and removed her veil. He looked at the minister who hurriedly said that he could kiss the bride.

Alex's lips pressed to hers as his arms encircled her waist and held her to him. She slid her hands up his arms and over his shoulders. This kiss was hungry and sent heat throughout her body.

Ashley tapped her on the shoulder. "Okay, that's enough."

Savannah signed, "Forever."

Alex returned the sign. Music began to play, and Savannah signed, "Walk."

They walked to the back of the patio where they greeted everyone.

Alex's mom was tearful. "I've gained another daughter."

"And I've gained an extra mother."

Alex's father embraced her in a big hug. "I knew you would be part of this family. I could see it in Alex's eyes. He saw you at Aldo's Silent Spaghetti that one night and he smiled and said, 'There's a pretty girl at the table over there. I'm going to marry her.' And I knew he wasn't joking.'"

From somewhere came a wailing cry of Dusty protesting something. That caused Alex's mom to go look for her grandson.

Savannah's mom hugged her daughter and then went to Alex. "I still don't understand how you will succeed, but I'll give you credit for trying. You must be doing something right. My daughter believes in you and so does your family."

Alex verbalized, "I will take good care of your daughter. She is everything to me."

Savannah's father clasped Alex for a moment and then attempted to sign. What Savannah got out of it didn't make much sense, but Alex smiled and answered him.

Professor Stockton gave Savannah a bear hug and so did his wife.

Savannah smiled as she signed, "I heard that your husband didn't know much ASL when you met."

Mrs. Stockton looked at her husband for a brief moment. "He was terrible."

Professor Stockton laughed. "Yes, I was almost in your position with Alex. You've come a long way, Savannah. Keep learning the language. You've got a challenging road in front of you, but you will prevail."

There were several mixed, hearing and Deaf, couples in the room. Savannah knew she and Alex would succeed. Alex was already talking about getting his doctorate in something having to do with architecture while he built his clientele. She couldn't imagine him teaching in a regular college, but she would never doubt his ability or determination to do something extraordinary.

The sun was setting as they all made their way inside. Savannah tossed her bouquet and Ben Weaver's fiancée, Kate, caught it.

Ashley groaned. "Always a bridesmaid and never the bride."

Matthew slipped his arms around her. "It's only a bouquet."

Ashley let out a deep sigh.

Alex removed the garter that Savannah wore and shot it into the air. Ben caught it.

"We know who is next." Savannah giggled so hard that she could barely sign.

Several friends and family members offered toasts, and

from Alex's facial expression, he would have preferred dying to drinking. She noticed that he really wasn't doing more than tipping the champagne to his lips. The meal was served, and it was delicious.

When it ended and the cake was cut, a small band started to play.

Alex's mom came to them. "You must dance."

Savannah looked at Alex. "Can you dance?"

Alex grinned. "I can't hear the music and I was blessed with two left feet. Are you certain that you want to attempt this?"

Savannah smiled. "I'll find the beat. Then you need to just step with it."

Alex nodded.

"Ready?"

He nodded.

She began to sway with the music and followed with a verbal count of one two.

"One, two," Alex mouthed with her.

He was probably her worst dance partner, but he tried. And when the music slowed, she leaned into him, and he began to sway with her. She smiled. "You now need to dance with your mother, while I dance with my father. When that song is done, you will dance with my mother and I will dance with your father."

Alex grinned and signed, "Are you wearing steel-toed shoes? You will need them to dance with my father."

Savannah rolled her eyes as they split apart. She danced with her father. He wasn't good either, but she had danced with him since she was old enough to stand on his feet and be carried around their living room.

Then she stopped and watched Alex with his mom. He couldn't hear the music or even feel it, and he had no clue how to dance. But seeing mother and son together was worth it.

Now it was her turn to dance with his father. "Ready?"

He shook his head. "My wife said we had to have music and dance. I do not know why."

"It's okay. I'll help you. Move as we count. Ready?"

He nodded.

"One, two, one, two."

He did what she considered a box step, except it was not timed to the music – not even close. She went along with it and smiled at him. He was broader than Alex and just seemed bigger, even though the two men were about the same height. She felt tiny and petite next to him. He accidentally stepped on her toes and she almost yelped.

"I'm so sorry. Did I hurt you?"

She squinted and wiggled her toes in her shoes. "I think I'm fine."

"Are you sure? Did I break anything?"

"No, I think I'll be fine. They only were slightly pinched." *If you call flattened like a pancake, slightly pinched.* "Let's dance our way to the edge and quit."

Next it was Alex's turn to dance with her mom. He signed wish me luck as he went to his mother-in-law.

Oh, this ought to be good. I don't think I've ever seen my mother dance.

Oh no! She began to chant, "One, two, three, one, two, three."

Alex caught the beat of the music by watching her. He held her mom and began. Savannah kept mouthing. "One two three."

Somehow Alex actually managed to stay in time and move her mom around the dance floor. When they stopped, there was cheering.

Her mom turned several shades of red as she slunk away and almost hid behind her husband. Alex beamed.

Savannah went to him. "You did great."

"She was like oil on Teflon. She was easy."

"Oil on Teflon?" She shook her head as she contemplated

that expression for a moment and tried not to dissolve into hysterics. "Ready to do it again?"

"Let me get rid of this jacket." He slipped it off and put it over the back of his chair. "Okay, I'm catching the hang of this."

She scrunched her nose. "Teflon? I'll try."

The next song was faster and Alex caught on to it, probably from watching a few music videos. Ashley cut in and danced with Alex, while Matthew took Alex's place with Savannah.

Savannah signed, "Esther."

Alex nodded. Esther wouldn't and Alex ignored her protests, tugging her to her feet. He kept a proper distance. He was slightly off from the music, but at least he had Esther on the dance floor. Her cheeks flushed, and she could barely look at Alex. They stopped after the music ended. Alex took Esther's hand, brought it to his lips, and kissed it. He signed, "Thank you."

Esther's cheeks bloomed a rosy red as she signed, "You're welcome."

She hadn't picked up too many words, but it was amazing how much she had learned just from being in the house with them. Savannah went to her. "That was so sweet of you to dance with Alex."

"I never danced growing up."

Savannah laughed. "I don't think Alex has danced too many times in his life. Kind of hard when you don't hear music."

"I know, but to dance and then with a man who was not my husband—"

"Oh, silly. He thinks of you like a sister, well, maybe my sister. But only like a sister. You are quite safe. Demitri doesn't need to worry. Alex would do anything for you."

Esther blushed. "How did I get such good friends?"

Savannah smiled and winked.

It was amazing to see some of the couples on the dance floor. Apparently, the Deaf enjoyed dancing, too. The Electric

Slide was a big hit.

Alex came to Savannah and smiled as he asked, "Ready?"

Alex waited for Savannah's response before taking her hand and leading her outside. Away from the crowd, they sat on the edge of the patio facing each other.

"I have never seen you look more beautiful than you have this evening."

"Thank you, but I felt a little like a carousel horse being decorated for the big event."

He laughed at her. "No, you are beautiful. You are a lovely bride." He turned his gaze to the ocean and then turned back to Savannah. "We are going to do well together. Don't let anyone discourage you or make you believe that I won't be able to provide for my family. I will succeed." His muscles tightened in his shoulders. "I probably will never make the money that Ben will. A large firm has hired him. His starting pay is more than I will ever be offered."

"Has Ian said anything about keeping you?"

He shook his head. "So far it looks good. It will keep me near you and I'm going to try very hard to pass the necessary exams as quickly as I can, but no matter how I look at it, I will have to do my time under an architect."

Savannah smiled. "Are you still thinking about your doctorate?"

He nodded. "Will you continue to go to school while I'm under someone else?"

"It would make sense, but it constantly puts a long commute on you."

He shook his head. "No, that's not a problem. My rent is fairly low. My car is paid off, and it's cheap to drive. We'll be fine."

"But if I'm in school—"

"Don't stop until you must. Knowledge is a wonderful thing. We never stop learning. We merely devote more time to it when we're in school."

Savannah intensely stared at him. "So no children for a while."

He raised his eyebrows and smiled. "No plans, but plans change, and babies happen. I won't complain. You are the one who will carry the baby." He furrowed his forehead. "No tricks. That is so wrong. If you want a child, that is fine with me. I will go with your decision." He grinned. "Tell me. I want to know what I'm doing."

"If I continue my education, a baby would slow me down."

"It's your call. We can afford a child. That's not a problem. I think it will be easier if we wait."

She shook her head. "I want *your* child."

He leaned in and kissed her. "With the possibility of a deaf child? Or would you prefer to adopt?"

"You are Deaf, and I can't imagine not having you. Dusty is deaf, and he's a wonderful baby."

Alex reached out and traced her ear with a finger before continuing to sign, "Good. Because there is nothing wrong with me or with Dusty, nor with my sister, my father, Emily…" he shook his head, "is too spoiled, and I am partially to blame for that. But there is nothing wrong with her. We are Deaf."

"Deaf is fine. Our child will grow up in a bilingual home with lots of love."

"I have an idea."

"What?" She tilted her head slightly.

"Let's consummate this marriage. Your bedroom or mine?"

"Now? There's a party in there."

"They can party. I've been waiting to do this for a very long time."

...Savannah's Letter Continued

Alex's ability to verbally speak has improved, but unless you are around him on a frequent basis, you might have a slight problem understanding him. He's not going to be thrilled with my writing that, but it's true. I think most of the time people do follow what he is saying if they listen carefully. He still mispronounces certain words and has difficulty with certain letter combinations. I think it's amazing that he does so well when he can't hear what he's saying.

Ian Kilpatrick asked Alex to become a partner. Alex and Ian worked together to design the beautiful building that contains their new offices. Ben Weaver also joined the partnership after being with a very large architecture firm for several years. Alex and Ben have their American Institute of Architecture (AIA) certification, and Alex joined the World Deaf Architecture (WDA) organization. Alex obtained his doctorate last year, but I think he just wanted to prove that he could do it. Besides, it looks great on the company sign and on the nameplate that sits on his desk.

I did manage to graduate with double majors, marketing and communications, and then went for my Master's in telecommunication technology. I've designed several things for the company, including the company's website.

A few days a week, I go into the office to help Alex when he meets with clients. They don't seem to mind that he's Deaf once they understand that they can communicate. Alex has established a great reputation for giving them what they want while keeping it functional, and green. And of course, the Deaf community comes to Alex often from far away. Ian prefers working on commercial buildings and Ben loves the housing developments. They're a good group. Ian says he's glad that the printers on campus weren't working that fateful day.

Ben and Kate married shortly after graduation. They don't have any human children, theirs come with fur and paws – four Irish Wolfhounds.

Esther is a CPA. She does the bookkeeping and taxes for Ian's company. Demitri is an emergency department doctor. Their little boy is adorable.

Ashley has moved to Texas with her husband Matthew, and she's become a stay-at-home mom.

Alex's childhood friend Chris and his wife Cami have two children with normal hearing. They call them CODA's, Children of Deaf Adults, and Cami has made certain they both sign. She's teaching the Deaf children at McKinley and Chris works in the administration offices at the same hospital where Demitri works.

My dad has learned to sign. He's been going to ASL classes in the evening. Finally, my mom realized that she needed to learn to sign, or she was going to miss out on all the fun of being a grandmother. I'm still not certain that she believes that Alex is doing as well as he is.

Alex and I have two children; a boy and a girl. AJ – Alex Junior – is the oldest and looks just like his dad. Clydie is still toddling. She's an adorable blend of her dad and me. Both children are Deaf and bilingual - they sign and speak. AJ started preschool last year to help him with ASL, speech, and all the normal things that little ones need to know.

People often watch Alex and me signing. But they seem super fascinated with the fact that our children sign. I did, and still do, sing to the children. Clydie often won't fall asleep at night until I rock and sing to her. Alex says it's the vibration of my body when I sing. We weren't planning on a third child but…Alyssa is due in a few more months.

My pediatrician keeps pushing us to get the children a

cochlear implant. Alex adamantly says no; they are Deaf and will grow up Deaf. As adults, they can decide. Until then, they will learn that they are Deaf. But Alex is urging them to speak. He feels as though they need to learn to communicate using all the tools available. I did point out that a cochlear implant would be another tool, but I also understand Alex's decision.

Emily got a cochlear implant last year. Within three months, she decided she hated it. She took it off and hasn't worn it since. Gwen swears it takes months to get accustomed to it and keeps telling Emily that she needs to give herself time. Dustin never takes his off except to sleep. Dusty is bilingual and already has an implant.

Much like my mother-in-law, I straddle two worlds. I understand what she's been through raising Deaf children and providing the support they needed as they've made their way into the world. I hope that I will do as well. She's also been very considerate and helpful to me, and for that, I'm extremely grateful.

Life is good. Alex says it's what we make it, how we look at what we have, and what we are willing to do. I'm fortunate because I have the most wonderful husband who loves me. His children are privileged to be part of the Deaf heritage and to speak a language that has roots probably as old as mankind.

You'd think the house would be silent - it's not. I swear it's as noisy as any other. But at the end of the day, with the children tucked into bed, I get to curl up in Alex's arms and listen to his heartbeat. He says he likes to feel mine.

About the Author

Born and raised not far from Philadelphia, close to her forefathers' lands, Elizabeth Ayers grew up with a strong sense of heritage. A tomboy, spent her days on the back of a horse and not always in proper English attire. She knew every creek and pond, swam in plenty, and learned never to let her feet touch the bottom of the pond if she shared the water with ducks.

Her family loved to travel, and she can tell you where she hasn't been more readily than she can tell you where she has. Before she married, she'd logged thousands of air miles and even lived through an emergency landing in a commercial airliner sans landing gear. She swears it was the noisiest landing ever but also the smoothest.

As a teen, she moved to a small island in the Atlantic. While living there she met her husband. He swore the minute he saw her he knew he'd marry her. According to Elizabeth, it took her a little longer -- a whole evening of chatting over cheese steaks before she realized she had fallen in love. He was twenty-four and she was seven years younger. The day she turned eighteen, they obtained a marriage license and a few days later they were married. They'd known each other less than five weeks.

Less than a year later, the newlyweds moved to Virginia, bought a brand-new house, had two cars in the driveway, and a newborn. It might have sounded exciting, but it was a rather quiet life. She gardened organically and spent most of her days learning new domestic skills.

She and her husband had two girls. They were good

readers, beyond the reading level of the books appropriate to their ages, so Elizabeth began to write stories for them. She got serious and decided to publish her children's stories. A friend's daughter was a traditionally published romance author, and after a little arm-twisting, she convinced Elizabeth to put aside her children's stories in favor of more adult fare. Elizabeth at the time said she hated romances because they weren't real. That author said to write them the way should be.

Unfortunately, Elizabeth's husband didn't see her first book published, but he was her cheering squad as she'd begun her writing career. His constant faith in her pushed her forward and kept her writing. His unexpected death forced her to decide if writing was what she really wanted to do. She swears that was the easiest choice she'd ever made, and thousands of readers agree.

Life is still quiet in her Antebellum home on her tiny Virginia street. Of course, if things get a little too quiet, the ghosts remind her they lived there first.

Find more amazing titles by E. Ayers

A Rancher's Woman
A Rancher's Dream
A Rancher's Request

The Wedding Vows Series
The River City Novels
and much more...

"I absolutely love the detail in Ayers' novel."
USA Today HEA Recommended Read
E. AYERS
Historical Fiction
A Rancher's Woman
Victorian Native American Western
A Creed's Crossing Historical Novel

"A Rancher's Dream is unique, poignant, and wonderful."
Jessie, 5 Star Reader Review
E. AYERS
Historical Fiction
A Rancher's Dream
Victorian American Western
A Creed's Crossing Historical Novel

LISA PINKHAM
PEARL
THE DOLL COLLECTION · BOOK ONE